Devon Boys

A Tale of the North Shore

by

George Manville Fenn

Devon Boys
A Tale of the North Shore
by George Manville Fenn

Copyright © 2024

All Rights reserved.

ISBN: 978-93-69070-72-5

Published by

DOUBLE 9 BOOKS

2/13-B, Ansari Road
Daryaganj, New Delhi – 110002
info@double9books.com
www.double9books.com
Tel. 011-40042856

ABOUT THE AUTHOR

George Manville Fenn was a very productive author of novels, a writer, an editor, and an educator from England. He was born on January 3, 1831, in Pimlico, London. He mostly learned on his own; he taught himself Italian, French, and German. During the years 1851–1854, he went to Battersea Training College for Teachers and then became the head of a state school in Alford, Lincolnshire. In the early 1850s, Fenn started to write short stories and pieces for newspapers and magazines. The Old Forest Ranger, his first book, came out in 1856. Afterward, he wrote more than 100 books, many of them for teenagers and young adults. He was one of the most famous writers of his time, and his books were well-liked and read by many people. He also worked as a reporter and writer for Fenn. Among the newspapers and magazines, he worked for was The Boy's Own Paper, which he ran from 1866 to 1874. He worked hard to make children's books better and was a strong supporter of education and reading. The Englishman Fenn passed away on August 26, 1909, in Isleworth.

CONTENTS

Chapter One
Self and Friends

Bigley Uggleston always said that it was in 1753, because he vowed that was the hot year when we had gone home for the midsummer holidays from Barnstaple Grammar-school.

Bob Chowne stuck out, as he always would when he knew he was wrong, that it was in 1755, and when I asked him why he put it then, he held up his left hand with his fingers and thumb spread out, which was always his way, and then pointing with the first finger of his right, he said:

"It was in 1755, because that was the year when the French war broke out."

Then he pushed down his thumb, and went on:

"And because that was the year we had a bonfire in June, because Doctor Stacey was married for the third time, and we burned all the birches."

Then he pushed down his first finger.

"And because that was the year we had an extra week's holiday."

Down went his second finger.

"And because that was the year the Spanish galleon was wrecked on Jagger Rock."

Down went the third finger.

"And because that was the year your father bought the whole of Slatey Gap."

Down went the fourth finger, so that his open hand had become a clenched fist held up, and then in his regular old pugnacious way he looked round the room as if he wanted to hit somebody as he snarled out:

"Now, who says I'm wrong?"

I could have said so, but what's the use of quarrelling with a fellow who can't help being obstinate. It was in his nature, and no end of times

I've known that when my old school-fellow was snaggy and nasty and quarrelsome with me, he'd have fought like a Trojan on my side against half the school.

But that fourth finger of Bob Chowne's settled it as to the time, for it was not in 1755 but in 1752, for there's the date on the old parchment, which sets forth how the whole of the Gap from the foreshore right up the little river for five hundred yards inland, and the whole of the steep cliff slope and precipice, each side, to the very top, was conveyed to my father, Arthur John Duncan, of Oak Cottage, Wistabay, lieutenant and commander in the Royal Navy of His Most Gracious Majesty King George the Second.

It doesn't matter in the least when it was, only I may as well say when, any more than it does that everybody who knew my father, including Doctor Chowne of Ripplemouth, said he must be mad to go and buy, at the sale of Squire Allworth's estate, a wild chasm of a place, all slaty rock and limestone crag and rift and hollow, with a patch of scraggy oak-trees here, some furze and heath there, and barely enough grass to feed half a dozen sheep, and that, even if it was cheap, because no one else would buy it, he was throwing good money away.

But I didn't think so that hot midsummer afternoon when I was back home, and had set out to explore the place as I had never explored it before.

That was not saying much, for I pretty well knew the spot by heart, but it was my father's now — "ours."

We three boys had ridden home together the day before, sitting on our boxes in Teggley Grey's cart, for he was the carrier from Ripplemouth to Barnstaple.

I say we rode, though it wasn't much of a ride, for every now and then the red-faced old boy used to draw the corner of his lips nearly out to his ears, and show us how many yellow stumps of teeth he had left, as he stopped his great bony horse, to say:

"I'm sure you young chaps don't want my poor old horse to pull you up a hill like this."

Of course we jumped down and walked up the hill, and as it was nearly all hill from Barnstaple to our homes we were always jumping down, and walked quite half of the twenty miles.

Old Teggley must begin about it too, as he sat with his chin nearly down upon his knees, whisking the flies away from his horse's ears with his whip.

"We'm bit puzzled, Mas' Sep Duncan, what your father bought that place for?"

"It's all for bounce," said Bob Chowne, "so as to be Bigley Uggleston's landlord. Look out, Big, or Sep 'll send you and your father packing, and you'll have to take the lugger somewhere else."

"I don't care," said Bigley. "It don't matter to me."

All in good time we got to the Gap Valley, where there was our Sam waiting with the donkey-cart to take mine and Bigley's boxes, and Bob Chowne went on to Ripplemouth, after promising to join us next day for a grand hunt over the new place.

The next day came, and with it Bob Chowne from Ripplemouth and Bigley Uggleston from the Gap; and we three boys set off over the cliff path for a regular good roam, with the sun beating down on our backs, the grasshoppers fizzling in amongst the grass and ferns, the gulls squealing below us as they flew from rock to rock, and, far overhead now, a hawk wheeling over the brink of the cliff, or a sea-eagle rising from one of the topmost crags to seek another where there were no boys.

Now I've got so much to tell you of my old life out there on the wild North Devon coast, that I hardly know where to begin; but I think I ought, before I go any farther, just to tell you a little more about who I was, and add a little about my two school-fellows, who, being very near neighbours, were also my companions when I was at home.

Bob Chowne was the son of an old friend of my father—"captain" Duncan, as people called him, and lived at Ripplemouth, three or four miles away. The people always called him Chowne, which they had shortened from Champernowne, and we boys at school often substituted Chow for Bob, because we said he was such a disagreeable chap.

I do not see the logic of the change even now, but the nickname was given and it stuck. I must own, though, that he was anything but an amiable fellow, and I used to wonder whether it was because his father, the doctor, gave him too much physic; but it couldn't have been that, for Bob always used to say that if he was ill his father would send him out without any breakfast to swallow the sea air upon the cliffs, and that always made him well.

Bigley Uggleston, my other companion, on the contrary, was about the best-tempered fellow that ever lived. He was the son of old Jonas Uggleston, who lived at the big cottage down in the Gap, on one side of the little stream. Jonas was supposed to be a fisherman, and he certainly used to fish, but he carried on other business as well with his lugger—business which enabled him to send his son to the grammar-school, where he was one of the best-dressed of the boys, and had about as much pocket-money as Bob and I put together, but we always spent it for him and he never seemed to mind.

I have said that he was an amiable fellow, and he had this peculiarity, that if you looked at him you always began to laugh, and then his broad face broke up into a smile, as if he was pleased because you laughed at him, and tease, worry, or do what you liked, he never seemed to mind.

I never saw another boy like him, and I used to wonder why Bob Chowne and I should be a couple of ordinary robust boys of fourteen, while he was five feet ten, broad-shouldered, with a good deal of dark downy whisker and moustache, and looked quite a man.

Sometimes Bob and I used to discuss the matter in private, and came to the conclusion that as Bigley was six months older than we were, we should be like him in stature when another six months had passed; but we very soon had to give up that idea, and so it remained that our school-fellow had the aspect of a grown man, but what Bob called his works were just upon a level with our own, for, except in appearance, he was not manly in the slightest degree.

Chapter Two
Our Cliffs

I believe the sheep began all the creepy paths in our part of the country—not sheep such as you generally see about farms, or down to market, but our little handsome sheep with curly horns that feed along the sides of the cliffs in all sorts of dangerous places where a false step would send them headlong six or seven hundred feet, perhaps a thousand, down to the sea. For we have cliff slopes in places as high as that, where the edge of the moor seems to have been chopped right off, and if you are up there you can gaze down at the waves foaming over the rocks, and if you looked right out over the sea, there away to the north was Taffyland, as we boys called it, with the long rugged Welsh coast stretching right and left, sometimes dim and hazy, and sometimes standing out blue and clear with the mountains rising up in the distance fold behind fold.

I say I think the sheep used to make the cliff paths to begin with, for they don't feed up or feed down, but always go along sidewise, unless they want to get lower, and then they make a zigzag, so far one way and so far another, backwards and forwards, down the slope till they come to where it goes straight down to the sea with a raw edge at the top, and the cliff-face, which keeps crumbling away, in some places lavender and blue where it is slate, and in others all kinds of tints, as red and grey, where it's limestone or grit.

In the course of time the sheep leave a regular lot of tracks like tiny shelves up the side of the sloping cliffs, and the lowest of these gets taken by the people who are going along the coast, and is trampled down more and more, till it grows into a regular footpath, such as we were going along this hot midsummer day.

Part of our way lay close to the edge of the cliff, where it was about four hundred feet straight down, but a dense wood of oak-trees grew there, and their trunks formed a regular fence and screen between us and the edge, so that the pathway was quite safe, though it would not have troubled us much if it had not been, being used to the place; but in a short time we were through the wood, and out on the open cliff—from shade to sunshine.

I ought not to leave that wood, though, without saying something about it, for just there the trees grew very curiously. Of course you know what an oak-tree is, and how it grows up tall and rugged and strong, but our oak-trees didn't grow like that. You've seen horses out in a field on a stormy day, I suppose, when the wind blows, and the rain beats. If they have no trees, hedges, or wall to get under, they always turn their backs to the wind, and you can see their tails and manes streaming out and blown all over them.

Well there's no shelter out there on our coast, only in the caves, and the oak-trees there do just the same as the horses, for they seem to turn their backs to the wind; and their boughs look as if they are being blown close down to the side of the cliff slope and spread out ready to spring up again as soon as the wind has passed. But they don't, for they stop in that way growing close down and all on one side, and they very seldom get at all big.

That was a capital path as soon as we were out of the wood, running up and down the slope sometimes four, sometimes six or seven hundred feet above the sea, just as it happened, and with the steep cliff above us jagged with great masses of rock that looked as if they were always ready to fall rolling and crashing till they got to the broken edge, when they would leap right down into the sea. Sometimes they did, but only when a thaw came after a severe frost. There was none of that sort of thing though at midsummer, and the overhanging rocks did not trouble us as we scampered along in the bright elastic air, feeling as if we were so happy that we must do something mischievous.

The path was no use to us, it was too smooth and plain and safe, so we went down to the very edge of the precipice, and looked over at the beautiful clear sea, hundreds of feet below, and made plans to go prawning in the rock pools, crabbing when the tide was out, and to get Bigley's father to lend us the boat and trammel net, to set some calm night and catch all we could.

"Think he'll lend it to us, Bigley?" asked Bob.

"I don't know. I'm afraid he won't."

"Why not?" I said. "He did last holidays."

"Yes," said Bigley; "but your father hadn't got the Gap then, and made him cross, for he said he was going to buy it, only your father bought it over his head."

"But had he got the money?" I said.

"Oh, yes. He's got lots of money, though he never spends any hardly."

"He makes it all smuggling," said Bob. "He'll be hung some day, or shot by some of the king's sailors."

Bigley turned on him quickly, but he did not say a word; and just then a stone-chat's nest took his attention. After that we had to go round the end of a combe, as they call the valleys our way, and there we stopped by the waterfall which came splashing down forming pool after pool in the sunny rocks.

It was not to be expected that three boys fresh from school could pass that falling stream without leaping from rock to rock, and penetrating a hundred yards inland, to see if we could find a dipper's nest, for one of the little cock-tailed blackbirds gave us a glimpse of his white collar as he dropped upon a stone, and then walked into a pool, in whose clear depths we could see him scudding about after the insects at the bottom, and seeming to fly through the water as he beat his little rounded wings using them as a fish does fins.

The nest was too cleverly hidden for us to find, so, tiring of the little stream, and knowing that there was one waiting for us in the Gap where we could capture trout, we went on along the cliff path, gossiping as boys will, till we reached the great buttress of rock that formed one side of the entrance to the little ravine, and there perched ourselves upon the great fragments of rock to look down at where the little stream came rushing and sparkling from the inland hills till it nearly reached the sea at the mouth of the Gap, and then came to a sudden end.

It looked curious, but it was a familiar object to us, who thought nothing of the way in which the sea had rolled up a bank of boulders and large pebbles right across the little river, forming a broad path when the tide was down, and as the little river reached it the bright clear stream ended, for its waters sank down through the pebbles and passed invisibly for the next thirty or forty yards beneath the beach and into the sea.

But when the tide was up this pebble ridge formed a bar, over which there was just room for Uggleston's lugger to pass at high-water; and there it was now in the little river, kept from turning down on its side by a couple of props, while the water rippled about its keel.

From where we were perched it looked no bigger than a row-boat, and the house that formed our school-fellow's home—a long, low, stone-built place thatched with reeds—seemed as if it had been built for dolls, while the fisherman's cottage on the other side, where an old sailor friend lived, was apparently about as big as a box.

The scene was beautiful, but to us boys its beauty lay in what it offered us in the way of amusement.

We were not long in deciding upon a ride down one of the clatter streams—a ride that, though it is very bad for the breeches and worse for the boots, while it sometimes interferes with the skin of the knuckles, and may result in injury to the nose, is thoroughly enjoyable and full of excitement while it lasts.

You don't know what a clatter stream is? Then I'll tell you.

Every here and there, where the slate cliffs run down in steep slopes to the valleys, you can see from the very top to the bottom, that is to say on a slope of some nine hundred feet, what look like little streams that are perhaps a foot wide at the top and ten or a dozen at the bottom where they open out. These are not streams of water, though in wet weather the water does trickle down through them, and makes them its bed, but streams of flat, rounded-edge pieces of slate and shale that have been split off the face of the rock and fallen, to go slowly gliding down one over the other, perhaps taking years in their journey. Some of the pieces are as small as the scraps put in the bottom of a flower-pot, others are as large as house slates and tiles, perhaps larger; but as they go grinding over one another they are tolerably smooth, and form a capital arrangement for a slide.

This thing determined upon we each selected a good broad piece big enough to sit or kneel on, and then began the laborious ascent, which, I may at once tell you, is the drawback to the enjoyment, for, though the coming down is delightful, the drag up the steep precipitous slope, with feet frequently slipping, is so toilsome a task that two or three slides down used to be always considered what Dr Stacey at Barnstaple School called *quantum sufficit*.

As a matter of course we were soon tired, but we managed three, starting from right up at the top, and close after one another, with the stones beneath us rattling, and sometimes gliding down swiftly, sometimes coming to a standstill; but if it was the foremost, those behind generally started him again.

In this case Bob went first, I followed, and Bigley came last, and though we two stuck more than once, he never did, his weight overcoming the friction of the stones to such an extent that, towards the last, he charged down upon us and we all rolled over together into a heap.

We tried again, but the fall had made Bob disagreeable. I don't think he was much hurt, but he pretended to be, and said that Bigley had done it on purpose.

It was of no use for Bigley to protest. Once Bob had made up his mind to a thing he would not give in, so after about half a slide down we stopped short without being driven on again by our companion, and the game was voted a bore.

"'Tisn't as if there were a couple of sailors at the top with a capstan, to haul you up again when you've slid down," said Bob.

"Ah, I wish there were!" cried Bigley, "I get so tired."

"No rope would pull you up; you're too heavy," sneered Bob. "Never mind, Sep, let's do something else. The clatter streams ain't half so slippery as they used to be. I s'pose we may do something else here though it is your father's place?"

"Don't be so disagreeable," I cried.

"Who's disagreeable?" he retorted. "I didn't make the stones stick and old Bigley come down squelch on us, did I?"

"Oh, if you want to quarrel, Bob, we may as well go home," I said.

"There, just hark at him, Big! Quarrel! Just as if I wanted to quarrel. There, I shall go."

"No, no, don't go, Bob," I cried.

"No, no, don't go, Bob," chimed in Big. "It's holidays now, and we can get up a row when we're at school."

The force of this, and its being waste of time now the long-expected holidays had come, made an impression on Bob, who sat down and began sending rounded pieces of slate skimming through the air towards the little stream.

"Didn't I tell you I didn't want to quarrel," he grumbled out. "I ain't so fond of—there, you chaps couldn't do that."

"Ha! Ha! Couldn't we?" I cried, as a stone he threw went plash into the stream, and I jerked a piece of slate so far that it went right over.

This made Bob jump up, and, as there was plenty of ammunition, the old contention was forgotten in the new, Bigley Uggleston joining in and helping us throw stones till we grew tired, when we looked round for something fresh to do.

"Let's climb right to the top of Bogle's Beacon," I said, as my eyes lit upon the highest crags at our side of the ravine.

"Oh, what's the good?" said Bigley. "It'll make us so hot."

"Get out, you great lazy fellow," cried Bob, whose lips had been apart to oppose my plan; but as soon as Bigley took the other side he was all eagerness to go.

"Oh, all right then," said Bigley. "I don't mind. If you're going I shall come too; but wait a minute."

As he spoke he set off at a trot down the slope, and as we two threw ourselves down to watch him, we saw him run on and on till he reached the smuggler's cottage, and go round to the long low slate-roofed shed where his father kept his odds and ends of boat gear, and then he dived in out of sight.

"What's he gone for?" said Bob.

"Dunno," I said lazily as I turned over on my chest and kicked the loose slates with my toes. "Yes, I do."

"No, you don't," said Bob sourly.

"Yes, I do; he's gone to get a bit of rope. Don't you remember when we climbed up last year we didn't get quite to the top, and you said that if we'd had a bit of rope to throw over the big stone, one of us might have held the end while the other climbed up?"

"No, I don't remember, and don't believe I ever said so."

"Why, that you did, Bob. What's the good of contradicting?"

"What's that to you, Sep Duncan?" he retorted. "You arn't everybody. I shall contradict if I like."

"But you did say so."

"I didn't."

"You did. Now, just you wait till old Big comes and see if he don't say so too."

"Yah! He'd say anything. What does he know about it?"

"Well, here he comes," I said.

"Let him come; I don't care."

"And he has got a coil of rope over his shoulder."

"Well, what do I care? Any fool might get a ring of rope over his shoulder."

"Yes, but what for?"

"Oh, I dunno; don't bother!" said Bob surlily.

Meanwhile Bigley Uggleston was coming along at a lumbering trot, and as soon as he was within hearing I shouted to him:

"What are you going to do with that rope?" And now for the first time I noticed that he was carrying a long iron bar balanced in his right hand.

Big did not answer, but came panting on.

"There, I told you so!" cried Bob; "didn't I say so?"

"I don't care if you did," I retorted; and just then our companion panted up to us and threw himself down, breathless with his exertions.

"What did you fetch the rope for?" I cried eagerly.

"To" —puff— "throw it over" —puff— "the big stone" —puff— "up atop, same" —puff— "as Bob Chowne said" —puff— "last year."

"There!" I cried triumphantly, turning on Bob.

I was sorry I had spoken directly after, for Bob tightened his lips and half shut his eyes as he rose slowly to his feet, thrust his hands in his pockets, and began to move off.

"Here, what are you going to do?" I cried.

"Going home."

"What for?"

"What for? Where's the use o' stopping? You keep on trying to pick a quarrel with a fellow."

"Why, I don't, Bob. I say, don't go. We're just going to have no end of fun."

"Yes," cried Big; "and I've brought one of my father's net bars to drive in the rock and fasten the rope to, and then no one need hold it."

"No, I sha'n't stop," grumbled Bob sourly. "Where's the use o' stopping with chaps as always want to quarrel?"

"I don't want to quarrel," I said.

"And I'm sure I don't," said Big. "I hate it."

"More don't I," growled Bob. "It's Sep Duncan; he's always trying to have a row with somebody."

"Here, come on," cried Big. "I've got the rope and the bar."

"No," said Bob, sticking his hands farther into his pockets and sidling off; "I'm going home."

"Oh, I say, don't spoil our fun, Bob," I cried.

"'Taint me; it's you," he said. "I sha'n't stay."

"Oh, if it's me I'm very sorry," I said, "I didn't mean to be disagreeable."

"Oh, well, if you're sorry and didn't mean to be disagreeable I'll stay," he said. "Only don't you do it again."

"Say you won't," whispered Big.

"Well, I won't do it again," I cried, though I felt all the time as if I wanted to laugh outright.

"Then I sha'n't say any more about it," said Bob, relenting all at once. "I say, Big, is that rope strong?"

"Strong enough to hold all of us," he replied. "Here, come along. It'll soon be dinner-time. I'm getting hungry now."

"Why, you're always hungry, Big," cried Bob as we began to climb the steep slope diagonally.

"Yes, I am," he assented. "I do eat such a lot, and then I always feel as if I wanted to eat a lot more."

It was a stiff climb over the loose slates and in and out among the rough masses of stone that projected every here and there; but the air grew fresher and cooler as we made our way from sheep-track to sheep-track, where the little brown butterflies kept darting up in our path; and as we stopped again and again, it was to get a wider view of the sail-dotted sea all rippling and sparkling like silver in the sun, while as we climbed higher still we began to get glimpses of the high hills along the coast to the west, and the great moor into which the Gap seemed to run like a rugged trough.

At last after many halts we reached the piled-up mass of rocks known as the Beacon—a huge heap of moss-grown grey fragments that stood on the very crest of the ridge.

It was a favourite place with us, and many an expedition had been made here to sit under the shelter of the great lump of rock that crowned the heap, a mass about fifteen feet high, and as many long and broad, the whole forming just such a cube as you find in the sugar basin, and whose sides were so perpendicular that we had never reached the top.

But this time, provided with rope, and, by Bigley Uggleston's forethought, with the iron bar, the ascent seemed easy, and we set about it at once.

Big soon found a place on the shoulder of our little mountain where blocks of a ton-weight and less lay around, some of them so weakened and overhanging that they looked as if a touch would send them thundering down into the gorge.

Between two of these Big drove in the long iron bar, the rope was thrown right over the rock, one end tied securely to the bar, the other held by Bigley on the other side, the great heavy fellow hanging on to it, and the question arose as to whether Bob or I was to make the first attempt.

I wanted to go, but I felt that if I did, Bob would be affronted, so I gave way and let him lead, giving him a hoist or two as he seized the rope, and climbed, and scratched, and kicked, and got up half-way and then slid down again.

"Here, Big," he shouted, "what's the good of bringing such a stupid little thin rope? It's no good."

"Can't you get up?" cried Big.

"No, nor anyone else. It's no use. Let's get back."

"No, no; let me try," I cried eagerly.

"Don't I tell you it's of no use," he said angrily. "Here, I'll go again and show you. Hold on tight, Big."

"Yes, I'm holding," came from deep down in Bigley's chest, and Bob made another attempt, scrambling up over my back and on to my shoulders, and ending in his struggles by giving me so severe a kick on the head that I leaped away, leaving him hanging by his hands, so that when he relaxed his hold he came down in a sitting position, with so hard a bump upon the stones that he seemed to bounce up again in a fit of fury to begin stamping about with rage and pain.

"Oh—oh—oh!" he gasped. "You did that on purpose."

"Oh, I say, you do make me laugh," spluttered out Bigley, who held on tightly to the rope to keep it strained.

"Yes, I'll make you laugh," cried Bob, flying at him and punching away, while Bigley held on by the rope, and the more Bob punched the more he laughed.

"Oh, I say, don't," he panted. "You hurt."

"I mean to hurt," cried Bob. "You and Sep Duncan got that up between you, and he did it to make you laugh."

"I didn't say you kicked me on the ear on purpose," I grumbled. "Oh, I say, Bob, your boot-toe is hard."

"Wish it had been ten times harder," he snarled.

"Oh, never mind," said Bigley, "I'm getting tired of holding the rope. Why don't you climb up? Make haste!"

"I'm going home," grumbled Bob. "If I had known you were two such fellows I wouldn't have come."

"Here, you get up, Sep," cried Bigley. "I'll stand close up to the rock, and you can climb up me, and then lay hold of the rope."

"No, no," I whispered; "it would only make Bob savage."

"Never mind; he'll come round again. He won't go—he's only pretending."

I glanced at our school-fellow, who was slowly shuffling away some twenty or thirty yards down the slope, and limping as he went as if one leg was very painful.

"Here, Bob!" I cried, "come and have another try."

He did not turn his head, and I shouted to him again.

SEP DUNCAN SCALES THE BEACON.

"Here, Bob, mate, come and have another try."

He paid no heed; but while I was speaking Bigley placed himself close to the great rock, reaching up as high as he could, and holding on by the rope with outstretched arms.

"Now, then, are you ready?" he cried.

The opportunity was too tempting to be resisted, and making a run and a jump, I sprang upon his broad back, climbed up to his shoulders, got hold of the rope, and steadied myself as I drew myself into a standing position, and then reaching up the rope as high as I could, I managed to get my toes on first one projection, then upon another, and in a few seconds was right at the top.

Bigley burst into a hoarse cheer, and began to jump about and wave his cap, with the effect of making Bob stop short and turn, and then come hurrying back more angry than ever.

"There: you are a pair of sneaks," he cried. "What did you go and do that for?"

"I helped him," said Bigley. "Hoo—rayah!"

"Yes, and I'll pay you for it," he snarled; but Bigley was too much excited to notice what he said; and, taking hold of the rope again, he planted himself against the rock to turn his great body into a ladder.

"Go on up, Bob, and then you two chaps can pull me up to you."

The temptation was too great for Bob, who began to climb directly, and had nearly reached where I stood, when I bent down and held out my hand.

"Catch hold, Bob!" I cried, "and I'll help you."

"I can get up by myself, thank you," he cried very haughtily, and he loosed his hold with one hand to strike mine aside.

It was a foolish act, for if I had not snatched at him he would have gone backwards, but this time he clung to me tightly, and the next minute was by my side.

"Oh, it's easy enough," he said, forgetting directly the ugly fall he had escaped.

"Here, now, you two lay hold of the rope and pull me up!" shouted Bigley. "I want to come too."

We took hold of the rope and tightened it, and there was a severe course of tugging for a few minutes before we slackened our efforts, and sat down and laughed, for we might as well have tried to drag up any of the ton-weight stones as Bigley.

"Oh, I say," he cried; "you don't half pull. I want to come up."

"Then you must climb as we pull," I said, and in obedience to my advice he fastened the rope round his waist, and tried to climb as we hauled, with the result that after a few minutes' scuffling and rasping on the rock poor Bigley was sitting down rubbing himself softly, and looking up at us with a very doleful expression of countenance.

"You can't get up, Big; you're too heavy," cried Bob, who was now in the best of tempers. "Here, let's look round, Sep."

That did not take long, for there were only a few square feet of surface to traverse. We were up at the top, and could see a long way round; but then so we could fifteen or twenty feet below, and at the end of five minutes we both were of the same way of thinking—that the principal satisfaction in getting up to the summit of a rock or mountain was in being able to say that you had mastered a difficulty.

Bob thoroughly expressed my feelings when, after amusing himself for a few minutes by throwing dry cushions of moss down at Bigley, he exclaimed:

"Well, what's the good of stopping here? Come on down again!"

"I'm ready," I said, "only I wish old Big had come up too."

"I don't," said Bob; "what's the good of wishing. I'm not going to make my hands sore with tugging. He had no business to grow so fat."

"I should like to come up," cried Bigley dolefully.

"Ah, well, you can't!" shouted back Bob. "Serves you right pretending to be a man when you're only a boy."

"I can't help it," replied Bigley with a sigh.

"Let's have one more try to have him up," I cried.

"Sha'n't. What's the good? I don't see any fun in trying to do what you can't."

"Never mind: old Big will like it," I said. "Come on."

Bob reluctantly took hold of the rope, and after giving a bit of advice to our companion, he made another desperate struggle while we pulled, but the only result was that we all grew exceedingly hot and sticky, and as Bigley stood below, red-faced and panting with his efforts, Bob put an end to the project by sliding down the rope to his side, so there was nothing left for me to do but to follow.

This I did, but not till I had had a good long look round from my high perch at the deeply-cut ravine with its rugged piled-up masses of cliff, and tiny river, to which it seemed to me I was now the heir.

Chapter Three
A Gunpowder Plot

We three boys sat down at the edge of the steepest side of the crags after this to rest, and think what we should do next, and to help our plans we amused ourselves by pitching pieces of loose stone down as far as we could.

Then the rope was dragged over the Beacon rock and coiled up, while I tugged and wriggled the iron bar to and fro till I could get it free.

"Let's go down to the shore now, and see if we can find some crabs," I said. "The tide's getting very low."

"What's the good?" said Bob picking up the iron bar, and chipping this stone and loosening that. "I say, why don't some of those stones rock? They ought to."

He began to wander aimlessly about for a few minutes, and then, finding a piece that must have been about a hundredweight, he began to prise it about using the iron bar as a lever, and to such good effect that he soon had it close to the edge.

"Look here, lads," he cried, "here's a game! I'm going to send this rolling down."

We joined him directly, for there seemed to be a prospect of some amusement in seeing the heavy rugged mass go rolling down here, making a leap down the perpendicular parts there, and coming to an anchor somewhere many hundred feet below where we were perched.

For there was not even a sheep in sight, the side of the valley below us being a rugged mass of desolation, only redeemed by patches of whortleberry and purple heath with the taller growing heather.

"Over with it, Bob," cried Bigley; "shall I help?"

"No, no, you needn't help neither," said Bob. "I'm going to do it all myself scientifically, as Doctor Stacey calls it. This bar's a fulcrum."

"No, no," I said; "that isn't right."

"Ha, ha, ha!" laughed Bigley.

"Then what is it, please, Mr Clever? Doctor Stacey said bars were fulcrums, and you put the end under a big stone, and then put a little one down for a lever—just so, and then you pressed down the end of the bar—so, and then—"

"Oh! Look at it," cried Bigley.

For Bob had been suiting the action to the word, and before he realised what he was doing the effect of the lever was to lift the side of the big stone, so that it remained poised for a few moments and then fell over, gliding slowly for a few feet, and then gathering velocity it made a leap right into a heap of *débris* which it scattered, and then another leap and another, followed by roll, rush, and rumble, till, always gathering velocity, amidst the rush and rattle of stones, it made one final bound of a couple of hundred feet at least, and fell far below us on a projecting mass of rock, to be shivered to atoms, while the sound came echoing up, and then seemed to run away down the valley and out to sea.

No one spoke for a few moments, for the feeling upon us was one of awe.

"I say, that was fine!" cried Bob at last. "Let's do another. You don't mind, do you, Sep?"

"N–no," I said, "I don't think it does any harm."

I spoke hesitatingly, as I could not help wondering what my father would have said had he been there.

"Come along," cried Bob, who was intensely excited now, "let's send a big one down."

His eagerness was contagious, and we followed him up a little along the edge of the steep cliff to find a bigger piece; but, though we could find plenty of small ones, which we sent bounding down by the help of the iron lever with more or less satisfactory results, the heavy masses all seemed to have portions so wedged or buried in the live rock that our puny efforts were without avail.

"I tell you what," said Bigley at last, "I know!"

"What do you know?" cried Bob with a sneer, for somehow, though he could easily have taken us one under each arm, Bigley used to be terribly pecked by both.

For answer Bigley pointed up at the ragged comb-like ridge above us.

"Well, what are you doing that for?" cried Bob.

"Let's send down the big boulder."

We looked up at the great stone which we had long ago dubbed the Boulder, because it was so much like one of the well-rolled pieces on the shore, and there it lay a hundred feet beyond us, looking as if a touch would send it thundering down.

"Hooray!" cried Bob. "Why, I say, Sep, he isn't half such a stupid as you said he was."

"I didn't say he was stupid," I cried indignantly.

"Oh, yes, you did!" said Bob with a grin; "but never mind now. Come on, lads. I say, it's steeper there, and as soon as it comes down it will make such a rush."

"Can't hurt anything, can it?" I said dubiously.

"Yes; it'll hurt you if you stand underneath," said Bob grinning. "Come along. What can it hurt? Why, it wouldn't even hurt a sheep if there was one there. My! Wouldn't he scuttle away if he heard it coming."

Bob was right, there was nothing to harm, and the displacement of a big stone in what was quite a wilderness of rough fragments would not even be noticed. So up we climbed, and in a few minutes were well on the ridge grouped on one side of the big boulder.

"Now, then," Bob cried; "you are strongest, old Big, and you shall help her. Look here; I'll get the bar under, and Sep and I will hoist. Then you put your shoulder under this corner and heave, and over she goes."

"Bravo, skipper!" I said, for he gave his orders so cleverly and concisely that the task seemed quite easy.

"Wait a moment," he cried. "I haven't got the bar quite right. That's it. My! Won't it go!"

"*Pah! Tah! Tah! Tah!*" rang out over our heads just like a mocking laugh, as a couple of jackdaws flew past, their dark shadows seeming to brush us softly as they swept by.

"Now, then, Big. Don't stand gaping after those old powder-pates. Now: are you ready?"

"Yes, I'm ready," cried Bigley.

"And you, Sep? Come and catch hold of the bar. Now, then, altogether. Heave up, Big. Down with it, Sep. Altogether. Hooray! And over she goes."

But over she did not go, for the great mass of stone did not budge an inch.

"Here, let's shift the bar, lads," cried Bob. "I haven't got it quite right."

He altered the position of the lever, thrusting in a piece of stone close under the rock so as to form a fulcrum, and then once more being quite ready he moistened his hands.

"Get your shoulder well under it, Big; shove down well, Sep, and we shall have such a roarer."

"Wait a moment," I said.

"What for?"

"Let's make sure there's nobody below."

"Oh! There's nobody," cried Bob; though he joined me in looking carefully down into the gorge; but there was nothing visible but a bird or two below, and a great hawk circling round and round high above us in the sunny air, as if watching to see what we were about.

"Oh! There's no one below, and not likely to be," cried Bob. "Now, then, my jolly sailor boys, heave ho. One—two—three, and over she goes."

No she didn't.

We pressed down at the lever, and Bigley heaved and grunted like an old pig grubbing up roots, but the grey mass of stone did not even move.

"Oh! You are a fellow, Big!" cried Bob, stopping to wipe his forehead. "You didn't half shove."

"That I did!" cried Bigley, rising up and straightening himself. "I heaved up till something went crack, and I don't know whether it's buttons, or stitches, or braces. Braces," he added, after feeling himself about. "Oh! Here's a bother, it's torn the buckle right off!"

"Never mind the buckle, lad. Let's send this stone over. I want to see it go; don't you, Sep?"

"Of course I do," I said. "Now, then, all together once more. Shove the bar in here, Bob."

"Oh, it's of no use to shove it there," he replied. "No; here's the place. Ah! Now we've got it."

"Shall I come there and help with the bar?" cried Bigley.

"No, you sha'n't come there and help with the bar," sneered Bob. "There ain't hardly room for us two to work, and you'd want a great bar half a mile long all to yourself. Only wish I was as strong as you, an' I'd just pop that stone over in half a minute."

"Would you?" said Big, staring at him sadly. "I can't."

"No, because you don't half try."

"Oh, don't I? Now you both heave again, and this time we'll do it."

"All right," cried Bob excitedly. "Now, then, all together, heave ho, my lads, heave ho! And this does it. One—two—three—and—"

"Oh, look at that!" cried Bigley, straightening himself again. "There now, did you ever see such a chap?" cried Bob, stamping with rage; "just as she was going over, and it only wanted about half a pound to do it, he leaves off."

"Well, how would you like your other brace buckle to get torn up by the roots?" said Bigley reproachfully.

"Brace buckles! Why, your brace buckles are always coming off," said Bob. "I wouldn't be such a great lumbering chap as you are for all Devonshire and part o' Wales."

"I can't help it," said Bigley sadly, as he tried to repair damages, and failing that, secured his clothing by tying his braces tightly round his waist. "I didn't want to grow so big all at once. Everybody laughs at me for it."

"Nobody minds your being big," cried Bob, "if you would only be useful. Your braces are always breaking."

"I'm very sorry, Bob, old chap."

"What's the good of being sorry now?" replied Bob. "You've spoiled all the fun. It's no use stopping if you chaps won't help."

"Why, we did help, Bob," I said, "and the stone didn't move a bit. It's too heavy."

"It did move, I tell you. If you want to quarrel you'd better say so, and I'll be off home. I don't want to fight."

"More do I, Bob," I replied; "but it didn't really move. Did it, Big?"

"If you say it didn't, Big, I'll give you a crack right in the eye," cried Bob fiercely, as he doubled his fist.

Bigley's mouth was opened to speak, but Bob was so energetic and fierce that it remained like a round O, and the great fellow looked so comical that I burst out into a fit of laughter which set Bob laughing too, and this made Big stare at us both in a puzzled way; but by degrees he caught the mood of the moment and laughed too, and the cloud that overhung our expedition drifted away.

"Well," said Bob at last in a disappointed tone, "I s'pose we may as well go down on the beach crabbing, for we can't move that stone."

"I know how we could move it," cried Bigley suddenly.

"Tchah! How?" I said.

"Same as my father moved the great rock out there in the cove. There was a big lump there that was always dangerous for the lugger when she was coming in."

"Well, what then?" said Bob contemptuously.

"Why," continued Big eagerly, "he waited till the spring tides and the water was terribly low, and then he put a lot of gunpowder in a hole under it and laid a train, and smeared a piece of rag with powder, and nicked the flint and steel till the rag caught fire, and then he ran away."

"Well?" I said.

"Well, then the rag sparked and spit fire till the train began to run, and then the train set light to the powder, and there was a big *bom boom*."

"A big what?" we both cried.

"A big *bom boom*," said Bigley.

"Why, you didn't say anything about a big *bom boom* being there before," cried Bob. "I don't believe there is such a thing."

"Now, how you do go on!" cried Bigley. "You know what I mean—a big bang when the powder went off."

"Then why don't you call things by their right name?" said Bob. "A bang's a bang and nothing else."

"Well, the powder went bang and knocked the big rock right off the place where it stood."

"What! Up in the air?" I said.

"Up in the air? No; over into the deep water, where it sank to the bottom."

"Well, you don't suppose we're such old stupids as to think it floated, do you?" cried Bob.

"No, of course not, but that's what it did."

"I don't believe it," said Bob stubbornly.

"You don't believe it?" I said, while poor Bigley stood staring at the last speaker.

"No. If that had been true old Big would have been bouncing about it at school, and told us that story, as he always does everything he knows, nine hundred thousand times, till we were all tired of hearing it."

"But I'd forgotten all about it till just now," pleaded Bigley.

"Ah, well," said Bob, who was sitting on the big stone swinging his legs to and fro, "I don't believe it, and if I did, what then?"

"Why, I thought," said Bigley eagerly, "if we were to put some powder under that stone, and make a train, and strew some wet powder on a piece of rag—"

"And light it, and make it fizzle, and then run away," cried Bob, mimicking Bigley's speech.

"Yes," cried the latter eagerly, "it would topple it over right down into the glen."

"There's an old stupid for you," said Bob, looking at me. Then turning to Bigley he said sharply, "Why, I haven't got my pockets full of powder, have I?"

"N–no," stammered Bigley, who was taken aback by his fierce way.

"And powder don't grow in the furze pops, does it?"

"N–no," faltered Bigley; "but—"

"Here, Sep Duncan," cried Bob, "go and see if any of the rabbits have got any in their holes. There, get out! I shall go home. What's the good of fooling about here?"

"But father's got lots of gunpowder in the shed," cried Bigley.

"Eh?" said Bob starting.

"I could go and get a handful. He'd give it me if he was at home, and he wouldn't mind my fetching some."

"Wouldn't he?" cried Bob, whose sour looks changed to eagerness. "Hooray, then! Cut off and bring your handkerchief full, and we'll send the stone sky-high."

"All right," said Bigley eagerly.

"And bring a flint and steel."

"Yes: anything else?"

"No, that'll do."

"But, I say," I ventured to put in, "wouldn't it be dangerous?"

"Dangerous! Ha, ha, ha! Hark at him, Big. Here's Miss Duncan very much afraid that the powder might go off and pop him. Oh, here's a game!"

"I'm not afraid," I said; "only I shouldn't like to do anything dangerous."

"Well, who's going to, stupid?" said Bob importantly. "Think I don't know what powder is. There, cut off, Big, and see how soon you can get back. We'll make a hole for the charge, same as they do in the quarry, and have it ready by the time you come. Run."

Chapter Four
The Explosion

Bigley wanted no further telling, but started off at full speed diagonally down the slope, while Bob, who was all animation and good temper again, seized the iron bar, and began to look out for a suitable place for the charge.

"Hadn't we better wait and see if he can get the powder?" I ventured to say.

"Not we," said Bob. "He'll be sure to get it, and then—oh, I say, Sep, it will be a game!"

Once more I began to feel misgivings as to whether it would be such a game; but I said nothing, only looked on sometimes at Bob, who, in imitation of what he had seen at the quarries, or the places where they blasted out shelves in the cliff-side for houses to be built, was busy driving in a hole right under the big rock by means of the bar, and sometimes at where Bigley was shuffling and sliding down the side of the Gap till he disappeared behind the shed.

"If he gets the powder I wouldn't put much in," I said.

"Why not?"

"Because it may be dangerous."

"There, get out! Just as if I didn't know what I'm doing. I've watched the quarry-men lots of times."

"Will it split the rock?" I asked.

"All depends how you put your charge," said Bob very sagely. "I'm going to make it lift the rock, and drop it down over the side, and then away it'll go and sweep a lot of those big bits with it, just as if they were skittles, and they'll all go down like a big clatter stream to the bottom."

"Here's a better place here," I said, crawling down on the opposite side of the rock.

"No, it ain't," said Bob in his opiniated manner, and without looking. "It ain't half so good. This is the place. Now go and look, and see if old Big's coming back."

I rose up again, and shading my eyes looked down to the cottage, beyond which the sea was glittering in the sun.

"No," I said; "not yet. Yes, he is: here he comes."

"Has he got it?" cried Bob.

"I don't know," I replied, "he's so far-off; but he has got something. He's waving his handkerchief."

"Here, hi! Stop! Don't do that!" cried Bob, jumping up and throwing his arms about. "You'll spill all the powder. There's an old stupid. He don't take any notice."

"Why, how can he at all that distance away? You couldn't make him hear if he was only a quarter as far."

Bob did not reply, but sat down watching, and I did the same, while poor old Bigley came panting and toiling up the slope in the hot sun.

"Oh, isn't he jolly slow," cried Bob. "I wish I'd gone myself. It'll take him all day."

"You'd have lain down and gone to sleep before you were half-way up the hill," I said maliciously, and Bob tightened his lips.

"Go on," he said sourly. "I know what you want. You want to fall out, but I sha'n't. I hate a fellow who always wants to get up a fight. I came here to-day to see if we couldn't have a bit of fun, so I sha'n't quarrel. Oh, I say, what a while he is! He's just like old Teggley Grey's horse, only he ain't so quick."

Poor old Bigley wasn't quick, certainly, for it was hot, and hard climbing to where we were perched. To have come straight up was next to impossible: the only way was to come sidewise, getting a little higher as you walked along; and toiling industriously at his task, Bigley at last reached the foot of the piled-up mass where we were waiting.

"Oh, I say, come up. Be quick. What a while you have been!" said Bob. "Got it?"

"Oh, it's all very well to talk," panted Bigley wiping his forehead, "sitting down there so quietly. It's hot."

"Never mind about it's being so hot," cried Bob. "Have you got it?"

"Got what?"

"Did you ever hear such a chap?" cried Bob. "The powder."

"Why, of course I have. Didn't I go on purpose to get it?"

We both thought that the intention was not always followed by the deed, but we said nothing in our anxiety to get the material for our experiment; and as Bigley had come to a halt, we had to go down about a hundred feet to help him climb up the rest of the way, when he drew out a pint tin can full of powder, the flint and steel, and a piece of rag, which he had taken the precaution to damp in the stream and then wring out before starting back.

We set to work at once making the damp rag into a fuse by rubbing it well with the coarse-grained gunpowder, and then, it being decided that we could not do better than leave the powder in the tin canister, whose opening answered admirably for the insertion of the rag fuse, Bob set to work to enlarge the hole he had made till it was big enough to admit the charge.

Then with great care the end of the rag was thrust into the powder, and held there with a piece of slaty chip, sufficient length of the rag being left to reach out beyond the side of the stone.

Next Bob took the tin and thrust it into its place far under the rock, and the only remaining thing to do was to light the fuse and get well out of the way.

"Who's going to nick the steel?" I said.

"Well," said Bob coolly, "as I've done nearly all the rest of the work you may as well do that."

I felt a moment's hesitation, nothing more, and taking the flint, steel, and tinder-box, with a brimstone match, I went down on my knees beside the stone, where the piece of rag lay out ready, and after a great deal of nicking I made one of the sparks I struck fall into the tinder-box, and, after the customary amount of blowing, produced enough glow to ignite the tip of the brimstone-dipped match, which by careful shading fluttered and burned with a blue flame nearly invisible in the noontide light.

It was an extremely risky proceeding, for we had dropped some of the powder in among the short dry moss and stones, and then, too, the rag was drying fast, and it was quite within the range of possibilities that when I lit one end it might communicate too rapidly with the powder in the canister, and the explosion would take place before I could get out of the way.

But Bob Chowne and Bigley were standing only a couple of yards behind me, ready to dodge behind some of the great rocks on the comb of the ridge, and I believe that in those days I possessed so much of the Spartan fortitude which pervaded our school, that I would sooner have been blown up than show fear. So I sheltered my match, bending lower and lower, till I could bring it to a level with the powder-smeared rag, which caught at once, and began to sparkle and scintillate, sending up a thin blue flame at the same time.

That was enough, and throwing the match away, I began to back towards the lookers-on, but hearing a scuffling noise among the stones, I looked round to see that they were both running.

"Come on!" shouted Bob. "Look sharp, Sep!"

As they had begun to run it seemed to be no shame for me to do the same, so I darted after them, and found them just on the other side of the ridge, lying down behind some of the great rocks.

"That's right," cried Bob. "Creep close; nothing can hurt us here. Are you sure you left the thing burning?"

"Quite," I said. "It must be off directly."

I don't know whether Bigley was aware of the fact, but he crept close between two rocks and behaved just as an ostrich is said to do, for he stuck his head right in and then seemed to consider that he was quite safe.

Suddenly, as we were listening impatiently for the explosion, an idea occurred to me.

"I say," I said, "what's the good of all this? We sha'n't see the stone go down."

Bob started up in a sitting position, and gave Bigley a tremendous slap which made him follow suit.

"Why, you are a chap!" he said as the idea came home to him too. "Why didn't you say so sooner?"

"I didn't think of it," I replied.

"Oh!" exclaimed Big dolefully, "what was the use of me taking all that trouble about the powder. I'm hot yet with climbing."

"It's all Sep Duncan's fault," cried Bob. "I never did see such a chap as he is. Well, what's to be done now?"

"Let's go on the top again and see it go," cried Big.

"Oh, no," I said, "it wouldn't be safe till the powder's gone off."

"You mean it wouldn't have been safe if I'd done what you wanted," cried Bob triumphantly. "I say, Big, he wanted me to put the powder under the stone on the other side, so that when it went off it would have blown the stone over this side instead of down into the Gap, only I wouldn't."

"Well, it does seem a pity after taking all that trouble," cried Bigley dolefully. "I say, isn't it time it started?"

"Yes," said Bob in his sour way. "I don't believe old Sep lighted the rag."

"That I'm sure I did, and it was smoking fast when I came away."

"Ran away, you mean, you coward!"

"Ho—ho—ho!" laughed Bigley.

"What are you laughing at, stupid?" said Bob.

"At you. Didn't you say to me, 'come on, Big, let's run for it now. It's all alight.'"

"Well, I thought it was then, old clever-shakes. Don't you be so precious ready with your tongue."

"Here, don't make all this bother," I said pettishly. "I did light the rag, and it has gone out again. Never mind, I can soon get another light."

"Let's wait a minute first," said Bob cautiously.

It was good advice, and we did wait I suppose quite a minute, but to us it seemed more than five, and considering now that it was quite safe, I jumped up and we went back to the ridge, looking eagerly towards the place where the stone hung over the Gap, but it was hidden from us by the great blocks we had run round, or else probably we might have seen what we smelt—the thin blue stream of smoke that curled up from beneath the great block.

As it was, our noses and not our eyes saved us, for I being in front, and just about to pass on to the open edge of the Gap, stopped suddenly and said:

"I can smell burning. Can't you?"

"I can smell the tinder," said Bob. "Go on and—"

He did not finish his speech, for the earth shook beneath our feet, and we saw a flash and a great puff of smoke, and quite a hurricane of bits of slate and stone and earth came flying by our ears, turning us into statues for the moment. Then I bounded forward, followed by my companions, to stand beneath a broad canopy of smoke that floated inland, and just in time to see the great stone go rumbling and bounding down the precipitous place like a pebble, gathering force moment by moment, till it seemed to glance from a stone and make one tremendous leap of quite a couple of hundred feet right into a clump of rugged masses of rock half-way down the precipice, and these it scattered and drove before it in one great avalanche of *débris* down and down and down till the bottom was reached, and what had increased into quite a little landslip settled into its new home with a sullen roar.

Chapter Five
We Dine with a Smuggler

We three boys stood gazing down at our work with a feeling closely akin to awe, staring at the rushing stone cataract which kept throwing off masses of grey foam which were great pieces of rock bouncing and leaping and bounding down as if delighted at being set free to move after being fixed to the earth since who could say when? No one spoke, no one moved till all was still below, and then, while I was wondering what my father would say, Bigley Uggleston suddenly made us start by tossing up his cap and shouting "Hooray!"

This roused Bob, who began to smile.

"I thought that would move it," he said coolly. "Why, what's the matter with you, Sep? Here, Big, look at him; he's quite white. Here's a game! He's frightened."

"No, I'm not," I said stoutly. "I was only thinking about what my father will say when he sees what we've done."

"Get out! Hark at him. One can't come down to the Gap now without old Sep Duncan dinning it into your ears about his father, and what he'll say, and all to show how proud he is, just because an old chap has bought a bit of land down by the sea. Why, what harm have we done?"

"Torn all that ragged place down the bottom of the cliff," I said dolefully. "It wasn't like that before."

"And what of it? Who's to know but what the stone tumbled down by itself? Nobody heard."

We looked guiltily round, but the Gap was perfectly solemn and silent, the only thing suggesting life after the two cottages and the lugger being the vessels out at sea between us and the Welsh coast.

"But it seems such a pity!" I said ruefully. "I didn't think the stone would make so much of a mark coming down."

"There he goes again!" sneered Bob. "Afraid of spoiling his father's estate. Oh, arn't we proud of two sides of a hole and a water-gully!"

I had some reason for my remarks, for as I looked down there below us, where the great mass had struck so heavily, there appeared to be a smooth grey patch as if the surface had been scraped away.

"Hi! Look, look!" cried Bigley. "See the rabbits!" We looked, and could see at least a dozen little fellows that had been scared out of their holes, scuttling about among the stones, their white cottony tails showing quite plainly in the clear air. But these soon disappeared, and the others yielding to my desire to go down and see what mischief had really been done by the fall, we all began to slip and slide and stumble down the precipitous place, keeping as nearly as we could in the course taken by the stone, till we came upon the bare-looking spot.

It was just as it had struck me; the great rock we had sent down had started a number more, and they had literally scraped off all the loose surface pieces and earth, and scoured the valley slope for a space of about three yards wide and fifty feet in depth down to the ancient rock. Below this the valley grew less steep, and the stone slide had had less force, beginning after a time to leave fragments behind, so that the place seemed little changed, except here half-way up the slope.

"Tchah!" exclaimed Bob; "nobody will notice this, and if they saw it from down below they wouldn't take the trouble to climb up."

His words seemed full of truth, for it seemed to me that nothing but the sheep and rabbits was likely to come rambling and climbing up here; so, feeling more at my ease, I began to look about with the eyes of curiosity to see if there was anything to be found.

My companions followed my example, and we examined the places that had been scoured bare, to see that they were very much like the cliffs down by the shore, being evidently of the slate common there, a coarse grey slate, stained with markings of lavender and scarlet pink, which, where it was freshly fractured, glistened in the sun like some portions of a wood-pigeon's breast.

There was nothing else to see, and my companions went on climbing down, while I lingered for a few minutes picking up a bit of broken stone here and another there, to throw them away again, all but one bit which looked dark and shiny, something like a bit of Welsh coal, only it wasn't coal, and that I put in my pocket.

"Come on!" shouted Bob; "we're going down to the shore."

I hurried after them, and we went lower and lower till we reached the little river, which ran glistening and rippling over the stones.

We had no tackle but our hands, and so the little trout that revelled in the clear water escaped that day; but we were obliged to stop at every swirling pool where the water grew deep and dark, to have a good stare at the little speckled beauties, and lay plots against their happiness.

These pauses took up a good deal of time, so that it was about one o'clock when we reached Uggleston's cottage, and, as it happened, just as its tenant was coming up from his boat, having just landed from some expedition along the coast.

He was not alone, for old Binnacle Bill, as we called him, was behind, carrying the oars and the mast with the little sail twisted round, so as to put them in Uggleston's lean-to shed.

As we drew nearer I began to wonder what sort of a reception we were going to receive from old Jonas Uggleston; and it struck me very forcibly then, how strange it seemed that he should be the father of my school-fellow, who was always well dressed, that is as school-boys are, while he was just like an ordinary fisherman of the coast, with rough flannel trousers rolled up, big fisherman's boots, blue worsted shirt, and an otter-skin cap, from beneath which his grisly hair stuck out in an untended mass, while his beard, that was more grisly still, half covered his dark-brown face.

He was a stern, fierce-looking man, with large dark eyes that seemed to ferret out everything one was thinking about, and as he came up he looked at us all searchingly in turn.

"Hallo, father! Been along the coast?" cried Bigley, striding up to him; and there was just a faint kind of smile on Jonas Uggleston's face as his son shook hands and then took his arm in a way that seemed to come like a surprise to me, for it seemed so curious that my school-fellow Bigley could like that fierce, common-looking man.

"Hallo, Big!" growled old Jonas grimly, "keeping your holidays then. Who've you got here? Oh! It's you, young Chowne, is it? Ah! I was coming over to see your father 'bout my foot as I got twisted 'tween two bits o' rock—jumping; but it's got better now. Home from school?"

"Yes, sir; we came home yesterday," said Bob, staring hard at old Uggleston's mahogany hands.

"And who's this, eh? Oh, young Cap'n Duncan, eh?" continued the old fellow, turning to me as if he were not sure. "So you've come home from school, eh?"

"Yes, sir," I said; "I came with them yesterday."

"Well, I know that, don't I?" he said sharply. "Think folk as don't go to school don't know nothing, eh?"

"Oh, no, sir," I said apologetically.

"'Cause they do, you know. And so we must buy the Gap, must we, and get to be landlords, must we, and want to turn parties as has lived here twenty or thirty years or more out of their houses and homes, must we? Now, look ye here, young gent, what I've got to say is—Bah! What a fool I am," he cried, smiting his open left hand with his fist. "What am I talking about? 'Tar'n't his fault."

I was standing aghast and wishing myself a long way off, when his whole manner changed and he patted me on the shoulder.

"'Tar'n't your fault, my lad, 'tar'n't your fault. So you've come home for the holidays, eh?"

"Yes, sir."

"Hah! Bigley, my big babby, often talks about you when he writes to me, lad. You're mates, eh?"

"Oh, yes," I said, finding his tone roughly kind now. "We sleep in the same room."

"Hah, yes! Well, and what have you chaps been about?"

"Oh, climbing about, and down by the stream, father," put in Bigley quickly.

"And you ar'n't hungry a bit, eh, lads? Well, I am," he said, without waiting for us to speak. "Let's go in and see what Mother Bonnet has got for us."

I was for hanging back, and so was Bob, who was jealous of the extra notice taken of me; but old Jonas Uggleston took hold of us both by the shoulders and marched us before him as if we were prisoners, and regularly pushed us in at the low door and into the low rustic-looking room, with its floor formed of big rough slabs of slate, and its whitewashed walls hung with all kinds of fishing gear and odds and ends, that looked very much as if they had come from different wrecks, so out of keeping were they with the plain, homely room, smelling strangely of sea-weed with a dash of fish.

"And I thought there'd be something ready to eat," said old Jonas. "That's right, Big, put some chairs to the table, and come to an anchor all of you."

He smiled grimly as he thrust both Bob and me into chairs and then turned to his son.

"Take the big pitcher, boy, and fill it from the cider barrel. It's in the back place yonder. Good cider won't hurt boys. It's only like drinking apples 'stead o' chewing of 'em. I'm going to dip my hands. Back directly."

He nodded and left the room with his son, leaving Bob and me staring at each other across the table.

"Don't it seem rum," he whispered, "having no table-cloth?"

I said it did, but then the table was beautifully clean, and so were the silver table-spoons, and the silver mug at the end where old Jonas sat. While, to make the table thoroughly attractive to us hungry boys, who had been walking all the morning, there was a good-sized cold salmon on a big dish; a great piece of cold ham; a large round loaf that looked as if it had been baked in a basin, and a plate of butter and a dish of thick yellow cream.

These substantial things had a good effect upon Bob Chowne, whose face began to look smooth and pleasant, and who showed his satisfaction farther by kicking me under the table, for he was afraid to make any more remarks, because we could hear Jonas Uggleston, in some place at the back, blowing and splashing as if he were washing himself in a bucket; and of this last there was no doubt, for we heard the handle rattle, then a loud splash, as if he had thrown the dirty water out of the window, and the bucket set down and the handle rattling again.

This made Bob kick me again painfully, and he grinned and his eyes seemed to say, "No jug and basin, and no washstand."

Just then Bigley came in with a great brown jug of cider, smiling all over his face.

"I say, I am glad father has asked you to stop," he said. "We'll get him to let us have the boat after dinner."

Just then old Jonas came in without his otter-skin cap, combing the thick grisly fringe round his head, the top of which was quite bare; and directly after from another door—for there were doors nearly everywhere, because Jonas Uggleston had built the cottage very small at first and then kept on adding rooms, and kitchens, and wash-house with stores—Mother Bonnet came in, an elderly plump woman, who always put me in mind of a cider apple when it was ripe.

Mother Bonnet was Binnacle Bill's wife, and lived at the cottage on the other side of the stream, but she came and "did for" Master Uggleston, as she called it; that is to say, she cooked and kept the house clean; and she bore in hand a dish of hot new potatoes, which were very scarce things with us and a deal thought of by some people for a treat.

She nodded to us all in turn, and was going away again, when Jonas shouted "Winegar," and Mother Bonnet hurriedly produced a big black bottle from a corner cupboard, and placed it upon the table.

That was about as rough a dinner as Bob Chowne and I had ever sat down to, but how delicious it was!

"'Live last night," said Jonas, digging great pieces of the salmon off with a silver spoon, and supplying our plates.

"You catch him, father?" said Bigley.

"Yes, Big. Weir."

"Weir," I thought to myself. "Weir? What does he mean by weir?"

"Eat away, my lads," cried Jonas Uggleston. "Big: have off some bread."

"When did you finish the weir, father?" said Bigley, with his mouth full, in spite of all Dr Stacey had said.

"Seccun April, boy. You can work it a bit, now you're down."

Bigley looked at us with eager eyes, but we were too busy to pay much attention, though I was anxious to see a weir that would catch salmon, and ready to ask questions as soon as the dinner was done.

"Pour out the cider, lad. It's a fresh cask, and it's good. I bought some at Squire Allworth's sale."

Bigley began to pour out for us, old Jonas having pushed his silver mug to my side, while he took a brown one from a shelf for his and Bob's use; and I was feeling sorry that he should have given me the silver mug, because Bob would not like it, when, just as old Jonas mentioned Squire Allworth's sale, his face changed again, and I saw his scowl as he looked at me.

"He's thinking about my father buying the Gap," I said to myself; but forgot it all directly, for the fierce look passed away as the old man lifted his cup.

"Taste it, boys, and it'll make you think of being in the sunshine in an orchard, with the sun ripening the apples. Now then: salmon getting bony. Who'll have some ham?"

We all would, and we were quite ready afterwards to attack and finish off a pot of raspberry jam which Mother Bonnet brought in with a smile; and the raspberry jam, the beautiful butter and bread, and the cream worked such an effect upon Bob Chowne that he exclaimed suddenly:

"Oh, don't I wish Dr Stacey would give us dinners like this!"

Old Jonas uttered a hoarse harsh laugh, which made me feel uncomfortable, for he did not look as if he were laughing, but as if he were in a very severe and angry fit with somebody.

"There," he said, when we had quite done, "be off, boys, now. I'm going to be busy."

"Yes, father," said Big. "May we have the boat and go out for a sail?"

Old Jonas turned sharply round on him, and looked as if he were going to knock his son down, so fierce was his aspect.

"No!" he roared.

"No, father?" faltered Bigley.

"No!" said old Jonas, not quite so fiercely. "Do you think I want to spend all next week on the look-out to find you chaps when you're washed ashore—drowned?"

"Oh, father! Just as if it was likely!"

"Haw, haw!" laughed old Jonas, and it did not seem like a laugh, but as if he were calling his son bad names. "You can manage a boat all of you, can't you, and row and reef and steer? Get out. Books is in your way, and writin', and sums, not boats."

"But father—"

"Hold your tongue. I don't want to lose my boat, and I don't want to lose you. May be useful some day. Doctor wants his boy too, teach him to make physic; and I ar'n't no spite again' young Duncan here, so I dunno as I partic'lar wants him throw'd up on the beach with his pockets full o' shrimps; so, No. Now be off. Go and look at the weir."

Chapter Six
A Sea-side Weir

"It's of no good," said Bigley, as we tramped down over the rough sand and pebbles. "When he says 'no' he means it. We could have managed the boat all right. I say, I'll get him some day to let Binnacle Bill take us, and we'll buy some twisty Bristol for him, and make him spin yarns."

"But where's the weir?" I said, as we were getting close down to where the sea was breaking, and where the fresh-water of the little river came bubbling up from among the boulders after its dive down below, and was now mingling with the salt water of the sea.

"Where's the weir?" cried Bigley. "Why, this is it."

"This?" said Bob, "why it's only a lot of hurdles." So it appeared at first sight, but it was ingeniously contrived all the same for its purpose; and in accordance with the habits of the salmon and other fish that are fond of coming up with the tide to get into fresh-water, and run up the different rivers and streams.

It was a very simple affair, and looked to be exactly what Bob had said—a lot of old hurdles. But it was strongly made all the same, and consisted of a couple of rows of stout stakes driven down into the beach, just after the fashion of the figure on the opposite page, with one row towards the sea, and the other running up beside where the stream water bubbled up and towards the shore. In and out of these stakes rough oak boughs were woven so closely, that from the bottom to about four feet up, though the water would run through easily enough, there was no room for a decent-sized fish to go through, while down at the bottom all this was strengthened by being banked up with stones inside and out, and all carefully laid and wedged in together, and cemented with lime.

Now when the tide was up all these posts and hurdles were covered with water, and as the fish swam up to meet the fresh stream, a great many would sometimes be over the ground inclosed by the weir, searching about for food washed down by the stream, or for the little shrimps and other water creatures that hung about the hurdles, which were a favourite place too with mussels, which cling to such wood-work by thousands. Now though they are easily frightened it does not seem as if fish have much brain, for sometimes they stopped swimming about inside these hurdles till the tide had run down as low as the tops of the posts, and then, feeling it was time for them to be off with the tide, they'd start to swim off, but only to find themselves shut in.

Sometimes it would be a shoal of grey mullet, sometimes a salmon or two that had tried to get up the stream, and could not get by the pebble bar; and there they would be swimming about, not feeling their danger till it was too late.

First of all they would try to get through the hurdles, and there they would keep on trying till some wise one amongst them thought that by swimming round the ends at A or B they would reach the open sea.

Sometimes they would do this and escape. They all follow one another like sheep in a flock; but generally they do not try to get round the ends till it is too late, for while there is still plenty of water at C there is very little at B and none at all at A, and the consequence is that the fish are left splashing when the tide goes out, in a few little shallow pools, where there is nothing to do but scoop them out with a bit of a net.

The tide was getting well down, and the hurdles were nearly all bare, but there was too much water for us to see whether there were any fish left, and so we stood on first one big boulder, and then upon another, as they were left dry, every now and then making a bold leap on to a rock, to stand there surrounded by water, and now and then obliged to jump back to avoid a wetting.

But at last the hurdles and stones at the sea end of the weir were completely left by the tide, so that we could walk down, and then, as the water shallowed more and more in the triangular inclosure, we looked out eagerly for fish.

"There they are—lots of 'em!" cried Bob excitedly, for he was too much interested to be disagreeable and say unpleasant things.

"Oh, those are only little ones," cried Bigley, as the little silvery fry kept flashing out of the surface. "They'll all go out through the holes. You'll see none of them will be left."

And so it proved; for as the water in the inclosure sank lower and lower the small fry were seen no more, but a swirl here and there showed that one, if not more, good-sized fish were left, and in the anticipation of a good catch we hopped about from stone to stone, and clambered along the hurdles.

"Hooray!" shouted Bob, who was now in a high state of delight, "isn't this better than learning our jolly old *hic—haec—hoc*, eh, Sep?"

"I should think so."

"Oh!"

There was a shout and a splash and we two roared with laughter, for Bigley had just then made a jump to gain a stone standing clear of the falling water, when, not allowing for the slippery sea-weed that grew upon it in a patch, his feet glided over the smooth stone and he came down in a sitting position in the water, which flew out in spray on all sides.

"Here! Hi! Net!—net!" shouted Bob. "Come on, Sep, here's such a big one—a Bigley big one. It's a shark, I know it is. Look at his teeth!"

"It's all very well to laugh," said Bigley, getting up and standing knee-deep in the water to squeeze the moisture out of the upper part of his clothes, "but how would you like it?"

"Ever so," cried Bob; "I'm as hot as hot. Mind how you go near him, Sep, he'll bite. Oh, don't I wish I had a boat-hook, I'd fetch him out."

"I don't care. It's only sea-water. I don't mind," grumbled Bigley wading about in the pool. "I say, boys, here's a salmon and a whole lot of mullet."

"Where, where?" cried Bob, and, without a moment's hesitation he jumped in and waded towards Bigley.

"There! Can't you see 'em? There they go!" cried Bigley pointing.

"No."

"Why, out yonder! They're lying there quiet now amongst the stones."

"Oh, won't I give it you for this, old Big!" cried Bob. "There are no fish there at all. You gammoned me to make me come in and get my legs wet like yours are. Never mind, I'll serve you out."

"Why, there are some fish," cried Bigley indignantly.

"Don't you believe him, Sep," said Bob. "It's all nonsense."

"Yes, there are," I said from where I had climbed over the deepest part by clinging to the hurdles, "I can see them."

"Oh no, you can't, my lad. You'd like me to come splashing through the water there for you to laugh at me, but it won't do. There isn't a single fish in the place, only old Bigley—old Babby as his father calls him. I say, Sep, what a game! Did you ever see such a babby?"

"Don't do that," said Bigley sharply.

"Don't do what?—splash you?" cried Bob. "There—and there."

He suited the action to the word, and scooping up the water, he sent it flying over our tall schoolmate.

"You know what I mean," said Bigley, speaking in a low angry tone such as I had never before heard from him.

"Why, what do you mean?" cried Bob offensively. "Do you want me to thrash you?"

"I want you to leave my father alone, and what he says to me," said Bigley sharply. "I don't mind your making fun of me. I don't mind what you call me; but that's his name he has always used since I was a little baby, and you've no business to say it."

"Ha—ha—ha!" laughed Bob, "here's a game. Do you hear, Sep! He says he was once a little baby. I don't believe it. Ha—ha—ha!"

Bigley did not take any notice, and I did not join in the laugh, so Bob made a movement as if he were going to wade out of the pool, and his lips parted to say something disagreeable. I knew as well as could be that he was going to say that he should go home if we were about to turn like that; but his legs were wet, and the walk home was long, and not pleasant to take alone. And then there were the fish in the pool to catch, and in spite of his expressions of unbelief he knew that there must be some. So he altered his mind, and changed his tone.

"I didn't want to upset you, Big, old matey," he said. "I didn't, did I, Sep Duncan? Here, what's the good of quarrelling when it's holidays? There, I won't call you so any more."

Bigley's face cleared in a moment, and with a couple of splashes he was at Bob's side with one hand extended, and the other upon his school-fellow's shoulder.

"It's all right," he said quickly. "Shake hands, and let's get the fish. There, I'll go for the prawn net and a basket."

He ran splashing out of the water, and up over the boulders towards the cottage, leaving me and Bob together.

"I wouldn't be as big as he is," said Bob, "and I wouldn't have such a nasty temper for thousands of pounds. Here, what are you grinning at?"

"At you." For there was something so comic in his speech, coming as it did from the most ill-tempered boy in the school—Dr Slacey had often said so, and Bob proved it every day of his life—that I burst into a hearty laugh.

Bob stood knee-deep in the water staring hard at me. For the first few moments he looked furious; then he seemed to grow sulky, and then in a low surly voice he said:

"I say, Sep, it isn't true, is it?"

"Isn't what true?"

"About the—about what old stay-sail said?"

"About you being disagreeable?"

"Yes. It isn't true, is it?"

I nodded.

"I don't believe it," he said impetuously. "I'm as good-tempered a chap as anybody, only people turn disagreeable with me. Well, you are a pretty mate to turn against me like that."

"I don't turn against you, Bob, and I don't mind your being disagreeable," I said; "but you asked me, and I told you the truth."

Bob stood quite still and thoughtful, as if he were watching the fishes, and he began to whistle softly a very miserable old tune that the shepherds sang out on the moor—one which always suggested winter to me and driving rain and cold bleak winds.

"Look here!" I said, for the water was draining away fast out of the pool now, the stones that banked up the bottom of the woven hurdle-work being visible here and there.

But Bob did not move. He stood there with his hands deep in his pockets and the water up to his knees still, the part where he was being deeper, and he kept on whistling softly to himself.

"Why can't you look, Bob?" I said. "You can see the fishes quite plain."

"I don't want to see 'em," he replied sulkily. "When are you going home?"

"Oh, not forever so long; not till tea-time. Here comes Big!"

Bob did not look round, but his ears seemed to twitch as the sound of our schoolmates' heavy tread came over the stones, for he lumbered along at a trot with a big maund, as we called the baskets there, in one hand, a great landing-net in the other. But as Bigley came to the edge of the pool Bob waded out and said in a low quiet voice:

"Shall I carry the basket?"

We both stared, for in an ordinary way Bob would have shouted, "Here, give us hold of the net," and snatched at it or anything else in his desire to take the lead.

"No, no," cried Bigley, though. "You two chaps are visitors. You have the first go, Bob, and then let Sep Duncan try. But it's no use yet."

He was quite right; there was too much room for the fish to dart about, and so we stood here, and crept there, to watch them as they glided about among the swaying sea-weed, all brown and olive-green, and full of bladder-like pods to hold them up in the water. Sometimes there was a rush, and a swirl in the pool. At another time we could catch sight of the silvery side of some fish as it turned over and glided through the shoal. Then for a few minutes all would be perfectly still and calm—so still that it was hard to imagine that there was a fish left in the place.

And all the time the tide kept on retiring, and the water in the pool lowering, till all at once there was a tremendous rush, a great silvery fish flashed out into the air, and then fell flat upon its side, making the drops fly sparkling in the sun.

"Salmon," cried Bigley, "and a big one."

"Well, let's catch him, then," cried Bob excitedly, the gloomy feeling forgotten now in the excitement of the scene.

"Go on!" cried Bigley, handing him the net, and armed therewith Bob began to wade about, hunting the salmon from side to side of the pool, under my directions, for being high up on the dry, I could see the fish far better than those who were wading.

But it was all labour in vain. Twice over Bob touched the salmon, but it was too quick for him, and flung itself over the net splashing him from head to foot, but only encouraging him to make fresh exertions.

"Here, you come and try!" he cried at last. "You're not tired. Do you hear? You come and try, Sep Duncan. They're the slipperiest fishes I ever saw."

I shook my head. I was dry, and meant to keep so now, and said so.

"It's of no use to try," said Bigley, "not till the water's nearly gone. You can't catch 'em."

"Why, you knew that all along!" I cried.

"To be sure I did; but you wouldn't have believed me if I'd said so. Let's wait. In half an hour it will be all right, and we can get the lot."

So we waited impatiently, wading and creeping from stone to stone, and trying to count the fish in the weir pool; but not very successfully, for some we counted over and over again, and others were like the little pig in the herd, they would not stand still to be counted.

All at once it seemed as if a big retiring wave left room for nearly all the water left to run out, and though another wave came and drove some back, the next one took it away, leaving room for the weir to drain, and with a shout of triumph we charged down now at the luckless fish, which were splashing about in about six inches of water among the sea-weed and stones.

I forgot all about not meaning to get wet, for I was in over my boot-tops directly. But what did it matter out there in the warm sunshine and by the sea!

It was rare sport for us, though it was death to the fishes. But the weir was contrived to obtain a regular food supply, and we thought of nothing but catching the prisoners and transferring them to the basket.

Bob was pretty successful with the net, but he only caught the mullet. The honour of capturing the eleven-pound salmon, for such it proved to be, was reserved for Bigley and me, as I managed to drive the beautiful silvery creature right up on to the stones, and there Bigley pounced upon it, and bore it flapping and beating its tail to the basket.

As we worked, the remainder of the water sank away, leaving only a pool of an inch or so deep, and from which Bob fished three small mullet, the total caught being eleven, the largest five pounds, and the salmon eleven, the same number of pounds as there were mullet.

We bore our capture up to the cottage in triumph, where old Jonas presented me and Bob with a fine mullet a piece, the salmon and the rest being despatched at once by Binnacle Bill to Ripplemouth for sale.

It was now getting so near tea-time that we set off for home, it being understood that Bigley was to come with us as far as my home, where we were all to have tea, after which he was to set off one way, and I was to go the other; that is to say, walking part of the way home with Bob.

This I did; but when we set off I could not help feeling how much pleasanter it would have been to have gone with Bigley, for I did not anticipate any very pleasant walk. And I was right; for, whether it was the new bread, or the strength of our milk and water, I don't know—all I do know is, that Bob was as sour as he could be, and insisted upon my carrying his mullet, because he said I should have nothing to carry going home.

Chapter Seven
I Startle my Father

My father was first up next morning, and had been out for an hour before I went down the garden to join him, and found him walking the quarter-deck.

You must not think by these words that he was on board a ship. Nothing of the kind. He called by that name a flat place at the bottom of the garden just at the edge of the cliff, where there was a low stone wall built to keep anyone from falling over a couple of hundred feet perpendicular to the rocks and beach below.

This was my father's favourite place, where he used to spend hours with his spy-glass, and along the edge of the wall, all carefully mounted, were six small brass cannon, which came out of a sloop that was wrecked below in the bay, and which my father bought for the price of old metal when the ship was broken up and sold.

I used to think sometimes that he ought to have called the place the battery, but he settled on the quarter-deck, and the quarter-deck it remained.

Always once a year on his birthday he would load and fire all the cannons, and it was quite a sight; for he used to call himself the crew and load them and prime them, and then send me in for the poker, which had all the time been getting red-hot in the kitchen.

Then he used to take the poker from me, and I used to stop my ears. But as soon as I stopped my ears, he used to frown and say, "Take out the tompions, you young swab!"

So I used to take out the tompions—I mean my fingers—and screw up my face and look on while with quite a grand air my father, who was a fine handsome man, with a fresh colour and curly grey hair, used to stand up very erect, give the poker a flourish through the air, and bring the end down upon a touch-hole.

Then *bang!* There would be a tremendous roar, and the rocks would echo as the white smoke floated upwards.

A quarter of a minute more and *bang* would go another gun, and so on for the whole six, every one of them kicking hard and leaping back some distance on to the shingle.

When all were fired, my father used to push them on their little carriages all back into their places; then he used to "bend," as he called it, the white ensign on to the halyards, and run it up to the head of a rigged mast which stood at the corner, and close to the edge of the cliff, and after this shake hands with himself, left hand with right, and wish himself many happy returns of the day.

It was not his birthday that one on which I ran down the garden to join him; but there he was by his guns, busy with his spy-glass sweeping, as he called it, the Bristol Channel and talking to himself about the different craft.

"Hallo, Sep, my boy!" he said; "here's a morning for a holiday landsman—or boy. Well, I didn't see much of you yesterday."

"No, father," I said; "I was out all day with Doctor Chowne's boy and young Uggleston."

"Rather a queer companion for you, my boy, eh? Uggleston is a sad smuggler, they say; but let's see, his boy goes to your school?"

"Yes, father, and he's such a good fellow. We went to his house down in the Gap, and had dinner, and Mr Uggleston was very civil to me, all but—"

"Well, speak out, Sep. All but what?"

"He spoke once, father, as if he did not like your having bought the Gap."

"Hah! Very likely; but then you see, Sep, I did not consider myself bound to ask everybody's permission when I was at the sale, much more Mr Jonas Uggleston's, so there's an end of that."

"He seemed to think he would have to turn out and go, father," I said, looking at him rather wistfully, for it appeared to me as if it would be a great pity if old Uggleston and Bigley did have to turn out, because we were such friends.

"If Mr Jonas Uggleston will behave, himself like a Christian, and pay his rent," said my father, "he'll go on just the same as he did under old Squire Allworth, so he has nothing to complain about whatever."

"May I go and tell him that, father!" I said eagerly.

"No: certainly not."

"I mean after breakfast, father."

"So do I, my boy," he replied. "Don't you meddle with such matters as that. So you had a good look round the place, eh?"

"Yes, father."

"See many rabbits?"

"Yes, father, plenty."

"That's right. I want to keep that place for a bit of shooting, and I'm thinking of buying a bigger boat, Sep, and I shall keep her there."

"Oh!" I cried, "a bigger sailing boat?"

"Yes, a much bigger one, my boy—big enough to take quite a cruise. You must make haste and get finished at school, my lad, and then I can take you afloat, and make a sailor of you, the same as your grandfather and great-grandfather used to be."

"Yes, I should like to be a sailor, father," I said.

"Ah, well, we shall see," he replied; "but that is not the business to see to now. The first thing is to take in rations, so come along and have breakfast."

I was quite willing, and in a few minutes we were seated in the snug cottage parlour with the window open, and the scent of the roses brought in by the breeze off the sea.

"Why, Sep," said my father, after I had been disposing of bacon and eggs and milk for some time, "how quiet you are! Isn't the breakfast so good as you get at school?"

"Heaps better, father;" for schools were very different places in those days to what they are now.

"Then what makes you so quiet?"

"I was thinking how nice it would be if it was always holidays."

"With the sun shining warmly like it is now, and the sky blue, and the sea quite calm, eh?"

"Yes, father."

"You young goose—I mean gander," he said laughing. "Pleasure that has not been earned by hard work of some kind is poor tasteless stuff, of which everybody would soon tire; and as to its being always hot and sunshiny, why, my dear boy, I've been out in the tropics when the sky has been for weeks without a cloud, the seams oozing pitch, and the rails and bolts and bell all so hot you could not touch them, and we would have given anything for a thick mist or a heavy rain, or a good puff of cool wind. No, no, my dear boy, England and its climate are best as they are. In all my travels I never found a better or more healthy place; and as to the holidays—bah! Life was not made for play. Kittens are the most playful things I know, but they soon give it up, and take to work."

"Yes, father," I said with a sigh, "but school exercises are so hard."

"The better lad you when you've mastered them. It's hard work to learn to be a sailor, but the more credit to the young man who masters navigation, and gets to know how to thoroughly handle a ship; better still how to manage his men, for a crew is a very mixed-up set of fellows, Sep."

"Yes, father, I suppose so. But I am trying very hard at school."

"I know you are, Sep. Have another egg—and that bit of brown. You've got room, I know. Make muscle."

He helped me to what I was by no means unwilling to take, and then continued:

"Of course you are trying hard, and I know it. Otherwise I shouldn't have been so glad to see you home for the holidays you've earned, and be ready to say to you, 'Never mind about holiday lessons, I don't approve of them, my lad; put them aside and I'll make excuses for you to the doctor. Work as hard as you can when you are at school, and now you are at home, play as hard as you can.' We must have a bit of fishing. I've got some new lines, and a trammel net to set, and we'll do a good deal of boating. You sha'n't stand still for want of something to do. What's that?"

"Only a stone, father," I replied, for in pulling out my handkerchief, the piece that I had put in my pocket on the previous day flew out, and fell with a crash in the fireplace.

"What do you want with stones in your pocket?" he said rather crossly, as he rose and picked up the piece to throw it out of the window; but, as soon as he had it in his hand, its appearance took his attention. He turned it over, weighed it in his hand, and then held it more to the light.

I went on eating my breakfast and watching him closely, for I did not want to lose that piece of stone, and I was afraid that he would ask me more questions about it, sooner than bear which I was ready to see him throw the piece of rock out of the window, when, if he threw it far enough, the chances were that it would go over the cliff and fall upon the beach.

Just as I feared, the questions came as he put on his glasses and examined the fragment more closely.

"Where did you get this, Sep?" he said—"on the beach?"

"No, father, up on this side of the Gap."

"Whereabouts?"

"About three hundred yards from Uggleston's cottage, and half-way up the slope, where the rocks stand up so big on the top."

"Hah! Yes, I know the place. It was lying on the slope, I suppose?"

"Well, ye–es, father."

"Humph, strange!" he muttered. "There can't be any metals there. Somebody must have dropped it."

I hesitated. I wanted to speak out, but I was afraid, for I did not know what he would say if he heard that we had blown up one of the rocks with gunpowder, and sent all those stones hurtling down the side of the cliff.

"Yes," continued my father, "somebody must have dropped it. A good specimen—a very good specimen indeed."

Just then he raised his eyes, and caught me gazing at him wistfully.

"Hallo!" he said, "what does that mean? Why are you looking so serious and strange?"

"Was I, father?"

"Yes, sir: of course you were. No nonsense. Speak out like a man, and a gentleman. Not quite the same thing, Sep, for a gentleman is not always a thorough man; but a thorough man is always a gentleman. Now, what is it?"

I did not answer.

"Come, Sep," he said sharply, "you're getting a great fellow now, and I want you, the bigger you grow, the more frank and open. I don't want you to grow into one of those men who look upon their father as someone to be cheated and blinded in every way, instead of as their truest and firmest friend and adviser. Now, sir, you have something on your mind."

"Yes, father," I said slowly.

"Hah! I thought as much. In mischief yesterday?"

"I'm afraid so, father."

"Well, out with it. You know my old saying, 'The truth can be blamed, but can never be shamed.'"

"Yes, father."

"Well, I'm sure my boy could not bear to be shamed."

"Oh, no, father."

"Of course not," he said quietly. "And I'm sure you've got manly feeling enough not to be afraid of being blamed; so out with it, sir, and take your punishment, whatever it is, as the son of a sailor should."

"Yes, father," I exclaimed with a sort of gasp, and then I told him what we had done with the powder.

"Humph! Nice fellows!" he exclaimed as I ended. "Why, you might have blown each other to pieces. Powder wants using only by an experienced man, and young Chowne, who seems to have played first fiddle, seems to know more about his father's powders than that out of a keg. Humph! So you blew down one of the lumps of stone?"

"Yes, father."

"Well, why didn't you say so at once?" he continued tartly, "and not shuffle and shirk. It was a foolish, monkeyish trick, but I suppose no great harm's done. What did you do it for?"

"To see the stones rush down, sir," I said.

"Humph! Well, don't do so any more."

"I will not, father," I said hastily.

"That's well. Now we will not say any more about it. Many stones come down?"

"Yes, father, they swept a bare place down the side of the cliff right to the old rock."

"Here, Sep," said my father excitedly, holding out the lump of mineral, "did you pick this up before or after?"

"After, father; where the rock was swept bare."

My father looked at me quite excitedly.

"Done breakfast?" he said sharply.

"Yes, father."

"Put on your hat and come with me to the Gap. Stop a moment. Did your school-fellows notice that piece of rock—did you show it to them?"

"No, father. I was alone when I found it."

"So much the better. Then, look here, Sep; don't say anything to them about it, nor about what you see to-day."

"No, father; but—"

"Don't ask any questions, boy. I am not sure but you may have made a very important discovery in the Gap. I had no idea of there being any metals there."

"And are there, father?"

"We are going to see, my boy. So now, keep your counsel. Put on your cap and we will walk over to the Gap at once, when you can show me the exact spot where you found this piece."

I grew as excited as my father seemed to be, but with this difference, namely, that as I grew warmer he grew more cool and business-like.

After I had given him some better idea of the place where the specimen had been found, he decided that we would not go round by the cliff path, and past Jonas Uggleston's cottage, but take a short cut over the high moorland ground at the back of the bay, and so on to the Gap, where we could descend just where we lads had blown down the rock.

It was not a long walk that way, though a hilly one, and before half an hour had passed we were close to the edge of the ravine, and directly after on the spot from whence the stone had been dislodged.

Here for the first time I noticed the handle of a hammer in my father's pocket as he stooped down and examined the place where the rock lay, and then shook his head. "No, not here," he said. "Go on first." I led the way and he followed, noting where the rock had bounded off, and then descending to where it had charged the other pieces and rushed on down, baring a portion of the side of the ravine, as I have said, to the very rock.

"Hah!" ejaculated my father suddenly, as he seemed to pounce upon a fragment of stone something like the first I held. "Here's another, and another, and another," I said. "Yes, plenty," he replied rather hoarsely, as he picked up a couple more pieces. "Place them in your pocket, boy."

As he spoke he looked about him up and down, and ended by uttering another sharp exclamation, for in one place there was a rugged patch of rock just like the fragments we held, and seeming as if the cliff-side there was one solid mass.

"Look here, Sep," he said quietly; "be smart, and gather up all the rough pieces of common grey slate you can find and throw them about here I'll help."

I set to work and he aided me vigorously, with the result that in a short time we had hidden the bright metallic-looking patch, and then he laid his hand upon my arm.

"That will do," he said. "Now, keep a silent tongue in your head. I'll talk more to you afterwards. Let's go home now. Stop," he cried, starting; "don't seem to look, but turn your head slightly towards the sea. Your eyes are better than mine. Who's that standing on the piece of rock over yonder. Can you see?"

"No, father, not yet."

"Look more to the north, boy. Just over the big rock that stands out of the cliff-side. There's a man watching us."

"Yes, I see, father," I cried.

"Who is it?" he whispered, as he led the way along by the steep slope so that we might descend and go up the Gap by the stream side and reach the shore.

"Yes, I know, I'm sure now," I cried. "It's old Jonas Uggleston."

"Humph! Of all men in the world," said my father. "Well, the place is my own now, and no one has a right to interfere."

He walked on silently for a few minutes, and then said softly: "I would rather no one had known yet." Then aloud to me: "Come, Sep, let's get home and see what these rocks are made of. I'm beginning to think that you have made a great find."

Chapter Eight
The Doctor and I Build a Furnace

My father was very silent as we walked swiftly back home, where he locked up the specimens we had obtained, and then after a few minutes' thought he signed to me to follow him and started for Ripplemouth.

About half-way there we met Doctor Chowne on his grey pony with Bob walking beside him, and directly after the doctor and my father were deep in conversation, leaving us boys together.

"What's the matter!" said Bob. "Your father ill?"

"No," I replied; "I think it's about business." How well I can recollect Doctor Chowne! A little fierce-looking stoutish man, in drab breeches and top-boots, and a very old-fashioned cocked hat that looked terribly the worse for wear. He used to have a light brown coat and waistcoat, with very large pockets that I always believed to be full of powders, and draughts, and pills on one side; and on the other of tooth-pincers, and knives, and saws for cutting off people's legs and arms. Then, too, he wore a pigtail, his hair being drawn back and twisted up, and bound, and tied at the end with a greasy bit of ribbon. But it was not like anybody else's pigtail, for, instead of hanging down decently over his coat collar, it cocked up so that it formed a regular curve, and looked as if it was a hook or a handle belonging to his cocked hat.

Before my father and he had been talking many minutes, the doctor turned sharply round in his saddle, with one hand resting on the pony's back. He was going to speak, but his hand tickled the pony, which began to kick, whereupon Doctor Chowne, who looked rather red-faced and excited, stuck his spurs into the pony's ribs, and this made him rear and back towards the cliff edge, till the doctor dragged his head round so that he could see the sea, when he directly ran backwards and stood with his tail in the bank.

"Quiet, will you?" cried the doctor, and, as the pony was not being tickled, he consented to stand still. "Here, Bob!" said the doctor then.

"Yes, father."

"Go home."

"Go home, father! Mayn't I go along with Sep Duncan?"

"I said go home, sir," said the doctor sternly; and Bob turned short upon his heel, and I saw him go along the road cutting viciously at the ferns and knapweeds at every step.

"Come along, Sep," said my father, and I followed them as they walked slowly back towards our cottage, my father holding on by the pony's mane as he talked quickly to the doctor.

For my father and Doctor Chowne were great friends, having once served for a long time in the same ship together; and so it was that, when my father left the service and settled down to his quiet life at the little bay, Doctor Chowne bought the practice off the last doctor's widow, and settled himself, with his boy, at Ripplemouth.

As I say, the doctor and my father were very great friends, such great friends that when one day my father felt himself to be dangerously ill, and sent over in great haste for Doctor Chowne, that gentleman galloped over and examined him carefully, and then began to bully him and call him names. He told him there was nothing the matter with him but fancy, and made him get up and go out for a walk, and told him afterwards that if they had not been such great friends he—the doctor—would have run him up a twenty-pound bill for attendance instead of nothing at all.

And there before me were those two, one walking and the other riding, with their heads close together, talking in a low eager tone, while I was thinking about how hard it was for Bob Chowne that he should be sent away, and began to wish that I had not found that piece of stone.

We reached home, and our Sam, who kept the garden in order, and cleaned the boots and knives, and washed the boat, was called to take the doctor's pony, after which Doctor Chowne whispered something to my father.

"Oh, no," my father said. "He found it, and we can trust him."

Doctor Chowne whispered something else, and it set me wondering how my father could be such good friends with a man who made himself so very disagreeable and unpleasant to every one he met; but all at once it seemed to strike me that I was always good friends with Bob Chowne, who was the most disagreeable boy in our school, and that though he could be so unpleasant, there was something about him I always liked; for though he bullied and hectored, he was not, like most bullying and hectoring boys, a coward, for he had taken my part many a time against bigger and stronger fellows, and at all times we had found him thoroughly staunch.

As soon as Sam had gone off with the pony, my father called Kicksey, our maid, a great, brawny woman of forty, who was quite mistress at our place, my father being, like Doctor Chowne and Jonas Uggleston, a widower.

Kicksey came in a great hurry, with her muslin mob-cap flopping and her eyes staring, to know what was the matter.

"Light the back kitchen fire," said my father.

"No," said Doctor Chowne, "put some wood and charcoal ready, and fetch a dozen bricks out of the yard."

"Is Master Sep ill?" cried Kicksey. "Oh, no: there he is. I was quite—"

"There, be quick," said my father; "and if anybody comes, go to the gate and say I'm busy."

Kicksey stared at us all, with her eyes seeming to stand out of her head like a lobster's, she was so astounded at this curious proceeding, but she said nothing and hurried out.

And here I ought to say that her name was Ellen Levan, only, when I was a tiny little fellow after my mother died, she used to nurse me, and in my childish prattle I somehow got in the habit of calling her Kicksey, and the name became so fixed that my father never spoke of her as Ellen; while our Sam, who was an amphibious being, half fisherman, half gardener, with a mortal hatred of Jonas Uggleston's Bill Binnacle, and the doctor's man, always called her Missers Kicksey and nothing else.

"Now, then, Duncan, are we to do this together, or is—"

He made a sign towards me.

"Let him stop and help," said my father. "I can trust Sep when I've told him not to speak. But can you stop? I understood you to say that you were going to see a couple of patients."

"Only old Mrs Ransom at the Hall, and Farmer Dikeby's wife. The old woman's got nothing the matter but ninety-one, and as for Mistress Dikeby, she has had too much physic as it is, and if I go she won't be happy till I give her some more, which she will be far better without. No: I am going to stay and see this through."

"I shall be very glad."

"And so shall I, Duncan. I said you were an idiot to buy that Gap, and I told you so; but no one will be better pleased than I shall if it turns out well."

He held out his hand and my father took it without a word.

"Now, then," said the doctor, "let's see the stuff."

My father opened the corner cupboard and took out the pieces of rock, and Doctor Chowne put on his glasses and examined them carefully, frowning severely all the time and without a word.

"Do you think it *is* tin?" said my father at last.

"No, sir, I don't," said Doctor Chowne, throwing down one of the pieces in an ill-humoured way. "I'll take my oath it isn't."

"Oh!" ejaculated my father in a disappointed tone; "but are you sure?"

"Sure, sir? Yes. I'm not clever, and I'm better at gunshot wounds and amputations than at medical practice, but I do know a bit about metals and mining. Why, didn't we touch at Banca in '44 and see the tin mining there?"

"Yes," said my father; "but I took no interest in it then."

"Well, I did, my lad. Tin? No. Tin would either be stream-tin, looking like so much grey stone, or else tin in quartz, all little blackish grains."

"Then this is—"

"Like the yellow iron you showed me once, and wanted to make me believe was gold—a mare's nest?"

My father looked at him with his brow all wrinkled up.

"No," said the doctor quickly, "it is not tin, Duncan, but very fine galena—"

"Galena?" said my father; and I stared at the glittering blackish ore like metallic coal.

"Yes, sir, galena-lead ore, and I shall be very much surprised if we do not find in it a large proportion of silver."

"Silver!" cried my father excitedly. "Then it is a great find."

"Great find, my boy? A very great find. Now get a hammer and let's powder some of this up, and see whether we can melt it. Got a pair of bellows?"

"Oh yes, big ones."

"Hah! That's right," said the doctor. "Now the way would be to take our powdered specimens to the blacksmith's forge, and melt them there, but that would be like letting the whole country-side know about it, and we've no occasion to do that. I suppose no one knows as yet?"

"No—I'm not sure," said my father; and he mentioned how Jonas Uggleston seemed to be watching him.

"That's bad. But never mind; the place is yours. Have you got your deeds?"

"No," said my father, "Lawyer Markley said they would be ready in a day or two. That was last week."

"Take the pony and ride over to Barnstaple at once, and get them. Don't come back without them, or, mark my words, there'll be some quibble or hindrance thrown in the way. Make quite sure of the place at once I say."

"But to-morrow, when we've tested these stones," said my father.

"My dear Duncan," cried the doctor, "I'm a disagreeable crotchety fellow, but you know you can trust me. Now, take my advice, and go directly. If I saw a patient in a bad way, should I put off my remedies till to-morrow; and if you saw that you were getting your ship land-bound on a lee shore, would you wait till to-morrow before you altered your course?"

DOCTOR CHOWNE CONDUCTS AN EXPERIMENT

"No," said my father smiling. "There, I'll go."

He started directly, and as soon as we heard the pony's hoofs on the road the doctor turned to me.

"Come along, Sep," he said, "and let's see if we can't make your father's fortune."

He was quite at home in our house, and I followed him into the back kitchen, where he set me at work powdering up the specimens with a hammer on a block of stone, while he built up in the broad open fireplace quite a little furnace with bricks, into which he fitted a small deep earthen pot, one that he chose as being likely to stand the fire, which he set with wood and charcoal, after mixing the broken and powdered ore with a lot of little bits of charcoal, and half filling the earthen pot. This he covered with more charcoal, shut in the little furnace with some slate slabs, and then, when he considered everything ready, started the fire, which it became my duty to blow.

This did not prove necessary after the fire was well alight, for the doctor had managed his furnace so well that it soon began to roar and glow, getting hotter and hotter, while, as the charcoal sunk, more and more was heaped on, till the little fire burned furiously, and the bricks began to crack, and turn first of a dull red, then brighter, and at last some of them looked almost transparent.

All this took a long time, and our task was a very hot one, for from between the places where the bricks joined, the fire sent out a tremendous heat, where it could be seen glowing and almost white in its intensity.

But hot as it was on a midsummer day, the whole business had a great fascination for me, and I would not have left it on any account.

The doctor, too, seemed wonderfully interested. Kicksey came about two o'clock to say that the dinner was ready, but the doctor would not leave the furnace; neither would I, and each of us, armed with a pair of tongs from the kitchen and parlour, stood as close as we could, ready to put on fresh pieces of charcoal as the fire began to sink.

"How long will it take cooking, sir?" I said, after the furnace had been glowing for a long time.

"Hah!" he said, "that's what I can't tell you, Sep. You see we have not got a regular furnace and blast, and this heat may not be great enough to turn the ore into metal, so we must keep on as long as we can to make sure. It is of no use to be sanguine over experiments, for all this may turn out to be a failure. Even with the best of tools we make blunders, my lad, and with a such a set out as this, why, of course, anything may happen."

"Anything happen, sir?" I said.

"To be sure. That ore ought to have been put in a proper fire-clay crucible."

"What's a crucible, sir?" I said.

"A pot made of a particular material that will bear any amount of heat. Now perhaps while we are patiently waiting here that pot in the furnace may have cracked and fallen to pieces, or perhaps melted away instead of the ore inside."

"Oh, but a pot would not melt, sir, would it?" I said.

"Melt? To be sure it would, if you make the fire hot enough. Did you ever see a brick-kiln?"

"Yes, sir."

"And did you never see how sometimes, when the fire has been too hot, the bricks have all run together?"

"And formed clinkers, sir? Oh yes, often."

"Well, then, there you have seen how a mixture of sand and powdered stone and clay will melt, so, why should not that earthen pot?"

"Then if that pot melts or breaks all our trouble will have been for nothing, sir?"

"Yes, Sep, and we must begin again."

"But shouldn't we find the stuff melted down at the bottom of the fire?"

"Perhaps; perhaps not; we might find it run into a lump, but we should most likely find it not melted at all, and then, as I said, we should have to begin over again."

"That would be tiresome," I said. "But never mind, we should succeed next time, perhaps."

"We should try till we did succeed, Sep, my lad. There, that's the last of the charcoal."

"Shall I fetch some more?" I cried.

"No, my lad, perhaps what has been burned may have melted it, so we'll wait and see."

"And take out the pot?"

"No, we couldn't do that. We must wait till it cools down. Maybe by and by I can take out a brick, and we shall be able to see whether the ore has melted."

I waited impatiently for this to be done, and about an hour later the doctor took the top brick from the glowing furnace with the tongs, and touched the charcoal embers, which fell at once down to a level with the top of the pot, the interior having burned away, so as to leave quite a glowing basket or cage of fire.

Chapter Nine
The Result of the Smelting

But there was nothing to see yet, and the brick was replaced, the fire roared once more, and for what must have been quite another quarter of an hour we waited before the doctor took out the brick again.

It was now possible to make out what seemed to be a regular ring red-hot in the midst of so much glowing ember with which the pot was filled; and into this the doctor thrust the poker, to find that it passed through what was light as feathers.

"I must be gentle," he said quietly, as he thrust the poker lower, till he could gently tap the bottom of the pot.

"It's quite sound," he said, as he gave the poker a stirring motion and ended by withdrawing it.

"I think we may let out the fire," he said; and we proceeded to bear away the slates we had used for screens, and then to take down the glowing bricks one by one, and toss them into the yard.

This done, I proposed throwing a bucket of water over the heap of embers, in the midst of which stood the pot.

"No, thank you, young wisdom," said Doctor Chowne. "I should like to have some result to show your father when he comes back. If you did what you say, the pot would fly all to pieces, and where would our work be then?"

"I say, Doctor Chowne," I said, looking at him rather wistfully, "I wish I knew as much as you do."

"Learn then," he said. "I did not know so much once upon a time."

As he spoke, he slowly and carefully drew the ashes down from about the pot, and as they were spread about the brilliant glow began to give place to a pale grey feathery ash, which flushed red, and then yellow, whenever the air was disturbed, while the earthen pot that had been red-hot changed slowly to a dull drab.

"There, Sep," said the doctor, "that pot will take pretty well an hour to get thoroughly cool, so we may as well go and have some dinner. What do you say?"

"I was thinking, sir," I said, "that if there is any metal in that pot now, it would be something like the lead when we are casting sinkers for fishing. Why couldn't we lift the pot with the tongs, and pour out what's at the bottom and run it into a mould."

"Have you got a mould, Sep?" he said.

"Yes, sir; three different sizes—up here on the shelf."

I went to a corner of the back kitchen, and reached down three dusty clay moulds, one of which the doctor took and set upon the floor.

"You are right," he cried. "There, take your tongs, and we'll catch hold of the pot together, and set it out here. Then, both together, mind, we'll pour out what there is into the mould."

It was easy enough. We each got a good hold of the pot, lifted it out with its glowing feathery charcoal ashes half filling it, and then, after setting it down to get a more suitable hold, we tilted it sidewise, and then more and more and more, but nothing came out save some glowing ashes, which fell beyond the mould in a tiny heap.

"Higher still, Sep, higher, higher," the doctor kept on saying; and we tilted it more and more; but still nothing came till, just as we were about to turn it upside down, there was a flash of something bright and silvery, and a tiny drop of fluid metal ran out on to the mould, and down the side.

"That's it. Up with it, Sep. A little more this side. Now then."

Up went the bottom of the pot higher still, and out came a little rush of glowing charcoal, and directly after a bit of heavy clinker, and that was all.

"Oh, I say, doctor," I cried, "what a pity!"

"Pity, my lad! I don't think so. Here, let me do it."

He lifted up the piece of hard clinker and set it upon the slate slabs by itself, and then taking hold of the mould with the tongs, he raised it and gave it a tap or two on the floor, to get rid of the feather ash, and I could see that there was what seemed to be a piece of thin lead beginning in a sort of splash running to the edge in a thread, then down the side of the mould, to finish off in a little round fat button of metal.

"Hah! I don't think we've done so badly after all, Sep," he said, as he placed the mould upon the table; "but first of all, brush those embers lightly aside, and let's see if there is anything left."

I took a wisp of birch and did as I was told, but there was nothing to be seen, and when the doctor took the pot out into the yard, and carefully examined it, he found nothing there, and brought the little clay vessel back.

"You must take care of that pot, Sep," he said. "It is nothing to look at, but a thing which will stand fire in that way may prove valuable. Now, then, my lad, bring that bit of refuse, and we will go in and have some dinner. These things will be quite cool by the time we have done."

We carried our treasures into the parlour, and, to Kicksey's great delight, had a wash and our dinner, while she obtained leave to clear away what she was pleased to call our "mess."

But the doctor did not let the dinner pass without carefully examining the rugged piece of metal and the button, and then the piece of refuse, the remains of the broken-up specimen.

For my part I was not at all dazzled by the result of our experiment, and at last, with my mouth full of jam and bread and cream, I said:

"But that's only a shabby little bit to get out of all those bits I broke up, isn't it, sir?"

"Do you think so, Sep?" he replied smiling.

"Yes, sir!"

"Well, I think quite differently. We put in rough stony uncleansed ore, and we have got out this piece. If there's plenty of it in the sides of the Gap, my boy, and it is properly worked, your father will be a rich man from the produce of the lead alone; and I feel pretty sure," he continued, as he examined the scrap of metal through his glass, "that there is a great deal of silver in this as well. Here, what are you doing?" he cried.

"I was looking to see if father was coming," I cried, as I turned back at the door.

"You need not look," he said quietly, "for it will be three hours at the least before he can get back. The pony must have a rest at the town."

I came back slowly, for I felt that what the doctor said was true, and it seemed to be all so curious that our bit of mischief should turn out so strangely that I did what was a very unusual thing for me in those days, sat down and thought.

The piece of metal was lying before me, and I took it up and examined it, turning it over and over in my hands, while I could not keep a strong feeling of doubt from creeping in.

"Perhaps the doctor is wrong," I said to myself, and this may be worth nothing at all; and as I thought in this fashion, I longed for my father to come back, so as to hear what he had to say about the value of the metal. For in those days I had a very frank loyal feeling towards my father, and a belief in his being about the best man anywhere in the neighbourhood, and that he knew better than anybody else.

The silence in the room was broken by the entrance of Kicksey to take away; and as she did so she took the opportunity of informing us that she had cleared everything away, and that the kitchen was as clean once more as a new pin.

As I have before said, the doctor, as my father's old friend and companion, was quite at home in our house, and, after refreshing himself with a pinch of snuff, he proceeded to have some tobacco in another form, for he went to the corner cupboard and got out the jar and a long pipe, which he filled and lit, and then sat there in silence, watching the piece of rugged metal.

As he sat watching the metal and surrounding himself with smoke, I sat and watched him, till it became so tiresome and dull that I rose quietly at last, and stole out into the garden and had a look at the sea, all aglow now with the evening sunshine, and looking curiously like the burning charcoal when it had been spread out on the kitchen floor.

It was very beautiful, but I had watched that too often, so I crossed the garden and went out into the lane to see if I could find anything amusing there.

For it seemed to me that it might be very nice for my father to have found a mine of lead and silver, and that it would be very interesting to see it dug out and melted, as we had melted those pieces that day—of course in a large way; but I did not feel as if I wanted to be rich, and I would a great deal rather then have been wandering out there on the cliff with Bob Chowne or Bigley Uggleston, when I heard a shout, and, looking in the direction, there, high up on the cliff path, and coming towards me with long strides, was my last-named school-fellow.

"Hallo, Big!" I shouted, running towards him; "where are you going?"

"Coming to look after you," he said. "Why didn't you come over again?"

"Because I was wanted at home," I replied. "You might have come over to me."

"I couldn't. I didn't like to. Father was put out this morning, because he saw you and your father on our grounds."

"Your grounds!" I said. "Oh, come, that is a good one."

"Well, father always talks about it as if all the Gap belonged to him. What were you doing there?"

"Having a walk," I was obliged to say.

"Oh, well, you might have stopped."

"Didn't I tell you my father wanted me," I replied in a pettish way. "I've only just got out again."

"I've been waiting at home to see if my father would come back. He started off to walk to Barnstaple."

"Your father has?" I cried involuntarily. "Why, that's where my father has gone."

"What! To Barnstaple, Sep?"

I nodded.

"I say," he said, "I hope they won't meet one another."

"Why?" I exclaimed.

"Because they might quarrel. I say, Sep, I wish your father and my father were good friends like we are."

I shook my head at that, and felt rather lofty.

"I don't see how that can ever be," I replied; and then I felt quite uncomfortable as I recalled my father being uneasy about old Jonas watching us that morning. I felt, too, that it would be much worse now if Jonas got to know that there was a mine upon the estate, and it seemed as if we were going to be at the beginning of a good deal of trouble.

"Father went up the Gap after you had gone," said Bigley, "and I saw him go right up to the place where we blew down the big rock, and when I saw him go there I went indoors and got his spy-glass and watched him out of the window."

"I say, you oughtn't to watch people," I said sharply.

"I know that," replied Bigley; "but I was afraid there was going to be a bother, and I wanted to tell you if there was."

"Well, what did he do?"

"Why, if he didn't seem to make it all out exactly just where we had been, and he followed down the place where the stone fell, and then went on down till he came to the rough part where the rock was all bared, and stooped and looked it all over and over. Oh, he has got eyes, my father has. I could see as plain as could be through the spy-glass that he picked up bits of the stone, and once he knelt down and I think he smelt the stones."

"Smelt them!" I exclaimed.

"Yes, to find out about the gunpowder. He has found it all out, I'm sure."

"So am I," I said sadly, but without telling Bigley I meant something else.

"And then he went right down slowly just where the big rock slipped along, and down to the stream, and washed his hands and came home."

"And did he speak to you about it?"

"No," replied Bigley. "I expected him to say a lot. I didn't mind, for I should have told him all about it, and I don't think he would have been very cross with me; but he didn't say a single word about it, though I saw him shake his fist several times when he was talking to himself, and soon after he set off to walk in to Barnstaple, and, as I told you, he hasn't got back."

Just then there was the clattering of hoofs, and I looked up and saw my father coming down the zigzag road.

"I must go now," I said. "Don't think me unkind, Big, old chap. Or you stop and I'll come out to you again."

"Yes, do," he said. "I'll go and sit down on the rocks till you come. Only, mind you do."

I promised that I would and we parted, one going down towards the sea, the other along the lane, where I met my father looking very hot and tired; but he seemed in good spirits, so I supposed that he had not met old Jonas.

"Well, Sep," he cried, "how about the experiment? What luck?"

"Oh, we melted the stones, father, and got out of them a little bit of lead."

"It was lead, then?" he said eagerly, as we reached the cottage.

"Yes, father, and Doctor Chowne says he thinks there's silver in it as well."

"You young dog!" cried the doctor, coming out pipe in mouth. "Why, you are telling all the news, and there'll be nothing left for me to do."

"Only show the stuff," I said.

"Ah, yes; show the result," said the doctor. "But come in, Duncan, the tea's waiting, and I want a cup myself."

"And I am regularly tired out," cried my father. "Here, Sam, feed the pony well, for he has worked hard."

Sam, who had heard the pony coming, took the rein and led it off to the stable, while I followed my father into the little parlour, where the doctor caught him by the arm.

"Here's the specimen, father," I said; but he did not turn his head, for the doctor was speaking to him.

"Did you get the deeds?" he said.

"Chowne, you're as good as a witch," cried my father.

"Why?"

"As I came out of the lawyer's office, who should I see but old Jonas Uggleston coming along the street, and as I went into the hotel I saw him turn in where I had been."

"But did you get the deeds?" cried the doctor.

"Specimen, Sep?" said my father. "Oh, that's it, is it? Well, it doesn't look worth all this trouble."

"Duncan, what a man you are!" said Doctor Chowne pettishly. "I've said twice over, Did you get the deeds?"

"I beg your pardon, Chowne. Yes, of course. He wanted to put me off, said I'd better let them stop with him, and that there was no hurry, and that a little endorsing was wanted."

"Oh, of course!" said the doctor.

"But when he saw that I was in earnest, and that I meant to wait for them, he set to work and got the business done—that is, all that was wanted. In fact, it was a mere nothing."

"And he wanted to keep them in his charge unsigned, with the chance of making more of the estate to somebody else if that somebody else turned up."

"Jonas Uggleston to wit?" said my father.

"Exactly. Duncan, old fellow, you see that you were just in time."

"That's what I felt, Chowne; but there the deeds are safe and sound; the Gap is thoroughly mine—my freehold."

"And you may congratulate yourself on being the owner of a valuable lead and silver mine."

"Then you feel sure of that, Chowne?" said my father, who seemed quite overcome.

"I am certain of it; but of course I can't say what is the quantity."

"Silver?"

"Probably. Lead, certain."

"Then, Sep, my boy—" cried my father excitedly, catching me by the shoulder.

"Yes, father," I said.

I believe now that my father was going to say something about my growing up to be a rich man; but he checked himself, and only said quietly:

"Come and sit down to tea."

Chapter Ten
We Bale the Rock Pool

Now there was very little done during the rest of our holidays; all I remember was, that instead of old Jonas Uggleston being very disagreeable, and making himself my father's enemy, he grew very civil and pleasant, and nodded to my father when they met, and called him "Captain."

He was wonderfully kind to me too, asking me into the house, and seeming very pleased whenever he knew that Bigley had come over to see me.

The news that there was lead and silver in the Gap soon spread, and a great many people came to see my father, and wanted to buy the little estate; but he said no, that he should work it himself, for he wanted some occupation; and he and the doctor planned it all out, how to begin in a small way; and men were set to work to wall in the part where the mine was to be opened, and to build sheds and pumping-house.

But after a few days this became monotonous to us boys, who had plenty of things to tempt us about the cliffs and the shore, and I'm going to put down one or two of our bits of adventure which we had about this time.

Our little bay or cove was one of three or four little bays within one big bay, formed by Norman's Head at the west and Barn's Nose in the east, and all round from point to point there was one tremendous wall or cliff of reddish or bluish rock, nowhere less than a couple of hundred feet high; and the only places where you could get down to the sea were at the heads of the coves, or where one of the little streams from the moor made its way down to the beach. Here and there when the tide was low lay patches of blackish sand, but the foot of the cliffs nearly all the way was one jumble of great rocks, beginning with lumps, say as big as a chest of drawers, and running up to rugged masses as large as cottages.

They did not look so big when you were up on the cliff path, six or seven hundred feet above them; but when the tide went down, and we boys went for a ramble over and among them, it was to find the smaller blocks nearly as high as our heads, while the big ones made the most magnificent climbing any lad could wish for who was an enemy to the knees of his breeches and the toes of his boots.

Of course we could have gone east or west along the cliff path as peaceably as the sheep; but what was a walk like that to wandering in and out among the sea-weed-hung masses, full of corners and ways as a maze; with rock pools amongst them, and chasms and rifts, and rock arches and hollows, and caves without end?

Some of these blocks were of a sort of limestone or grit, and they were rugged and rounded at the corner, and lumpy, but the slaty rocks were generally flat-sided, and split off regularly, forming smooth flat forms that often rose one above another in rough steps, so that you could easily climb to the tops, or, where they had fallen and split away from the cliff, and lay resting against one another, you could walk under what seemed to be like great stone lean-to sheds, whose floors were as often as not water as pure and clear as crystal.

It was a wonderful place, and never ceased to attract us, for there was always something to find when the tide had gone down leaving the rocks bare.

All the things that lived or grew upon them had been seen by us hundreds of times, but after some months at school they always seemed new again, and we got our little pawn nets and baskets, and went prawning with as great zest as ever.

There are plenty of ways to go prawning, I daresay, but I'll tell you how we managed. We each used to have a small ring net, fixed at the end of a six-foot stick that answered two or three purposes, and, with our little baskets slung at our backs, set off along the shore.

I remember one morning very well. It was about three weeks after finding the lead vein that Bob Chowne and Bigley came over to the Bay, and we started, our Sam saying that it was going to be a very low tide.

Off we went down by the little waterfall which came along by the back of our house, and down to the beach, getting as close to the sea as the rocks would let us, and looking out for the first pool where the sea had left a few prisoners.

We were not long in seeing one, and then the thing was to approach as quietly as possible and look in.

These pools were generally fringed with sea-weed, great greenish-brown fronds in one place, dark streaks of laver in another, and lower down the bottom would be all pink with the fine corallite, while all about the sea-anemones would dot every crack and hole, like round knobs of dark red jelly, where the water had left them high and dry, spread out like painted daisy flowers, where they were down in the pool.

No matter how cautiously we approached, something would take fright. Perhaps it would be a little shore crab that betrayed itself by scuffling down amongst the corallite or sea-weed, perhaps a little fierce-looking bristly fish, which shot under a ledge of the rock all amongst the limpets, acorn barnacles, or the thousands of yellow and brown and striped snaily fellows that crawled about in company with the periwinkles and pelican's feet.

Those were not what we wanted, but the prawns, which would be balancing themselves in the clear water, and then dart backwards with a flip of their tails right under the sea-weed or ledges.

I remember that day so well because it was marked by a big black stone, of which more by and by; and everything connected with our doings that morning seems to stand out quite clear, as the Welsh coast did under the clear blue sky.

We reached our first pool, and Bob Chowne shouted, "There's one!" while I was certain I saw two more. Then Bob and Bigley softly thrust in their nets, and it became my duty to poke about among the sea-weed and under the ledges where we had seen the prawns take shelter.

At about the second stirring of the overhanging weed on one side, out darted a big prawn. "I've got him!" cried Bob, and we all shouted "Hooray!" but when the net was raised, dripping pearls in the bright sunshine, the prawn was not there, for, preferring open water to nets, it had shot between the two and taken shelter under the ledges on the other side.

But there he was, for there was no way out to where the sea sucked and gurgled among the rocks three or four yards away, and we continued our hunt, not to dislodge this one, but three more, one being larger, and two much less.

For a good ten minutes they dodged us about, hiding in all manner of out-of-the-way corners, till all at once it seemed as if they must have gone. The water, that had been brilliantly clear when we started, was now thick with sand and broken sea-weed, and Bigley lifted out his net to clear it and to let the water settle a little before we started again.

"I don't know where they've got to," said Bob sourly. "Prawns are not half so easy to catch as they used to be."

"Hallo! Why, here's one," cried Bigley just then, as he found one of the biggest kicking about among the sea-weed that he had turned out of the bottom of his net.

This first capture was soon transferred to the basket, and the fact of one being taken so encouraged Bob that he set to with renewed energy, and the result was that we caught two more out of that pool, the biggest of all—at least Bob Chowne said it was—having to be left behind in the inaccessible crack where he had hidden himself.

Another pool and another was visited with excellent luck, for the tide was down lower than usual, and prawns seemed plentiful, there having been plenty of time for them to collect since they were last disturbed, for we boys were the only hunters on that deserted shore. So on we went, one poking about among the weeds till the prawn darted backwards into the nets held ready, and we had soon been able to muster over a dozen.

Then, all at once, we came upon quite a little pool right under a large mass of rock with a smaller and deeper pool joined to it by a narrow channel between two blocks of stone, and farther from the sea.

We caught sight of several prawns darting under cover as we came in sight, but, to our disgust, found that we could not attack them, the pool being so sheltered by overhanging rocks that the only possible way seemed to be by undressing and going into what was quite a grotto.

Travellers tell us how the natives of some far-off islands dive into the sea and do battle with sharks; but no boy ever lived who could dive into a pool and catch a prawn in his native element—at least I never knew one who could, and we were going to give it up after a few frantic thrusts with our nets, when an idea occurred to me.

"Here, I know!" I cried. "Let's bale out the little low hole, and that will empty the big one."

"To be sure," cried Bob. "Go it! But we've got nothing to bale with."

"Big's shoes," I cried as I caught sight of them hanging from his neck, tied together by their thongs, and each with a knitted worsted stocking plugging up the toes.

Big made not the slightest objection, but laughed as he pulled out his stockings and thrust them into his breeches' pockets.

The next minute he and I were scooping out the water at a tremendous rate, making quite a stream flow down from the upper part under the rock, and it soon became evident that in less than an hour both would be dry.

We worked away till I was tired and gave place to Bob Chowne, Bigley all the while working away and sending out great shoefuls over the lower edge of the rocks.

I sat down to rest, and as I watched where the water fell I suddenly made a dart at something thrown out, but it only proved to be a prickly weaver.

Five minutes later, though, Big threw out a prawn which had come down with the current, and this encouraged him to work harder, but Bob began to be tired, and he showed it by sending a shoeful of water at me, making me shout, "Leave off!"

Then he sent one flying over Bigley, who only laughed and worked on for a few moments till Bob was not looking, and then sent a shower back.

Bob jumped out of the hole like a shot and turned upon Bigley angrily:

"You just see if I'm going to stop down there and be smothered with water. Yah! Get out, you ugly old smuggler."

As he spoke he flung Bigley's great shoe with a good aim down by his feet, and splashed him completely all over.

Some lads would have jumped out and pursued Bob in a fury, but Bigley only brushed the water out of his eyes and began to laugh as if he rather enjoyed it.

"Come on, Sep," he cried to me; "you and I will finish, and if he comes near we'll give him such a dowsing."

I went to his help, and we worked so well that no less than six more prawns came down to our pool, and were scooped out; and at last the upper one was completely emptied, but it was nearly an hour's work.

"Now then, I'll go in," said Bob, and he crept in through the rift between the two pools, and under the overhanging rocks.

"Oh!" he cried as soon as he was in, "what a jolly place! And—ugh! Here's a conger."

"No!" we cried together.

"Yes there is, long as my arm, and he's squirming about. Here, give me a landing-net. I'll poke him, and make him come out to you chaps."

We handed him the net, and he began banging and thrusting at the rock for some time without result.

"Well, isn't he coming?" I cried.

"No; he gets up in a corner here so that I can only feel his slippery tail with the stick, and he won't come out."

"Take hold of it with your hand and pull," said Bigley.

"Oh yes, I daresay. Just as if I didn't know there's only one place where you can hold on."

"Where's that?" said Bigley.

"With your hand in his mouth. You come and put yours in."

Of course Bigley did not respond to the invitation, and the banging and rattling went on for a few minutes longer.

"Why don't you chaps stand away from the light? I can't see," cried Bob. "That's better: now I can tell. Look out, boys, look out! Here he comes."

"Catch him in the net, Bob," I shouted.

"Yah! Don't talk stuff," was the answer. "Look out! Is he coming your way?"

"No!" we both shouted, and then "Yes!" for there was a quick movement in the channel between the two pools, and the next instant a large eel was splashing and writhing in the water and sea-weed of the pool which we had baled.

"Here he is, Bob!" we shouted; and, as we finished the struggle which resulted in our getting the eel into one of the nets, and then out on the open rocks, and in a position to make it cease its writhings, Bob Chowne backed out to look on and help us gloat over our capture, which proved to be a plump young conger of a yard long.

"Well, that's something," said Bob. "Now I'm going after the prawns. No, you go, Sep," he said. "I don't see why I should do all the work."

I went into the dripping grotto nothing loth, and by careful search among the wet weed I found first one prawn and then another, till I had thrown out six, the work being tolerably easy, for the little horny-coated fellows made known their presence by their movements, flipping their tails sharply and making a noise that betrayed their hiding-places.

The grotto-like place, shut in by some rocks overshadowed by others, was so gloomy that it was hard to make out everything, but twice over I noted a bit of a rift on my left all fringed with sea-weed and slippery with anemones, where it was not rough with limpets and barnacles.

"Was it down here, Bob, down on the left, that you found the conger?"

"No," he shouted, "on the right."

I looked round, and found the crack where the conger must have been, and then came a summons from without.

"Well, can't you find any more?"

"No," I said; "but there's a big hole here. Perhaps there's another conger."

"Put your hand in and pull him out, then," cried Bob with a sneer.

I did not answer, for I felt now very plainly how much easier it is to give orders than to obey them. But a little consideration taught me that there was nothing to fear, for if there was a conger in the hole the chances were that he would have thrust his head into the farthest corner, and that it would be his tail that I should touch.

"Now, then," cried Bob. "Ar'n't you going to find any more prawns?"

"I don't know," I said, as I carefully introduced my hand and arm, going down on one knee so as to get closer, and so by degrees hand, arm, and shoulder had nearly disappeared, as I touched the far end of the cleft.

"Nothing," I said to myself, as I felt about with my cheek touching the wet slippery sea-weed. Then I uttered a loud "Ugh!" and started away.

"What's the matter?" cried my companions.

"I don't know," I cried. "Here's something alive in a hole here."

"Well, why don't you pull it out?" cried Bob.

"I—I don't know," I said. But I'm afraid I did know. The feeling, though, that my companions were laughing at me was too much, and with a sudden burst of energy I thrust my hand right into the rift again, felt down cautiously till my hand touched, not the slimy serpentine form of an eel, but the hard back of a shell-fish, and as I touched it, there was a curious scuffling down beneath my fingers that told me it was a crab.

"Hooray, boys!" I shouted. "Crab!"

"Have him out, Sep! Mind he don't nip you!" they shouted; and after a minute's hesitation I plunged my hand into the hole again, knowing that I must feel for a safe place to get hold of the claw-armed creature, so that I should not have to suffer a severe pinch or two, from its nippers.

I was pretty quick, but the crab was quicker, and as I caught it the left claw seized tight hold, but only of my sleeve.

My natural instinct was to start back, and this had the effect of dragging the crab out of its lurking place, and I ran to the opening holding out my arm, just as the crab dropped with quite a crash into the little channel, and then began running sidewise back towards me and the darkness.

I stopped my prisoner with my foot, and he scuffled back and into the little empty pool, where he tried hard to hide himself under the sea-weed fronds, but Bigley worked him out, and by clever management avoided the pincers, which were held up threateningly, and popped him into one of the baskets.

"It's my turn now," said Bigley. "Think there's anything else?"

"I don't know," I said. "Try."

"What's the good of saying that?" said Bob laughing. "He couldn't get in."

"Oh, couldn't I?" cried Bigley. "You'll see. Mind that eel don't slip out. Now you'll see."

He rolled up his sleeves nearly to the shoulder, and picking out the widest spot began to crawl in, dragging himself slowly through, and at last drawing his legs in after him, and standing in a bent position right under the rock.

"There!" he cried triumphantly. "Who can't get in? Now then, where are these cracks?"

"Right up at the other end," I cried; and he groped on into the narrower part, Bob and I looking into the slippery grotto-like place enjoying his slow cumbersome manner, and paying no heed to the fact that the tide had turned, and that already a little water had run into the little pool where we had baled.

"Found anything, Big!" we shouted, though he was only a couple of yards away.

"N–no. Nothing here. I'm going to try this other hole. Oh, I say, isn't it deep?"

"Mind! Mind!" shrieked Bob, and Bigley scuffled back.

"What—what is it?" he panted.

"Ha-ha-ha-ha!" roared Bob. "Did he bite you?"

"What a shame!" grumbled Bigley in his gruff voice. "I didn't try to scare you. I don't care though. You won't frighten me again."

He crept back, and we could hear him grunting and panting.

"I say, it is deep," he said. "I've got my arm in right to the shoulder and there's nothing here. Stop a minute; here's a crack round this corner where I can get my hand. It's quite a big opening with water in it, and slippery things in the rock, and—Ugh!—oh!—ah!"

Chapter Eleven
A Terrible Danger

Bigley dragged his arm out of the crack and came scuffling back to us, and as soon as he reached the opening we could see that he looked quite pale.

"Why, Big, what is it?" I cried eagerly.

"Don't frighten him. He has seen the ghost of an old cock shark," cried Bob Chowne grinning.

"Oh, I don't know," he panted. "Something soft, and cold, and alive."

"Why, it was a jelly-fish," we said together. "Did it sting?"

"No. You wouldn't find jelly-fishes in a hole like that. It felt like a tremendously great polly-squiggle with a big parrot's beak, and my hand nearly went in."

"Get out!" said Bob, "there are no big ones."

"How do you know?" retorted Bigley. "That felt just like a large one."

"Did he take hold of you with his suckers?" I said.

"No, I didn't give him time."

"If it had been a polly-squiggle it would have got you fast directly with its suckers," I said oracularly.

"Never mind what it was, old Big. Go in and fetch it out again."

"No; one of you two go, I don't like," said Bigley. "You can't see where you're putting your hand; and suppose he bites it off?"

"Why, then, you could have a wooden peg," said Bob sneeringly. "Here, come out, my poor little man, and let me go in. I'll soon fetch out my gentleman, you see if I don't. Here, come out."

Bob Chowne never meant to go in. His face said as much as he looked round at me; but his words had the effect he intended, for Bigley grunted and went back as far as the narrow crack in the grotto would allow, and boldly thrust in his hand.

"Mind, Big," I said seriously, "be ready to snatch away your fist."

He did not answer, but we heard him draw his breath hard; then there came a splashing noise, and directly after our school-fellow backed towards us.

"I've got him," he shouted, his voice sounding hollow and strange.

"What is it?"

"I dunno," he cried, and then, wrenching himself round, he dropped something soft down upon the rock.

"Why, it's a crab!" I cried.

"A soft one," shouted Bob. "He can't nip now."

As he spoke he poked the curious-looking object with his finger, making it wince and threaten with its claws, but they were perfectly soft, and it was evident that the creature had only just crept out of its old shell, and was hiding away in the dark hole waiting for the new armour to form.

"Well, he is a rum one," said Bob, growing bolder. "Why, he's just like a counterfeit is when you pull his tail out of a whelk shell."

"Not quite so soft," I said, gaining confidence and handling the crab in turn, for it was not so fleshy feeling as the back part of hermit crabs, which we called counterfeits in our part of the world.

"What shall we do with if?" said Big. "It isn't good to eat now."

"Kill the nasty, bloaty thing, and throw it in for bait for the fishes."

"No, no," I said, "put it down and let it creep back. It will grow into a fine crab, and we know its hole and can come and get it some day when the tide's down."

"That's it," said Big; and taking the pulpy, soft crab, which pinched at his hands without the slightest effect, he crept back and thrust it into its hiding-place once again.

We two were looking in after him when—*thud!*—*plash!*—came a wave, breaking just below us and drenching us from head to foot, while a quantity of the water rushed into our baled-out hole, filled it, and began running swiftly up the channel, so swiftly that we saw at a glance it would only take another or two to fill the upper pool.

"Here, come out, Big. Quick!" I cried. "Tide's coming in. Now, Bob, get the baskets and nets."

I ran down a few yards, and was only just in time to snatch mine up before a wave washed right over the spot where they had lain. For the tide was coming in rapidly, and, as I have shown, we were on a part of the shore that was only bare about once a month.

"All right," cried Bob. "I've got mine and old Big's."

"Where are Big's shoes?" I said.

"Down by the pool. Come on, Big, old chap," shouted Bob.

"I'll get them," I said, and I ran to the bottom pool and had to fish them out of the bottom where they had been left.

As I took them out I felt ready to drop them, but I did not, for I flung them and my net and basket as far up the shore as I could, and held out my hands to Bigley, who was looking out at me from the grotto-like place.

"Why don't you come out?" I cried. "Can't you see the tide's coming in?"

"Yes—yes," he said in a curious hollow voice, "I can see, but I can't move. I'm stuck fast. Help!"

I felt a chill of horror, and in those moments saw the tide rising higher and higher till it had filled the little cavern and drowned my poor school-fellow, we his companions being unable to drag him out.

Those thoughts only occupied moments, but they made an impression that I have never forgotten, and I don't think I ever shall have the memories weakened.

I saw it all plainly enough. Poor fellow! He had been startled by the incoming tide and tried to creep out, but not in about the only part that would permit of his passing, but in the first that offered, and he had become fixed, and, as in a few words he explained, the harder he tried to free himself the tighter prisoner he became.

"Here, Bob! Bob!" I shouted in such a tone of anguish that he came running from the back of the rocks to where I was standing knee-deep in water.

"Get out!" he shouted as soon as he saw me. "You can come. Look here, if you play me a trick like—"

"No, no, don't go," I shouted. "Bob: he's fast!"

Bob dashed down to me now as quickly as the rough place would let him. He had thrown down his load at my first appeal for help, and as he came splashing through the water he looked horribly pale.

He saw the position in an instant, and stood by me too much horrified to act; and, as he told me afterwards, his thoughts were just like mine. How long would it take to go to the Gap and bring Bigley's father with a boat?

"Can't you get any farther?" I cried at last as a fresh wave came rushing in, and nearly swept me off my legs.

"No; I'm fast; I can't move," said Bigley in a hoarse whisper. "Run for help."

"No, no," shouted Bob. "Don't go, Sep. We must get him out."

The curious dreamy feeling of helplessness had left us both now; and, taking hold of our companion's hands, we set our feet against the rock and dragged with all our might, while poor Bigley struggled and strained, but all in vain. He had by his unaided efforts got to a certain distance and then stopped. Our united power did not move him an inch.

We stopped at last panting, and all looking horror-stricken in each other's faces. It was a calm enough day, but down there among the rocks the tide rushed in with such fierce power and so rapidly that we were being deluged by every wave which broke, while at intervals the greater waves threatened to be soon big enough to sweep us away.

"Don't stop looking," cried Bob Chowne frantically. "Sep, Sep! Pull, pull!"

He dashed at poor Bigley again, and we dragged with all our might; but the efforts were vain, and again we stared at each other in despair.

"Try again!" I cried breathlessly, and with a horrible feeling coming over me as I once more seized my school-fellow's hand.

Bob followed my example, and again we dragged and hauled at the poor fellow, whose great eyes stared at us in a wildly appealing way that seemed to chill me.

It was of no use. We could not stir him, and we stopped again panting, as a bigger wave struck us and drove us against the rocks, and ran gurgling up into the grotto where poor Bigley was fixed.

"Shall I run for help?" groaned Bob, who was crying and sobbing all the time.

I shook my head, for I knew it was of no use, and then dashed at poor Bigley again, to catch hold of his hand, not to drag at it, but to hold it in both mine.

I don't know why I did it, unless it was from the natural feeling that it might encourage and comfort him to have someone gripping his hand in such a terrible time.

I tried not to think of the horror as the water splashed and hissed about us, and gurgled horribly in the grotto; but something seemed to be singing in my ears, and I heard again the shrieking of a poor boy who was drowned years before by getting one leg fixed in a rift among the rocks when mussel gathering and overtaken by the tide.

He, poor fellow, was drowned, for they could not drag him out, and it seemed to me that our poor schoolmate must lose his life in the same way unless we could devise some means to rescue him.

We looked round despairingly, and for a moment I tried to hope that the tide might not, upon this occasion, rise so high; but a glance at the top of the rocks showed them to be covered with limpets and weed, indicating that they were immersed at every tide, as I well enough knew, and I could not suppress a groan.

"Sep," said poor Bigley, drawing me closer to him, with his great strong hand, and gazing at me with a terribly pathetic look in his eyes. "Sep, tell poor father not to take on about it. We couldn't help it. An accident. Tell him it was an accident, will you?"

I could not answer him, and I turned to Bob Chowne, who was standing with his fingers now thrust into his ears.

"Bob!" I cried. "Bob, let's try again!"

He sprang to poor Bigley's other hand, and we dragged and tugged with slow steady strain and sharp snatch, but without any effect; and every now and then, as we pulled, the waves came right up, and drove us against the rock.

"It's of no use, boys," said Bigley at last. "I'm fast."

"Help!" yelled Bob Chowne with all his might; but in that great solitude his voice had no more effect than the wail of a sea-bird. There was not a soul in sight either on cliff path or the shore. Out to sea there were sails enough, small craft and goodly ships going and coming from Bristol and Cardiff; but no signals on our part were likely to be seen. And besides, if they had been understood, it would have been an hour's row to shore from the nearest, and before a quarter of that time had elapsed the rocks where we stood would be under water.

"Big, Big!" I cried piteously in my despair and wonder to see him now so pale and calm; "what shall we do?"

"Nothing," he said in a low whisper. "Only be quiet now; I'm going to say my prayers."

I dropped down on my knees by him and hid my face, and how long I knelt there I don't know; but it was till I was lifted by the tide and driven heavily against the rocks.

"It's of no use," said Bigley then, after a tremendous struggle. "I can't get out. You must go."

"For help?" I said.

"No; run both of you, or you'll be drowned."

As he spoke a wave came in, broke and deluged us, and I don't know what my words would have been if Bob Chowne had not wailed out:

"Nobody sha'n't say I didn't stick to my mate. I sha'n't go. I won't go. Sep Duncan may if he likes, but I shall stop."

He caught frantically at poor Bigley's collar as he spoke, set his teeth, and then closed his eyes.

"No, no! Run, Bob; run, Sep!" panted Bigley, as if he was being suffocated; "the water will be over us directly, and you must go and tell poor father where I am."

"I sha'n't go and leave you two," I said sullenly; and I also caught hold of him, set my teeth, and swung round as a bigger wave than ever came rolling smoothly in, and regularly seemed to leap at us as it broke upon the rocks, and after deluging us, rushed up, and came down again in a rain of spray.

What followed seems wild and confused, for the sea was rising fast, and we were deluged by every wave, while the greater ones that came every now and then threatened to snatch us away; but everything was as if it occurred in a dream.

Somebody said to me once that Bob Chowne and I behaved in a very heroic manner, standing by our school-fellow as we did; but I don't think there was much heroism in it. We couldn't go and leave him to drown. I wanted to run away, and Bob Chowne afterwards said that he longed to go, but, as he put it, poor fellow, it seemed so mean to leave him to drown all alone.

At all events we stayed, and, as I say, what followed appears to me now to have been dreamy and strange. The water came splashing over us always, but every now and then a great solid wave drove us together, lifting us to strike against the rocks, and then letting us fall heavily, but only to leap in again, and snatch us up as they beat, and swirled, and hissed, and dragged at us like wild creatures, and if we had not held on so tightly to poor Bigley, we must have been washed outwards from the shore.

As I say I don't know how long this lasted, only that we were getting more and more helpless and confused, when a tremendous wave came rolling in and struck full in the grotto-like opening where poor Bigley was wedged. I felt as if my arms had been suddenly wrenched from their sockets, and then I was being carried out by the retiring wave.

It was so natural to us sea-side boys that I involuntarily struck out, tossing my head so as to get the water out of my eyes, and then I saw that Bob Chowne was swimming too, a short distance from me.

My next glance was in the direction of the little cave now some ten yards away, about whose mouth the water was rising and falling; and as I looked, there was nothing but water; then Bigley seemed to crawl out quickly into the next rising wave, and then he too seemed to be swimming towards the shore.

It appeared to be so impossible that I could not believe it, or do anything but swim in amongst the rocks where the long slimy sea-tangle was washing to and fro; but there was no fancy about it, as I found, for Bigley was standing knee-deep in the water, and ready to give us each a hand as we staggered in.

"Why, Big," I exclaimed, "how did you manage to get out?"

He could not answer me, nor yet Bob Chowne, when he repeated the question, but walked slowly and heavily up towards the cliff, and sat down upon a dry stone, to rest his head upon his hands, while we respected his silence.

It was some time before he could speak, and when he did, it was in a dull half-stupefied way, to explain what was simple enough, namely, that when that last big wave came, it struck him violently and buried him deep, the blow, and the natural effort to escape from the water, making him shrink backwards into the hole, a task he achieved without much difficulty; while, when, as the wave retired, he made another effort to pass out, he involuntarily tried where the rocks were a little farther apart, or placed his body in a different position, for he glided out over the slimy rock with ease.

His explanations were, however, like our questions, confused; and we had only one thought now, which was to get home and obtain dry clothes, so we parted as we reached the nearest combe, Bigley going one way barefooted, and we the other, Bob Chowne afterwards going home in a suit of mine.

Chapter Twelve
We make another Slip

I'm afraid that we thought very little about Bigley's escape from a horrible death, for by nine o'clock the next morning he was over at the Bay, and while we were talking outside, Bob Chowne came trotting up, holding on to the mane of his father's pony, for the doctor had ridden over to see my father.

Half an hour later we were down on the beach to look for our baskets and nets which had been covered by the tide, and which we were too much exhausted to hunt for after our escape.

For a long time we had no success, for, until the tide ran lower, we were not quite sure of the spot; but we hung about hour after hour till the cluster of rocks were uncovered, and as soon as the water was low enough we were down at the place, and, but for the labour necessary to bale out the lower pool, we should, I am sure, have crawled in again to try how it was Bigley was held.

It did not take much examination to show that, however, for it was plain enough now to see how one part of the opening was a good deal narrower than the other; and here it was that Bigley had become fast, never once striving in his horror to get back, but always forward like an animal in a trap.

As I stood there looking, the whole scene appeared to come back again, and I shuddered as I seemed to see my school-fellow's agonised face gazing appealingly in ours, and for the moment the bright sunny day looked overcast.

"Come away," I said nervously; "let's look for the nets."

"Ha, ha, ha!" laughed Bob, who had quite recovered his spirits and took up his usual manner; "look at old Sep! He's frightened, and thinks it's his turn to be stuck in the rock."

"Never mind; let's look for the nets," said Bigley, who seemed to be more in sympathy with me, and we set to work, finding one before long, buried all but a scrap of the net in the beach sand and shingle.

This encouraged us, and we hunted with more vigour, finding another wedged in between some blocks of rock, and soon after we discovered something that we had certainly expected would have been swept out to sea, namely, one of the baskets.

It was the one which contained the crab, and it had been driven into a rock pool surrounded by masses of stone, which had held it as the tide retired.

To our great satisfaction the crab was still inside alive and uninjured; but we found no more relics of our expedition. The other baskets were gone with the eel and prawns, and the third net was wanting. I must except, though, one of Bigley's shoes, which had been cast up four hundred yards from the rock pool, and lay at high-water mark in a heap of sea-weed, battered wreck-wood and shells.

I am not going to enumerate all our adventures during those holidays; but I must refer to one or two more before passing on for a time to the more serious matters in connection with the silver mine in the Gap, where, while we were enjoying ourselves on the shore or up one of the narrow glens baling out holes to catch the trout, business matters were progressing fast. Our mishap was soon forgotten, and we determined to have another prawning trip, for, as Bob Chowne said, there was no risk over it, if we didn't go and stick ourselves between two stones ready for the tide to come in and drown us. "But it was an accident," said Bigley gravely. "Oh, no, it wasn't," cried Bob; "an accident's where you can't help it—where a boat upsets, or a horse falls down, or a wheel falls off, or you slip over the edge of the cliff."

"Well, that was an accident too," I said; "wasn't he nearly drowned?"

"No," cried Bob, "not nearly; and how could it be an accident when he crept into the hole, and turned round and stuck fast when he tried to get out?"

It was of no use to argue with Bob that morning, as we three ran down to the shore after finding that old Uggleston's lugger was at sea, crushing the weed under our feet, and enjoying the curious salt smell that ascended to our nostrils. We had another net, and a big basket, borrowed of our Sam. It was not so handy as our old ones, for two of us had to carry it; but as I said it would hold plenty, and we could lay a bit of old net over the prawns to keep them from flicking themselves out.

"I don't believe we shall catch any to-day," said Bob, who was in one of his hedgehog fits, as Bigley used to call them. But he was wrong, for after walking about a mile along the shore, so as to go right away from the cottages, the first pool we stopped at gave us three fine fat fellows.

In another we were more successful, and as we roamed: farther and farther away the better became our sport.

This time we went on past the Gap, and under the tremendous cliffs that kept the sun from shining down upon the shore in winter. Then on and on with our numbers always increasing, for we passed very few pools that did not contain one prawn at least.

"I tell you what," said Bob, as we stopped to rest, net in hand; "we'll go to old Big's this afternoon, and get Mother Bonnet to boil the prawns, and then have a thorough good feast. You'll find us some bread and butter, won't you, Big?"

"Of course," he replied; "but we haven't got them home yet."

"No," said Bob, "we haven't got them home; but you're not going to get stuck in a hole this time, are you?"

Bigley shook his head, and the remarks were forgotten, as we discovered, just washed in by the tide, a good-sized cuttlefish, that was quite dead, however, having been killed I suppose by being bruised against the rocks, so we were not favoured with a shower of ink.

A little farther on we came to a bare smooth patch of dark sand, over which the sea ran gently, sweeping before it a rim of foam which sparkled and displayed iridescent colours like a soap-bubble. Here we found our first jelly-fish, a beautifully clear disc of transparency about the size of a penny bun, and from which, when we plunged it in the first rock pool, hung down quite a lovely fringe of the most delicate hues.

Perhaps it was too nearly dead from being washed ashore, for it did not sting, as some of these creatures do slightly, when encountered while bathing.

We thought the jelly-fish curious, but it was not good to eat, so it was left in the little rock pool with a few tiny shrimps, to get well or die, and we went on kicking over the little shells, getting our feet wet, and finding more prawn-haunted pools, as we made for one big rock which lay close to the water's edge, a quarter of a mile farther on, where it stood up in the midst of a clump of smaller ones, the beach around being tolerably level for some distance.

"That's where old Binnacle always goes when he wants to find a lobster," said Bigley; "and I shouldn't wonder if we get one, for he hasn't been there lately."

"How do you know?" I said.

"Because he hasn't sold one, nor given us one, nor had one himself."

"There, hark at him!" cried Bob. "How can you tell?"

"Easy enough."

"But how?"

"Haven't lobsters got shells?"

"Yes."

"And aren't they red?"

"Why, of course they are."

"Well, don't they always throw the shells out on the heap by the pig-sty?" cried Bigley. "And there hasn't been one there since I came home. Old Bill has been too busy making a new net to go lobstering."

"I say, what a day for a bathe!" cried Bob suddenly, as we approached the big rock which formed out here a point, from which a series of smaller rocks ran right to sea, for the heads of some were level with the surface, and others only appeared at times.

"Why, you couldn't bathe here," said Big; "you ought to know that."

"Why not?" cried Bob.

"Because the tide hits against those rocks, and then runs right out to sea like the river runs down the Gap after a storm."

"Oh, I don't believe all these old stories," cried Bob contemptuously; "and suppose it did run out, couldn't I swim out of the stream and come ashore?"

"No."

"Oh, couldn't I? Precious soon let you see."

"Hi! Look there," cried Bigley, "there's father's boat."

"Where?" I said.

"Out yonder. He has been with Binnacle Bill to Swincombe, and that's them coming back."

"Why, you can't see anything but a bit of sail," cried Bob scoffingly, as he shaded his eyes and looked far-off into the west.

"No, but I know the shape of it," cried Bigley. "There isn't another boat hereabouts with a sail like that."

"I don't believe you know it," cried Bob. "It's a Frenchman, or a Dutchman, or a Welsh boat."

"Well, you'll see," said Bigley decisively, and the matter dropped, for we were close up to the big rock now, a mass that stood about a dozen feet above the beach, and to our great delight there were several little pools about, all of which seemed to be well occupied by the toothsome delicacies we sought.

The baskets were set down and we were soon hard at work catching prawn after prawn; but, though we peered into every crack, and routed about as far as we could reach, there was no sign of a lobster large or small.

"Never mind," said Bob sourly, "they're rather out of season if you do catch them now. I don't mind."

For another half hour or so, with the tide coming whispering and lapping in, we went on prawning, getting a dozen fine ones.

Then Bob insisted upon bathing, and it was only by an effort we stopped him from going into the water at so dangerous a spot.

It was Big who took off his attention at last, by telling him that he could not scale the big rock and get on the top.

"Tchah!" cried Bob sneeringly; "why, I could almost hop on it."

We laughed at him, and he began to peer about for one of the surrounding pieces to form a step to help him part of the way, but all were too distant, the great stone lying quite isolated. There was one spot, though, where the big stone was split, as if some gigantic wedge had been driven in to open it a little way, and here, as it was encrusted with limpets, there seemed to be a good prospect for us to climb up the roughened sides.

As it proved it was like many tasks in life, it looked more difficult than it really was, and by the exercise of a little agility and some mutual help we contrived to get to the top, where there was a large depression like a caldron, scooped out by the action of the sea upon a heavy boulder lying therein, and which looked as if, when the waves beat, it must be driven round and round and to and fro.

We all sat down with our legs in the hole, following Bigley's example as he set himself to watch the coming of his father's boat, which was growing plainer now every minute, and trying, by spreading all the sail she could, to reach the Gap.

"I wonder how long she'll be?" said Bob, sitting there with his chin upon his hands.

"About an hour," replied Bigley.

"What! Coming that little way? Why, she's close here."

"It isn't close here, and the boat's a good six miles away, I know," replied Bigley. "Distances are deceiving by the sea-side."

"Hark at the doctor," cried Bob; "he's going to give us a lecture. I say, this isn't school."

It was very pleasant seated there on that smooth, warm platform of rock in the glowing sunshine, and with the soft sea-breeze fanning our cheeks. There was plenty of room, and before long we were all lying down in various attitudes. Bob turned himself into a spread-eagle by lying upon his back, and tilting his cap over his nose as he announced that he was going to sleep.

We both laughed and did not believe him, as we each took up the position most agreeable to him, Bigley stretching himself upon his breast, folding his arms and placing his chin upon them, so as to gaze at his father's boat with undivided attention.

As for me, I lay on my side to stare at the great wall of cliff that ran along the land, and curved over and over into great hills and mounds.

It was very beautiful to watch the many tints in the distance, and the bright colours of the broken rock. The upper parts were of a velvety green; then in the hollows where the oak-trees flourished there were endless tints, against which the soft grey of the gulls, as they floated along, seemed to stand out bright and clear.

We three lads had been walking and climbing and exerting ourselves for hours now, and the strange restful sensation of stretching one's self on that warm, smooth mass of rock was delicious.

To make it more agreeable, the soft wind fanned our faces, and the sea seemed to be whispering in a curious lulling way that was delightful.

I remember raising myself a little to look at Bob Chowne in his lazy attitude. Then I stared at Bigley, who had doubled back his long legs, as he watched the boat, whose sails seemed to be coming nearer now, and then I sank back in my former attitude, to gaze at the cliffs and the soft blue sky flecked with silvery gauzy clouds.

Then one of the big grey gulls fixed my attention, and I lay staring at it hard, and watching its movements, as I wondered why it was that it should keep flying to and fro, for nothing apparently, turning itself so easily by a movement of the tail, and curving round and round without an effort.

That gull completely fascinated me. Sometimes it floated softly so near that I could plainly see its clear ringed eye and the colour of its beak, the soft white of its head and under parts, the delicate grey of its back, and the black tips of its wings, which formed soft bends that sustained the great bird with the slightest exertion. For now and then it beat the air a little, then the wings remained motionless a minute at a time, and the secret of flying seemed to me to be to float about in that clear transparent air, just as a fish did in the sea.

It was very wonderful to watch it, feeling so dreamy and restful the while. The gull seemed to have fixed its eyes on me, and to know that I was noting all its graceful evolutions, and I felt that it was flying and floating and gliding to and fro, and round and round, now up, now down, on purpose to show off its powers to me, for it never occurred to me that the bird was waiting till my eyes were closed to make a pounce down upon the big basket and help itself to the prawns.

No, it all seemed done for my special benefit, and lulled by the lapping of the sea, and with the fanning motion of the gull's wings having a curiously drowsy effect, I lay there watching—watching, till I seemed to be able to float with the gull, and to be gliding onward and onward through space, up and down, up and down, in a soft billowy, heaving movement, with the blue sky above me, the green cliff-side draped with oak and ivy below, and all about me, and pervading me and sustaining me as the sea did when I swam, there was the soft pure air.

Was I a gull or myself? I did not know, only that I seemed to be floating deliciously on with wide-spread invisible wings, and that there was no such thing as the earth and shore, over which I laboriously plodded, for me.

It was one soft dreamy ecstasy, such as comes to the weary sleeping in the summer breeze out in the open air. Now and then I seemed to hear the wild softened harshness of the gull's cry, then all was still again, and I was floating on and on, wishing nothing, wanting nothing, only to go on, when all at once a huge roc-like bird seemed to sweep over between me and the sunshine, to grasp me as Sindbad was seized, and raise me up.

But this roc spoke and cried harshly:

"Quick! Wake up! You have been to sleep."

"Sleep?" I said, rousing myself. "Sleep?"

"Yes; we've all been to sleep, and—Here, Bob! Wake up! Wake up!"

He shook Bob Chowne, who was so sound that it was with difficulty he could be made to sit up, and in that little interval I realised why it was that Bigley looked so scared.

It was plain enough: tired out with our prawning, we had been thoughtless enough to let our weariness get the better of us, and while we had slept the enemy had not only approached, but surrounded us and cut us off from the shore. In fact, as we stared about us, a wave struck the rock and sent its soft spray right up to where we were standing.

"Here, what's the matter?" cried Bob. "I say, what is it? Oh, I say, where are the prawns?"

Prawns? They and the baskets were far away now, while the nets might be anywhere. Between us and the shore the water for a good hundred yards was six feet deep at least, and there was a swim of a hundred and fifty before we could begin to wade, while, if we did not start at once, there would be a swim of nearly half a mile, for the points of the little bay where we were would soon be covered, the rocks were perpendicular, and to stay in the bay was to be drowned.

Chapter Thirteen
A Perilous Swim

"I say, what shall we do?" cried Bob.

"We must take off our clothes and swim for it," said Bigley.

"No, no," I cried, for the idea was appalling. "Let's stay here."

"What, and be swept off?" said Bob. "No; Bigley's right. We must swim for it. No, I see! There's your father's lugger, Big. Let them come and take us off."

"They durstn't come in on account of the rocks," said Bigley slowly.

"Then, let them send the boat. Let's hail them."

"Yes, they might send the boat," said Bigley thoughtfully, "and they would if we could make them understand."

"Shout," cried Bob.

"What's the use when they're nearly two miles away."

"'Tisn't so far, is it?" I said in an awe-stricken whisper.

"Almost," he said. "The wind's against them, and they're beating up very slowly, and keeping off so as to run straight in when they get past the point. You see they don't want to go in at the Gap till it's high-water and the pebble bar is covered."

"But they must hear us," cried Bob, "and send a boat to fetch us off. I don't know that I could swim so far as the shore, and we should have to undress and lose all our clothes. Here, ahoy! Boat—oh! Ahoy!"

The sound died away in the vast space, but there was no movement aboard of the lugger, and after each had hailed in turn, and we had all shouted together, we looked at each other in despair.

"Oh," cried Bob, "what a set of stupids we are! Only just now we went and got into trouble, and lost our nets and baskets, and now we've been and done it again. Here, Big, it's all your fault, what are we going to do?"

Bigley looked to sea, and he looked to shore, and then down at the water, that kept lapping round the rock and rising and falling. The small blocks all about us had long been covered, and at its most quiescent times the sea was now within some three feet of the top, while as the waves swayed and heaved, they ran up at times nearly to where we stood.

The peril did not seem very great, because we did not quite realise our position; but stood disputing as to which would be the better proceeding — to try and swim ashore, or to wait till we could attract the notice of those on board the boat.

Several attempts were made to do the latter, for the stripping to swim with the loss of our clothes was not a course to be thought upon with equanimity; and though we shouted and waved handkerchiefs, the lugger pursued its slow way, and it was quite plain that we were not seen.

Meanwhile the water was steadily rising up the sides of our little island rock, and our position was beginning to wear a more serious aspect.

"We shall have to swim ashore, boys," said Bigley, speaking in a tone which seemed to indicate that he would rather do anything else.

He looked towards the cliff as he spoke, and being so much taller than we, of course he had a much better view.

"Oh!" he exclaimed, with a look of horror, "the tide is round both points, and we shall have to swim right along ever so far before we can land."

"No, no," cried Bob, "let's swim straight in."

"I tell you," cried Bigley, "if we do, we shall be drowned."

"What nonsense!" cried Bob. "Why, we'd climb up the rocks."

"There is not a place where you could climb," said Bigley gloomily. "I know every yard all along here, and there isn't a single spot where you could get up the cliff."

"It's too far to swim," I said gloomily. "I know I can't go so far as that. Could you, Bob?"

He shook his head.

"Oh, yes, you could," cried Bigley excitedly. "It would be swimming with the stream, you know, and it would carry us along — I mean the tide would, and you've only got to think you could do it, and you would."

Bob Chowne shook his head, and I began to feel chilled and oppressed by the task we had before us.

"No, I couldn't swim so far," cried Bob suddenly. "It would take a strong man who could keep on for hours to do that."

"I tell you that you could do it," cried Bigley, who seemed to be quite passionate now. "Don't talk like that, Bob, or you'll frighten Sep Duncan out of trying."

"I'm not going to try," I said gloomily. "It would be no use. I could swim to the shore but not round the point."

"What's the good of talking like that?" cried Bigley. "You both can swim it, and you must."

"Why, I don't believe you could, Big," cried Bob in a whimpering tone.

"I do," said the great fellow doggedly, "and I'm going to try, and so are you two fellows."

"That we are not," we cried together.

"Yes, you are, for it's our only chance, unless they see us from the boat. You'll have to try, for the water will be up and over here before long, and what will you do then?"

"Drown, I s'pose," said Bob.

"Nonsense!" cried Bigley, who astonished us by the eager business way he had put on. "Who's going to stand still and drown, when he can swim to a safe place? Here, let's try and get 'em to see us aboard the lugger," he cried. "All together! Let's wave our caps and handkerchiefs."

We did all wave our caps and handkerchiefs, together and separately, but the boat went slowly on, as if there was no one in danger, and we turned and looked at each other in despair.

"They must be asleep," said Bob angrily. "Oh, it's too bad."

"No," said Bigley sadly. "They can't be asleep, because there's someone steering, and someone else attending to the sails when they go about. It's only because they cannot see us. The rocks and cliffs hide us from them."

"Why, we can see them," said Bob bitterly.

"Yes, because they are against the sky," I said. "We are against the cliff. Oh, look at that!"

My schoolmates wanted no telling, for they were looking aghast at the way in which the water had washed up, and lapped over the edge of the rock upon which we stood. It fell directly, but it had risen high enough to show that in a few minutes it would sweep right to where we were, and in a few more completely cover the stone.

At this Bigley began to wave his jacket frantically, but the boat still glided slowly on with its sail lit up by the sunshine, and the sea glittering as far as we could see.

"It's of no use; we must swim," cried Bigley; but we neither of us stirred, though he began resolutely to take off his big shoes. We saw what he was doing, but our eyes were strained towards the boat, which was much nearer now, making a long reach in towards the land, and it seemed so strange that those on board should be calmly sitting there, while we were in such peril, looking longingly for a sign that we were seen.

And still the water slowly rose, threatening several times, and then making a bold leap which carried it right over the stone, though it barely wetted our feet.

As it came over, Bigley stooped down quickly and caught up his shoes and clothes to keep them dry, and it seemed very ridiculous to me that he should trouble himself about that, when in a few more minutes they must be afloat.

Another wave and another came over us, and though I kept on waving my handkerchief at times, there seemed to be no hope of help from the lugger. So in a fit of despair, after a glance towards the shore, I began to follow Bigley's example and undress, feeling that it was forced upon me, and that I must make an effort and swim for my life.

Bob Chowne stood with his forehead all wrinkled up watching me for a few minutes, and then he began to undress slowly; but a wave came and rose right up to our knees as it swept in, telling us plainly enough that before many minutes had passed we should be unable to stand there, and in frantic haste we tore off our garments, and followed Bigley's lead in tying them together in a bundle, in the faint hope of being able to take them in our teeth and carry them ashore.

We were ready none too soon, for the tide rose rapidly, and it was evident that the time had come for our plunge.

"I'll go first, boys, and you follow," cried Bigley. "Now, don't hurry, and try and keep together. I won't swim fast. Ready?"

There was no answer.

"Are you ready, I say? I want to give the word, and for us all to take the water together."

Still neither of us answered; and we stood there, bundles in hand, unwilling to quit the firm rock on which we stood knee-deep, for the treacherous sea.

"I say, boys! Are you ready!" cried Bigley again.

Still there was no answer, and the reluctance to stir would have continued longer, but an unexpected termination was put to our indecision by a larger wave sweeping over us, and making Bob Chowne slip and stagger.

He tried hard to recover himself, and we to catch him, but the wet rock was bad for the feet, or he placed his foot upon a piece of sea-weed. At all events over he went with a splash and disappeared.

We two followed, bundles and all, and as Bob rose we were one on each side, and started swimming level with the shore so as to round the point between us and the western side of the Gap.

Driven to it as we were, Bob Chowne and I forgot our dread and began to swim steadily and well; but we had not been in the water five minutes before I found that we had undertaken to do that which was impossible, and that we had quite forgotten all about this being a dangerous spot for bathing.

I think we all discovered it about the same moment, but Bigley was the first to speak.

"Be cool, boys, as the doctor says," he called out to us. "This is no use. We're not going with the tide, but fighting against it."

"But the tide's coming in," I said.

"Yes, underneath," cried Bigley; "but the top part of the water's running out like a mill-race, and we must go with it now. Follow me."

There was no help for it. The tide carried us along into a tremendous current, caused by the meeting of two waters at the point formed by the ridge of rocks which ran down into the sea, and to my horror, as I swam steadily on, still holding to my bundle, I found that we were in a line with the cliff about which I had watched the gull flying, but that it was getting farther and farther away.

It was all plain enough. We were well in the fierce current that ran off the point, and being carried straight out to sea.

My first idea was to shout this to my companions; but I felt that if I did I should frighten them, and I knew well enough that as soon as anyone grew frightened when he was swimming the best half of his power had gone.

It was a great thing to recollect, and I held my tongue. It was hard work, and something seemed to keep prompting me to shout the bad news, but somehow I mastered it, and instead of swimming faster made myself take my strokes more slowly, so as to save my breath.

Bigley told me afterwards, and so did Bob Chowne, that they felt just the same, and would not shout for fear of frightening me, swimming steadily on, though where we did not know.

"I say, how warm the water is!" cried Bigley; and we others said it was. Then I thought of something to say.

We had each tied our clothes up as tightly as we could in our pocket-handkerchiefs, and so it was a long time before they were regularly saturated and heavy.

"I say," I cried, "my bundle's just like a cork, and holds me up beautiful. How are yours?"

Bob Chowne panted out that his was better, and to prove hew good and buoyant his was Bigley thrust it before him, and swam after it, giving it pushes as he went.

All this took up our attention for a little while from the horror of our position, for a horrible position it was indeed. It was a glorious sunny day, and sea and sky were beautiful, but the fierce current that set off from the point was sweeping us rapidly away, and it was only a question of how long we could keep on swimming—a quarter of an hour, half an hour, an hour—and then first one and then another must sink, unless in our efforts to save the first weak one we all went down together, and the glittering sea flowed over our heads with only a few bubbles of air to show where we had been.

We must have been swimming twenty minutes when Bigley uttered a shout, and looking up, Bob and I for the first time caught sight of a little dinghy coming towards us, and far beyond it the lugger lying with her sails flapping in the breeze.

The boat was a long way off, but the man in it had evidently seen us, and was coming down to our help, and a thrill of exultation ran through me, as I struck out more vigorously to reach the haven of safety.

The minute before we were all swimming steadily and well, but the sight of help coming seemed to have completely unnerved us, and in place of taking slow long regular strokes, and steady inspirations, with the sides of our heads well down in the water, we all quickened our strokes and strained our heads above the surface, while, as if moved by the same thought, we all together shouted "Boat!"

"Ahoy!" came back from what seemed a terrible distance, and the feeling of fear I had begun to experience increased more and more.

A couple of minutes earlier I had not thought about the distance I could swim, but had kept on swimming. Now I could think of nothing else but was it possible that I could keep on long enough for the boat to reach me; and, instead of steadily trying to decrease the distance, and so help the boatman, I began to make very bad progress indeed.

"Hooray!" shouted Bigley just then. "Keep up, boys, and don't lose your bundles. It's father, and he'll soon pick us up."

Bundles?—bundles? Where was my bundle?

I dared not turn my head to look, but it was not by me, and I must have let it float away just when most excited by the coming of the boat, but I could say nothing then.

"Steady!" shouted Bigley again, checking his own speed, for he had been getting ahead of us, and he waited till we were abreast of him, both swimming too heavily and fast.

"Don't do that," he cried. "Go steady. Go—"

He said no more, poor fellow, for the curious dread that unnerves people in the water, and robs them of the power and judgment that are their saving, seemed to have attacked him, and he began to swim in a more and more laboured fashion.

His example affected us, and away went all coolness. We were all swimming, and the tide was carrying us along towards the boat, that seemed to be getting farther away instead of nearer to my dimming eyes. Then in my rapid splashing I struck up the water, and grew confused; and feeling all at once that I was regularly exhausted, I turned over on my back to float.

It was an unlucky movement, for I did it hastily and with the consequence that my head went under. I inhaled a quantity of the stinging briny salt water, and raising my head as I choked and sputtered, I turned back again, struck out two or three times, and then began to beat the surface frantically like a dog which has been thrown into the water for the first time.

I can remember no more of what occurred during the next few minutes, only that I was staring up at the sky through dazzling water-drops; then that all was dark, and then light again, and not light as it was before. Then it was once more dark, and then I was sitting in a boat half blind, shivering, and helpless, with the boat rocking about tremendously, and Bob Chowne over the side holding on to the gunwale with one hand, to my wrist with the other.

It all seemed very wild and strange; but my senses were coming back fast, and in an indistinct manner I saw someone swimming and plashing the water about twenty yards from the boat. It was a man in a blue woollen shirt, and his head was bald and shining in the sun, as I saw it for a moment, and then, whoever it was, reared himself high as he could in the water, and then struck off and swam away from us out to sea.

He did not go far, but stopped suddenly and shouted to us; and as he did so, I saw a gleam of something white, and then that he was holding someone's face above water.

THE LUGGER'S BOAT SAVES THE DROWNING BOYS.

THE LUGGER'S BOAT SAVES THE DROWNING BOYS.

Chapter Fourteen
Just in Time

"Ahoy, lad!" he shouted. "Shove a scull over the stern, and scull her this way."

This roused me, and I jumped up to seize a scull, but felt giddy and nearly fell, for Bob Chowne had hold of my wrist.

"Take hold of the gunwale, Bob," I panted, as I tried again, and this time felt better, getting an oar over behind, and sending the boat along, as I had learned to years before.

It was slow and awkward work, with Bob hanging on to the side with his eyes fixed, and his face white; but I got her along, and before I had been sculling many minutes, a great brown hand was thrown over on the opposite side to where Bob clung, and Jonas Uggleston said hoarsely:

"Lay in your oar, mate, and lean over, and take hold of Bigley here. Get your arm well under him. That's right. Keep his head out of the water. I'm about beat for a bit."

I obeyed him in a dreamy way, getting Bigley's arm over into the boat, while I knelt down and put mine round him, and held him close to the side.

"Can you hold on, youngster?" said old Jonas hoarsely. This was to Bob Chowne, who stared at him wildly, and did not speak.

"Nice chance for me," growled old Jonas. "There, hold fast, my lads. I'm going to get in over the starn."

The boat rose and fell and rocked as he came round, passed me hand over hand, to pause by the stern, and I thought he was going to climb in; but he altered his mind, and went on round by where Bob Chowne clung, held on with one hand, while he thrust his right arm under the water, and the next moment he had hoisted Bob right up and rolled him over into the boat, where he lay for a few moments apparently quite helpless.

"Now, young Duncan," said old Jonas, "you hold him fast. I'll get in this side. She won't go over."

It was done in a moment; he let himself sink down, and turn, gave a spring as I turned my head round to watch him; the gunwale of the boat seemed to go down level with the water, and he was on board, while, before I could realise it, he was bending over me to get his arms under poor Big's and drag him into the boat, this time sending the gunwale so low that a quantity of water came in as well.

Old Jonas set his son up in the stern with his back against the rowlock, and it was no easy job, for Big was limp, and tremendously heavy; but the bumping about seemed to do him some good, for, just as I was about to ask in a voice full of awe if he was dead, poor Bigley uttered a low groan.

"Hah! He's coming to, then," said old Jonas, panting heavily, as he seated himself on the middle thwart. "Here, you young doctor, take that pannikin, and bale out some of that water you're lying in. You don't want another bath, do you?"

Bob Chowne got up on to his knees in the bottom of the boat, shivering and blue, and stared wildly at us all in turn.

"Cold, eh?" growled old Jonas. "Well, then, I'll bale, and you two row to the lugger."

He glanced round at his son, who was showing signs of returning animation; but it evoked no sympathy before us, whatever he might have felt, for he only frowned as, in a shivering mechanical way, we two wretched boys seized an oar apiece, sat down on the wet thwarts and began to row.

"Now, then," shouted old Jonas, "look where you're going. Pull, doctor! Easy, captain! That's better."

Between his words he kept sending out pannikins of water rapidly to ease the boat, for it was above our ankles as we sat and pulled.

"Nice fellows all of you!" grumbled old Jonas. "Why, you all look blue. Fool's trick! Who put it up?"

"I—I don't know what you mean, Mr Uggleston," I said.

"Who proposed to swim off to the lugger? Was it Bigley?"

"N—no, Mr Uggleston," I panted, half hysterically, as I tugged at the oar, an example followed by Bob Chowne, who was very silent and very blue.

"Soon as I get you aboard, I'll give you all a good rope's-ending, and chance what your fathers say," grumbled old Uggleston, as he sent the water flashing over the side. "I suppose it was my Bigley as set you at it, wasn't it?"

"No, sir," I said, as I rapidly grew more composed now. "We were on the rock yonder, and had to swim for it. We wanted to get to shore."

"And the current took you out, eh? Of course it would. Then you weren't swimming for the lugger, eh?"

"Oh, no, sir," I cried; "we had forgotten all about the boat."

"Then, where were you going to swim to—Swansea?" he cried.

"I don't know, sir," I said dolefully.

"No more do I," he snarled. "'Cross the sea to Ireland, eh? And no biscuit and water. Ah, you ought to be all rope's-ended. How came you on the rock?"

I told him.

"Lucky I saw you all standing on it white-skinned against the black rocks. I see you all dive in and took my spy-glass, and see you swimming this way, and when I told Binnacle Bill, he said just what I thought, that you was swimming out to the lugger, and wouldn't do it, and so I took the boat and come to you, and I'm sorry I did now."

"Sorry, sir?" I said.

"Ay, sorry. You're a set o' young swabs. What's the good of either of you but to give trouble. Here, where are your clothes? Under the cliff?"

"No, sir," I said dolefully. "We undressed on the big flat rock there, and tied them up in bundles."

"Bundles? Where are they then?"

"Lost mine," said Bob, speaking for the first time.

"Oh, you're coming round then, are you?" cried old Jonas. "You've lost yours then; and has my Bigley lost all his kit?"

"Yes, sir; we've all lost our bundles, unless they get thrown up by the tide."

"Which they won't," snarled old Jonas. "Rope's end it is, for if I don't thrash that big ugly cub of mine as soon as I get him aboard, I'll—Now then, what are you yawing about that way for? Easy, captain! Pull, doctor, will you? Now, both together. Regular stroke. That's better. And so's that," he said, as he scooped out the last few drops of water with the tin pannikin, and finished off by sopping the remaining moisture with a piece of coarse flannel stuff which he wrung out over the side.

Bob and I did not speak, but tugged at our oars, as absurd-looking a crew as was ever seen upon the Devon coast, while we kept looking pityingly at poor Bigley.

Poor fellow! He had placed his arms one on either side, resting upon the gunwale, and appeared to be hard set to keep his head up from his chest. Then he had one or two violent fits of coughing, and ended by sitting back in the bottom of the boat with a weary sigh and closing his eyes.

"Look, sir, look!" I cried in agony, for I thought Bigley must be dying.

"Well, I am looking at him, boy. He's coming round. I can't do anything for him here, can I? Pull hard, you young swabs, both of you, and let's get aboard. I don't know what folks want to have boys for."

We rowed hard, bending well to our oars, and after a few minutes I ventured to speak again, for Bigley looked terribly ill.

"Do you think he's getting better, sir?" I said.

"Better, boy? Yes," he said, not unkindly, for I suppose my anxiety about his son moved him. "He'll be all right when I've warmed and laced him up with the rope's end. I'm going to make you all skip as soon as I get you aboard and there's room to move."

"But he looks so ill, sir," I said, quite ignoring the rope's-ending.

"Of course he does, my lad. So would you if you had gone down as far as he did, and swallowed as much water. Easy. In oars."

I did not know we had rowed so far, but just then the boat bumped up against the side of the lugger, and old Jonas rose, took the painter as he stepped into the bows, and handed it to Binnacle Bill, whose grim old face relaxed into a grin as he saw our plight.

"What have you got, Master Uggles'on?" he said. "White seals?"

"Ay, something o' the sort," grumbled old Jonas. "Here, boys, on board with you."

We needed no second order, but scrambled over the side into the lugger, while, at a word from his master, Binnacle Bill unbolted the piece of the lugger's bulwarks that answered the purpose of a gangway, and as, by main force, old Jonas lifted up Bigley, the old sailor leaned down, put his arm round the poor limp fellow, and lifted him on deck, where he lay almost without motion.

The next thing was to make fast the little boat astern, after which Binnacle Bill seized the tiller, the sails filled, and the boat began to glide through the sunny sea, while Bob and I picked out the sunniest spot we could find, and watched old Jonas as he bent over Bigley and poured a few drops of spirit between his teeth from a bottle he had fetched from the little cabin.

"Rowing's put you two right," said Jonas. "Ah, I thought that would do him good."

Certainly it did, for in a few minutes' time Bigley was able to sit up in an oil-skin coat of his father's, while we two were accommodated with a couple of Jersey shirts, which when worn as the only garment are nice and warm, but anything but becoming.

The little lugger tacked and tacked again before we could make the mouth of the Gap; and, probably because he was too busy over Bigley and the boat, old Jonas said no more about the rope's end, but ran us right in over the pebble bar into the little river, when Binnacle Bill was sent over to our cottage to fetch some clothes for me and Bob, he being about my size, and till they came we lay in old Jonas's bed.

Then a tremendous tea was eaten, Bigley being well enough to join in, and afterwards in cool of the evening old Jonas rowed us round and along the coast to see if we could pick up our bundles; but they had either sunk or gone off to sea, and we returned without.

Bigley was evidently very poorly, but he wouldn't give up, and started to walk part of the way back with us.

I noted one thing as we were going. Bob Chowne and I held out our hands to say "Good-night," and to thank old Jonas for saving our lives.

"Oh, it was nothing," he said, shaking hands very warmly with Bob Chowne, but taking no notice of mine. "It's all right. Good-bye, lads, but don't do it again."

We said we would not, and started off home, where we both expected severe scoldings; but before we had gone fifty yards up the cliff path old Jonas hailed us with a stentorian, "Ahoy!"

"What is it, father?" shouted Bigley.

"Bring those boys back," roared old Jonas. "I forgot to give 'em the rope's end."

I need not tell you we didn't go back. But when we parted from Bigley half a mile further on, I said to him:

"Why wouldn't your father shake hands with me?"

"Hush! Don't take any notice," said Bigley in low voice; "he's very angry still about Captain Duncan buying the Gap and finding the silver mine. That's all!"

"That's all!" Bigley said. But it was not.

Chapter Fifteen
Back to School

I tried very hard not to meet Doctor Chowne when he next came over to our cottage, which was two days after the escape from drowning, for he was very frequently in confab with my father.

They went into the little parlour, and so as to be out of the way I went into the cliff garden to watch the sea seated astride of one of the gates; but, as luck would have it, my father and the doctor came out to talk in the garden, and as there was no way of escape without facing them, I had to remain where I was and put on the boldest front I could.

"Oh, you're there, are you, Mr Sep?" exclaimed the doctor grimly.

"Yes, sir," I said.

"That's right; I only wanted to ask a favour of you."

"What is it, sir?" I said.

"Oh, wait a minute and I'll tell you," said the doctor in his grimmest way. "It was only this. You see I'm a very busy man, twice as busy as I used to be since your father has taken to consulting me. What I want you to do is this—"

He stopped short and stared at me till I grew uncomfortable.

"This, my lad," he continued. "To save time, I want you to tell me when you are going to try next to kill my boy."

"To kill Bob, sir?"

"Yes, I want to be ready, as I've so little time to spare. I want to order mourning from Exeter, and to give orders for the funeral."

"I—I don't understand you, sir," I stammered.

BOB CHOWNE DOING FENANCE IN HIS OLD CLOTHES.

"Not understand me, my lad! Why, I spoke plainly enough. You've tried to kill my Bob twice; third time never fails."

"Doctor Chowne!" I exclaimed.

"Your most humble servant, sir," he continued sarcastically. "I only wanted to add, that I should like you to do it as soon as you can, for he is costing me a great deal for clothes and boots."

"There, there, Chowne," said my father, taking pity upon me, "boys will be boys. I daresay your chap was just as bad as mine, and old Uggleston's baby quite their equal."

"They lead my Bob into all the mischief," cried the Doctor sharply.

"Oh, no doubt, no doubt," said my father in his driest way.

"And I should like to know as near as I can when it's to come to an end?"

"There, there, never mind," said my father good-humouredly. "Give them another chance, and if they spoil these clothes we'll send into Bristol for some sail-cloth, and have 'em rigged out in that."

"Sail-cloth!" cried the doctor, "old carpet you mean. That's the only thing for them."

"Holidays will soon be over, Chowne, and we shall be rid of them."

"Yes, that's a comfort," said the doctor; and, as he turned away, I looked appealingly at my father, who gave me a dry look, and taking it to mean that I might go, I slipped off and went in to Ripplemouth.

I soon found Bob, sitting in a very ragged old suit, out of which he had grown two years before, and he looked so comical with his arms far through his sleeves, and his legs showing so long beneath his trouser bottoms, than I burst out laughing.

"Yah! That's just like you," cried Bob viciously. "I never saw such a chap. Got plenty of clothes, and it don't matter to you; but look at me!"

"Well, I was looking at you," I said. "What an old guy you are!"

"Do you want me to hit you on the nose, Sep Duncan?" he said.

"Why, of course not," I said. "I came over to play, not fight. Where are your Sunday clothes?"

"Where are they?" snarled Bob, speaking as if I had touched him on a very sore spot. "Why, locked up in the surgery cupboard along with the 'natomy bones and the sticking-plaster roll."

"What! Has your father locked them up?"

"Yes, he has locked them up, and says he isn't going to run all over the country seeing patients to find me in clothes to lose—just as if I could help it."

"But haven't you been measured for some more?"

"Yes, but they won't be done yet, and father says I'm to go on wearing these the rest of the time I'm at home."

I looked at him from top to toe as he stood before me, and it was of no use to try to keep my countenance. I could not, and the more I tried the more I seemed to be obliged to laugh.

As for Bob he ground his teeth and clenched his hands, but this only made him look the more comic, and I threw myself in a chair and fairly roared, till he came at me like an angry bull; but as I made no resistance, only laughed, he lowered his fists.

"I can't help it, Bob; I was obliged to laugh," I cried. "There, you may laugh at me now; but you do look so droll. Have you been out?"

"Been out? In these? Of course I haven't. How can I? No: I'm a prisoner, and all the rest of my holiday time is going to be spoiled."

"Oh, I say, don't talk like that, old boy," I cried. "Why didn't you keep the suit I lent you?"

"I don't want to be dependent on you for old clothes," he said haughtily.

"Well, I'd rather wear them than those you have on, Bob. Oh, I say, you do look rum!"

"If you say that again I shall hit you," cried Bob fiercely.

"Oh, very well, I won't say it," I said; "but I say, wouldn't you wear a suit of old Big's?"

I said it quite seriously, but he regularly glared and seemed as if he were going to fly at me, but he neither moved nor spoke.

"Never mind about your clothes," I said. "Big's sure to be over before long. Let's get out on the cliff, or down by the shore, or go hunting up in the moor, or something."

"What, like this?" said Bob, getting up to turn round before me and show me how tight his clothes were.

"Well, what does it matter?" I said. "Nobody will see us."

"It isn't seeing you," he replied, "it's seeing me. No, I sha'n't go out till I get some clothes."

Bob kept his word, and for the rest of the holidays when I went out it always used to be with Bigley Uggleston. But we did not neglect poor Bob, for we went to see him nearly every day, and played games with him in the garden, and finished the gooseberries, and began the apples, contriving to enjoy ourselves pretty well.

As for the doctor, it was his way of dealing with his son, and I suppose he thought he was right; but it was very unpleasant, and kept poor Bob out of many a bit of enjoyment, those clothes being locked away.

I said that Bob would not go out. I ought to have said, by daylight, for he used to go with us after dark down to the end of the tiny pier, where we sat with our legs swinging over the water, each holding a fishing-line and waiting for any fish that might be tempted to take the raw mussel stuck upon our hooks.

But somehow that narrow escape of ours seemed to act like a damper upon the rest of our holidays, and I spent a good deal of my time with Bigley, watching the preparations made by the masons at the works in the Gap.

We all declared that we were not sorry when one morning old Teggley Grey's cart stopped at our gate to take up my box. Bob Chowne's was already in, and he was sitting upon it, while Bigley was half-way up the slope leading over the moor waiting by the road-side with his.

I said "Good-bye" to my father, who shook my hand warmly.

"Learn all you can, Sep," he said, "and get to be a man, for you have a busy life before you, and before long I shall want you to help me."

I climbed in, and old Teggley drew out the corners of his lips and grinned as if he was glad that Bob Chowne was so miserable. For Bob did not move, only sat with his hands supporting his face, staring down before him, bent, miserable, and dejected.

"What's the matter, Bob?" I said, trying to be cheerful. "Got the toothache?"

"Yes," he said sourly, "all over."

"Get out! What is it? Father made you take some physic?"

"Yes, pills. Verbum nasticusis, and bully draught after."

"What! Has he been scolding you?"

"Scolding me! He never does anything else. I sha'n't stand it much longer. I shall run off to sea and be a cabin-boy."

"Hi, hi, hi!"

"What are you laughing at?" snapped Bob, turning sharply upon old Teggley.

"At you, Mars Bob Chowne, going for a cabin-boy."

Whop!

That last was a severe crack given to admonish the big bony horse old Teggley drove; but he was a merciful man to his beast, and always hit on the pad, the collar, or the shafts.

"S'pose I like to go for a cabin-boy, 'tain't no business of yours, is it?" cried Bob snappishly.

"Not a bit, my lad, not a bit. I'll take your sea-chest over to Barnstaple for you when you go."

"No, you won't," grumbled Bob viciously, "for I won't have one."

"Ahoy! Bigley," I shouted, looking out from under the tilt. "Hooray for school!"

"Aha! Look at him—look at him!" shouted Bob, whose whole manner changed as soon as he saw Bigley's doleful face. "I say, old Grey, here's a little boy crying because he is going back to school."

Bigley did not say anything, only gave Bob a reproachful glance as he handed his box up to the carrier, and then climbed in.

"Gently, Mars Uggles'on," cried the old carrier, who seemed to consider that he had a right like other people to joke Bigley about his size; "gently, my lad, or you'll break the sharps. I didn't know I was going to have a two-horse load."

"Look here, old Teggley Grey!" cried Bigley firing up; "if you say another word about my being so large, I'll pitch you out of the back of the cart, and drive into Barnstaple without you."

"Do, Bigley, do," cried Bob in ecstasy. "Here, I'll hold the reins. Chuck him out."

"Don't talk that way, Mars Bob Chowne," whined the old man. "You wouldn't like me to be hurt."

"Oh, just wouldn't I!" cried Bob spitefully. "Pitch him overboard, Bigley, old boy, and hurt him as much as you can."

"No, no, you wouldn't, Mars Bob Chowne. You wouldn't like me to have to be carried home on a wagon, and your father have to tend me for broken bones and such."

"I tell you I would," cried Bob savagely; "and I hope you'll bite your tongue, and then you won't be so ready to ask questions. There!"

"Me ask questions!" exclaimed the old carrier in an ill-used tone. "As if I ever did. Well, never mind, he'll know better some day."

The old man sniffed several times quite severely, and sat bolt upright at the side of the cart, looking out at his horse's ears, and left us to ourselves. Bob's fit of melancholy was over, and he was ready to make remarks upon everything he saw; but neither Bigley nor I spoke, for we were intent upon something the latter told me.

"I don't want to tell tales," he said to me in a low tone, "but father makes me miserable."

"But do you think it is so bad as you say?"

Bigley nodded.

"He goes and sits on a stone with his spy-glass where he can see them, but they can't see him, and he stops there watching for hours everything they do, and comes back looking very serious and queer."

"Well, what does it matter?" I said. "He won't hurt us. He can't, because he is my father's tenant, and if he did he'd have to go."

"Don't talk like that, Sep," whispered Bigley. "It's bad enough now, and it would be worse then."

"I say, what chaps you two are!" cried Bob Chowne. "Why don't you talk to a fellow?"

No one answered, and Bob turned sulky and went and sat on the front of the cart, where he began to whistle.

"What do you mean by being worse?" I said.

Bigley shook his head.

"I don't know; I can't say," he whispered. "I mean I don't want father to be very cross."

"I say, Big," I whispered. "Your father really is a smuggler, isn't he?"

Bigley looked sharply round to gaze at old Teggley Grey and Bob Chowne, creeping as he did so nearer to the tail-board of the cart, and I followed him.

"I oughtn't to tell," he whispered back.

"But you'll tell me. I won't say a word to a soul," I said.

"Well, I don't know. I'm not sure, but—"

Bigley paused, and looked round again before putting his lips close to my ear and whispering softly:

"I think he is."

"I'm sure of it," I whispered back; "and I know he goes out in his lugger to meet French boats and Dutch boats, and makes no end of money by smuggling."

"Who told you that?" whispered Bigley fiercely.

"Nobody. It's what everybody says of him. They all say that he'll be caught and hanged some day for it—hung in chains; but of course I hope he won't, Big, because of you."

"It's all nonsense. It isn't true," said Bigley indignantly, "and those who talk that way are far more likely to be hung themselves. But I wish your father hadn't bought the Gap."

"I don't," I said. "He had a right to buy it if he liked, and I don't see what business it is of your father. Why don't he attend to his fishing?"

Bigley looked up at me sharply, to see if I had any hidden meaning.

"He does attend to his fishing," he said angrily; "and if he hadn't been attending to his fishing he wouldn't have been out in his boat that day, and saved you from being drowned."

I never liked Bigley half so well before as when he spoke up like that in defence of his father; but I was in a sour disappointed mood that day, because the holidays were over and I was going back to school, so I said something that was thoroughly ungenerous, and which I felt sorry for as I spoke.

"Yes, he saved us all from being drowned, I suppose," I said; "but he hadn't been fishing, for there were no fish in the boat."

"Just as if anybody could be sure of catching fish every time he went out," cried Bigley angrily. "There, you want to quarrel because you are miserable at having to go back to school, but I sha'n't. I hate it. Go and fall out with old Bob Chowne."

This made me feel angry and I drew away from him, for it was trying to make out that I was as quarrelsome as Bob Chowne delighted to be. But I felt so horribly in fault directly after that I went back to my place and sat by him in silence.

After a time the old carrier turned to us with a request that we would get out and give the horse a rest up the hill.

We all obeyed, two of us jumping out over the tail-board, the other by the front, and leaping off the shaft.

It was plain enough that the holidays were over, and that the joyous hearty spirit of the homeward-bound was there no more, for Bob Chowne took one side of the road in front of the horse, and the old carrier the other, while Bigley and I hung back behind and walked slowly after them on opposite sides after the fashion of those in front.

Then came the stopping of the cart, and mounting again and descending a couple more times, before we reached Barnstaple, dull, low-spirited, and ready to find about a score of boys just back, and looking as doleful as we did ourselves.

Chapter Sixteen
Our Silver Mine

School life has been so often narrated, that I am going to skip over mine, and make one stride from our return after Midsummer to Christmas, when we all went back home in a very different frame of mind.

The country looked very different to when we saw it last, but it was a mild balmy winter, with primroses and cuckoo-pints pushing in the valleys, and here and there a celandine pretending that spring had come.

The roads were dirty, but we thought little about them, for we knew that the sea-shore was always the same, and, if anything, more interesting in winter than in summer.

I was all eagerness to get home and see what had been done in the Gap, for my father in his rare letters had said very little about it.

Bigley was equally eager too. Six months had made a good deal of difference in him, for, young as he was, he seemed to be more manly and firm-looking, though to talk to he was just as boyish as ever, and never happier than when he was playing at some game.

He, too, was ready enough to talk about the Gap, and wonder what had been done.

"I hope your father has made friends with mine," he kept on saying as we drew nearer home. "It will be so awkward if they are out when you and I want to be in. Because we do, don't we?"

"Why, of course," I cried. "And it will be so awkward, won't it?"

"No," I said stoutly, "it won't make any difference; you and I are not going to fall out, so why should we worry about it? I say, look at Bob Chowne!"

Bigley turned, and there he was once more seated upon his box, right up on the big knot of the cord, just as if he liked to make himself uncomfortable. Then his elbows were on his knees and his chin was in his hands, as he stared straight before him from out of the tilt of the big cart.

"Why, what's the matter, Bob?" I said.

"Nothing."

"Why, there must be something or you wouldn't look like that. What is it?"

"Oh, I don't know; only that we're going home."

"Well, aren't you glad?"

"Glad? No, not I. What is there to be glad about? I haven't forgotten last holidays."

"What do you mean?" said Bigley and I in a breath.

"Oh, wasn't I always getting in rows, because you two fellows took me out and got me in trouble. I haven't forgotten about that old suit of clothes."

"But I say, Bob," I cried, "didn't you do your part of getting into trouble?"

"Oh, I don't know. Don't bother, I'm sick of it. I'm tired of being a boy. I wish I was a man."

"Nay, don't wish that," cried the old carrier, who had been hearing everything, though he had not spoken before. "Man, indeed! Why, aren't you all boys with everything you can wish for? How would you like to be a man and have to do nothing else every day but sit in this here cart, and go to and fro, to and fro, from year's end to year's end, and never no change?"

As we drew near the Bay Bob Chowne grew more fidgety and despondent, but we tried to cheer him up by making appointments to go fishing and exploring the shore; but my first intent was to run over to the Gap, and see what was going on there.

As the carrier's cart descended the hill and we came in sight of the cottage, I saw some one at the gate, and leaning out on one side I saw that it was my father and the doctor, but before I could say so there was a jerk which nearly threw me off, and I heard a familiar voice cry:

"There you are, then. Out with your box, lad. Here's Binnacle Bill come to carry it. How do, young gentlemen! Well, young doctor, I've got that rope's-ending saved up for you whenever you like to come."

Old Jonas did not offer to shake hands with either of us, but Bigley did after handing out his box.

"You'll come on to-morrow," he said quickly.

"Yes, we'll come," I said, answering for both; and I observed that old Jonas smiled grimly, though he did not speak.

Then Bob and I were alone and jogging down the zigzag road, traversing another five hundred yards before we reached our gate, where my father and the doctor were waiting for us.

"Brought the lads home quite safe, captain," said old Teggley Grey. "Shall I take Mars Robert's box on to the town, doctor?"

The old carrier remained unanswered, for we were both being heartily shaken by the hand, while old Sam came up smiling to carry in my box.

"Yes, take on the other box, Grey," cried the doctor. "We shall walk home, Bob."

"After a good tea," put in my father; and I found that meal awaiting us all, and very hearty and cosy it looked after the formal repasts at school.

"Why, you've both grown," said the doctor, as we sat down in the snug old room, where every object around seemed to be welcoming me.

"Yes, that they have," said my father. "Your Bob has the best of it too."

"Trifle," said the doctor, "trifle. Well, sir, how many suits of clothes shall you want this time? I've never heard any more of the ones you lost."

I saw Bob turn red and take a vicious bite out of a piece of bread and butter.

"They're nearly six months older now," said my father smiling, as he performed the feminine task of pouring out the tea, "and they'll be more careful."

"Will they?" said the doctor emphatically. "You see if the young varlets are not in trouble before the week's out, sir."

"Let's hope not," said my father. "Come, boys, help yourselves to the ham and eggs."

"Come, boys, help yourselves to the ham and eggs!" said Bob Chowne to me, as soon as we were alone. "Who's to help himself to ham and eggs when he's having the suit of clothes he lost banged about his unfortunate head? It regularly spoiled my tea."

"Why, Bob," I cried, "you had three big cups, six pieces of bread and butter, two slices of ham, three eggs, a piece of cake, and some cream."

"There's a sneak—there's a way to treat a fellow!" he cried, growing spiky all over, and snorting with annoyance. "Ask a poor chap to tea, and then count his mouthfuls. Well, that is mean."

"Why, I only said so because you declared you had had a bad tea."

"So I did—miserable," he retorted. "I seemed to see myself again sitting at home in those old worn-out clothes, and afraid to go out at any other time but night, when no one was looking."

"Now, Bob: where are you?" cried his father. "I'll take him off at once, Duncan, or he'll eat you out of house and home."

"Hear that?" cried Bob, "hear that? Pretty way to talk of a fellow, isn't it. I don't wonder everybody hates me. I'm about the most miserable chap that ever was."

"Not you, Bob. Come over to-morrow."

"What for?"

"Oh, I don't know. We'll go rabbiting or something."

"Now, Bob!" came from the doctor.

"Here, I must go. Good-bye. I'll come if I can. I wish I was you, or old Bigley, or somebody else."

"Or back at school," I said laughing.

"Yes, or back at school," he said quite seriously; and then his arm was grasped by his father.

"Just as if I was a patient," he grumbled to me next day. "Father don't like me. He only thinks I am a nuisance, and he's glad when I'm going back to school. I shall run off to Bristol some day and go to sea, that's what I shall do."

But that was the next day. That evening I stood with my father at the gate till Bob and his father were out of sight in the lane, and then we went back into the parlour, where my father lit his pipe and sat smoking and gazing at me.

"Well, Sep," he said after a pause, "don't you want to know how the mine is getting on?"

"Yes, father," I said; "but I didn't like to ask."

"Well, I'll tell you without, my boy. I've not got much profit out of it at present, because the expenses of starting have been so great; but it's a very fine thing, my boy."

"Is it going to make you rich, father?"

"I hope so, boy, for your sake. There's plenty of lead, and out of the lead we are able to get about four per cent of silver."

"Four per cent, father!" I said; "what—interest?"

"No, boy, profit. I mean in every hundred pounds of lead there are four pounds of pure silver, but of course it costs a good deal to refine."

"And may I go and see it all to-morrow?" I asked.

"To be sure; and I hope, after a year or two, you will be of great use to me there."

I felt as if I could hardly sleep that night when I went to bed. There had been so much to see about the place, so much talk to have with old Sam and Kicksey, that it hardly needed the thought of seeing the mine next day to keep me awake.

I thought I should never go to sleep, I say; but I awoke at half-past seven the next morning, feeling as if I had had a thoroughly good night's rest, and as soon as breakfast was over I started with my father on a dull soft winter's morning to see the mine.

Bob and Bigley were to come over; but I felt that it would be twelve o'clock before Bob came, and that I should meet Bigley; so no harm would be done in the way of breaking faith in the appointment.

We walked sharply across the hill and descended into the Gap, but before we had gone far we met old Jonas Uggleston.

"Morning!" he said pleasantly. "Morning, squire!" to me. "Seen my Bigley yet?"

"No."

"Ah! He has gone your way. Tell him I want to see him if he comes."

We said we would, and old Jonas went his way and we ours.

"Why, father," I said, "how civil he has grown!"

"Yes," said my father gravely, "he has; but I would almost rather he had kept his distance. Don't tell your school-fellow I said that."

"Of course not, father," I said confidently; and we went on to the mine—the silver mine, and I stood and stared at a part of the valley that had been inclosed with a stone wall. There were some rough stone sheds, a stack of oak props, and a rough-looking pump worked by a large water-wheel, which was set in motion by a trough which brought water from the side of the hill, where a tiny stream trickled down.

There was one very large heap of rough stone that looked as if barrows full of broken fragments were always being run along it, and turned over at the end, for the pieces to rattle down the side into the valley; there was a small heap close by, and under a shed there was a man breaking up some dirty wet stuff with a hammer.

That was all that was to see except some troughs to carry off dirty water, and the rough framework and trap-doors over what seemed to be a well.

"Why, Sep," said my father laughing, "how blank you look! Don't you admire the mine?"

"Is—is this a silver mine, father?" I faltered.

"Yes, my lad, silver-lead. Doesn't look very attractive, does it?"

I shook my head.

"But is it going to be worth a great deal of money?"

"Yes, my boy; only wait and you'll see. But I suppose you expected to see a hole in the earth leading down into quite an enchanted cave—eh?—a sort of Aladdin's palace, with walls sparkling with native silver?"

"Well, not quite so much as that, father," I replied; "but I did expect to find something different to this."

"So do most people when they go to see a mine, Sep, and they are horribly disappointed to find that they have not used their common sense. They know that if they dig down into the earth to make a well, in twenty feet or so, perhaps less, they come to water; and it has never occurred to them that if they dig down to form a mine, it must naturally be a wet dark muddy hole just like this one upon which you look with so much disgust. But wait a bit, my boy. We shall soon have furnaces at work and be smelting our ore and converting some of it into silver. There'll be more to see then. You don't care to go down?" he said, leaning his hand upon a windlass over the trap-doors.

"Is there anything to see, father?" I said rather dolefully.

"To see! Well, there are the sides of a big well-like hole which you can see from here. Look!"

He threw open a trap-door, and I gazed into a well-like place with a couple of ropes hanging down it, and I noted that the walls were made of the stone that had been dug and broken out. The place looked dark and damp, and there was the trickling of dripping water. That was all.

"Well, Sep, what do you say?—will you go?"

"Is it all like this, father?" I said.

"Yes, precisely, my lad. Shall I have you let down?"

"No, thank you," I said; "I think I'll stop up."

He nodded and smiled, and after staying with him for a time while he examined some of the ore that the man was breaking up he set me free, but not till I had asked him how many men he had at work, and been told that at present there were only six.

Chapter Seventeen
We have a Little Fishing

I went away to see if I could find Bigley, feeling very much put out, and full of hope that Bob Chowne, when he came, would not ask me to take him to see the mine.

For, truth to tell, I had made rather a fuss about that mine, talking about silver-lead in a very important way at school; and, as I recalled my words, I felt quite a shudder of horror as I thought of all the boys in my class coming and standing at the mouth of the mine, and bursting into a roar of laughter at this being the silver cavern in the earth.

There was no likelihood of any of them coming save Bob Chowne; but there was no knowing what he would say when we got back if I offended him and he was in one of his teasing fits.

I walked down to the end of the Gap, past the cottage, and was just going to ask if Bigley had come back, when I saw old Jonas and Binnacle Bill, with another man, putting off in the lugger, which was lying by a buoy about a quarter of a mile from the shore.

After five months at school it seemed such a pretty sight to see the red sails hoisted and fill out, and the lugger begin to move slowly over the smooth water, that I sat down on a stone and watched the boat, wishing I were in her, till she gradually grew more distant, and there was a dull thud close beside me.

I looked round but saw nothing, and I was turning to watch the lugger again, when I heard a fresh pat on the slate rubbish by me, and soon after a piece of flat, thin shale struck the clatter stream behind me.

"Some one throwing," I said to myself, and looking up, there, about six hundred feet above me on the cliff path, were Bigley and Bob Chowne.

I shouted to them, and they ran to the nearest clatter stream and began to slide down standing. Sometimes they came swiftly for a few yards; sometimes they stopped and each had a check, a fall, and a roll over, but they were up again directly, and in less than half the time it would have taken them to walk they were down by my side.

"Here, where have you been?" cried Bob, who was in the highest of glee. "Old Big says it's such a dark quiet day that the fish are sure to bite, and he's going to ask his father to let us have the boat, and row out."

"But Mr Uggleston isn't at home."

"No, that he isn't," said Bigley, who had just caught sight of the lugger. "That is tiresome."

"But they haven't taken the boat," cried Bob, "so it don't matter."

"Yes, it does," said Bigley gravely, "because I shouldn't like to take the boat without leave."

"Why, of course you wouldn't if your father was at home," said Bob quickly; "but I'm quite sure Mr Uggleston wouldn't like us two to be disappointed when we'd come on purpose to go."

"Oh, I don't think he'd mind," said Bigley.

"But I know he would," cried Bob, who spoke in the most consequential manner. "Your father is rough, but he is very good at bottom."

"Why, of course he is," cried Bigley.

"Then he wouldn't like us to be cheated out of our treat, so you get the mussels for the bait, and some worms, and let's go."

Bigley hesitated. He wanted to go, for the sea was as smooth as a mill-pond—a rare thing in winter; and perhaps we should have to wait for some time before another such day arrived.

He looked at me and I wanted to go too. That was plain enough, and the chance seemed so tempting that, even if I did not openly abet Bob, I said no word to persuade Bigley not.

"You'd got all the lines and bait ready, hadn't you?" said Bob cunningly.

"Yes, everything's ready, and I meant to ask father as soon as I got back. Here, hi! Mother Bonnet, how long will father be?"

"Oh, all depends on the wind," said the fresh-looking old lady coming out, smiling and smoothing her hair. "They've gone across to Swansea, my dear. It will be a long time 'fore they're back."

"There, you see, you can't ask, and it's no use to signal to them in the lugger, because they couldn't understand, so you've got to take the boat, and we shall be back long before they are."

"But it would be so horrible if we were to meet with any accident this time," said Bigley. "You know how unlucky we were over the prawns. There, we'd better not go!"

"There's a Molly for you!" cried Bob. "Just because we got in a muddle twice over in catching prawns and crabs you think we're always going to be in a mess."

"No, I don't," said Bigley; "but it would be so queer if we got into a scrape the very first time we go out."

"Get out! Oh, I say, you do make me grin, old Big. There, go and get your lines, and a gaff, and the basket of bait. Let's be off while the sea is so smooth."

Bigley hesitated, and after a good deal of banter from Bob, and an appeal to me, he went off, sorry and yet pleased, to get the lines and bait.

"And now he'll be obliged to go, Sep. Don't let's give him time to think, or he's such an old woman he'll back out."

"But—"

"Get out! Don't say but. There, we won't go out far, only to the mouth there by the buoy, and we can catch plenty of fish without any trouble at all."

I gave way—I couldn't help it, and we two went on, so that when Bigley came with the baskets and lines we were waiting for them, and his scruples were nearly overcome.

"Think it will matter if we take the boat?" he said dubiously, for he evidently shared our longing to go.

I said no, I did not think it would, for we could clean it out after we had done fishing, and we had been boating so often with other people that I for one felt quite equal to the management of the little vessel.

But all the time there was a curious sensation of wrong-doing worrying me, and I wished that I had not been so ready to agree. It was as if I felt the impression of trouble that was coming; but I kept the feeling to myself.

"Well," said Bigley, "I did mean to ask for leave."

"Of course you did," cried Bob Chowne; "but as your father is off you can't. Come along, boys, and let's get a good haul this time."

He seized the bait-basket and made the shells of the mussels rattle as he trotted down towards where the little five-pointed anchor or grapnel lay on the beach, and began to haul in the boat.

As the light buoyant vessel came gliding over the smooth surface, and grated and bumped against and over the stones, the thoughts of whether we were doing right or wrong grew faint, and then, as the bait-basket was thrown in, and the lines followed, they were forgotten.

"In with you, lads!" cried Bob, making a spring, and leaping from a dry stone right into the boat; but his feet slipped, and he came down sitting in the basket of mussels with an unpleasant crash.

"Now, look here!" he cried in a passion, "if you fellows laugh at me I won't go."

Of course this made us all the more disposed; but we turned our backs and went down upon our knees to begin seeing to the hooks upon one of the reeled-up lines.

"There, you are laughing both of you!" cried Bob, who was easing the pain he felt, or thought he was, by lifting up and setting down first one leg and then the other.

"That we are not!" I cried, and certainly our faces were serious enough, as we hurriedly popped the lines over the bows, when I jumped in, and, catching up the little grapnel, Bigley took one big stride with his long legs, and was on the gunwale, which went down nearly to the water with his weight; but as the boat rose again, the impetus of the thrust he gave her in leaping aboard carried her out a couple of lengths.

There was no thought now of any wrong-doing, as Bob and I seized an oar apiece and began to paddle as the boat rose and fell and glided over the swelling tide.

"Pull away, Sep!" cried Bob. "Here, old Big, you're sitting all on one side and making the boat lop. Get in the middle or I'll splash you!"

Bigley moved good-humouredly, and the boat danced beneath his weight.

"Heave ho! Steady!" shouted Bob. "Don't sink us, lad. I say, what a weight you are! Let's put him ashore, Sep. He's too big a Big for a boat like this."

"Make good ballast," said Bigley, laughing good-humouredly. "Boats are always safer when they are well ballasted."

"I daresay they are, but I like 'em best without Big lumps in 'em. I say, how far out shall we go?"

"Oh, about a quarter of a mile, straight out, over the Ringlet rocks. You pull, I'll watch the bearings, and drop out the grapnel. Pull hard!"

We rowed away steadily, while, to save time, Bigley took out his pocket-knife and, taking a board from the bait-basket, laid it upon the seat, and began to open the mussels and scrape out the contents of the shells ready for placing them upon the hooks when we reached the fishing ground.

For I may tell you that knowing the bottom well has a great deal to do with success in sea-fishing. A stranger to our parts might think that all he had to do was to row out in a little boat a few hundred yards, and begin to fish.

If he did that, the chances are that he would not catch anything, while a boat three or four lengths away might be hauling in fish quite fast.

The reason is simple. Sea fish frequent certain places after the fashion of fresh-water fish, which are found, according to their sorts, on muddy bottoms; half-way down in clear deeps; among piles; in gravelly swims; at the tails of weeds; or under the boughs of trees close in to the side of river or lake.

So with the sea fish. If we wanted to catch bass, we threw out in places where the tide ran fast; if we were trying for pollack, it was along close by the stones of the rocky shore; if for conger, in deep dark holes; and if for flat-fish, right out in deep water, where the bottom was all soft oozy sand.

Upon this occasion we had decided for the latter, and with Bigley giving a word now and then to direct us, as he watched certain points on the shore, we rowed away for quite half a mile, but keeping straight out from the Gap.

"Now we're just over the Ringlets," cried Bigley suddenly.

"Heave over the anchor then!" I shouted.

"No, go on a bit farther, about fifty yards, and then we shall be on the muddy sand. I know."

We boys pulled, and then all at once Bigley shouted "In oars!" and we ceased rowing as the grapnel went over the side with a splash, and the cord ran across the gunwale, grating and *scrorting* as Bob called it, till the little anchor reached the bottom, and the drifting of the boat was checked.

"I say, isn't it deep?" I said.

"Just about nine fathoms," said Bigley. "You'll have plenty of hauling to do."

"I say, look!" I cried, as I happened to look shoreward, "you can see right up the Gap nearly to the mine."

"Isn't the sea smooth?" said Bob. "It's just like oil. Now then, first fish. Put us on a good big bait, Bigley, old chap."

The hooks were all ready with the weights and spreaders, and Bigley began calmly enough to hook and twist on a couple of the wet and messy raw mussels for Bob, and then did the same for mine, when we two began to fish on opposite sides of the boat, letting the leads go rapidly down what appeared to be a tremendous distance before they touched the ooze.

It seemed quite a matter of course that we two were to fish, and Bigley wait upon us, opening mussels, rebaiting when necessary, and holding himself ready to take off the fish, should any be caught.

I never used to think anything about Bigley Uggleston in these days, only that he was overgrown and good-tempered, and never ready to quarrel; and it did not seem to strike either of us that he was about the most unselfish, self-denying slave that ever lived. I know now that we were perfect tyrants to him, while he, amiable giant that he was, bore it all with the greatest of equanimity, and the more unreasonable we were, the more patient he seemed to grow.

We fished for some few minutes without a sign, and then Bob grew weary.

"It's no good here, Big, they won't bite. Let's go on farther."

"Bait's off, perhaps," suggested Bigley.

"No, it isn't. I haven't had a touch."

"Perhaps not, but the flat-fish suck it off gently sometimes. Pull up."

Bob drew in the wet line hand over hand, till the lead sinker hit the side of the boat; and Bigley proved to be right, both baits were off his hooks, and as they were being rebaited I hauled in my line to find that it was in the same condition.

By the time Bob's lead was at the bottom, my hooks were being covered with mussel, and I threw in again.

As mine reached the sandy ooze, and I held the line in one hand, there was a slight vibration of the lead, but it passed away again, and I fished, to pull up again at the end of a few minutes and find both baits gone.

Bob's were the same, and so we fished on till he declared that it was of no use, that it was the tide washed the bait off, and that there wasn't a fish within a hundred yards. "But I'm sure there are lots," said Bigley. "Why, how can you tell?" cried Bob. "You can't see two feet down through the water, it's so muddy."

"I know by the baits being taken off," replied Bigley decidedly. "There are fish here I'm sure, and—"

"I've got him," I shouted, beginning to haul in, for I could feel something heavy at the end of the line which had given several sharp snatches as I hauled.

"Oh, what a shame!" cried Bob. "I don't see why they should come first to old Sep. Here, I know what it is. Only an old bow-wow."

"No, it isn't," I exclaimed as I caught a glimpse of something white, looking like a slice of the moon far down below the boat. "It's a flat-fish, and a big one."

I proved to be right, as I hauled it flapping over the side, and Bigley seized what proved to be a nice plaice, and took the hook from its jaws.

As the line, being rebaited, was thrown in again, there was a serious examination of the prize, which was about to be transferred to the basket brought to hold our captures, when Bob shouted, "I've got him!" and began to haul in with all his might.

We both adjured him to be careful, but in his excitement he paid no heed, only dragged as hard as he could, and hoisted in a long grey fish, at which he gazed with a comical aspect full of disgust.

I laughed, and as I laughed he grew more angry, for his prize was what he had previously called a "bow-wow" and attributed to me. For it was a good-sized dog-fish, one which had to be held at head and tail lest in its twining and lashing about it should strike with its spine and do some mischief.

"Here, let me take him off," cried Bob.

"No, no; you mind the line isn't tangled," cried Bigley; but Bob gave him a push, the dog-fish, which was nearly a yard long, was set free, and began to journey about amongst Bob's line, while, when he placed his foot upon its head, the fierce creature bent half round, and then let itself go like a spring, with the effect that it struck Bob's shoe so smart a blow with one of its spines that the shoe was pierced by the toe, and it required a tug to withdraw the spine.

"Are you hurt, Bob?" we both cried earnestly.

"No, not a bit. My toes don't go down as far as that. Ah, would you?"

This was to the fish, which was lashing about fiercely.

"Let me do it, Bob. I'll kill it in no time, and I know how to manage him."

"So do I," said Bob independently, as he made another attack upon the dog-fish, which resented it by a fresh stroke with its spine, this time so near to Bob's leg that he jumped back and fell over the thwart.

"I say, that was near," he cried. "You have a try, Big."

Our school-fellow wanted no second bidding, and taking hold of the line, he drew the fish's head under his right foot, pressed down its tail with his left, took out the hook, and then with his knife inflicted so serious a cut upon the creature that, when he threw it over, it only struggled feebly, as it sank slowly and was carried away.

"There's a cruel wretch!" cried Bob. "Did you see how vicious he was with his knife?"

"It isn't cruel to kill fishes like that," retorted Bigley. "See what mischief they do hunting the other fish and eating everything. See how they bite the herrings and mackerel out of the nets, only leaving their heads."

"He wouldn't have said anything if the dog had spiked him," I said.

"Why, so he did spike me," cried Bob; "and—"

"I've got another," I cried, beginning to haul up, and as I hauled Bob sent his freshly-baited and disentangled hook down to the bottom.

I had caught another flat-fish about the size of the first, and directly after Bob caught one. Then there was a pause, and I took another dog-fish, and after that we fished, and fished, and fished for about half an hour and caught nothing.

It was December, but the air was still, and we did not feel it in the slightest degree cold. I suppose it was the excitement kept us warm, for there was always the expectation of taking something big, even if the great fish never came.

Just as we were thinking that it was of no use to stay longer the fish began to bite again, and we caught several, but all small, and then all at once, as I was lowering my lead, I cried out:

"Look here! I can't touch bottom."

"Nonsense!" said Bob, lowering his line, but only to become a convert, and exclaim accordingly.

"Why, we're drifting," cried Bigley, going to the line that held the anchor, to find that it had been dragged out of the muddy sand, and that we had slowly gone with the tide into deeper water, whose bottom there was not length enough of rope for the grapnel to touch.

"I'll soon put that right," cried Bigley, unfastening the line and letting about three fathoms more run out, but even then the anchor did not reach bottom, and without we were stationary it was of no use to fish.

"Haul in your lines, lads," cried Bigley, setting us an example by dragging away at the cord which held the anchor. "We must row back a bit. We've drifted into the deep channel. I didn't know we were out so far."

"Oh, I say, look!" cried Bob. "It's beginning to rain, and we've no greatcoats."

"Never mind," said Big, getting hold of the anchor as we drew in our leads, and laid them with the hooks carefully placed aside, ready for beginning again.

"Now, then, who's going to pull along with me!"

"You pull, Sep," said Bob. "I want to count the fish."

I took an oar, and just as I was about to pull the boat's head round I looked towards the mouth of the Gap, which was nearly three-quarters of a mile away, and though at present the smooth sea was just specked here and there by the falling drops, over shoreward there was what seemed to be a thick mist coming as it were out of the mouth of the Gap, and a curious dull roar towards where we were.

"Going to be a squall," said Bigley. "Pull away, Sep, and let's get ashore."

Easy enough to say—difficult enough to do, as we very soon found, in spite of trying our very best.

Chapter Eighteen
The Following Night

I have told you who did not know what our coast was like—one high wall of cliffs and hills from six hundred to a thousand feet high, with breaks where the little rivers ran down into the sea, and these breaks, after the fashion of our Gap, narrow valleys that run into the land with often extremely precipitous walls, and a course such as a lightning flash is seen to make in a storm, zigzagging across the sky.

If you do not know I may as well at once tell you what is often the effect of rowing or sailing along such a coast as ours: You may be going along in an almost calm sea for hours, perhaps, till, as you row across one of these valleys or combes, the wind suddenly comes rushing out like an enormous blast from some vast pipe. All the time, perhaps, there has been a sharp breeze blowing high up in the air, the great wall of rock preventing its striking where you are, but no sooner are you in front of the opening than you feel its power.

Beside this, all may be calm elsewhere, while down the steep-sided valley a keen blast rushes, coming from far inland, high up on the moor, where it has perhaps behaved like a whirlwind, and having finished its wild career there, has plunged down into the combe to make its escape out to sea.

It was just such a gust as this last which suddenly came upon us, raising the sea into short rough waves, and bearing upon its wings such a tremendous storm of sharp cutting rain and hail, that, after fighting against it for some time and feeling all the while that we were drifting out to sea, we ceased rowing and allowed the boat to go, in the hope that the squall would end in a few minutes as quickly as it had come on.

The rush of the wind and the beating and hissing of the rain was terribly confusing. The waves, too, lapped loudly against the sides and threatened to leap in; and while we glanced to right and left in the hope of being blown in under shelter of the land, we found that the boat was rushing through the water, our bodies answering the purpose of sails.

We crouched down together, not to diminish the power of the wind, but in that way to afford each other a little shelter from the drenching rain.

"It can't last long," shouted Bigley, for he was obliged to cry aloud to make himself heard above the shrieking of the storm.

But it did last long and kept increasing in violence. The heavens, in place of being of the soft bluish-grey that had been so pleasant when we came out, had grown black, the rain all about us was like a thick mist that shut out the sight of the cliffs, and with it the power of seeing the hissing water descend into the sea for a few yards round, we forming what seemed to be the centre of the mist.

And there we were, drive, drive before the wind at what we felt was quite a rapid rate, till all at once the rain passed on, leaving us wet, and cold, and wretched, and ready to huddle more closely still for the sake of warmth.

But though the rain had passed on, and it was clear behind us as it was dark ahead, while we could see the mouth of the Gap and the lowering cliffs, the wind did not cease, but seemed to be blowing more angrily than ever—with such force, indeed, that we could hardly make each other hear.

There was an unpleasant symptom of danger, too, ready to trouble us, in the shape of the waves, which made the boat dance up and down and then pitch, as it still went rapidly on farther out to sea.

"Ready?" shouted Bigley, as I sat with my teeth chattering in the piercing wind.

I nodded, for I did not care to open my mouth to speak; and, in obedience to a sign, I held the water while he began to pull round as fast as he could and get the boat's head to the wind.

For a minute or so we were in very great danger, for as soon as we were broadside to the wind the waves seemed to leap up and the wind to strive to blow us over; but by sheer hard work Bigley got her head round, and then we pulled together, with the boat rising up one wave and plunging down another in a way that was quite startling.

Bob Chowne did not speak, only crouched down in the bottom of the boat and watched us as we tugged hard at the oars, under the impression that we were rowing in. But we soon knew to the contrary. We were only boys, the boat was a heavy one and stood well out of the water, and as we pulled the wind had tremendous power over our oars. In fact all we did was to keep the boat's head straight to the wind, and so diminished the violence of its power over us, while of course this was the best way to meet the waves that seemed to come directly off the shore.

"Come and pull now, Bob," I shouted after tugging at the oar for a long time. My feeling of chilliness had passed away, and I was weary and breathless with my exertions.

I kept on pulling while Bob came to my side, and as he took the oar I gradually edged away and crept under it to go and take the place where he had crouched.

It was a black look-out for us; for it was already growing dim, and we knew that in half an hour it would be quite dark. The wind was still rising and the sea flecked with little patches of foam; while, as I looked towards the Gap, I could not help seeing with sinking heart that not only were the high rocks growing dim with the shades of the wintry night, but with the distance too.

You know how quickly the change comes on from day to night at the end of December. You can imagine, then, in the midst of that sudden storm, how anxiously I watched the shore, and tried to persuade myself that we were getting nearer when I knew that we were not.

If I had had any doubt about it, Bigley, who had been used to sea-going from a little child, put an end to it by suddenly shouting:

"It's of no good; we are only drifting out. I'm going to try and get under shelter of the cliff."

Then, shouting to Bob to ease a little, he pulled hard at the boat's head to get her a little to the west instead of due south, and then shouted to our companion again to pull with all his might.

Bob did pull—I could see that he did; but we did not get under the shelter of the cliff, for the change in the position of the boat presented more surface to the wind, and we could feel that we were drifting faster still.

We tried not to lose heart; but it was impossible to keep away a certain amount of despondency as we realised that all our pulling was in vain, and as we grew wearied out Bigley said that it was of no use to row. All we were to do was to keep the boat's head well to the wind.

I crept after a time to Bigley's place in answer to a sign from him, for we had grown very silent; and as he resigned his oar to me and I went on pulling, while he crept aft to sit in the stern, it seemed as if it had all at once grown dark above us. The shore died away, all but one spot of light—a tiny spot that shone out like a star, one that we knew to be in the cottage where Mother Bonnet had no doubt a good hot cup of tea waiting for us, who were perishing with the cold and gradually drifting farther and farther away.

We could not talk for the wind. Besides, too, it was very hard work to talk and row in such a sea; so I sat and thought of how hard it was to be situated as we were, and to have again got into trouble in what was meant for a pleasant recreation.

I thought all this, and I believe my companions had very similar thoughts as we danced up and down on the short cockling sea.

Then all at once, as the darkness overhead seemed to have grown more intense, and the sea with its foam to give the little light we enjoyed, we were aware of a fresh danger.

The wind and the hissing and beating of the sea made a great deal of noise, but that loud washing splash sounded louder to us, and so did the rattle of a tin pot which Bigley seized, and lifted the board from over the bit of a well and began to bale.

For one of the waves had struck the bows, risen up, and poured three or four gallons of water into the boat.

Bigley was ready for the emergency, though, directly, and we saw the rise and fall of the tin pan as he swept it up and down and sent the water flying on the wings of the wind.

Before he had baled the boat out the first time another wave swept in, and he had to work hard to clear that out; but he soon had that done after correcting our rowing, for I was pulling harder than Bob, and the consequence was that the boat was not quite head to wind and did not ride so easily as she should.

Darker and darker, with the faint star in the Gap quite gone now, and all around us the hissing waste of waters upon which our frail shell of a boat was tossed! It was so black now that we could hardly see each other's faces, and in a doleful silence we toiled on till all at once there was a sobbing cry from Bob Chowne, who fell forward over his oar. Then the boat fell off and a wave came with a hissing rush over the bows.

"Back water, Sep!" yelled Bigley as he dragged Bob Chowne away, seized his oar, and began pulling, when the boat seemed to be eased again and rose and fell regularly; but a quantity of water kept rushing to and fro about poor Bob Chowne, who kept receiving it alternately in his back and face.

"Sit up and bale, Bob!" shouted Bigley. "Do you hear? Take the pannikin and bale."

Bob did not move, and Bigley shouted to him again.

"Take the pannikin and bale. Do you hear me? Take the pannikin and bale."

"I can't," moaned Bob. "I can't. Let me lie here and die."

Dark as it was I could just make out Bigley's actions, for I was in the fore part of the boat, and he before me.

"Bale, I say! Do you hear? Bale!" he shouted in his deep gruff voice.

"I can't," moaned Bob piteously.

"Then we shall sink—we shall go to the bottom."

"Yes; we're going to die," groaned Bob.

"No, we're not," cried Bigley in a fierce angry way that seemed different to anything I had before heard from him. "Get up and bale!"

"No, no," groaned Bob again.

"Get up and bale!" thundered Bigley, and I felt hot and angry against him, as I heard a dull thud, and it did not need Bob Chowne's cry of pain to tell me that Bigley had given him a kick on the ribs.

"Oh, Big!" I cried.

"Row!" he roared at me; and then to Bob: "Now, will you bale?"

"Yes," groaned Bob, struggling to his knees, and, holding on with one hand, he began to dip the baler in regularly and slowly, throwing out about a pint of water every time.

"Faster!" shouted Bigley; "faster, I say."

"Oh!" moaned poor Bob; but he obeyed, and it seemed a puzzle to me that our big companion, whom we bantered and teased, and led a sorry life at school, should somehow in this time of peril take the lead over us, and force us to behave in a way that could only have been expected of a crew obeying the captain of a boat.

I bent forward to Bigley as we kept on with the regular chop chop of the oars, making no effort to get nearer to the shore, only to keep the boat's head level, and I whispered in his ear:

"Shall we get to shore again!"

"Yes," he said confidently; "only you two must do what I tell you. I must be skipper now. Go on, you, Bob Chowne!" he roared. "Heave out that water. Do you want me to kick you again?"

Bob whimpered, but he worked faster, scooping the water clumsily out and throwing it over, the side, and, after he had done, and been sitting crouched at the bottom, Bigley seemed to attack him again unkindly, as if he were going to take advantage of his helplessness, and serve him out for many an old piece of tyranny.

"Now, then," he shouted—and it seemed to be his father speaking, not our quiet easy-going school-fellow, but the rough seafaring man who had the credit of being a smuggler — "Now then, you, Bob Chowne," he roared, "get up, and come and take Sep Duncan's oar."

"I can't," he groaned piteously, and he let himself fall against the side of the boat. "I'm so cold, I'm half dead."

"Oh, are you?" shouted Bigley. "No you ar'n't, so get up and creep over here."

"I can't," cried Bob again.

"Then I'll make you," cried Bigley fiercely, and lifting his oar out of the rowlocks he sent it along the gunwale, till he made it tap heavily against the back of Bob Chowne's head.

"Oh!" shrieked Bob, and I felt my cheeks burn, cold as I was.

"Now, will you come and work, you sneak?"

"I — I can't."

"Get up, or I'll come and heave you overboard," roared Bigley. "I won't have it."

"Oh — oh!" sobbed poor Bob.

"Let him be, Big," I cried. "I'm not very tired."

"You hold your tongue," was the response I had in an angry tone. "You be ready to give up your oar when he comes. Now, then, up with you, or I'll do it again."

Bob Chowne groaned piteously and crawled forward.

"Why can't you let a fellow die quietly?" he sobbed out, and then he crept over the seat where Bigley was rowing, so as to get to where I still tugged at my oar in hot indignation.

"Die, eh?" shouted Bigley with a forced laugh. "Yes, you'd better. Leave us to do all the pulling, would you? Oh, no, you don't. I'm biggest and I'll make you pull."

"Oh — oh — oh!" whimpered Bob. "Why can't you let a poor fellow be?"

"Be! What for?" shouted Bigley to my astonishment, for I could not have believed him guilty of such brutality. "Yes, I'll let you be. I'll make you work, that's what I'll do. I wish I'd a rope's end here."

"It's too bad, it's too cruel, Big," I cried passionately. "How can you behave so brutally to the poor fellow!"

"Here, you stick to your own work," cried Bigley fiercely. "Look, you're letting me do all the work. Keep her head to the wind, will you?"

His orders were so sharp and fierce that I found myself obeying them directly, and went on baling while Bob whimpered, and Bigley kept on hectoring over us, as I ladled out a little water now and then.

The wind blew as fiercely as ever, and we knew that we were rapidly being carried out farther and farther, right away to a certain extent towards the Welsh coast, but of course being also in the set of the tide, and going out to sea. The cold was terrible whenever we ceased pulling from utter weariness, but we managed among us to keep the boat's head to wind hour after hour, and danced over and over the waves till by degrees the fury of the wind died out, though we could not believe it at first. Soon, though, it become very evident that it was sinking, and I heard Bigley utter a sigh of relief.

It was quite time that the little gale did pass over, for during the last half hour the water had been coming into the boat more and more, so that it had become necessary for one of us to keep on baling, for the waves seemed to be getting more angry; a sharp rain of spray was dashed from their tops into our necks, and soaking our hair, and every now and again there was a blow, a splash, and a rush of water through the boat.

It was quite true, though we at first thought that we must be under shelter of the land; the wind was sinking fast, and the waves lost their fierce foaminess. They rose and fell, and leaped against the boat, but it was with less splash and fury, and then, as the danger died away, so did our remaining strength. Bigley and I, who were now rowing, or rather dipping our oars from time to time, slowly threw them in, and the boat lay tossing up and down at the mercy of the waves; but no water dashed in over the gunwale, and Bob Chowne's hand with the baler rested helplessly by his side.

No one spoke out there in the darkness, but we sat in the terrible silence, utterly exhausted, and rapidly growing chilled through and through in our saturated clothes. I remember looking out, and away through the darkness towards the shore as I thought, but I could see nothing till I raised my eyes toward the sky, and then I saw that the clouds had been driven away by the wind, and the stars were out, while straight before me there was the only constellation I knew—the Great Bear.

I was too weary for it to trouble me, but I learned then that the boat must have turned almost completely round since we had left off rowing, for where I had thought the land lay was out to sea, and the Welsh coast—in fact I had been looking due north instead of due south.

It did not trouble me much, for I was hungry and thirsty, and then I felt sleepy, and then shivering with cold, while a few minutes later I felt as if nothing mattered at all, for I was utterly wearied out.

Bigley was the first to speak, but it was not in the fierce tone of a short time before. He seemed to have changed back into our big mild school-fellow as he said:

"Come on over here, Sep, and let's all creep together. It won't be so cold then."

I noted the change in his tone, but I could not say anything, only obey him.

"Come, Bob," I said, as I climbed over the thwart, and tried to stand steadily in the dancing boat.

But Bob did not move or speak, and we others crept close to his side, beginning by edging up and leaning against each other, shivering the while, but the improvement was so great at the end of a few minutes, that we thrust our arms under each other's soaked jackets, and held on as closely as we could, to feel bitterly cold outside but comfortably warm on the inner.

The stars came out more and more, the wind died away, and the short dancing motion by very slow degrees subsided into a regular cradle-like rock, that, in spite of the cold, had a lulling effect upon us; and at last I seemed to be thinking of the miserable-looking mine in the Gap, and my father scolding me for going away without asking leave, and then everything seemed to be nothing, and nothing else.

Chapter Nineteen
A Friend in Need

I suppose it was an uneasy movement made by Bob Chowne that awoke me, and as I started away, and looked round at the darkness, and felt the motion of the boat, I trembled, and could not for the time make out where I was, or what all this peculiar sensation of cramped stiffness meant.

The stars were shining, and twinkling reflections flashed from the water; the boat rocked to and fro, and the cold was horrible. This feeling of bitter cold or else the stupefied sensation brought on by exhaustion seemed to keep me from thinking, and it was a long time before I quite realised the truth.

Then I wanted to wake up Bigley and Bob Chowne, to get them to start rowing again, for the sea had gone down, there was hardly a breath of wind; and, though I could see nothing, I felt that the land could not be very far away.

I raised my hand to shake Bigley; but I did not, for the inclination was stronger to creep close up to him, and try to warm myself; and this I did, clinging closely to him and Bob Chowne; and then, as I crouched shivering and cramped in the bottom of the boat, I felt as if all the cold and darkness had suddenly sunk away and I was in oblivion.

I don't know how long I slept, but I remember starting up again and wondering why the boat was moving so curiously, and then I found that I was being shaken, and a hoarse voice said:

"Sep! Sep! Wake up."

"What's matter?" I said drowsily.

"It's dark and cold, and we'd better begin to row again. The sea has gone down."

"Has it?" I said sleepily. "Never mind. It don't matter."

"Yes, it does. Wake up. I want to talk to you."

"No, no. Let me go—sleep," I said.

"I sha'n't. Wake up. Let you and me row for a bit, and then we'll make Bob. Come along."

Bigley half pushed me over the thwart to that in front, and placed the oar in my hands; then, taking the other, he thrust it in the rowlocks, and asked me if I was ready.

"Ready? No," I said angrily. "I want to lie down and sleep. I'm so cold. Let me lie down."

"But you can't," he said. "Now, then, let's row. It will warm you."

"But where are we to row?" I said dolefully, and with a curious sense of not caring what happened now.

"I'll show you. Look!" he cried, "you can see the north star."

"Bother the north star!" I grumbled. "I don't want to see the north star."

"But if we keep staring straight up at that as we go, we are sure to reach our shore—somewhere."

I yawned and shivered.

"Must we row, Bigley, old fellow?" I said dolefully.

"Yes. Now, then. Both together."

I let my oar fall in the water with a splash, and then began to pull, feeling dreadfully stiff and cold, and aching so that I could hardly use my arms.

"Pull away!" cried Bigley; and I did pull away, making an angry snatch at the water each time, for I was in pain and misery; but in a short time the stiffness wore off, the aching was not so bad, and, to my great delight, a curious sensation of glow began to run through me, and I was beginning to feel comfortable, when Bigley exclaimed:

"In oars! I'm going to wake up Bob."

He leaned forward and shook Bob, who resented it by kicking, and then throwing out a fist which struck the side of the boat a sharp rap.

"Bob! Bob Chowne! Wake up!" cried Bigley taking him by both shoulders and shaking him.

Bob hit out again, striking Bigley this time viciously in the chest, and the result was another sharp shake, for Bigley seemed disposed to take up his father's tone again.

"What is it?" whimpered Bob. "I am so precious cold. Let me alone, will you?"

"Just you get on that thwart and row, will you?" cried Bigley in a deep fierce growl; and Bob slowly, and with many a groan and sigh, took his place, and began to row straight away into the darkness.

It was a wise thing to do, for it made us warmer, tired as we grew, and so we kept on change and change about for quite an hour, when I saw something which made me shout.

"We're close home; there's the light."

Bigley looked out in the direction I pointed, and watched for a minute before he spoke.

"No," he said; "it's moving. It's a light on board a ship." It was out of our course, but it seemed the wisest thing to do; and with visions of dry warm blankets, and something hot to drink, we tugged away at our oars, but never seemed to get a bit nearer to the light, which kept disappearing and then coming into sight again, looking if anything smaller than before.

How long the time seemed, and how bitterly cold it was! By degrees our clothes seemed to be not quite so heavy and wet; but, though I could get my arms and hands warmed, my legs and feet seemed to have lost all their feeling, no matter what I did to bring it back.

It was still dark all around, though overhead the sky now sparkled with points of light, one of which that we kept seeing in the distance might very well have been on the shore, only that we felt sure that we saw it move.

And so hour after hour we tugged away at the oars, changing about, and the one who was off lying down to go to sleep directly in spite of the wet and cold, for sheer exhaustion was stronger than either.

At last the whole affair seemed to grow misty and dreamlike, and I was only in a half-conscious state, when all at once I noted that the sky looked pale and grey behind us, and this showed that we were rowing to the west.

But for a long time there was nothing but that pale grey look in the sky to indicate that morning was coming; indeed, once, or twice as it became cloudy, it seemed to be darker.

By degrees, though, out of the dull drowsy, weary confusion of that bitter night the day did begin to dawn; and in a hopeless way we tried to make out how far we were from the shore. But for a long time we could distinguish nothing but what seemed to be high hills, having long missed the stars now on account of the clouds.

Then we thought these must be clouds too, for it seemed impossible that it could be land, and both Bigley and I said so to Bob.

But he was sulky and dejected, and would not take any notice of us, treating us both as if it was all our fault that we had been driven out to sea, though we were quite as miserable as he; and at any moment I felt ready to throw myself down in the bottom of the boat and give up.

At last, though, as there comes an end to all dismal nights, this also had its finish, and we made out, as we lay on the cold grey sea of that fine winter morning, that we were about five miles from the Welsh coast, and home lay as near as we could tell right beyond the range of our vision, far away to the south-east.

"What's to be done?" Bob said dolefully. "Hadn't we better row ashore here, and ask for something to eat?"

Big said *No*, decidedly, for he had caught sight of a good-sized vessel some miles away to the south-east.

"If we get ashore here we shall be farther away from home," he argued; "and I've heard my father say there's sharp currents about this coast, which would be too much for us, and besides, father is sure to come out to look for us this morning, so let's try and get back."

"And some ship is sure to see us, and give us something to eat," I said hopefully. "Come, Bob, rouse up. We shall get across all right."

Setting the boat's head as nearly as we could guess toward the opposite shore, we began to row; and, though it was winter time, we were not long before we were pretty warm, and Bob Chowne unwillingly took his turn.

But we made poor progress. Miles take a great deal of getting over with a small boat in the open sea at the best of times. So rowed as ours was by three weary hungry boys, as may be supposed, we did not make the best of way.

We saw several vessels and tried to signal them, but no one took any notice of us till about midday, when a very large lugger that was beating across from the Devon shore began to bear down upon us, and before long, to our great joy, we were able to make out the figures looking over her bulwarks, one of whom waved something in answer to our frantic tossing up of our caps and holding a jacket on the blade of an oar.

Then we set to work and rowed as hard as we could, making very little progress though, for wind and tide were against us. But the big lugger came rushing on, and we could see now that there were dark foreign-looking men on her deck.

It did not matter to us, though, what they were, so long as they would take us on board, for we were starving and faint, and had long ago come to the conclusion that we should not be able to row across before dark, half the day being gone, and the night would come down very early seeing the time of year.

Bigley and I were in ecstasies, and even Bob began to look a little more cheerful as the lugger came closer, and then rounded up with her head to the wind, and lay with her dark red sails flapping.

We rowed up to her side, and a man threw us a rope.

Chapter Twenty
The Captain of the Lugger

"Eh ben!" he shouted. "Eh ben! Eh ben!" while half a dozen yellow-faced little fellows with rings in their ears looked down upon us and grinned.

All at once they made way for a quick dark-looking body, with tiny half grey corkscrew ringlets hanging round under his fur cap, not only at the sides but all over his forehead. It was a man evidently, but he looked like an elderly sharp-eyed wrinkled-faced woman, as he pushed a big lad aside, and putting his arms on the bulwark, stared down at us.

"Vell, lad, vot you vant?" he said.

"Hungry, sir. Blown off the shore, sir," I cried. "We can't row back. Can you understand? No parly vous."

"Bah, stupe, thick, headblock, who ask you parlez-vous? I am England much, and speak him abondomment. How you do thank you, quite vell?"

"No, sir; we're starving, and cold and—and—and—tell him Big, I can't."

I was done for. I could not keep it back, though I had said to myself Bob Chowne was a weak coward, and, dropping on the thwart, I let my face go down in my hands, and tried to keep back my emotion.

"Ah, you bigs boys, you speak me," I heard the French skipper say. "How you come from? Come, call yourself."

"Uggleston, of the Gap," said Bigley, as boldly as he could. "Blown off shore, sir, in the squall."

"Aha! Hey, hey? Ugglees-tone. Ma foi, you Monsieur Jonas Ugglees-tone?"

"No, sir; I am his son," said Bigley.

"What say, sare, you Monsieur Jonas Ugglees-tone, you b'long?"

"Yes, sir; I belong to him. Will you give us something to eat?"

"Aha! You Engleesh boys, big garçon, always hungries. Vais; come aboard my sheeps. Not like your papa—oh, no. I know him mosh, very mosh. Know you papa, votr' père, mon garçon. Come-you-up-you-come."

He said it all as if it were one word, so curiously that it seemed to help me to get rid of my weakness, and I was about to stand up in the boat when the French skipper said to Bigley:

"Look you! Aha. Boy ahoy you. What sheep you fader?"

"Do you mean what's the name of my father's lugger, sir?"

"Yes; you fater luggair—chasse marée. I say so. Vat you call. Heece nem?"

"The *Saucy Lass*, sir."

He leaned over and looked at the stern of the boat and nodded his head.

"Yais, him's olright. Ze *Saucilass*. Come you up—you come, boys. All you. Faites."

This last was to one of the men, who, as we climbed over the side of the French lugger, descended into our boat, and made her fast by the painter to the stern.

The skipper shook hands with us all, and smiled at us and patted our shoulders.

"Pauvres garçons!" he said. "You been much blow away ce mornings, eh?"

"No, sir, last night," said Bigley.

"How you say? You lass night dites, mon garçon."

"We were fishing, sir, and the squall came, and we've been out all night."

"Brrrr!" ejaculated the French skipper, shrugging his shoulders and making a face, then seizing me he dragged me to a hole away in the stern deck, and pushed me down into quite a snug little cabin with a glowing stove.

"Come—venez. All you come," he cried, and he thrust the others down and followed quickly.

"Pauvres garçons! Warm you my fire. Chauffez vous. Good you eat bread? Good you drink bran-dee vis vater? Not good for boy sometime, mais good now."

He kept on chattering to us, half in English, half in French; and as he spoke he cut for us great pieces of bread and Devon butter, evidently freshly taken on board that day. Next he took a large brown bottle from a locker, and mixed in a heavy, clumsy glass a stiff jorum of brandy with water from a kettle on the stove. Into this glass he put plenty of Bristol brown sugar, and made us all drink heartily in turn, so as to empty the glass, when he filled it again.

"It is—c'est bon—good phee-seek—make you no enrhumée—you no have colds. No. Eat, boys. Aha! You warm yourselves. Hey?"

We thanked him, for the glowing stove, the sheltered cabin, the hot brandy and water, and the soft new bread and butter, seemed to give us all new life. The warm blood ran through our veins, and our clothes soon ceased to steam. The French skipper, who had, as we rowed to the side of the lugger, looked about as unpleasant and villainous a being as it was possible to meet, now seemed quite a good genius, and whatever his failings or the nature of his business, he certainly appeared to be deriving real pleasure from his task of restoring the three half-perished lads who had appealed to him for help, and the more we ate, the more he rubbed his hands together and laughed.

"How zey feroce like ze volf, eh? How zey are very mosh hunger. Eat you, my young vrens. Eat you, my young son of ze Jonas Ugglee-stone. I know you fader. He is mon ami. Aha! I drink your helse all of you varey."

He poured himself out a little dram of the spirit and tossed it off.

For a good half hour he devoted himself to us, making us eat, stoking the little stove, and giving us blankets and rough coats to wear to get us warm again. After that he turned to Bigley and laid his arms upon his shoulders, drooping his hands behind, and throwing back his head as he looked him in the face.

"You like me make my sheep to you hous, yais?"

"Take us home, sir. Oh, if you please," cried Bigley.

"Good—c'est bon—my frien. I make my sheep take you. Lay off, you say, and you land in your leettle boats. My faith, yes! And you tell you fader the Capitaine Apollo Gaultière—he pronounced his surname as if it was Goo-awl-tee-yairrrre—make him present of hees sone, and hees young friens. Brave boys. Ha, ha!"

He nodded to us all in turn, and smiled as he gave us each a friendly rap on the chest with the back of his hand.

"Now you warm mosh more my stove, and I go on le pont to make my sheep."

"But do you know the Gap, sir?" said Bigley eagerly.

"Do I know ze Gahp? Aha! Ho, ho! Do I not know ze Gahp vis him eye shut? Peep! Eh? Aha! And every ozer place chez ze cote. Do I evaire make my sheep off ze Gahp to de leettl business—des affaires vis monsieur votre père? Aha! Oh, no, nod-a-dalls."

He gave his nose a great many little taps with his right forefinger as he spoke, and ended by winking both his eyes a great many times, with the effect that the gold rings in his ears danced, and then he went up the little ladder through the hatchway, to stand half out for a few minutes giving orders, while we had a good look at the lower part of his person, which was clothed in what would have been a stiff canvas petticoat, had it not been sewn up between his legs, so as to turn it into the fashion of a pair of trousers, worn over a pair of heavy fishermen's boots.

Then he went up the rest of the way, and let in more light and air, while the motion of the vessel plainly told us that her course had been altered.

"Well," said Bob Chowne, speaking now for the first time, "he's the rummest looking beggar I ever saw. Looks as if you might cut him up and make monkeys out of the stuff."

"Well, of all the ungrateful—"

I began a sentence, but Bob cut me short.

"I'm not ungrateful," he said sharply; "and I'm getting nice and warm now; but what does a man want to wear ear-rings for like a girl, and curl up his hair in little greasy ringlets, that look as if they'd been twisted round pipes, and—I say, boys, did you see his breeches?"

I nodded rather grimly.

"And his boots, old Big; did you see his boots?"

"Yes, they looked good water-tighters," said Bigley quietly, and he seemed now to have settled down into his regular old fashion, while Bob Chowne was getting saucy.

"And then his hands! Did you see his hands?" continued Bob. "I thought at first I could not eat the bread and butter he had touched. I don't believe he ever washes them."

"Why, he had quite small brown hands," said Bigley. "Mine are ever so much larger."

"Yes, but how dirty they were!"

"It was only tar," said Bigley. "He has been hauling new ropes. Look, some came off on my hand when he had hold of it."

"I don't care, I say it was dirt," said Bob obstinately. "He's a Frenchman, and Frenchmen are all alike—nasty, dirty-looking beggars."

"Well, I thought as he brought us down in the cabin here, and gave us that warm drink and the bread and butter, what a pity it was that French and English should ever fight and kill one another."

"Yah! Hark at him, Sep Duncan," cried Bob. "There's a sentimental, unnatural chap. What do you say?"

"Oh, I only say what a difference there is between Bob Chowne now and Bob Chowne when he lay down in the bottom of the boat last night, and howled when old Big made him get up and row."

"You want me to hit you, Sep Duncan?"

"No," I said.

"Because I shall if you talk to me like that. Old Big didn't make me. I was cold and—"

"Frightened," I said.

"No, I wasn't frightened, sneak."

"Well, I was, horribly," I said. "I thought we should never get to shore again. Weren't you frightened, Big?"

"Never felt so frightened before since I got wedged in the rocks," said Bigley coolly.

"Then you are a pair of cowards," cried Bob sharply. "I was so cold and wet and stiff I could hardly move, but I never felt frightened in the least."

I looked at Bigley, and found that he was looking at me; and then he laid his head against the bulkhead, and shut his eyes and laughed till the tears rolled down his cheeks, and I laughed too, as the picture of ourselves in the open boat came before me again, with Bigley ordering Bob to get up and row, and him shivering and sobbing and protesting like a child.

"What are you laughing at?" he cried. "You've got out of your trouble now and you want to quarrel, I suppose. But I sha'n't; I don't want to fight. Only wait till we get across, you won't laugh when old Jony Uggleston comes down on you both for taking the boat. I shall say I didn't want you to, but you would. And then you've got my father and your father to talk to you after that."

But in spite of these unpleasant visions of trouble, which he conjured up, Bigley and I still laughed, for, boy-like, the danger passed, its memory did not trouble us much. We had escaped: we were safe; Bob was making himself ridiculously comic by his hectoring brag, and all we wanted to do was to laugh.

In the midst of our mirth, and while Bob Chowne was growing more and more absurd by putting on indignant airs, the hatchway was darkened again by the French skipper's petticoats and boots, and directly after he stood before us smiling and rubbing his hands.

"Aha, you!" he said. "You better well, mosh better. I make you jolly boys, eh?"

"Yes, sir, we are much better now," I exclaimed, holding out my hand. "We are so much obliged to you for helping us as you have."

"Mon garçon, mon ami," he exclaimed; and instead of shaking hands, he folded me in his arms and kissed me on both cheeks. I stepped back as soon as I was free, and stood watching as he served Bigley the same, and then took hold of Bob, whose face wore such an absurdly comical aspect of horror and disgust, that I stood holding my breath, and not daring to look at Bigley for fear I should roar with laughter.

"Dat is well," exclaimed the skipper. "It is done, my braves. Good— good—good. You tink I speak Engleish magnificentment, is it not?"

He looked round at us all, and nodded a great many times. "Now you are warm dry, come on ze pont and see my sheep. Ze belle chasse marée. She sail like de bird. Is it not? Now come see."

We went on deck, and found as he took us about amongst the crew of seven men, all wearing petticoat canvas trousers, that the big lugger was very dirty and untidy, wanting in paint, and with the deck, or pont as the skipper called it, one litter of baskets, packages, and uncoiled ropes. On the other hand she seemed to be very long and well shaped, and her masts, which were thick and short, had large yards and tremendous sails, which in a favourable wind sent her through the water at a very rapid rate.

"Aha! You lofe my sheep," said the skipper, as he watched our faces. "You tink she run herselfs very fas, eh?"

We expressed our pleasure, which was the greater that we could see now that the two bold masses which formed the entrance to the Gap were right before us; but even now, as far as we could judge, six or seven miles away.

We took a good deal of notice of this, for it showed us how far we had been driven out by the fierce little gale of the previous night; and as I looked over the stern at where our boat was being towed along in the foam, and was thinking that we must have had a narrow escape, the French skipper clapped me on the shoulder, laughed, and said:

"You wonder you not go to feed ze fishes at ze bottom? Yes, much; et moi aussi. Ah, mon brave, you nearly go, and—no boat—no boy—no noting. Hah!"

I shivered as I realised the truth of what he said, and was musing over what was to come, when Bigley came to me, for the skipper had gone to his men.

"Don't tease Bob," he said. "Don't say anything to him about being queer last night, nor about me bullying him. He couldn't help it."

"Oh, I sha'n't say anything," I said.

"He couldn't help it," whispered Bigley again. "No more could I."

We all grew very serious then, for as we neared the shore, there was the question to think over about meeting our fathers, and what they would say. Would they be exceedingly angry with us, or talk quietly about our narrow escape?

I found that my companions were thinking as I was, for Bigley said quietly:

"I'm afraid my father will be very cross."

"So am I," was my reply, when Bob came to where we were gazing over the bulwark shoreward, and said sulkily:

"I say, I don't want to be bad friends with you two. My father's sure to give me a big wigging for letting you persuade me to go. Well, I don't mean that," he added with a droll twinkle of the eye, as he saw us stare, "what I mean is, hadn't we all better stick together, and share the blame?"

"Yes, of course, Bob," I said; and I felt quite pleased with his frankness, when if he didn't go and spoil it all again by saying:

"I thought it would be best, because it would be nicer for you."

Our conversation was stopped by Captain Gualtière coming up, and pointing westward.

"Look you!" he exclaimed, "see, mes amis, la *Saucy Lass*."

"So it is," cried Bigley eagerly, as he shaded his eyes, and gazed at the lugger in full sail about a couple of miles away, and making for the same point as we—"so it is: it's father's lugger."

"Oui, my young frien," said the French skipper; "and he has been to sweep ze sea to try and find you boys."

Chapter Twenty One
The Knife Bob Wanted

In half an hour the luggers were close together off the Gap with their sails flapping, and the French skipper jumped into the boat with us, and rowed to the *Saucy Lass*, on board of which we had long before descried my father and the doctor along with old Jonas Uggleston.

We leaped up the side eagerly, and yet with fear and trembling, not knowing what our reception might be, and a few words explained all.

"Humph!" said old Jonas, "nice chase we've had after you. Well, I suppose I mustn't after all."

He picked up a capstan-bar, and balanced it in his hands before throwing it down under the little bulwark with a loud clatter.

"Mustn't what, father?" said Bigley.

"Knock you down with that, as you've had such a rough time of it. I was in hopes that you were all three drowned."

"And he went himself to see and find ze bodies, and sheat ze sharks!" cried the French skipper laughing, and clapping us on the shoulders.

"Perhaps Captain Duncan, my landlord, would like to use that bar on his boy!" growled old Jonas sourly.

"No!" said my father bluffly, "I can preserve discipline, Mr Uggleston, without treating my boy like a dog. Come, Sep, my lad, let's get ashore."

"The doctor, then?" said old Jonas, with his eyes twinkling maliciously.

"What, to knock my boy down, Uggleston? No, thank you, sir. I've little things at home that will put him to bed for a fortnight and keep him quiet without giving myself a job to mend his broken bones."

He looked at Bob, and I saw my school-fellow turn yellow and shudder as if he were about to take a dose of some horribly nauseous medicine. Just then Bob caught my eye, and I suppose he saw that I was amused, for he doubled his fist, and showed his teeth in a snarl just like a disagreeable dog who had been threatened by a stranger with a stick.

"My faith, gentlemen," said the French skipper, "ze boys is brave boys and make fine sailor. Zey fight zis bad storm. Zey vin ze storm, and behold me here ve are!"

"Captain Gualtière," said my father, holding out his hand, "as an old sailor, sir, to one of the same noble profession, I thank you for your kindness to my son."

"Mon capitaine, I you embrace with my heart whole!" cried the French skipper. "It is vell, Capitaine Ugglees-stone. Ve vill land ourselves. Mon vieux brave—to your home, and trink von 'tit verre of ze bon spee-reete vis ze friens. Come." Jonas Uggleston nodded his head and exchanged a peculiar look with the Frenchman.

"Let's get ashore," he said. "You, Bill, I'll come out again by and by. Get her fast to the buoy."

Binnacle Bill growled and crept behind us boys to watch his opportunity, and give us each a nod, a wink, and a furtive shake of the hand.

Then the boat was hauled alongside, we descended, and Bigley pulled us ashore, where, almost in silence, and evidently a very uncomfortable party, we walked up to the cottage where Mother Bonnet was in waiting, and her first act was to rush at Bigley, hug him, kiss him soundly on both cheeks, and burst into tears.

I was afraid it was coming my way, and drew back; but it was of no use, for the old woman seized me, and I had to be kissed in the same way, while Bob Chowne submitted to the same operation with a worse grace than mine.

"Not a wink of sleep—not a wink of sleep—not a wink of sleep all night!" the old woman kept on sobbing over and over again. "Master Bigley—Master Bigley, I was afraid I should never see you any more!"

"Brave vomans? Ha, ha! Brave vomans!" cried the Frenchman.

"Look here, Duncan!" said the doctor. "I don't think we'll trouble Mr Uggleston any more. We want to get back home."

"Yes," said my father; "but—"

He made a movement with his head towards the French skipper.

"Oh, come along, Captain Duncan," growled old Jonas surlily. "You must drink a glass with him. I won't poison you this time."

"Thanks, Uggleston," said my father quietly; and, intimate as I was with Bigley, school-fellows and companions as we were, I could not help noticing the difference, and how thoroughly my father was the gentleman and Jonas Uggleston the commonplace seafaring man.

"Here, Mother Bonnet!" cried old Jonas, "the boys want something. You see to them."

The old woman took us into her kitchen, as she called it, and attended to our wants; but I could hear what went on in the other room, and the French skipper's words as they all partook of something together.

Ten minutes after, my father called me by name, and I found him waiting with the doctor outside, the Frenchman beaming on all in turn.

"Ve are ze old amis, le vieux—ze old Jonas and myselfs. Sare, I am been glad I receive ze boys on my sheep."

"And I thank you, captain," replied my father. "You have saved my boy's life. Will you accept this in remembrance? It is old but good."

My father drew out his plain gold watch, and I saw the Frenchman's eyes glisten as he stretched out a not very clean hand.

But he snatched it back directly.

"Mais non—but no!" he exclaimed. "I not have hims. We are sailors all. Some day I am in open boat, and you take me in your sheep, and say 'Ma foi! Pauvre fellow, you cold—you hoongrai—you starve youselfs.' And you give me hot grogs, and varm fires, and someting to eats. I no give you ze gold vatch. Mais non—mais non—mais non. Voilà. I take zat hankshife, blue as ze skies of France, and I wear him roun' my necks. Give me hims."

My father smiled and then unknotted the bright blue silk neckerchief he wore, and accompanied it with a hearty shake of the hand.

"Thank you, captain," he said warmly.

"And you—merci. We go to war some day. Who know I may be prisonaire. I may come to fight against you, and then. Eh bien, ve fight, but you take me prisonaire, ma foi. I am vis ze shentleman, and it is good."

"And now it's my turn," said the doctor. "Will you keep this, captain, from me?"

"Ma foi. Yais, oui," cried the French skipper, whose eyes sparkled with pleasure as the doctor handed him a very bright peculiarly-formed knife. "I keep hims. Vat is ze mattaire vis ze young shipwrecked open boatman?"

"Nothing—nothing at all," said Bob Chowne hastily; but he had certainly uttered a groan.

"As for you, Uggleston," cried the doctor, "I sha'n't offer you a present, for you'll want me some day to mend your head, or cut off a leg or a wing. Only, recollect I'm in your debt."

"As for me, Mr Uggleston," said my father.

"There—there, that will do," cried old Jonas surlily. "We ar'n't such very bad friends, are we?"

"I hope not," said my father, and we took our leave, being embraced by the French skipper, who said that we should meet again, shaking hands with old Jonas, and giving Binnacle Bill a crown piece, which my father slipped into my hand for him, making the old red-faced fellow's eyes twinkle as he exclaimed:

"Ba–c–co!"

Then we started homeward in the lowest of spirits, we two boys expecting the most severe of lectures; but to our intense surprise and delight we were allowed to drop behind, for our elders were deep in conversation about the mine.

Then it was that, after hanging more and more behind, Bob Chowne relieved his feelings.

"It was a shame—it was too bad!" he kept on grumbling.

"What was too bad—what was a shame?" I cried.

"Why, for father to give old Parley Vous that knife!"

"Why?" I said wonderingly.

"Why? Because it was such a good un. I've tried to coax him out of it lots o' times. It was as sharp as sharp, and he used to use it to cut off fingers and toes, and that sort of thing. He never would give it to me, because he said it was good for operating, and now that old Frenchee Frenchee will use it for toasting frogs over his nasty little stove."

"Here, you boys, come up here," said the doctor just then.

We crept up very unwillingly, for the lecture was evidently going to begin.

"I thought we'd tell you," said the doctor in his grimmest fashion, "we're going to find out a school where there are no holidays, and send you there."

But they did not, for in due time we went back to Barnstaple, and I had the last of my education there.

Chapter Twenty Two
"How you have growed, lads; how you have growed!"

It seems a long time to look forward to, but when it has gone how everyone finds out what a scrap of our lives three years appear to be.

I am going to jump over three years now, and come to an exciting time when we lads were leaving school at midsummer for good.

Those were exciting times, and we all were as much infected as the rest of English folk, for we were at war with France, and there was drumming, and fifing, and enlisting, and men marching off to join their regiments, and we boys were fully determined to arrange with our respected fathers as soon as we got home to get us all commissions in cavalry regiments, and failing commissions, we meant to petition for leave to enlist to fight for our country.

Bob Chowne and I of course knew better, but in spite of this knowledge we were constantly feeling that there was something wrong with our companion Bigley.

He was just the same easy-going fellow as of old; ready to submit to any amount of bullying and impertinence from us, except in times of emergency, when he would quietly step to the front in the place Bob and I shirked, and do what there was to be done, and as soon as it was over go back patiently into the second rank, leaving us in the front.

But as I say, though we knew better, it always seemed to us as if something particular had taken place in Bigley, he who used to tower above us, a big fellow with whiskers, a deep voice, and broad shoulders, had now shrunk, so that he was no longer like a man and we both like small boys, for he seemed to have come down so that he was only a trifle taller than we were, and very little broader across the chest. It was the whiskers and the thick down upon his chin which made nearly all the difference.

We used to laugh about it together, and Bigley would say that it was rum, and only because he had started two years sooner than we did—that was all.

Of course the fact was that Bigley had not shrunk in the least. He had not come down, but Bob Chowne and I had levelled matters by growing up, so that at seventeen we were as big as Devon lads of that age know how to be.

While we had changed, old Teggley Grey had not. He always seemed to have been the same ever since we could remember, and his horse too, but he shook his head at us.

"Mortal hard work for a horse to carry such big chaps as you. How you have growed, lads; how you have growed!"

I looked at him as he spoke, and it seemed to me that it was he who had changed. But it did not matter; we were full of plans for the future. Big as we were, we could take plenty of interest in fishing and such other sport as came in our way, and we were talking eagerly about what was to be done first, and how we were to contrive it without having some mishap, when old Teggley summoned us to get down and walk.

"Wouldn't be acting like a Christian to ask a horse to drag you three big lads up a hill like this. I did think," he grumbled, "that with all this talk about making good roads, something would have been done to level ourn. Mortal bad they be for a horse sewer*ly*."

"Why, what could you do to the roads?" I said, as I stood on the step looking at the quaint old fellow. "Do, lad? Why, there's plenty of stuff ar'n't there? Cutoff all the tops of the hills, and lay in the bottoms, and there you are, level road all the way."

We seemed to have only been away a few days, as, after parting from Bigley, Bob and I reached the cottage, where, just as of old, were my father and the doctor.

I remember thinking that they both looked a little older and greyer, but that was all. But that was soon forgotten in the interest and excitement of what was going on around me, for I had, I found, gradually been growing older, and ready to take an interest in matters more important than hunting prawns and groping for crabs down on the rocky shore.

Chapter Twenty Three
Old Sam is Unhappy

Seventeen, and grown as big as Bigley, with the consequence that I could not help thinking a good deal of what people said to me when I went in to Ripplemouth or down to the Gap.

The salute I generally met was:

"Why, Master Sep Duncan, you are growing quite a man."

I suppose I was in appearance, but, thank goodness, I was still only a boy at heart.

Plenty to see, plenty to hear.

The fishermen and people at the tiny port were always looking out to sea, and shutting their eyes and shaking their heads.

"Ay, and we need look out, master," they would say. "Strange doings now. Who knows how soon they Frenchies will come down upon us and try to take the town. But we're going to fight 'em to a man."

I remember even then laughing to myself as I went home one morning after being disappointed in finding Bob Chowne, who had gone on a round with his father, for I asked myself what the French, whom the Ripplemouth people saw in every passing vessel, would gain by making a descent upon our rock-strewn shore.

But when I ventured to hint at their being more likely to attack Plymouth or Portsmouth, old Teggley Grey, who was down on the pier loading up with coal that had come over in a sloop from Monmouth, shook his head.

"Ay, it be well for you, lad, with all they big cannon guns in front o' your house ready to sink the Frenchy ships; but we ar'n't no guns here, on'y the one in the look-out, and she be rusted through."

Oddly enough, when I reached home there was no one in the house. My father had gone down to the mine, and I was thinking about going after him, but being hot with my walk, I strolled down first into the garden on the cliff, but only to stop short, for there was a curious hissing sound in the air.

"What, a snake!" I said to myself. And then, "No, it's too loud."

I stood listening, and I learned directly what caused the hissing, which gave place directly to a peculiar humming, and then after more hissing a familiar raspy voice roared out, its owner imagining he was singing:

"For we be sturdy English lads,
And this here be our land;
And ne'er a furren furreneer
Shall ever in it stand."

Then came a great deal of hissing before the strain was taken up again, and accompanied by a good deal of scuffling on the beach-strewn path.

"They say they'll have the English soil,
These overbearing French;
So if they come they'll find it here
In six-foot two o' trench."

"Why, Sam," I said, "what are you doing?"

"Ah, Mas' Sep: can't you see? Washing out the bull-dogs' throats to make 'em bite the Peccavis when they come."

I laughed as I looked at the old man, who was busy at work with a mop and pail cleaning out the old cannons on my father's sham fort.

"Why, Sam, what's the good of that?"

"Good, my lad?" he cried, ramming the wet mop down one of the guns and making the water spurt out of the touch-hole like a little fountain, "Good! Why, we'll blow the Frenchy ships out of the water if they come anigh us."

"Why, there's no powder," I said.

"Powder! Eh, but there is: lots, my lad."

OLD SAM PREPARING FOR A FRENCH INVASION.

"But there are no cannon-balls."

Old Sam stopped short with the mop right in the gun, and loosening one hand, he tilted his old sou'-wester hat that he wore summer and winter with no difference, only that he kept cabbage-leaves in it in summer, and stood scratching his head.

"No cannon-balls!" he said. "No cannon-balls!"

"Not one," I said; "only the big one indoors we use for a door-weight, and that would not go in."

"Well, now, that be a rum un, Master Sep, that be a rum un. I never thought o' that. Never mind, it don't matter. They Frenchies 'll hear the guns go off and see the smoke, and that's enough for them. They'll go back again."

"Go back again," I said laughing. "Why, they'll never come."

"Get out, lad! You're too young to understand they things. You wait a bit, and you'll see that they will come and find us ready for them too."

"With six-foot two of trench, eh, Sam?" I said.

"Eh? What? What do you mean?"

"Why, weren't you singing something about burying them all. Here, sing us the rest."

"Nay, nay, nay, my lad; I can't sing."

"Why, I heard you, Sam."

"Ay, but that's all I know; and I must get on with my job afore they come."

"Before they come, Sam! Why, they'll never come. Go and hoe up your cabbages and potatoes and you'll be doing some good."

"Nay, lad, this be no time for hoeing up cabbage and 'tater. Why, what for?—ready for the French?"

"French!" I said with a laugh as I leaned over the low wall and looked down the perpendicular cliff at the piled-up masses of fallen fragments. "No French will ever trouble us."

For it looked ridiculous to imagine that a foreign enemy would ever attempt to make a landing anywhere beneath the grand wall of piled-up rock that protected our coast from a far more dangerous enemy than any French fleet, for the sea was ready to attack and sweep away even the land, and this a foreign fleet could never do.

I sat on the edge looking down at the ivy, and toad-flax, and saxifrage, and ferns that climbed and clustered all over the steep cliff-face; and as I sat looking and enjoying the sea-breeze and the rest from all school labours, old Sam went on cleaning out the guns and expressing in his way the feelings of nearly everybody round the coast.

"Is my father over at the mine?" I said.

"Ay, my lad; he's always there. Going over?"

"Yes, Sam, when I'm rested. They're very busy now, I suppose."

"Wonderful, Master Sep, wonderful. Who'd ha' thought it?" he exclaimed, sticking the mop handle on the path and resting his bare brown arms upon the wet woollen rags that formed the top.

"Who'd have thought what, Sam?"

"Why, as there'd be lead and silver under they slates down at the Gap. Always looked to be nothin' but clatter, and old massy rock and no soil."

"Ah, it was a discovery, Sam," I said.

"Discovery, my lad! Why, when they said as the Captain had bought the old place I went into my tool-shed and sat down on a 'tater heap and 'most cried."

"'Most cried, Sam—you?"

"Ay, my lad, for I thought the Captain had gone off his head and everything would be in rack and ruin."

"Instead of which my father is making quite a fortune out of it, Sam."

"Ay, I s'pose so, my lad, but fortuns aren't everything. It makes him look worried, it do, and he've give up his garden, as is a bad sign. I don't like to see a man give up his garden. It means weeds."

"Well, then, why don't you hoe them up, Sam?" I said sharply.

"Hoe 'em up, lad? I can't put a hoe in his mind, can I? That's where the weeds grows, my dear lad. Why, he never takes no interest in his guns now, and if I hadn't set to this morning to scour 'em out and give 'em a regular good cleaning, where would they have been when the French come?"

Chapter Twenty Four
Down the Silver Mine

I left Sam picking out the touch-holes with a piece of wire, walked across the high ground of the wind-swept moor and descended into the Gap, a well-beaten track now marking the way.

It was too rough for wheels, but filled with the heavy hoof-marks of donkeys, which were used largely for carrying wood, charcoal, and sea-coal to the mine; and as I stood up by the spot where years before Bob Chowne, Bigley, and I had blown up the big stone and set it rolling down into the valley, it was wonderful what a change had taken place.

Where we had swept the side of the ravine clear with an avalanche of rock, there had now sprung up quite a tiny village built of the rough stones dug from the mine. There was a large water-wheel slowly turning and sending down the water led to it from above, in company with that which it pumped out of the mine, all thick and discoloured, in quite a torrent to the beautiful little stream below, which now ran turbid and in which the trout were all dead.

There was a row of stoutly-built sheds, and a big place with a high chimney where the ore was smelted. Then there were offices, and a building where the purified metal was passed through another furnace, and in addition a place where the metal was kept.

There seemed a total alteration in the place till I directed my eyes towards the sea, where all appeared to be unchanged. There were the two cottages—Binnacle Bill's, with some newly washed white garments hanging over the rocks; and Jonas Uggleston's, with its stone sheds and outbuildings bristling with spars and wreck-wood that had been thrown up, and with nets and sails spread out to dry.

Beyond lay his lugger; and the boat drawn up on the beach, suggesting to my mind the horrors of that night when we were blown off the shore.

I stood looking at the scene, with the bare sea beyond and the vast cliff towering up a thousand feet on my left, and then began to descend the rugged slope, making straight for the building which my father used as his counting-house and office.

"Well, Sep," he said, smiling, "I'm glad to see you."

I noticed that he looked care-worn and anxious, and his aspect reproached me, for I felt as if it was too bad of me to be making holiday while he was working so hard.

"Can I help you, father?" I said.

"Help me! Yes, my boy, I hope so—a good deal; but I don't want to be too hard upon you. Take a good look round for a few days, so as to rest a little while, and then you shall come and help me here; for, Sep, an affair like this is not without plenty of anxiety."

"Oh, father!" I said, "I shall have plenty of time for amusement; let's see if I can't help you now."

He looked more and more pleased as he heard my words.

"No," he said, "not yet. You shall have a look round first for a few days, and perhaps you may be able quietly to pick up the cause of something that is troubling me a great deal."

"Troubling you, father!" I said.

"Yes, my lad, troubling me, for things are not going as I could wish. 'Tis just as if, as fast as I get a few steps forward, someone pulls me back."

"But I thought the mine was very prosperous, father?" I said.

"So it is, my boy, and I am getting it better and better; but there is always mischief being done, or else some accident occurs, and I can't tell how."

"Do you suspect anybody?"

"Well, er—no!" he said emphatically. "But, there—never mind now. I'm busy with some calculations; go and have a look round."

I left his office and had "a look round," the place seeming to have far more interest for me than it had before. Men were busy wheeling broken ore and taking it from one heap to another; the great pump was hard at work sucking out water; and the wheel was winding up buckets of produce from out of the deep shaft.

I went and had a look there and shrank back, it seemed so repulsive and dark; but as I did so I saw one of the men smiling, and this made me turn red.

"Look here," I said sharply, "can I go down there?"

"Oh, yes, if you like, master," he replied, staring at me wonderingly now.

"Then I will," I said. "I'll have a look at the furnace first, and then I'll go down."

"Ay, do," he said; "and you're just in time. They're going to run off the metal in a few minutes."

I recalled our experiment at home with the little built-up furnace, when the ore was first tried, as I walked to the stone-built house, where from out of the centre came a low dull roar; from cracks and chinks and crannies blindingly bright rays of light shot out and seemed to cut the darkness, which, after the sunshine of out of doors, seemed to be black and terrible. Now and then there came a peculiar crackling, as if something were snapping and flying to pieces under the great heat, and it was some time before I could see anything but the brilliant pencils of light that cut the gloom.

By degrees, though, I made out that a couple of men were moving here and there, and that each of them carried a long black rod of iron.

The flames seemed to flutter and burn and to be rushing upward with tremendous force, while I could fancy that I heard the metal bubbling in its bed, where it was seething and throwing off wonderful flames, as I could judge by the gleams I saw.

"Stand back, young master," said one of the men roughly—"there, right up in the corner here. You won't hurt now. Just going to run her off."

I backed into the corner he pressed me to, where there was a broad shutter or screen, and I was getting so accustomed to the darkness now that I could see just below, and in front of a place where golden tears seemed to be dropping from a chink at the bottom of the furnace, several long square trenches in the black charcoal floor, and the next minute I made out that these trenches were all connected together by a little channel.

"The moulds," I thought to myself, and I looked eagerly now at one of the men, who shouted something by way of warning to his fellow-worker; and then, as the man stepped behind a similar screen of wood-work to that which sheltered me, the one who uttered his words of warning thrust and hammered with his long iron rod at the foot of the furnace.

I did not quite see what he did afterwards, but he seemed to dart out of the way, and then a stream of what looked like liquid gold came gushing out, sputtering, snapping, and sending into the air myriads of glorious firework-like sparks of blue and orange and scarlet and gold, and so brilliant that they lit up the whole building and made my eyes ache and my cheeks tingle.

Where a minute before there were so many black trenches were now so many dazzling ingots, over which played and fluttered many-tinted flames that kept on waving and undulating as if they were liquid, and swayed from side to side, giving forth with the molten metal a glow that scorched my face.

For the first few seconds the molten metal had run off quickly and filled the moulds; now what came was sluggish and not half so brilliant; and I noticed that by a quick movement of a long iron rake one of the men drew some of the earth and charcoal which formed the floor on one side, so as to alter the course of the running molten contents of the furnace, and instead of its passing into moulds it seemed to settle down in a patch.

This, too, was most brilliant to the eye; and from it endless dazzling coruscations darted up and played about, but for a much shorter period; and in place of the ruddy glow of the metal, which rapidly cooled down to look like silver, this last melting grew sombre and stony, ending by looking of a blackish-grey.

I was still watching the fading away of the brilliant display, when there was a familiar voice at the door of the building, and my father stepped in to make inquiries about the running off of the molten ore, and as he examined the result, he expressed his satisfaction.

"Mind!" he cried to me, as I was about to touch one of the ingots of lead with my toes. "My good boy, these will not be cool enough to touch yet. They retain the heat for a long while."

He stopped talking to me for some time, and explained how the men were closing the bottom of the furnace again with fire-clay, and that they would now go on pouring in at the top barrows full of charcoal and broken-up ore. How that dark grey stuff was the molten stones and refuse which remained after the metal had been cleared, and then he laughed at what he called my innocence, as I asked him if the ingots, as he called the square masses which now looked quite white, were silver.

"No, my boy," he said; "we are not so rich as that. If those pieces of coarse metal, when melted down again, and submitted to a fresh process, give us three pounds' weight of silver out of every hundred pounds of lead we shall do well. Now then, would you like to go down the mine?"

He spoke as if he expected to hear me decline; but I had made up my mind to go, and he looked quite pleased when he heard me say that I was ready.

"Well," he said, as we reached the top of the shaft, "I'll go down first, and you can follow. We can get candles at the bottom."

If I had had any ideas of a silver mine being a cavern full of beautiful sights, I was very soon deceived, for as I stood there at the top, I saw my father step on to the top rounds of a rough-looking ladder, and begin to descend slowly till he reached a platform, when he called to me to follow.

"Hold tight," he said. "But there, I needn't tell you after your cliff climbing."

I was just about to descend when a voice behind me made me turn.

"Going down, Sep?"

I turned to confront Bigley Uggleston, who looked at me imploringly.

"Ask him if I may come down too?"

"Who's that?" said my father sharply. "Oh, I see. Yes, he can come."

Bigley flushed up with pleasure, and I let him go down next, and then followed, to find that a gallery went off on a level with the platform; but my father had already descended to the next platform below, and when we followed him there, it was to find he had reached another.

To get to this we passed another gallery, and then stood by where my father was lighting a couple of candles, as he rested upon some wood-work, beneath which we could hear the trickle and splash of falling water, while away from our right, down a long passage propped here and there with pieces of timber, came the dull echoing sound of blows.

"Well, my lads, what do you think of the enchanted cave?"

I looked about me by the light of the dim candles and saw that the shaft was divided by a wood partition, one side being reserved for the ladders, the other for the pump to work and the stout rope to go up and down and draw the buckets, there being openings in the wood-work opposite each of the galleries.

"Well, you don't say anything," said my father.

"It's very dark, sir," replied Bigley.

"Yes," said my father; "and it's darker still farther in. What do you say, will you go on?"

"If Sep does."

"Oh, yes," I said, "I shall go;" not that I wanted to go any farther, but I felt that I could not draw back; though I would very gladly have been up in the bright sunshine instead of in the damp gloomy hole, shut in by ladders and wood-work, and with, the falling water seeming as if it was gathering force, and ready to rise as it does in a well.

But there was no time for thinking. My father was leading the way along the large square-shaped gallery, the candles casting curious shadows which glided along the walls, as if our company had been joined by some of the spirits of the mine.

As we went on, my father stopped from time to time to hold his light against the wall, for us to see where the lead ore glistened, and promised to be thick when he was disposed to work in another direction.

We could hear the water trickling still along a channel which had been cut on one side of the gallery, and every here and there great drops gathered on the wood-work that propped the roof, and fell with a plash making Bigley whisper to me:

"Suppose the sea was to break in."

He spoke as I say in a whisper, but it was heard by my father, who answered quietly:

"We should have to go down much lower before we were on a level with the sea at high-water mark, my lads. If anything were likely to do us any harm, it would be the brook."

He stopped soon after, for we had reached the end of the gallery, giving way while a workman wheeled by us a barrowful of ore, similar to a heap which two others were hewing and picking out of the wall.

"Well, my lads, what's it like?" said my father.

"Cleaner and richer and better, I should say, master," said one of the men. "It's a wonder, but I'm thinking you'll have to put more power on there to pump. Farther we goes, the worse the water gets."

"I've been thinking so myself," said my father quietly. "It sha'n't stop you, my lads, I'll see to that."

My father picked up a specimen of the ore, and placed it in his pocket; the men resumed their picking and hewing, and we two lads inspected the lode and the walls of the mine, and then, after looking at it up, down, and in every direction, to try and find something more interesting than the square passage with its dripping walls and patches of black mineral that glistened in a dull manner when the light was moved, we ended by staring at my father.

"Well," he said smiling; "had enough?"

"Is there no more to see than this?" I said in a disappointed tone.

"There is another gallery below here, and two above, but they are just the same. Shall we go and see them?"

"If Bigley likes," I said rather gruffly.

"No, I don't think I want to see any more," he replied.

My father laughed, and went on in front with one candle while I followed with the other, till we reached the foot of the shaft.

"Silver mine sounds better than it looks, eh, my lads!" he said.

We neither of us answered, for it seemed like damping his enterprise. But he did not heed our silence, for he began to climb slowly up the ladders, and as he reached the first platform, we followed, and then on and on with the water splashing and the pump going, and now and then the creaking sound of the windlass coming down to us as the men over the bucket shaft wound up each heavy load of ore.

"There, I'm going back into my office," said my father. "You, lads, have had enough mining for to-day. I shall not want you, Sep."

"Don't the open air look clear and fresh?" I said as soon as we were alone, and I gazed round at the patches of green upon the hills, and the bright sea out at the end of the Gap.

"Yes," said Bigley, with a shiver. "I shouldn't like to work in a mine. I say, I suppose your father's getting very rich now, isn't he?"

"I suppose so," I said.

"That's what the people say. Binnacle Bill says he has got heaps of silver locked up in the strong place below the office under iron doors. Have you seen it?"

"No," I said; "and I shouldn't think it's true. Hallo! Look yonder. Why, there's Bob Chowne!"

Bob it was, and the mine, the coming of the French, and everything else was forgotten, as we went down to the beach, ready enough for a ramble beneath the rocks, after six months' absence from home.

Chapter Twenty Five
Friends and Enemies

At seventeen one's ideas are very different to what they are at fourteen, and matters that seemed of no account in the earlier period looked important at the more mature. For it used to seem to us quite a matter of course that Bigley's father should have a lugger, and if the people said he went over to France or the Low Countries with the men who came over from Dodcombe, and engaged in smuggling, why, he did. It was nothing to us.

We never troubled about it, for Bigley was our school-fellow, and old Jonas was very civil, though he never would let us have the boat again. But now that we were getting of an age to think and take notice of what was said about us, Bob Chowne began to suggest that he and I ought to make a change.

"You see it don't seem respectable for me, the son of the doctor, and you of the captain, who is our mine owner, to be such friends with one whose father is a regular smuggler."

"How do you know he is?" I said.

"How do I know? Oh, everybody says so. Let's drop him."

"I sha'n't," I said, "unless father tells me to Bigley can't help it."

"Then you'll have to drop—I mean I shall drop you," said Bob haughtily.

"Very well," I said, feeling very much amused at the pompous tone in which he spoke. Not that I wanted to be bad friends with Bob Chowne; but I knew that he was only in one of his "stickly" fits, as we used to call them, and that it would soon be over.

"Very well, eh?" exclaimed Bob. "Oh, if you choose to prefer his society to mine, Good morning."

He walked off with his nose in the air, and, half annoyed, half amused, I went over the hill to the mine, where my father was busily examining some specimens of the lead that had been cut off the corners of some newly-cast ingots.

"Well, Sep," he said. "Coming to help?"

I replied that I was, somewhat unwillingly, for I had caught sight of Bigley coming up the valley, and I wanted to join him, and try and show that I did not intend to give up an old school friend because his father's name was often on people's lips.

"Who's that you are looking for?" said my father.

"Only young Uggleston, father," I said.

I looked at him intently and felt troubled, for he frowned a little, and, before I knew what I was saying, the words slipped:

"You don't mind Bigley Uggleston coming here, do you, father?"

"Yes—no," he said, sitting up up very stiffly. "I don't like your giving up old companions, Sep, or seeming to be proud; but there are beginning to be reasons why you should not be quite so intimate with young Uggleston."

"Oh, father!" I exclaimed dolefully. "Why, I thought that you and old Uggleston were good friends now."

"Oh, yes; the best of friends," said my father sarcastically. "He pays his rent regularly, and we always speak civilly to each other when we meet."

As he spoke there was a look in his face which seemed to say, "We don't like each other all the same."

"Look here, Sep," continued my father. "You are getting a big fellow now, and I am going to speak very plainly to you; of course, you understand that this is in confidence; it is quite private."

"Yes, father," I said sadly.

"Then you must understand that, though Jonas Uggleston is my tenant here, he is not a very satisfactory one, for there can be no doubt that he carries on rather a risky trade; but, so long as the authorities do not interfere with him, and he behaves himself, I am not going to take upon myself the task of being his judge."

"No, father."

"At the same time I cannot be intimate with him. I don't like him, and I don't like the companions who come over from Stinchcombe to man his lugger, and I'll tell you why. Do you know that, now this little mine is developing itself, I very often have blocks of silver here to a considerable amount."

"I have often thought you must have, father."

"You were quite right, and they are stored below this floor in a strong cellar cut and blasted out of the solid rock. I have good doors and keys, and take every precaution; but at the same time I often feel that it is very unsafe, and of course I send it into town as often as I can."

"But you don't think, father—"

"That Jonas Uggleston would steal it? I hope not, my boy; but at the same time I feel as if I ought not to expose myself to risks, and I prefer to keep Jonas Uggleston at the same distance as he has before stood. We can be civil."

"I'm sorry," I said.

"Sorry?"

"Yes, father," I replied, "because I like Bigley Uggleston."

"So do I, my boy. I like his quiet modesty under ordinary circumstances, and the sterling manner in which you have told me that he has come to the front in emergencies. But stop: I don't ask you to break with him, for he may be useful to us after all. There, let me finish these figures I am setting down, and I'll talk to you again."

I sat down and watched him, and then looked round the bare office, with its high up window close to the ceiling, and ladder leading to the two rooms above. Spread over the floor was a large foreign rug that my father had brought from the Mediterranean many years before, and this rug was stretched over the middle of the large office as if it had been brought from the cottage to make the place more homelike and comfortable. But it struck me all at once that the rug had been placed there to hide a trap-door. Then, as I sat looking about, I noticed that the door was very thick and strong, and that there were bars at the window in which the glass was set.

I might have noticed all this before, but it did not seem of any consequence till my father talked of the bars of silver and their value, and as I sat thinking, the place began to look quite romantic, and I thought what a strange affair it would be, and how exciting if robbers or smugglers were to come and attack it, and my father, and Sam, and the men from the mine to have to defend it, and there were to be a regular fight.

Once started thinking in that vein my mind grew busy, and I felt that if I were at the head of affairs I should arrange to have plenty of swords and pistols, and that made me think of old Sam and the cannon down the cliff garden.

I laughed at that, though, as being absurd, and began to think directly after that my father's sword and pistols that always used to hang over the chimney-piece in the little parlour were not there now.

"Why, I daresay he has brought them down here," I said to myself; and I looked round, half expecting to see them, but they were not visible, and I came to the conclusion that they must be in the cupboard in the corner.

My heart began to beat, and a curious feeling of excitement took possession of me, as my imagination had a big flight. I began to see myself armed with a sword helping my father, who, being a captain, would be a splendid leader.

"But we ought to have plenty of swords and guns," I thought, and I determined when my father began to speak to me again, to propose that he should have a little armoury in the cupboard.

Then I began to think about old Jonas, and the possibility of his getting a lot of men and coming and making an attack. There had been a rumour that he and his people had once, many years ago, had a fight with the king's men; but when Bob Chowne and I talked to him about it, Bigley fired up and said it was all nonsense. But it occurred before he was born.

It had never occurred to me before that this was a strange declaration. For how could it be all nonsense and yet have occurred before he was born?

It seemed now as if it was not all nonsense.

One thought brought up another, and I found myself thinking that, if I was helping my father defend the treasure of silver here in the store, and fighting bravely, as I felt sure I should, Bigley would be helping his father to make the attack, and I saw myself having a terrific cutlass combat with him somewhere out on the slope. Then I should have had a great deal of training from my father, who was an accomplished swordsman, and I should disarm old Big and take him prisoner, and then when night came, for the sake of old school-days, I should unfasten his hands and let him escape.

My thoughts ran very freely, and I was fully determined to grind the sword that I had not seen, and which perhaps had not yet been made, as sharp as a razor. It would be very easy, I thought, when I got it, to make old Sam turn the grindstone at home, while I put on a tremendous edge and tried it on the thin branches of some of the trees.

"What an exciting time it would be!" I thought, and I could not help wishing that I should have to wear some kind of uniform, for a bit of gold lace would go so well with a sword. Then I stopped short, for in all my planning there was no place for Bob Chowne, who was regularly left out of the business.

"Oh, how stupid!" I thought directly after. "He would be the surgeon's— his father's—assistant, and bind up everybody's wounds."

I'm afraid I was, like a great many more boys, ready to have my imagination take fire at the idea of a fight, and never for a moment realising what the horrors of bloodshed really were.

"Poor Bob!" I thought to myself. "He wouldn't like that, having to do nothing but tie and sew up wounds." He was so fond of a fight that he would want to be in it; and I concluded that we would let him fight while the fight was going on, and have a sword and pistols, and afterwards I could help him bandage the wounds.

Then I came back to Bigley, and began to think that, after all, it would be very queer for him to be fighting on one side and me on the other, and it did not seem natural, for we two had never had a serious quarrel, though I had had many a set-to with other lads, and had twice over given Bob Chowne black eyes, the last time when he gave me that terrible punch on the nose, when it bled so long that we all grew frightened, and determined to go to the doctor's, and it suddenly stopped.

I don't know how much more nonsense I should have thought if my father had not made a movement as if to get up, and that changed the current of my thoughts.

But he went on writing again, and this time I began watching a large chest that stood in one corner of the room, bound with clamps of iron, and it looked so heavy and strong that I concluded that it must be full of ingots of silver ready to send away.

I grew tired of looking at that box, and as my fancy did not seem disposed to run again upon fighting and defence, I sat listening to the scratching of my father's pen and the ticking of the clock, and then to the dull roar of the furnace, while mingled with it came the clattering of hammers, the creaking of the great windlass, and the rushing and plashing of falling water.

Just then there was a tap as of some one's knuckles at the door, and in obedience to a look from my father I got up and opened it, to turn quite red in the face, for there stood my old school-fellow about whom so much had been said—Bigley Uggleston.

Chapter Twenty Six
Forearmed as well as Forewarned

"Who is it?" said my father.

"Bigley Uggleston," I replied, feeling very awkward.

"Oh, come in, my lad," said my father quietly; and as I held the door back for him to enter, it suddenly struck me what a frank, handsome-looking fellow he had grown.

I felt more awkward still, for it seemed to me that I was going to listen to some very unpleasant remarks about our companionship being broken off; but to my surprise my father said quietly:

"Come after Sep?"

"Yes, sir. I thought if he was not busy—"

"Well, but he is," said my father smiling. "He was about to unpack that box for me—I was just going to set him the task."

Bigley drew back, but my father said good-humouredly:

"Why don't you stop and help him?"

"May I, sir? I should like to."

"Go on, then, my lads. Take the lid off carefully, Sep. There is a screw-driver in that cupboard."

I went eagerly to the cupboard and opened it, to give quite a start, for there, hanging upon nails at the back, were the pistols and sword I had remembered were absent from home.

I found the screw-driver in a sort of tool-chest, and as Bigley and I took it in turns to draw the screws, my father cleared the table.

"Be careful," he said. "You can lay the things out here. I shall soon be back."

He left us together, and, all eagerness now, I worked away at the screws, which were very tight, and there were four on each side of the lid, and others in the clamps, which had to be removed before the lid could be raised.

"I am glad I came, Sep," said Bigley. "I was wondering why you hadn't been down to me."

"Were you?" I said, feeling very uncomfortable.

"Yes. What's in the box?"

"I don't know," I said. "I thought it was blocks of metal, packed to send away."

I hesitated before I said metal. I was going to say silver; but I felt, after my father's words, as if I ought to be cautious.

"I believe I know what's inside," said my companion.

"Well, what?" I cried, as I tugged at another screw which refused to go round.

"New tools for the mine."

"Why, of course!" I exclaimed. "Here: you go on. I can't manage this screw. How stupid of me not to think of it!"

"There he goes!" said Bigley, giving the screw a good wrench. "How many more are there? I see: these two."

He attacked them one after the other, talking the while.

"I wonder you don't know what's in the box," he said. "I thought your father told you everything—so different to mine, who never says anything to me."

"He does say a great deal to me, but he didn't tell me about the box."

"There, then!" cried Bigley, taking out the last screw and seating himself suddenly upon the chest. "We've only got to lift the lid and there we are. Who has first peep?"

"Oh, I don't care," I said laughing. "You can."

"Here goes, then!" cried Bigley. "Take care of the screws."

I swept them into a heap and placed them on the table as Bigley threw open the lid, which worked upon two great hinges, and then removing some coarse paper he drew back.

"You'd better unpack," he said. "Don't make a litter with the shavings."

For as the paper was removed the box seemed to be full of very fine brown shavings mixed with fine saw-dust.

I swept the shavings away and felt my hands touch a row of long parcels, carefully wrapped in a peculiar-looking paper; and as I took them out, and shook them free of the saw-dust, handing them one by one to Bigley to place upon the table, my heart began to beat, and the blood flushed into my cheeks.

"Why, they're not mining tools!" cried Bigley excitedly. "Whatever are you going to do? They're swords."

"Yes," I said huskily; "they're swords—cutlasses."

"Why, you knew all the time!" cried Bigley.

"No; I did not," I said. "I had no idea."

"But how comical!" he cried. "What are you going to do with them?"

I did not answer, for all my thoughts of half an hour before seemed to have rushed back, and I felt that I had been wondering why my father had not done that which he really had; and, though Bigley evidently could not realise the object of the weapons being there, it certainly seemed to me that my father felt that there was danger in the air, and that he meant to be prepared.

"What are you thinking about?" cried my companion. "Why don't you speak?"

"I was thinking about the cutlasses," I said.

"Well, it is a surprise!" cried Bigley. "Oh, I know. Your father's an old sea captain, and they say the French are coming. He's going to arm some men as volunteers."

All this time I was handing out the wrapped-up weapons, as we supposed them to be—as we felt they must be—and Bigley was arranging them upon the table side by side.

"That's the end of those," I said, and Bigley counted them. Twelve.

"Twelve swords," he said. "I say, Sep, let's ask him to make us volunteers too."

But I was unpacking the next things, and felt in no wise surprised by their weight and shape, to which the brown paper lent itself pretty clearly.

"Pistols!" cried Bigley, as I handed the first. "Oh, I say, Sep, do you think there'll be any uniforms too?"

"No," I said, "not in a box like this. Here, catch hold!"

I handed the first pistol to him, and he laid it beneath the swords.

"I know how many there ought to be!" he cried—"twenty-four. A brace of pistols and a cutlass for every man. Here, pitch them and I'll catch."

There was nothing to prevent my handing them to him; but, boy-like, it seemed pleasant thus to turn work into play, and I began to pitch one by one the little heavy packages as I drew them out of the chest.

Bigley nearly let one fall, but he saved it, and laughingly placed it in the row he was making, till, counting the while, he exclaimed—

"Twenty-three! Is that next one the last?"

"Yes," I said, as I pitched it to him and it was placed in the range upon the table. "You were right."

"Is there anything else?"

"Oh, yes," I said; "the box isn't half empty."

I dived down and brought out next a long sword, more carefully wrapped, and in superior paper to those which had been previously taken out. Then followed a squarish case or box in paper, and for a few moments we were undecided as to what it might be, concluding that it must be a pistol-case with a brace of superior weapons inside.

Still the chest was far from empty, and on continuing the unpacking I found that I was handing out short carbines, such as artillerymen or horse-soldiers would use.

"Twelve!" cried Bigley, who was growing more and more excited. "What next?"

The next thing was a small square box wrapped in something soft, and occupying the bottom corner of the chest, while the rest of the space was occupied by small boxes that were not wrapped in paper, but fastened down with copper nails, and on each was painted the big figures—250.

I handed out eight of these little boxes, and they, being pretty heavy, were placed close beside the wall of the office.

"That's all," I said, and, concluding that it was the proper thing to do, we replaced the shavings and saw-dust in the chest, shut down the lid, put the loose screws in a piece of paper, and tied them to one of the clamps before pushing the chest aside and making all tidy.

This done, we hovered, as it were, about the table with longing eyes and itching fingers, ending by looking at each other.

"I say," said Bigley; "didn't your father say that we were to unpack the box?"

"Yes, and we've done it," I replied rather sulkily.

"Well, oughtn't we to take the things out of the paper, and lay the paper all neatly and save the string?"

"Think so?" I said longingly.

Bigley hesitated, took up a packet, turned it over, balanced it in his hand, laid it down again, and rearranged several of the others without speaking, but he heaved a deep sigh.

"Think we ought to unpack them further?" I said.

"No," said Bigley unwillingly. "I don't think it would be right. Do you?"

"No," I said with a sigh; "but I should like to have a look."

We two lads went on hovering about the table, peering at first one packet and then at another, feeling them up and down, and quite convincing ourselves that certain ones were a little more ornamental than others. There was no doubt about it, we felt. They were swords, pistols, and carbines.

"Here, I know," I exclaimed.

"Know what, Sep?"

"The boxes, 250."

"Well, what about 'em?"

"Cartridges," I said. "Two hundred and fifty in each."

"So they are," cried Bigley with his eyes dilating; and, however much we may have been disappointed over the silver mine, the counting-house now seemed to be a perfect treasure cave, such an armoury had it become.

"I say, they won't go off, will they?" cried Bigley.

"Pshaw! Not they. I say, wouldn't old Bob like to be here now?"

"Ah, wouldn't he?" said Bigley. "Why, it's like being in a real robbers' cave."

"No," I said; "not robbers'," and I recalled the thoughts I had indulged in earlier in the day.

"No; of course not," said Bigley thoughtfully; "it isn't like a robbers' cave. I say, don't it look as if there were going to be a fight?"

I nodded, and wondered whether there would be.

"Should you like to be in it if there was?" I said in a curious doubting manner.

Bigley rubbed one ear, and picked up a sword.

"I don't know," he said. "Sometimes I think I should; but sometimes I feel as if it would be very horrid to give a fellow a chop with a thing like this, just as if he was so much meat. I would, though, if he was going to hurt my father," he cried with his eyes flashing. "I'd cut his arm right off. Wouldn't you?"

"Dunno," I said, and I began wondering whether there would ever be any occasion to use these weapons, and I could not help a shrinking sensation of dread coming over me, for I seemed to see the horror as well as the glory of shooting down human beings, and more than ever it occurred to me that if trouble did come, my old school-fellow might be on one side and I on the other.

"I say," said Bigley suddenly; "we've only undone one box, oughtn't we to undo the other?"

"What, that?" I said, looking at a shorter smaller box on end in the corner behind the door.

"Yes."

"Father didn't say I was to."

"But that looks as if it came from the same place."

"Why, Big," I cried eagerly, "that must have the uniforms in it."

"Hurray! Yes," he cried. "Wonder whether they're scarlet?"

"No," I said. "They're sure to be blue, like the sailors'."

"Oh! I don't know about that," he cried. "Marines wear scarlet. I daresay they're red."

"Should you open the box if you were me?"

"Well, no," said Bigley; "perhaps not. He didn't tell us to. But oh, how I should like to take the paper off one of these pistols!"

"So should I," was my reply, with a longing look at the array of quaint-looking parcels; "but we mustn't do that, though I do feel as if I could do it up again just as neatly."

"No; don't try," cried Bigley. "Let 'em be. We can think what's inside. I shouldn't wonder if some of them are mounted with brass, and have lions' heads on the butts."

"Yes, and the swords too—brass lions' heads, holding the guards in their mouths."

"Why, we haven't seen any belts."

"No; they would be with the uniforms. I say, I wonder whether the cutlasses are very sharp?"

"And whether they are bright blue half-way up the blade; you said your father's sword was."

"Yes," I replied; "and inlaid with gold. It was given to him when he left his ship."

"Here, come out!" cried Bigley, laying hold of my hand.

"Come out? What for?" I said.

"Because it's the best way. I always run off when I see anything very tempting that I want to touch, and ought not to."

"Get out!" I cried.

"I do, Sep, honour bright, and I feel now as if I should be obliged to undo some of those papers, and try the pistols, and pull the swords out of the sheaths. Let's go out."

I laughed, for I felt very much in the same way, only it seemed to be so cowardly to go, and Bigley came to the same way of thinking, the result being that we kept on picking up the different packages and feasting our imaginations by means of touch, till suddenly the door opened, and my father came in.

Chapter Twenty Seven
Ready for the French

"Well, boys," said my father, "unpacked? That's right, but you might as well have undone them." We each dashed at a package, whipped out our knives, cut the string, and rapidly unrolled the contents, till Bigley held a pistol, and I a cutlass, of the regular navy pattern both.

My father took the sword from my hand, drew its short broad blade, and made it whiz through the air as he gave a cut, guarding directly, and then giving point.

"Hah!" he said, as we watched him breathlessly, "I used to have two hundred and fifty stout Jack-tars under me, boys, every one of whom handled a cutlass like that."

CAPTAIN DUNCAN TESTING THE WEAPONS.

"Two hundred and fifty," I said; "just as many as there are cartridges in those boxes."

"How did you know that they were cartridges?" he said smiling.

"Well, we guessed that they were, father," I replied colouring. "It seemed as if there must be cartridges for the pistols."

"Right, my boy," he replied.

"And of course cartridges are not wanted for cutlasses," I continued.

"No," he said laughing; "you load your cutlasses with muscles."

"But they want belts," I ventured to observe.

"To be sure," said my father. "There they are in that box. You shall unpack them when we've undone these. Let me look at that pistol, Uggleston."

Bigley handed him the pistol, and my father drew the ramrod, thrust it down the barrel, and gave it two or three taps to make sure that it was not loaded. Then replacing the ramrod he cocked it, held it at arm's length, and drew the trigger.

There was a little scintillation as the flint struck the cover of the pan, and he cocked and drew the trigger again, we two watching him with intense interest, and longing to try the pistol ourselves, but not liking to ask permission.

"There, work away!" he said, "save the string, and lay the brown paper in heaps; it may come in useful."

We set to work, while my father took a hammer and some large nails from a drawer, and, standing on a stool, drove the nails in a row along a board at one side of the office, and as we unpacked he took the weapons from us and hung them up, a cutlass between two pistols, arranging the nails so that the arms looked ornamental, while at the same time they were quite ready to hand in case they should be wanted.

It took us some little time, but at last the task was done, and the cartridge chests stowed away in a cupboard, but not till each one had been carefully wrenched open, the copper nails taken out, and the lids replaced loose on the top.

"There, Master Bigley," said my father dryly. "That's what I call being ready for action." Bigley nodded.

"If those boxes were put away unopened, the chances are a hundred to one that on the occasion of their being wanted the chisel and hammer would not be in their places. Now, then, we'll undo that other box."

I could not help seeing, or thinking I saw, a peculiar meaning in my father's way of saying all this, but Bigley did not understand it I felt, and we set to at once over the other chest, dragging it into the middle of the room and prising off the lid, for this one was only nailed.

It was not so heavy either, but as we had made up our minds that it contained the uniforms, we were not surprised.

The lid was more tightly nailed down than seemed to be necessary; but we had it off at last, and then drew out a dozen parcels, which, on being opened, proved to be white buckskin belts for the waist, with a frog or pouch to hold and support the cutlasses, and a cross belt of a broader kind, to which was attached a cartouche-box, ready to hold the ball-cartridge when required.

Another row of nails was driven in for the belts, which were hung in pairs, and then we drew out a couple more boxes of cartridges, and that was all.

"Why, what's the matter, Sep?" said my father, smiling at my disappointed countenance.

"I was wondering where the uniforms were," I said.

"Uniforms, boy?" said my father. "When my two hundred and fifty lads attacked the Spanish frigate and took her, they wore no uniforms. Every man stripped to his shirt and trousers, put a handkerchief round his waist, threw away his hat, rolled up his sleeves, and tucked up his trousers. They fought the Spaniard bare-armed, bare-headed, bare-footed; and if we have to fight, we can do the same, and drive off our enemies too."

"The French, father?" I said, feeling quite abashed.

"Ay, my boy, or anyone else. These uniforms look very attractive, but there's a great deal of vanity in them, and we are too busy to give way to that."

"Yes, father," I said meekly, and as I said it I thought about something else.

"There, you lads can go now. Thank you for helping to arrange my little armoury."

We should both have liked to examine those arms a little more. We should even have liked to try one of the pistols, and shoot at a mark, but this was a regular dismissal, and we went out, going quietly down to the stream, all stained now with the dirty water from the mine, and for some time we preserved silence.

"What are you thinking about, Sep?" said Bigley at last.

"I was thinking how nicely those belts would go with a uniform," I said.

"Were you? How funny!" said Bigley. "That's just what I was thinking."

"What, about a uniform?"

"Yes."

"Blue?"

"No, scarlet."

I went down to the shore with Bigley, and we had a good ramble, after which he fetched the glass, and we climbed up to the place on the rocks where his father used to station himself to look out—for fish, Bigley said; but my father often said they were very rum fish—and there we swept the horizon to see if we could make out the lugger, but she was not in sight, and after a time we grew tired of this and lay down in the warm sunshine upon the cliff, where Bigley dropped off to sleep.

I did not feel sleepy, though, but full of thought. Above all, I could not help thinking over my father's behaviour that day. It was evident that he feared attack by making such preparations, and no doubt I should soon see him drilling the work-people he had gathered around him, and I dwelt a good deal, being tolerably observant, upon the fact of his letting Bigley see all his preparations. I was asking myself why he had done this, and what reason he had for it, when Bigley woke up and said that it was time to go and get something to eat.

I did not answer and say it was, but a silent monitor gave me a hint that he was quite correct, and so we went to the cottage, and Mother Bonnet gave us quite a feast of bread and butter and fried fish, which form no bad refreshment for two hungry boys.

Chapter Twenty Eight
Drilling our Men

My father's armoury was a good deal talked about, but when regular drilling was commenced at the Gap it excited no surprise. The grey-beards of Ripplemouth talked it over, and said they were glad that Captain Duncan had woke up and was ready to defend the Gap when the French came to our part of the coast, and they said they expected great things of him.

"Ha, ha, ha!" laughed Bob Chowne one day, as he came over; "heard the news?"

"No," I said; "have the French come?"

"No, not yet; but the Ripplemouth people are going to ask your father to help them make a fort on the cliff over the harbour, and they're going to get some guns from Bristol."

"What nonsense!" I said. "Here, I'm going over to the Gap; will you come?"

"No, I don't want to come to the old lead pump and see your father's people make the water muddy. What are you going to do?"

"Sword drill."

"Oh! I don't care for sword drill."

"Bigley's coming too," I said; "and we're going through it all."

"It's stupid work standing all in a row swinging your arms about like windmills, chopping nothing, and poking at the air, and pretending that someone's trying to stab you. I wouldn't mind if it was real fighting, but yours is all sham."

"Then we're going to do some pistol-shooting at a mark with ball-cartridge."

"Pooh! It's all fudge!" said Bob yawning. "I wouldn't mind coming if you were going to do something with real guns."

"Why, they're real pistols."

"Pistols! Yes—pop-guns. I mean big cannons."

"Ah, well," I said, "I'm sorry you will not come, but I must go."

"That's always the way when a fellow comes away from our old physic-shop and takes the trouble to walk all these miles. You're always either out or going out."

"I can't help it, Bob," I replied, feeling rather ill-used. "My father expects me. I have to help him now. You know I like a game as well as ever I did."

"Ah, well, it don't matter. Be off."

"I'm very sorry," I said, glancing at the old eight-day clock; "but I must go now."

"Well, didn't I say, Be off?" cried Bob.

"Good-bye, then!"

I offered him my hand, but he did not take it.

"If you'll walk round by the cliff I'll come part of the way with you," he said ill-humouredly.

"Will you?" I cried. "Come along, then."

I did not let him see it; but I had felt all the time that Master Bob meant to come. He had played that game so many times that I knew him by heart. I knew, too, that he was wonderfully fond of the sword practice, in which he had taken part whenever he could, and to get a shot with a pistol or a gun gave him the greatest pleasure.

"He won't come away till it's all over," I said to myself; and we walked on round by the high track watching the ships going up to Bristol, till all at once, as we rounded the corner leading into the Gap, Bob exclaimed:

"Why, there's old Jonas's boat coming in!"

"Where?" I said dubiously.

"Why, out there, stupid!" cried Bob, pointing north-west.

"What! That lugger?" I said. "No, that's not his. He went out four days ago, and isn't expected back yet. That's more like the French lugger we rode in—Captain Gualtière's."

"Yah! Nonsense!"

"Well, but it is," I said. "That has three masts; it's a chasse marée. Jonas's boat has only two masts—a regular lugger."

"You've got sand in your left eye and an old limpet-shell over the other," grumbled Bob. "French boat, indeed! Why, no French boat like that would dare to come near England now. I s'pose that's a French boat too!"

He pointed to another about a mile behind.

"No," I said; "that looks like a big yacht or a cutter. I shouldn't wonder if it's a revenue cutter."

"Well, you are a clever chap," said Bob mockingly—"setting up for a sailor, and don't know any more about it than an old cuckoo."

"I know what our old Sam and my father and Binnacle Bill have taught me," I said quietly.

"No, you don't—you don't know anything only how to be surly and disagreeable to your visitors."

"I say, Bob," I said, "is it true what people say?"

"I don't care what people say."

"Why, that your father gives you so much physic that it makes you sour?"

I repented saying it directly, for Bob stopped short. "Want me to chuck you off the cliff?" he said fiercely.

"No, that I don't," I said, pretending to be horribly frightened.

"Because, just you look here—"

"Ahoy—oy!"

"Ahoy—oy! Ahoy—oy!" I shouted back in answer to the faint cry that came from below, where we could see Bigley waving his hat.

It was easier work for us to go down the precipitous slope than for him to climb up; but he did not seem to study that for he came eagerly towards us, while we slipped and scrambled down, ignoring the path, which was a quarter of a mile away.

Bob did not speak as we were scrambling down, and the exertion made him forget his ill-temper, so that he was a little more amiable when we came within speaking distance of Bigley.

"Going to the drill?" he shouted; and then without waiting for an answer, "So am I. Has your father come back, Sep?"

"Come back!" I said. "What do you mean? He came on here."

"Yes," said Bigley; "and then he got our boat and went off in her—so Mother Bonnet said. I was not here."

"Why, where has he gone?" I asked.

"I don't know. I thought he had rowed round to the Bay."

I shook my head and began to wonder what it meant.

"Father has been round to Penzance or Plymouth, I think," said Bigley. "He'll be back soon, I expect."

"What's he gone after?" said Bob shortly.

"I don't know," said Bigley, colouring a little. "Fishing or trading or carrying something, I expect."

"I don't!" sneered Bob. "I know."

"That you don't," said Bigley quietly; "even I don't."

"No!" sneered Bob; "you never know anything. People at Ripplemouth do. He has gone on a jolly good smuggling trip, I know."

I saw Bigley's eyes flash, and for a moment I thought that he was going to say something harsh, and that we were going to have a quarrel through Bob Chowne's propensity for saying disagreeable things; but just then I happened to turn my head and saw a boat coming round the western corner of the entrance to the Gap.

"Why, there's father!" I cried. "Where can he have been!"

That exclamation changed the conversation from what was a terribly touchy point with Bigley, who always felt it acutely if anyone hinted that his father indulged in smuggling.

"I know," said Bob Chowne, changing his attack so that it was directed upon me. "Well, if my father was so precious selfish as to get a boat and go out fishing without me, I should kick up a row."

"Why, you are always making rows without," I said testily. "My father has not been fishing, I'm sure."

"There he goes again," cried Bob in an ill-used tone. "That's Sep Duncan all over. I say, Big, he was trying to pick a quarrel with me up on the cliff when you came, and I wouldn't. Now he's at it again."

"Well, I sha'n't stop to quarrel now," I replied. "Come on down and meet father."

We were a good three hundred feet above the shore when I spoke, and starting off the others joined me, and we went down over the crumbling slates and then past the pebble ridge to where the little river bubbled up again through the stones before it reached the sea, and then in and out among the rocks, to stand and wait till my father rowed in.

"Ah, boys," he cried, as the boat grounded, and we dragged it up over a smooth patch of sand, "you are just in time to help."

"Been fishing, father?" I said.

"No; only on a little bit of investigation along the coast; but I found I had not time as it was drill day. There, make the boat fast to the buoy line, and let's get up to the mine, and we'll all go this afternoon when the drill's over."

"This afternoon?" I said eagerly.

"Yes; the weather's lovely and warm, and you fellows can row me."

I felt ready to toss up my hat and cheer, and I saw that Bigley was ready to do the same; but we both felt that we were getting too old, so we refrained.

"I'm afraid I can't go, Captain Duncan," said Bob in an ill-used way. "My father will be at home expecting me."

"No, he will not, Bob," said my father smiling; "he will not be back from Barnstaple till quite late. Come along, my lad, and we'll have some lunch, and then begin drill. Had Sam started with the basket, Sep?"

"No, father," I replied; "but I saw Kicksey packing it when I came away."

"Sure to be there," said my father; and he led the way up the Gap with Bigley, to whom he always made a great point of being kind, partly because he was my old companion, and partly, as I thought, because he wanted to smooth away any ill feeling, and to make up for the break between us that kept threatening to come.

This upset Bob, who hung back and began to growl about not being sure he could stop to drill, and thought that, as we reached the end of the cliff path, he ought to go now, and altogether he required a great deal of coaxing to get him along, or rather he professed to want a great deal, till we reached the mine, where all was going on just as of old, the wheel turning, the water splashing, furnace roaring, and the pump keeping on its regular thump.

Old Sam was standing at the counting-house door with a big basket, the one he always brought over, filled with provisions for our use, as so much time was spent at the mine; and as my father pulled out a big key, Sam took in the basket, cleared the table, and threw over it a white cloth, upon which he spread the provisions.

For a few minutes after we had sat down—Bob Chowne having to be fetched in, after sliding off so that he might be fetched back—we could not eat much for feasting our eyes on the bright swords and pistols; but young appetites would have their way, and we were soon eating heartily till the meat pasty and custard and cream were completely destroyed.

"A very bold attack," said my father smiling. "Now that ought to make muscle. Off with your coats, my lads, and roll up your sleeves."

As he spoke he went to the door, and blew an old silver boatswain's whistle, when work was dropped, and the men came running up quickly from furnace, and out of the pit and stone-breaking sheds, till ten stout work-stained fellows stood in a row, showing the effect of the drill and discipline already brought to bear.

"Like the old days on the quarter-deck," said my father to Bob Chowne. "Now, Sep, serve out the arms."

I had done this several times before, and rapidly handed to each man his cutlass and belt, which was as quickly buckled on. Then one each was given to Bob Chowne and Bigley, and I was left without.

"Humph, twelve," said my father counting, as he saw me unarmed. "You can take that new sword, Sep."

I could not help feeling pleased, for this was the officer's sword which had come down with the others; and as I buckled on the lion-headed belt I had hard work to keep from glancing at Bob Chowne, who, I knew, would feel disgusted.

There was no time wasted, for my father at these drills kept up his old sea-going officer ways; and in a few minutes we were formed into two lines before him, opened out, proved distance with our swords, so as to have plenty of room, and not be likely to cut each other; and there for a good hour the sun flashed on the blades, as the sword exercise was gone through, with its cuts, points, and guards, the men taking to it eagerly as a pleasant change from the drudgery of the mine, and showing no little proficiency already.

"There," said my father at last, after the final order to sheathe swords had been given. "Break off. No pistol practice to-day. Your hands will be unsteady."

"Always the way!" I heard Bob Chowne grumble. "I stopped on purpose to have a bit of pistol-shooting, and now there's none. See if I'd have stayed if I had known."

I had to run to the door of the great stone-built counting-house and receive the swords as the men filed up, and for the next ten minutes I was busy hanging all in their places.

When I had finished the men had all gone back to their work, and after a look round, my father said a few words to a big black-looking Cornishman, who had lately been selected as foreman from his experience about mines, locked up the counting-house, and turned to us.

"Now, boys," he said, "we'll go back to the boat."

Bob Chowne's lips parted to say that he could not stop; but he had not the heart to speak the words, and we went back to the beach, to enter upon an adventure that proved rather startling to us all, and had a sequel that was more startling, and perhaps more unpleasant still.

Chapter Twenty Nine
We Lose our Boat

"We're going to take the boat again, Mrs Bonnet," said my father, as we passed Uggleston's cottage.

"Oh, I'm sure master would say you're welcome, sir," said the rosy-faced old lady. "It's a beautiful afternoon for a row."

Ten minutes after we were well afloat, and Bigley and I were pulling, making the water patter under the prow of the boat, as it rose and fell on the beautiful clear sea. Below us were the rocks, which could be seen far enough down, all draped with the brown and golden-looking weed; and we felt as if it was a shame not to have a line over the side for pollack or mackerel on such a lovely afternoon. But there was to be no fishing, for my father evidently had some serious object in hand, telling us how to pull so as to keep regularly along at a certain distance from the mighty wall of rock that was on our left till, about a mile from the Gap, where there were a great deal of piled-up stone in huge fragments that had fallen from the cliff, he suddenly told Bigley to easy, and me to row. Then both together, with the result that we pulled right into a little bay where the cliff not only seemed to go up perpendicularly, but to overhang, while in one place at the bottom a dark patch or two showed where caves ran right in.

As we neared the shore he bade us cease rowing, and taking one of the oars he threw it over the stern, and sculled the boat in and out among the rocks that were half covered by the sea, threading his way carefully, and finally beaching her on a soft patch of sand.

We all leaped out, and the little anchor was thrown ashore to keep the boat safe while we went away.

"For neither of you will care to be boat-keeper," said my father smiling.

"What are you going to do?" I asked as we walked up together.

"Don't ask questions, my boy," he replied quietly. "If I tell you, of course you cannot, without seeming mysterious, refuse to tell your companions, and I do not care to say much at present. It does not matter, but I prefer not to talk."

We walked up straight to the caves, which were very beautiful, covered as their mouths were with ivy and ferns, while over each a perfect sheet of dripping rain fell like a screen and threatened to soak anyone who attempted to enter.

We did not attempt it, for my father led us away to the west, and soon after, hammer in hand, he was examining the cliff-face and the various blocks of stone that had fallen down in days gone by.

We walked on for a time, but it soon became too monotonous, and we took to something to amuse ourselves, to my father's great satisfaction, for he evidently now preferred to be alone.

We did not watch him, but to me it seemed evident enough that he was searching for minerals, of which he believed that he had seen some trace.

As for us, we rather enjoyed our ramble, for this was a part of the shore that we had not explored for some time, and the number of pools and hollows among the stones were almost countless, while at every turn we had to lament the absence of our baskets and nets.

Sometimes we climbed on to some difficult-looking pile, at other times we crept in under the cavernous-looking places, where, at high tide, the sea rushed and roared. Wearying of this, we explored the edge where high-water left its marks, to examine the curious shells washed up, and the varieties of sea-weed driven right under the perpendicular wall of rock, that towered up above us fully two hundred feet before it began to slope upwards as a hill.

Then after laughingly saying that if the French came, they would have to bring very long ladders and use them at low tide if they wanted to get into England, we sauntered back towards where we had left my father, but chose our path as nearly as we could close down by the edge of the water.

The tide was coming up fast, but this was all the better, as it was likely to bring in objects worthy of notice; but we found nothing, and at last the time had so rapidly glided away that evening was coming in as it were on the tide.

We looked about us, and found that we were well inside the little bay where we had first landed, its two arms stretching well out as jagged points on either side, among whose rocks the sea was foaming and plashing, although it was quite calm a little way out.

"No getting back, boys, now," said Bigley, "if it wasn't for the boat."

"Yah! Nonsense!" cried Bob. "If the tide was to catch me in a bay like this, I should make a run and a jump at the cliff, catch hold of the first piece of ivy I could see, and then go up like a squirrel."

"Without a tail," I added laughing.

"Hark at clever old Sep Duncan," sneered Bob. "He'd walk up the cliff without touching. It's a strange thing that we can't come out without your saying something disagreeable, Sep."

"I'm very sorry," I said with mock humility, for I had just caught sight of Bigley's face, and he was grinning.

"Well, don't do it again, then," said Bob pompously, and then we listened, for a voice hailed us from somewhere among the wilderness of piled-up rocks.

"Ahoy, there! Ahoy!"

"Here we are, father!" I shouted, and trudging on we met him coming down from a place where he had evidently been sitting smoking his pipe.

"Didn't you hear me hail before?" he said as we met.

"No, father."

"Why, I've been shouting at intervals for this last hour, and I should have been uncomfortable if I had not thought you had common sense enough to take care of yourselves."

"Oh! We minded that, sir," said Bob importantly. "We are older now than we used to be."

"Yes," said my father dryly, "so I supposed. Well, let's be off; we've a long row, and then a walk, and it's time to feed the animals, eh, Bob Chowne?"

"Yes, sir," said Bob; "but I've got ever so much farther to go before I can get anything to eat."

"No, you have not," said my father in his driest way. "I should think there will be enough for us all at the Bay."

"I—I didn't mean," said Bob in a stammering way; but he had turned very red in the face, and then he quite broke down and could get no further, being evidently thoroughly ashamed of the way in which he had spoken.

My father noticed it, and changed the conversation directly. "Found anything very interesting?" he said; "anything good among the rocks?"

"No, father," I said; "nothing much."

"Why, you blind puppy!" cried my father; "nothing? Don't you know that every pool and rock hole teems with wonders that you go by without noticing. Ah! I shall have to go with you, boys, some day, and show you a few of the grand sights you pass over because they are so small, and which you call nothing. Why, how high the tide has risen!"

"Didn't we leave the boat just beyond those rocks, sir?" said Bigley.

"Yes," said my father. "One of you will be obliged to strip and wade out to it. No, it couldn't have been those rocks."

"No, sir," said Bob Chowne; "it was round on the other side of this heap."

He pointed to a mass of rock lying right in the centre of the embayment, a heap which cut off our view on one side.

"I suppose you must be right, Chowne," said my father; "come along."

"I feel sure it was here, father," I said; "just out here."

"No it wasn't," cried Bob pettishly. "I remember coming round here after we left the boat."

Bigley and I looked at each other, but we said nothing, only followed my father and Bob Chowne as they went round to the other side of the pile of rock, and there lay the sea before us with the tide racing in, and sweeping over the rocks, but no boat.

"It's very strange," said my father; "we must have left it in one of these places."

"Perhaps it was behind the other heap, sir," said Bob eagerly.

"What heap?" said my father.

"That one, sir," said Bob, pointing towards the west.

"Impossible!" cried my father, and then he stopped and waited, while Bigley, who had, by getting on my back and shoulders, managed to climb up the highest part of the mass which stood like an island out of the stones and sand, shaded his eyes with his hand, and looked all round.

It was so still that the lapping of the evening tide sounded quite loud, and the querulous call of a gull that swept by was quite startling.

"Well," said my father, "can you see the boat? No no, don't look out there, my lad, look in here close."

"She isn't in here close," said Bigley quietly.

"She must be, Big," cried Bob. "Here, let me come."

"I see her!" cried Bigley just then. "No. Yes. There she is, sir!" he said, pointing to the east. "She's broke adrift, and is floating yonder half a mile away towards the Gap."

"Tut, tut, tut!" ejaculated my father. "Are you sure?"

"Yes, sir," said Bigley, "I'm quite sure. I was quite sure before that we left her where we looked first, but I didn't like to say so."

"Here, give me your hand," said my father. "You, Sep, let me try and get up over you. Bob Chowne, you had better stand by him to strengthen him. I'm heavy. Reach down, Bigley, and give me your hand."

My father was active enough, and with our help scrambled up on to the top of the rock, where he gave one glance at the speck Bigley pointed out, and then uttered an impatient ejaculation.

"Come down," he said. "You're quite right, my lad. But how can that boat have got away? The grapnel was good."

"I'm afraid I know," said Bigley sadly. "I don't think anyone looked to see if the painter was made fast to the ring. I didn't."

"And as I'm an old sailor, who ought to have known better, I confess that I did not," said my father. "Well, boys, it's of no use to cry over spilt milk. If the boat is not recovered unhurt, Mr Jonas Uggleston will have a new one, and I must apologise for my carelessness. Now, then, we must walk home."

Bigley looked at him in rather a curious way; and as I divined what he meant I glanced at the two points which projected and formed the bay, and saw that they were being swept by the waves to such an extent that it would have been madness to attempt to get round either wading or swimming.

"Yes," said my father, speaking as if someone had made this remark to him, "it would be impossible to get round there. Come along, boys, help me down; I can't jump. Let's see for a place to climb the cliff."

We helped him down by standing with our heads bent upon our arms, as if we were playing at "*Saddle my nag*," then he lowered himself till he could rest his feet upon our shoulders, and the rest was easy.

"We mustn't lose time," he said, as he stood on the rough shingle; "the tide is running in very fast."

It was quite true, and before long it would certainly completely fill the bay.

Chapter Thirty
A Night on the Rocks

It was very satisfying in a case of emergency to have with us some one so old and staid and full of authority as my father, who set the example to us lads of hurrying close up to the cliff right at the head where the caverns ran in, and the rain-like water streamed down from the ferns and saxifrages to form a veil that now looked golden in the glow from the west.

"Hah!" said my father decisively, "no standing here; and it would not be safe to go into the cave, the water rises six or seven feet here right up the cliff."

It was so all round, as we plainly saw by the sea-weed that clung in the crevices, and the limpets and barnacles on the smooth places right above the heads of us boys, while every here and there at our feet we could see the common red sea creatures, which look like red jelly when the tide is down, and like daisyfied flowers when it is up.

"No stopping down here, boys," cried my father. "Now, then, where's the best place to climb the cliff? You two try one way, Chowne and I will go the other."

We separated, and Bigley and I ran right round the steep wall, looking eagerly for a spot where foothold could be obtained, but it was generally overhanging, while elsewhere it rose up perfectly straight, so that a cat could not have run up it. Only in one place where there was a great crack did it seem possible to climb up any distance, and that crack seemed to afford the means of getting to a shelf of rock just beneath a tremendous overhanging mass, some fifty feet above where we stood.

This was very near the eastern arm of the little bay, where the tide was fretting and splashing and gurgling among the rocks, and threatening every minute to come right up amongst the stones that filled the foot of the crack.

"Let's look more carefully as we go back," said Bigley; and we did, but our only discovery was the entrance to another cave, which seemed to be quite a narrow doorway or slit behind some tall stones piled right above it, and shutting it from the sight of anyone walking by. In fact, we had missed it as we came.

"That might be a good place," said Bigley; "but it wouldn't be safe to try, for perhaps the sea fills it right up every tide."

We went on back, looking eagerly upwards, and stumbling over the stones that strewed our path, till we met my father and Bob Chowne.

"Well," said my father, in his short stern way, as if he were addressing his sailors on board ship. "Report!"

"No way up to the top, sir," said Bigley.

"No, father, none," I said.

"No way?" said my father, and he frowned severely; "and there is no way up whatever at our end. Boys, we shall have to venture out, and swim round the point."

Bob Chowne shuddered, and I felt a curious sensation of dread creeping over me which I tried to shake off.

"But there seems to be a way up to a shelf of rock, father," I said; "close there by the point."

"Ah!" he cried.

"But no higher."

"Never mind," he said sharply. "Go on first. Quick!"

It was quite necessary to be quick, for the water was already lapping among the stones at the foot of the chink and mounting fast.

"Yes, I see," said my father. "There! Lose no time. Up with you, Uggleston. You next, Chowne. Climb your best, boys, and help one another."

The climb was awkward and steep, but possible, and by one giving another a back and then crouching on some ledge and holding down his hand to the others, we got on up and up, till the big ledge was reached, and proved to be some twenty feet long by about nine broad in the middle, but going off to nothing at either end, while it went in right under a tremendous projecting portion of the cliff, that looked as if it would crumble down and crush us at any moment.

"Hah!" ejaculated my father breathlessly, as he partly dragged himself up, and was partly dragged by us on to the shelf. "What a place! Why, we must be at least eighty feet above the shingle."

"As much as that, father?"

"Yes, my boy; so mind all of you. No rolling off. Now, then, is there any other way of getting higher, and so on to the slope?"

A very few minutes' examination satisfied him that there was none.

"No; only a fly could get up there, boys," he said merrily. "Well, we are safe and quite comfortable. This will be another adventure for you. Why, my lads, I shall never have the heart to scold you for getting into scrapes after leading you into this one. It is easier to get into trouble than out."

"Shall we have to stay here very long, father?" I said.

"Only all night, my boys, so we must make ourselves as comfortable as we can. We shall have to divide ourselves into two watches and make the best of it. Certainly we shall not be able to climb down till daylight to-morrow morning."

"What! Do you mean for us to go to sleep in turns?"

"Or sit up, which you like, my boys," he said quietly. "And no very great hardship either. You have not touched upon our greatest difficulty."

"What's that, sir?" said Bob.

"Nothing to eat, my boy, and we are all very hungry."

"Oh!" groaned Bob; and if ever the face of boy suggested that he had just taken medicine, it was Bob Chowne's then.

"Worse disasters at sea, my lads; we shall not hurt. The worst is that people at our homes will not know what we know, and be very much troubled about us. If the boat is picked up they will fear the worst. For my part, I hope it will not be found."

"But are we safe, sir?" said Bob, with tribulation in his voice.

"Perfectly, my lad, so long as you don't roll off the ledge, which, of course, you will not do. There, boys, let's look on the bright side of it all, and be very thankful that we have reached so comfortable a haven. Make the best of it, and think you are on an uninhabited island waiting for rescue to come, with the pleasant knowledge that it won't be long."

"Oh, I don't mind," I said.

"Nor I," cried Bigley.

"I rather like it," said Bob, with a very physicky face.

"Then, choose your places, boys," said my father, "and we'll sit and sing and tell stories, after we have grown tired of watching the glorious sunset; for, my lads, while we are talking see what a magnificent sea and sky are spread before you."

We looked out from our niche under the stony canopy, to see that the sky was one blaze of orange, and gold, and fiery red, which in turn seemed to stain the sea, as if it was all liquid topaz, and sapphire, and amethyst, like the old jewels that had belonged to my mother, and which I had sometimes seen in my father's desk. Nothing, I suppose, could have been more lovely, nothing more grand. If we looked to the left, the rocky cliff was all glow hero, all dark purple shadow there, and the clustering oaks that ran right up to the top were as if they were golden green. If we looked to the right, the cliffs seemed as if on fire where the rock was bare, and as our eyes fell to where the tide was coming in, the waves, as they curled over, were burnished, and flashed and glowed like liquid fire.

It was all grand in the extreme, but somehow I felt, as did Bob and Bigley, that a well-spread tea-table with some hot fried ham and some eggs, with new bread, would have been worth it all.

I am almost ashamed to put this down, but my companions confided their feelings to me afterwards, and it is perfectly true.

By degrees the bright colours on the sea and overspreading the sky faded out, and all grew dark, save where there was a glow in the north. The stars had come out bright and clear, and covered the sky like so many points of light looking down at themselves in the mirror-like sea. The tide came up fast, and as the waves heaved and swayed and ran in, it seemed as if they were sweeping before them myriads and myriads of stars, for the water was covered with light, some being the reflections from the sky, others the curious little specks that we used to see in the water in warm weather.

We sat and talked and lay close to the edge to watch the waves come sweeping in more and more, till the little bay was covered and the tide rose over the outlying rock, the water sounding wild and strange as it washed, and splashed, and sighed, and sucked in amongst the stones. Then, by slow degrees, as we gazed down we found how necessary it had been for us to climb up to our perch, for the tide rose and rose, higher and higher, till it must have been seven or eight feet up the rocks below us; and now it was that we listened with a peculiar creeping sensation to the swell, as it rolled in and evidently right up into the caves which we had seen.

"Why, those places must go a long way into the cliffs," said my father as we listened. "Hark at that."

It was a curious creepy sound of hissing and roaring, as if there were strange wild beasts right in amongst the windings of the cave, and they had become angry with the sea for intruding in their domain.

"Seals!" said Bob Chowne decisively.

"No," said my father, "it is only the imprisoned air escaping from some of the cracks and crevices into which it is driven by the sea. Why, boys, those caves must be very large, or at all events they go in a long way. You ought to explore them some day at low water. Warm enough?"

We all declared that we were, and sat gazing out at the soft transparent darkness overhanging the sea, which was wonderfully smooth now, in spite of the soft western breeze that was blowing; and at last the silence seemed to have become perfectly profound. So silent were we that every one started as my father said suddenly:

"Look here, boys, suppose I tell you a story."

The proposal was received with acclamation, and he lay back against the cliff and related to us one of his old sea-going experiences, to the very great delight of all.

Chapter Thirty One
The Smugglers' Landing

After my father had finished his story it was arranged that watch should be set, and the arrangement made was that Bob Chowne and I should take the first spell, and it was to last as long as we liked—that is to say, we were to watch until we were tired, and then call my father and Bigley, who would watch for the rest of the night.

Bigley said he should not sleep, but he followed my father's example and lay down, while in a few minutes his regular breathing told that he had gone off; and before long, as Bob Chowne and I sat talking in a low tone, we knew that my father was asleep as well.

And there we two lads sat on the shelf of rock listening to the sobbing and sighing of the tide, and staring out to sea. Sometimes we talked in a low voice about how uncomfortable some people would be about us, and Bob said it was like my luck—that I had my father with me, while his and Bigley Uggleston's would be in a terrible way.

"And a nice row there'll be about it," he said dolefully. "There never was such an unlucky chap as I am."

"And Big?"

"Oh, Big! Pooh! His father never takes any notice about him."

Then we talked about the drilling, and the silver mine and my father's success, and what a fine thing it was for me; and about school-days, and what it would cost to get a new boat for old Jonas, and about Bob going up to London to be a doctor; and we were prosing on, but this gave him a chance to become a little animated.

"I don't want to be a doctor," he said fiercely; "but I'll serve some of 'em out if I'm obliged to be. I'll let them know!"

"What stuff!" I said. "Why, I should like to be a doctor, and if I was I'd go in for being surgeon on board a ship."

"Why?" said Bob.

"So as to go all round the world, and see what there is to see."

"Ah!" said Bob, "I hadn't thought about that; but it isn't half so good as having a mine of your own, as you'll have some day. I wish we could change fathers, but I suppose we couldn't do that."

We did not argue out that question, but went on talking in a low prosy tone, as we sat there with our backs supported against the cliff; and I suppose it must have been Bob's low muttering voice, mingled with the darkness, the natural hour for sleep, and the murmuring of the waves, that had so curious and lulling an effect upon me, for all at once it seemed that the water was running down from the mine shaft where it was being pumped up, the big pump giving its peculiar beats as it worked, and the splash and rush of the water sounding very soft and clear.

Then I seemed to be down in the mine, and it was very dark and cold, and I climbed up again and sat down on the ground to listen to the washing of the water, the hurrying of the stream, and the regular beat of the pump; and then I was awake again, staring out into the darkness that hung over the sea. For a few minutes I was so confused that I could not make out where I was. It was cold and I was shivering, and the rushing of the water and the beat of the pump was going on still.

No, it was not; for I was up there on the shelf of rock miles away from our mine, and I had been set to keep watch with Bob Chowne; and here was he, close by me, breathing heavily, fast asleep.

I felt miserable and disgraced to think that I should have been so wanting in my sense of duty as to have slept, and Bob was no better.

"Bob! Bob!" I whispered, shaking him.

"Yes," he said with a start; "I know—I wasn't asleep."

"Hush! Listen!" I said. "What's that noise?"

We both listened, and my heart throbbed as I heard a regular plash and thud from off the sea.

"Boat," said Bob decidedly. "Shall I hail it?"

"No," I replied quickly.

"Why not? It's a boat coming to fetch us."

I could not think that it was, and creeping to where my father lay I shook him.

"Yes. Time to watch?" he said quietly.

"Hush! Listen!" I said.

He sat up:

"Boat," he said, "close in."

"Is it coming to fetch us, father?" I whispered.

"No, boy; if it were, those on board would hail."

"What shall we do—shout?" I asked him.

"Certainly not. Here, Bigley, sit up, my lad! All keep perfectly still and wait. We do not know whose boat it may be."

He was our leader, and we neither of us thought of saying a word, but sat and listened to the low plash and roll of the oars of some big boat that seemed to be very close in; and so it proved, for at the end of a few minutes we could distinctly see something large and black looming up out of the darkness, and before long make out that it was quite a large vessel that was being worked with sweeps or large oars till it was close in; and then there was the noise of the oars being laid inboard, and the sound of orders being given in a low firm voice.

"Keep perfectly still," my father whispered to us; but it was unnecessary, and we sat together there on the rock shelf, the projecting portion making our resting-place quite black, as we watched and listened to what was going on.

Then for about three hours there was a busy scene below us. Men seemed to have dropped down into the water from both sides of the vessel. Some went up to the cliff-face away to our left where the caverns lay, and at the end of a minute the light of a couple of lanthorns gleamed out and then disappeared in the cave.

Hardly a word was spoken save on board the vessel, where those upon deck seemed from time to time to be doing something with poles to keep her from getting aground as the tide fell.

It must, I say, have been for nearly three hours that the busy scene lasted, and a large body of men kept on plashing to and fro with loads from the vessel to the cavern and back empty-handed. Everything seemed to be done as quietly as if the men were well accustomed to the task. Not a word was spoken, except by one who seemed to be leader, and the only sounds we heard were the tramping upon the slate-sprinkled sand and the splashing as they waded in to reach the vessel's side.

It was evident enough that they were landing quite a store of something of another from the vessel, and I knew enough of such matters to be sure that it was a smuggler running a cargo. For the first few minutes I felt that it must be the French coming to take us unawares; but the French would have landed men, not packages and little barrels.

It was a smuggler sure enough, and hence my father's strict order to be silent, for the smugglers had not a very good character in our parts, and ugly tales were told of how they had not scrupled to kill people who had interfered with them when busy over their dangerous work.

I was watching them eagerly, when, all at once, I turned cold and shivered, for it had suddenly struck me that old Jonas was away with his lugger, and that this must be it landing its cargo, while all the time, so close to me that I could have stretched out my hand and touched him, there lay my school-fellow—the old smuggler's son.

"He must suspect him," I said to myself; and then, "What must he feel?"

And all the while there below us was the busy scene—the men coming and going and the cargo being landed, till all at once there was a cessation. Those who returned from the cave stayed about the vessel, and seemed, as far as we could make out, to be climbing on board, and as I suddenly seemed to be making out their figures a little more clearly, my father whispered, "Lie down, boys, or you will be seen. The day is beginning to dawn."

We obeyed him silently, and lay watching, seeing every minute more clearly that the dark-looking vessel, which loomed up very big, was being thrust out with long oars, and beginning to glide slowly away in a thick mist which hung over the sea a hundred yards or so from shore. Then as it reached and began to fade, as it were, into the mist, first one then another dark patch rose from the deck.

"Hoisting sail," I said to myself. "Two big lug-sails. It is the *Saucy Lass*—old Jonas's lugger, and it looks big through the fog."

Just then in the coming grey dawn I saw another patch rise up, following a creaking noise, and I could make out that it was a third sail, when I knew that it could not be the *Saucy Lass*, but must be a stranger.

I was so glad, for Bigley's sake, that my heart gave quite a heavy throb; and, unless I was very much deceived, I heard my father draw a long breath like a sigh of relief.

As we gazed at the sails and the dark hull in the increasing light, everything looked so strange and indistinct that it seemed impossible for it all to be real. The sails began to fill, and the vessel glided silently away without a voice on board being heard, till it was so far-off that my father said:

"I think we may begin to talk, my lads, now."

"I say, sir," cried Bob excitedly, "weren't those smugglers?"

"I cannot say," replied my father coldly.

"Let's get down now and look," said Bob.

"I think," said my father, "that we had better leave everything alone, and, as soon as the tide will allow us, get home to breakfast. You, Bob Chowne, if I were you, I should keep my own counsel about this, and you too, Sep."

I noticed that he did not say anything to Bigley, who was kneeling down gazing after the vessel in the mist which was dying away about the land, and appeared to be going off with the vessel, surrounding it and trying to hide it from those on shore, as with the faint breeze and the swift tide it glided rapidly away.

Soon after there was a warm glow high up in the east. Then hundreds of tiny clouds began to fleck the sky with orange, the sea became glorious with gold and blue, the sun peeped above the edge, and it was day once more, with the vessel a couple of miles away going due west.

Chapter Thirty Two
Doing One's Duty

We did not have to stay very long before we descended. My father said it would be better to stop, and while we were waiting Bob Chowne asked whether we were going to search the cave and see what was there.

"No!" said my father in very decisive tones.

"But you said something about us lads exploring it, sir, yesterday—I mean last night."

"Yes, my lad, I did," replied my father so sternly that Bob Chowne was quite silenced; "but I have changed my mind."

I noticed that he still did not say anything to Bigley, and that my old school-fellow was very silent, in fact we were none of us in a conversational frame of mind, but every now and then the idea kept creeping in that old Jonas must know about that cave, and the purpose for which it was used; and then I seemed to understand my father's thoughtful manner, for it was as though this discovery was likely to widen the breach between them.

In about an hour's time my father proposed that we should climb down, and feeling very stiff and cold we began to descend.

I went first, lowering myself from ledge to ledge, with my father lying down and holding my hands, and then following me, though really it was not very difficult, for we boys had been up and down far more dangerous places after gulls' eggs in our earlier days.

But, though we could go down in the bay, we could not get out of it as yet, for the tide was some distance up the point we wanted to pass. The eastern one was clear, and we could have gone that way, and, after two miles' walk and scramble along the beach, have found a place where we could climb up, but that was not our object, and we waited about looking at the falling tide, and watching the rapidly disappearing three masts of the lugger. Then, too, we noted the tracks on the beach, some of which were quite plain, but they did not show higher up by the cavern, and we knew that they would all disappear with, the next tide.

The temptation was very strong to go in and explore the place, but neither Bob nor I hinted at it, and Bigley was exceedingly quiet and dull. In fact he went away from us after a time and sat down on the top of a rock close to the eastern point, a rock to which he had to leap, for it was still in the water, and there he sat waiting till he could get to another and another, and at last waved his hand to us, when we followed him and got round on to the shore on the other side.

It was no easy task even there, for the beach was terribly encumbered with rocks, but by creeping in and out, and by dint of some climbing, we managed to get along, and at last reached the Gap just as Doctor Chowne was about setting off back to get a boat at Ripplemouth and come in search of us, after having been up all night waiting for Bob's return, and then riding over to the Bay to hear from Kicksey that we had not been back, and then on to the Gap, to find that we had all gone out in Jonas Uggleston's boat, and not been heard of since.

"Well," said the doctor, after hearing a part of our adventure, "I suppose I must not thank Bob for this job, eh, Duncan? It was your fault, you see. My word, sir, you did give me a fright."

"I'll take all the blame, Chowne," said my father; "but let me tell Mrs Bonnet that we're all right, poor woman, and then let's walk across to my place to breakfast."

There was no need to go and tell Mother Bonnet, for she had caught sight of us, and came at a heavy trot over the pebbles to display a face and eyes red with weeping, and to burst forth into quite a wail as she flung her arms about Bigley, and hugged and kissed him.

"Oh, my dear child! My dear child!" she cried, "I've been up and down here all night afraid that you was drowned."

Just then I noticed that Bob Chowne was backing behind his father, and feeling moved by the same impulse, I backed behind mine, for we were both in a state of alarm for fear that the good-hearted old woman should want to hug and kiss us too. Fortunately, however, she did not, for all her attention was taken up by Bigley, and we soon after parted, Bigley going with Mother Bonnet towards old Jonas's cottage, and we boys following our fathers to reach the cliff path and get home.

"You will not come along here on the pony," said my father as the doctor mounted his sturdy little Exmoor-bred animal.

"Indeed but I shall," replied the doctor. "Why not?"

"It will be so dangerous for a mounted man."

"Tchah!" exclaimed the doctor, "my pony's too fond of himself to tumble us down the cliff; but there, as you are so nervous about me I will not ride. Here, Bob, you ride the pony home, and I'll walk."

"Ride him home along the cliff path, father?" said Bob, looking rather white.

"Yes, of course. Captain Duncan is afraid of losing his doctor, and you are not so much consequence as I. Here, jump up, and ride on first. Then we shall see where you fall."

Bob looked at me wildly.

"Not afraid, are you?"

"N–no, father," cried Bob desperately; and setting his teeth, he put his foot in the stirrup, mounted, and rode on along the high path with the rock on one side and the steep slope on the other, which ran down to where the perpendicular cliff edge began, with the sea a couple of hundred feet below.

"I don't think I'd do that, Chowne," I heard my father say in remonstrance.

"Bah, sir! Give the boy self-reliance. See how bravely he got over his scare. Haven't liked him so well for a week. Do you think I should have let him get up if there had been any danger?"

"But there is danger," said my father.

"Not a bit, sir. The pony's as sure-footed as a mule. He won't slip."

No more was said, and in this fashion we walked home, with Bob in front on the pony and me by his side, for I ran on to join him, my father and Doctor Chowne coming behind.

Old Sam was outside as we came in sight of the cottage, and the old fellow threw his hat in the air as he caught sight of us, and then came to meet us at a trot, after disappearing for a moment in the house.

"I said you'd come back all right. I know'd it when they told me about the boat," he cried to me as he came up.

"Boat! What about the boat?" I said.

"One o' the fishermen picked her up, and as soon as I heered as her oars and hitcher were all right, I said there was no accident. The rope had loosed and she'd drifted away."

"But how did you know we had gone off in the boat, Sam?" I said eagerly.

"How did I know?" he said. "Think when you didn't come back a man was going to bed and forget you all?"

"Well, I hardly thought that, Sam," I said.

"Because I didn't, and I went right over to the mine and asked, and you weren't there, and then I went to Uggleston's and heerd you'd gone out in the boat, and that's how I know'd, Mast' Sep, sir."

"Here, Sam, run back and tell Kicksey to hurry on the breakfast," said my father.

"Hurry on the braxfass, captain," said Sam grinning, "why, I told Kicksey to put the ham in the pan as soon as I see you a-coming."

The result was that we were soon all seated at a capital breakfast and ready to forget the troubles of the night, only that every now and then the recollection of the smuggling scene came in like a cloud, and I could not help seeing that my father was a good deal troubled in his mind.

Nothing, however, was said, and soon after breakfast the doctor went off with Bob Chowne.

As soon as we were alone my father began to walk up and down the room in a very anxious manner, and once or twice he turned towards me as if about to speak, but he checked himself and went on with his walk.

At last the silence became so irksome that I took upon myself to speak first.

"Are you going over to the mine, father?" I said.

"Yes, my boy," he replied. "But you had better go and lie down for an hour or two."

"Oh, no, father," I said. "I'm not tired. Let me go with you."

He nodded, and then stood thoughtful, and tapping the ground with his foot.

All at once he seemed to have made up his mind.

"Look here, Sep," he said; "you are growing a great fellow now. I've been helping you all these years; now you must help me."

"Tell me how, father, and I will," I said eagerly.

"I know you will, my boy," he replied, "and I'm going to treat you now as I would a counsellor. This is a very unfortunate business, my boy."

"What, our seeing the smugglers last night?"

He nodded.

"Did you think, then, like I did, that it was Jonas Uggleston's boat?"

"I did, my boy."

"But it was not, father."

"No, my boy; but—"

"You think Jonas Uggleston knew the boat was coming, and he knows all about that hiding-place, father?"

"Is that what you have been thinking, Sep?"

"Yes, father."

"And so have I, my lad. Now, though I am, as I may say, still in the king's service, and I feel it my duty to go and inform the officers of what I have seen, on the other hand there is a horrible feeling of self-interest keeps tugging at me, and saying, 'mind your own business. You are bad friends enough with Jonas Uggleston as it is, so let matters rest for your own sake and for your son's.'"

"Oh, father!" I exclaimed.

"Then this feeling hints to me that I am not sure of anything, and that I have no business to interfere, and so on. Among other things it seems to whisper to me that old Jonas will not know, when all the time he must. Now come, Sep, as a thoughtful boy, what should you recommend me to do?"

"It's very queer, father," I said rather dolefully; "but how often one is obliged to do and say things one way, when it would be so easy and comfortable to do and say things the other way."

"Yes, Sep," he replied, turning away his face; "it is so all through life, and one is always finding that there is an easy way out of a difficulty. What should you do here?"

"What's right, father," I said boldly. "What's right."

He turned upon me in an instant, and grasped my hand with his eyes flashing, and he gripped me so hard that he hurt me.

As we stood looking in each other's eyes, a strange feeling of misery came over me.

"What shall you do, father?" I said.

"I don't quite know, Sep," he replied thoughtfully. "I think I shall wait till Jonas Uggleston gets home, and then tell him all I have seen."

"But it seems so hard on poor Bigley," I said dolefully.

"Ah!" shouted my father. "Stamp on it, Sep; stamp it down, boy. Crush out that feeling, for it is like a temptation. Duty, honesty, first; friends later on. It is hard, my boy, but recollect you are an officer's son, and *officer* and *gentleman* are two words that must always be bracketed together in the king's service. There's that one word, boy, for you to always keep in your heart, where it must shine like a jewel—duty—duty. It is the compass, my lad, that points always—not to the north, but to the end of a just man's life—duty, Sep, duty."

Chapter Thirty Three
Old Uggleston is too Sharp for the Revenue

We did not go over that afternoon till it was growing late, for my father had a number of letters to write, and when we did go along the cliff, and reached the descent to the Gap, to our surprise there lay Jonas Uggleston's lugger, and we knew he had come home.

"Hah!" ejaculated my father after drawing a long breath. "I shall have to speak at once. He does not seem to have landed yet."

For the lugger was swinging to the buoy that lay about a hundred yards out, and we could see figures on board.

There was a brisk breeze blowing down the Gap, and the lugger was end-on towards us, rising and falling on the swell, while the sea was all rippled by the wind.

"Look, father," I said, as we went on down, seeing each moment more and more of the opening to the sea; "there's a boat coming ashore."

"Man-o'-war's," cried my father excitedly. "Look at the way the oars dip, Sep. Hah, it's a treat to see the lads handle them again. There she is!" he cried. "Look! Why, it's the revenue cutter."

She had just rounded a bend as he spoke, and there, sure enough, was a large cutter with snow-white sails lying off the point that formed the east side of the Gap, head to wind, and waiting evidently for the return of the boat that had come ashore.

My father walked rapidly on, and we reached the shore nearly at the same time as the boat, from which sprang an officer, and to our surprise Jonas Uggleston stepped out more slowly.

Just then Bigley appeared, I never knew where from; but I think he must have been watching from among the rocks, and in a quick husky voice he said to my father:

"Captain Duncan, please, pray don't say that you saw that cargo landed last night."

"My poor lad!" said my father kindly. "But tell me; have the cutter's men been aboard the lugger?"

"Yes, sir, searching her, I think; and you see they chased her in, and now they're bringing father ashore a prisoner."

He could say no more, for the cutter's officer came up.

"You are Captain Duncan, I think?" he said.

"Yes," said my father, returning his salute. "Whom have I the pleasure of addressing?"

"Lieutenant Melton, His Majesty's cutter *Flying Fish*."

They both saluted again, and old Jonas, who looked curiously yellow, and with his eyes seeming to search the officer's, drew nearer.

"Look here, Captain Duncan, I have been for some time on the look-out for this man."

"Well, sir, you have caught him," said my father coldly.

"Yes, sir, I have, and I have overhauled the lugger, but without success."

Old Jonas glanced at me and then at my father, who did not speak, only bowed, and the officer went on.

"Now, then, Captain Duncan; you know this man to be a notorious smuggler, do you not?"

"I have heard him called so."

"And you know it, sir."

"I never detected Mr Uggleston in any act of smuggling," replied my father more coldly, for the officer's hectoring manner offended him, and I felt that if he told what he knew, it would be to someone more in authority.

I glanced at old Jonas, and his eyes twinkled with satisfaction.

"This is prevarication, sir," cried the lieutenant; "but I am not to be put off like this. Come, sir, I received information about a very valuable contraband cargo that has been run from Dunquerque. It has been landed here successfully during the past night or the night before. Now, sir, if you please, where was that cargo landed?"

My father was silent, but his face was flushed, and I saw Jonas Uggleston dart a curious look at him as he screwed up his face, and at the same moment Bigley grasped my hand.

"I see," said the officer, "I shall have to question the boys. Once more, sir, I ask you as an officer and a gentleman, do you not know where that cargo was landed?"

"Sir," said my father, "your manner is dictatorial and offensive to a man of higher rank than yourself; but you ask me this question as one of his majesty's servants, and I am bound to reply. I do know where a cargo was landed, but it was not from this man's boat."

"But he was in the business, captain," said the lieutenant with a laugh. "Now, sir, if you please, where was it?"

"In the second bay to the westward, sir," said my father coldly; and Jonas Uggleston gave his foot a stamp, and uttered a fierce oath.

"You see, he is in the business," said the lieutenant laughing. "There, Uggleston, you have betrayed yourself."

I heard Bigley utter a piteous sigh, and I looked round at him to see the great drops standing on his forehead.

"I am so sorry, Big," I whispered; but he did not reply. He went and took hold of his father's arm.

Old Jonas turned round fiercely, but he smiled directly, and whispered something to Bigley, who fell back with his head drooping, and in a dejected way.

"Now, Captain Duncan, if you please, you will come with us on board the lugger, and we'll run along to the second bay," said the lieutenant; "it will not take long."

"Sir," said my father, "I have replied to your questions as I was bound, but I am not bound to act as your pilot."

"Sir," said the lieutenant, "I demand this service of you as his majesty's servant. Kindly step on board the boat. Now, Uggleston."

I shall never forget old Jonas's fierce scowl as he walked down to the boat, into which he stepped, and remained in the bows, while my father went into the stern-sheets, and was followed by the lieutenant. The bare-legged sailors ran the light gig out, and sprang over the side, seized their oars and backed water, turned her, and began to row with a light springy stroke for the lugger.

"Big, old mate," I said, "I am so, so sorry."

"Don't talk to me," he groaned. "I never said anything: but I was always afraid of this."

"Don't be angry with father," I said appealingly. "He was obliged to speak."

"I can't talk to you now—I can't talk to you now," the poor lad groaned more than spoke, as we stood there close to where the waves came running in.

The lugger had a good many men on board as she lay out there, quite three hundred yards away, though it had seemed only one from high up in the Gap, and the cutter was quite half a mile from where we stood, and more to the east.

All at once Bigley lifted up both his arms, and stood with them outstretched for quite a minute.

"What are you doing that for?" I said.

He made no answer but remained in the same position, and kept so while I watched the boat rising and falling on the heaving tide, with every one distinctly visible in the evening sun.

As I have said the lugger lay with her bows straight towards the Gap; but all of a sudden she began to change her position, the bows swinging slowly round, and I realised that the rope by which she had swung had been cast off, for the buoy was plainly to be seen now several fathoms away.

Just then I saw old Jonas start up in the bows of the boat and clap his hands to his mouth, his voice coming clearly to us over the wave.

"You, Bill! You're adrift! Lower down that foresail, you swab, lower down that foresail! Throw her up in the wind!"

This sail had begun to fill, but a man ran to the tiller, and the lugger's position changed slowly, the sails flapping and the bows pointing gradually in our direction again.

All this while the men in the cutter's gig were pulling with all their might, and rapidly shortened the distance, till the bow man picked up a boat-hook, and stood ready to hold on.

It was all so clear against the black side of the lugger, that we missed nothing, and to my surprise, I saw old Jonas draw back as if to let the bow man pass him, and then there was a tremendous splash, the bow man was overboard, and old Jonas had made a leap driving the light gig away with his feet, catching the side of the lugger, and swinging himself aboard.

It was so quickly and deftly done that the cutter's gig was driven yards away, and Jonas was aboard before the lieutenant had recovered from his surprise.

Then the men pulled their hardest, and the distance between lugger and boat diminished fast, but as it did the sails began to fill, and the position altered, for a man had run to the tiller, while half a dozen more stood at the side, one of whom was old Jonas.

Bigley uttered a curious hissing noise as he caught my hand, while we stood straining our eyes, and as we stared wildly there was a cheer, and we saw the boat touch the lugger's side, the sailors and the lieutenant spring up, and they made a dash to leap on board.

Chapter Thirty Four
I seem to be an Enemy to an Old Friend

I don't know which of us lads gripped his companion's hand the harder as we saw the struggle begin.

"They'll half kill him," groaned Bigley; and then he remained panting there with his eyes starting as we saw the men on the lugger, headed by old Jonas, make a brave defence of their deck, being armed with capstan-bars and cudgels, while the revenue cutter's men had cutlasses which flashed in the evening sunshine as if they had been made of gold.

We could hear the sound of the blows, some sounding sharp, which we knew to be when the bars struck on the sides of the lugger; some dull, when they struck upon the men; while others made a peculiarly strange chopping noise, which was of course when sword encountered cudgel.

"It's all over," groaned Bigley at last, as the sailors seemed for the moment to have mastered the lugger; but just then I saw old Jonas tumble one man over the side into the boat, and another over the bulwark into the water with a great splash, and all the while the sails of the lugger were full, and the little vessel was beginning to move faster and faster through the water.

One of the men in the gig was still holding on by the bulwark as the struggle went on, but I suddenly saw old Jonas bring down a cudgel smartly upon his head, the blow sounding like a sharp rap, when the man fell back, and my father caught and saved him from going overboard.

The next moment there seemed to be a gap between the lugger and the gig, and we could see the heads of three men in the water swimming, and the next minute or two were occupied in dragging them in, two being sailors, and the other the lieutenant, who stood up in the stern-sheets and shook himself.

"Heave to!" he roared after the lugger; "heave to, or we'll sink you!"

"Ha, ha, ha, ha!" came in a mocking laugh, that from its hoarse harshness was evidently old Jonas's, and the lugger heeled over now and began to skim through the water.

"Why, they're going to run for it," I cried excitedly.

"But the cutter will sink them," panted Bigley. "Oh, father, father, why didn't you take me too?"

"Never mind that, Big," I cried. "Look, they're going to row to the cutter."

For the oars were dipping regularly now as the gig was turned towards the cutter, aboard which there was an evident change. Her main-sail, which had been shaking in the breeze, gradually filled; we saw the stay-sail run up, and the beautiful boat came gliding towards the gig so as to pick her up with her crew before going in pursuit.

"How quickly she sails!" cried Bigley. "Once they've got their men on board they'll go like the wind."

"But they haven't got them on board yet," I said, unable in spite of myself to help feeling a little sympathy for the man who was making such a bold effort to escape. "Why, they're taking my father prisoner instead of yours, Bigley. I hope they'll bring him back."

"Look!" cried Bigley; "father's getting up a topsail, and that'll help them along wonderfully."

"Look!" I cried; "the cutter's close up to the gig now."

"Hurrah!" cried Bigley; "there goes the topsail. Look how tight they've hauled the sheets, and how the lugger heels over."

"The cutter has the gig alongside," I cried as excitedly, for, though I did not want old Jonas caught, my father was there.

"Why, they're running out another spar," cried Bigley, "so as to hoist more sail. Look at the lugger, how she is spinning along!"

JONAS UGGLESTON'S LUGGER ESCAPES THE REVENUE CUTTER.

"Yes," I said; "but look at the cutter now!"

Bigley drew a long breath as he saw with me that the gig's crew were on board the cutter, and that the boat was being hoisted up, while, at the same time, with the speed to be seen on a man-of-war, even if it be so insignificant a vessel as a revenue cutter, sail was being hoisted, and she was off full chase.

First we saw the jib-sail run up and fill. Then up went the gaff topsail, and as it filled the cutter seemed to lie over, so that we could not see her deck, while the white water foamed away from her bows, and she left a long streak behind.

She was now well opposite to the Gap, down which the breeze blew straight. In fact the cutter seemed to have too much sail up, and rushed through the water at a tremendous rate.

"She'll soon catch the lugger going like that, Big," I said. "Look! Your father's not going straight away; he's going more off the land."

"Yes, because he knows what he's doing. He wants to get more out so as to catch the wind. You'll see in a few minutes the cutter won't go half so fast. Hah! I was afraid of that."

For just then there was a puff of smoke from the cutter, and we could just make out, by the way it dipped, the round shot that went ricochetting over the sea.

"That will stop him," I said gloomily.

"No, it will not," said Bigley angrily. "You don't know my father. He'll keep on as long as the lugger will swim."

I shook my head as I strained my eyes at the exciting chase going on before me.

Bigley was right, for in place of lowering sails in token of submission, the lugger ran out another from her bows, and kept on her rapid flight, altering her course though, so as not to offer so fair a mark to the cutter, and the cutter seemed to spit out viciously another puff of white smoke, and then there was a dull thud and an echo among the rocks.

We could not trace the course of the shot, but it evidently did not hit its mark, the first having probably been aimed ahead.

"They can't hit her," cried Bigley, clapping his hands. "Oh, I wish I was aboard."

"What, to be shot at?" I said.

"Let them shoot!" he cried. "I should like to be there. Now, then, what did I tell you? The cutter is not going half so fast now."

He was quite right, for, as the white-sailed vessel got beyond the entrance to the Gap, she was more and more under the shelter of the huge headland and the mighty cliffs that ran on for miles, and instead of lying over so that we half expected to see her keel, she rode more steadily and upright in the water, and her speed was evidently far less.

Another white puff of smoke, and another shot sent skipping after the lugger, but with what result we could not see. The firing made no difference, though, to the lugger, which continued its course towards the west, and Bigley gave me a triumphant look from time to time.

The firing had now become regular, and had brought down all the miners from the pit, and Mother Bonnet, to see the exciting chase. One climbed up the side of the Gap here, another there, and then higher and higher, and seeing the advantageous position they occupied I turned quickly to Bigley.

"Run and get the glass, Big," I said, "and then we'll climb right up to the top of the head."

Big shook his head.

"Father has it in the lugger," he said; "but let's climb up all the same."

We knew the ways of the great headland better than the people, and were about to start upon our climb when Mother Bonnet came up and caught Bigley's arm.

"Think they'll get away, Master Big?" she whispered with her face mottled with white blotches.

"I'm sure of it," he cried triumphantly. "It will soon be dark, too, and father will run in and out among the rocks where the cutter daren't follow."

"To be sure he will," said the old woman with a nod and a smile. "They will get away if—if—Oh! There goes that horrible gun again!"

The poor creature turned white and hurried away from us to get a better view of the chase, while Bigley and I climbed right up by degrees to the very highest point of the headland and sat upon the rocks watching the long chase, with the cutter, in spite of her superior rig and sailing powers, seeming to get no nearer to her prey, while the evening shadows were descending, and the two vessels kept growing more distant from the Gap.

The cutter continued firing at regular intervals, and once we thought that the lugger was hit. But if she was the shot made no difference to her attempts at escape; and though we stayed up there in our windy look-out, fully expecting to see her lying like a wounded bird upon the water with broken wing, no spar came down, and at last the fugitive and the pursuer had become specks in the distance, fading completely from our sight.

"It's no use to stay any longer," I said. "Let's go down now."

Bigley strained his eyes westward and seemed unwilling to stir.

"It will be so dark directly we shall have a job to get down," I said. "Your father's sure to get away."

"Yes," said Bigley; "they'll never catch him now. He'll get right away in the darkness."

Just then there was a familiar hail from below.

"Chowne, ahoy!" I responded; and as we reached to about half-way down we encountered Bob coming up panting and excited.

"You are a nice couple!" he began to grumble. "I do call it mean."

"What is mean?" I said.

"Why, to have all the fun to yourselves and never send for a fellow. If it hadn't been for the firing I shouldn't have known anything about it. I wouldn't have been so shabby to you."

"Why, I didn't think about you, Bob," I said.

"That's just like you, Sep Duncan. But I say, what a game!"

"I don't see much game in it," I said sadly. "Big's father is in the lugger, and mine—"

"In the cutter trying to catch him," cried Bob. "Oh, I say, what a game!"

"Look here!" said Bigley in a deep husky voice, "come down along with me, Sep, and take hold of my arm. I feel as if I wanted to fight."

I did as he asked me and we went down, with Bob very silent coming behind, evidently feeling that he had said too much.

Bigley went straight to the cottage, where Mother Bonnet was waiting for him and ready to catch him by the shoulder.

"There now, my dear! It's of no use for you to hang away," said the old woman. "I've got a nice supper ready, and you must eat or else you won't be able to help your poor father if he should come back."

"But he won't come back," said Bigley. "He will not dare."

"I don't know what he may not do when it's quite dark," said the old woman. "There! You come and sit down, and you too, my dears, for you must be famished."

Bigley yielded, and Bob and I were going away, but Bigley jumped up and stopped us.

"I'm not bad friends, Bob," he said, holding out his hand. "You didn't mean what you said, only when a fellow speaks against my father it hurts me, and—"

"I'm so sorry, Big," exclaimed Bob eagerly, and they shook hands.

I was glad, but still I was going away. Bigley stopped me though.

"I sha'n't eat if you don't," he said.

"But I can't now after what has happened," I said.

"It wasn't your fault," replied Bigley gloomily. "Your father was obliged to speak. Come and sit down."

I was so faint and exhausted that I yielded, and we three lads made a tremendous meal, to Mother Bonnet's great delight.

This ended, the inclination was upon us all to go fast asleep after the broken night we had passed; but Bigley jumped up and led the way to the door.

"Come along," he said. "The cutter will be back soon to clear off the cargo, and I want to hear what they say."

He walked out and we followed him to the beach, which was quite deserted; and we three lads began to walk up and down, too much excited to feel sleepy now, and kept on gazing out to sea for the returning cutter.

Chapter Thirty Five
Bigley does not Think his Father is a Dog

We went up to the cottage two or three times, to find Mother Bonnet keeping up the fire and the table laid for a second supper; and then we went back to the beach.

Everything was perfectly still. The mine people had long before gone to bed, but we watched on, feeling sure that something was going to happen; and so it was that about half-past twelve we heard oars, and soon after made out a boat which was being pulled by four men, while as soon as we were seen a voice cried from the boat:

"Ahoy! Who's there?"

"Father!" cried Bigley excitedly.

"Hush! Who's there?" said old Jonas as we felt quite stunned with surprise.

"Only Bob Chowne and Sep Duncan, father."

"No one else?"

"No one."

"Pull, my lads!" cried old Jonas; and as the boat grated on the beach he leaped ashore.

"I shall not be a quarter of an hour," he said. "Keep her afloat. Here, Bigley."

He caught his son's arm and they went up to the cottage together at a trot, and in less than a quarter of an hour they were back again, and old Jonas clapped me on the shoulder.

"Look here, Duncan," he said, "I always liked you, my boy, because you and Bigley were such mates."

"Are you going to take Big away, sir?" I said.

"No, boy, but I'm going to ask you to be a true mate to him still. He's going to stay with Mother Bonnet."

"I will, sir," I said.

"That you will, my lad," he cried, shaking hands. "Now, Bigley, no snivelling—be a man! Good-bye! I'll write."

He shook hands with his son, seized a bag they had brought down between them, and the next minute he was on board the boat and they disappeared into the darkness.

"How came he back again, Big?" I whispered as we listened to the beat of the oars which came from out of the gloom.

"Doubled back along with the French boat *La Belle Hirondelle*. They saw her about ten miles away."

"Was it the *Hirondelle* we saw last night!" I said.

"Yes," said Bigley shortly. "Be quiet."

"I think your father might have said good-bye to me, Bigley Uggleston," said Bob Chowne shortly. "I've done nothing to offend him. But it don't matter. Never mind."

There seemed to be nothing to wait for, but we hung about the beach till daylight, and then went in and had some breakfast, which Mother Bonnet, who was red-eyed with weeping, had ready for us, and then we went down to the beach again.

By this time the mine people were out once more, and they came and had a look, but there was nothing to see, and no one told the sturdy fellows or their families that Jonas Uggleston had been back. As for me, I only meant to tell my father when he returned.

So the mining people went to work, and we lads stood gazing out to sea, till suddenly Bob Chowne shouted:

"I can see the cutter."

He was quite right, for it proved to be the cutter, but there was no prize coming slowly behind; and when at last she came close in, the boat was lowered, and we saw my father step in and come ashore with the lieutenant, we were ready to meet them.

I wanted to speak to my father about what had happened in the night, but I had no opportunity, and it seemed that he had only been brought ashore so that he could go up to the mine, give some orders, and then return, when he was to show the lieutenant where the cave lay to which the smugglers had taken their cargo of contraband goods.

The lieutenant walked up to the mine works with my father, and as he evidently wished me to stop, I remained by the cutter's boat with my companions, and, boy-like, we began to joke the sailors for not catching the lugger.

They took it very good-temperedly, and laughed and said no one had been much hurt.

"He was too sharp for us," the coxswain said grinning; "and—my! How he did do the skipper over getting away. He's a cunning old fox, and no mistake."

"How did you lose the lugger?" I said.

"Oh, it was too dark to do any more, and she went right in among the rocks about Stinchcombe, where we were obliged to lie to and wait for daylight. He's a fine sailor, I will say that of him."

"What, your lieutenant?" I said.

"Oh, he's right enough. I meant smuggler Uggleston. He's got away, and it don't matter; we're bound to have a lot o' prize-money out of the cargo we're going to seize."

"Are you going to seize it this morning?" I asked.

"Yes, my lad; and here comes the skipper back along o' the old cappen."

They were close upon us already, and we boys looked eagerly at the lieutenant, longing to go with them, but not being invited of course.

It was too much for Bob Chowne though, who spoke out.

"I say, officer," he cried, "we three saw the cargo landed night before last."

"You three boys?"

"Yes," said Bob, "we were all there."

"Jump in then, all of you," said the lieutenant.

We wanted no further asking, and the men pushed off and rowed straight for the little bay, where in due time we arrived in face of the caves.

"And a good snug place too," said the lieutenant. "Good sandy bottom for running the lugger ashore. Nice game must have been carried on here. Come, Captain Duncan," he continued in a jocular tone, "you knew of this place years ago."

"I give you my word of honour, sir," replied my father coldly, "that I was quite unaware of even the existence of the caverns till a few days ago; and even then I did not know that they were applied to this purpose."

"Humph! And you so near!"

"You forget, sir, that my house is two miles and a half along the coast, and I have only lately purchased the Gap."

My father was evidently very much annoyed, but as a brother officer he felt himself bound in duty to put up with his visitor's impertinences, and accordingly he said very little that was resentful.

The men rowed on steadily, and as my father grew more reserved in his answers the officer turned to Bob Chowne.

"So you were there when the cargo was landed, were you?" he said.

"Yes," replied Bob coolly.

"Yes, *sir*," said the lieutenant sharply, "recollect that you are addressing an officer."

"Doctors don't say *sir* to everybody they meet," retorted Bob quickly.

"Doctors?"

"Well, my father's a doctor, and I'm going to be one, so it's all the same. I can make pills."

The lieutenant frowned and looked terribly fierce; but his men had burst into a hearty laugh at the idea of Bob making pills, so he turned it off with a contemptuous "Pooh!"

"Well," he said, "how came you to be there when the cargo was landed?"

"Thought you knew," said Bob; "we were shut in by the tide. Our boat had drifted away."

"You three boys?"

"Yes, and Captain Duncan," replied Bob.

"And what did the smuggler say to you?" said the lieutenant, turning sharply on me.

"Say to us, *sir*?" I replied.

"Yes, answer quickly, and don't repeat my words."

"I didn't know smugglers spoke to people they could not see. Hasn't my father told you that we were in hiding?"

The lieutenant was about to say something angry; but we were coming alongside of the bay, and my father stood up, very unwillingly as I could see by his manner, and guided the men so that they might avoid the rocks.

"I suppose we could almost run the cutter in here, Captain Duncan, eh?"

"Oh, yes, I think so," said my father, "on a very calm day. There is deep water all along, and a way could be found with ease."

"Such as the lugger people knew, of course. Steady, my lads, steady; that's it, on that wave."

The men followed his instructions, and the boat was beached pretty close to the entrance to one cavern, the water being high, and we all jumped out.

"Get the lantern!" cried the lieutenant; "and light it now, coxswain."

This was done, and two men being left in charge, the officer gave the order, swords were drawn, and he led the way in.

As he reached the mouth he placed two men as sentries at the entrance of the other hole where the water rained down, and turned to my father.

"You need not enter unless you like, captain. We may have a brush, for some of the scoundrels are perhaps still here. By the way, where's the ledge where you people were hidden?"

"Up there," said Bob promptly, and I saw the officer scan the place.

"What, coming?" said the lieutenant.

"Yes," replied my father; "but I think these lads ought to stand aside in case of danger."

"Yes," was the short response. "Here, boys, you stop here. You are not armed," he added with a sneering laugh.

"I only wish we had your father's cutlasses here, Sep," whispered Bob, "and we'd show them."

We stood back as the man went first with the lantern, closely followed by the lieutenant with his drawn sword; and we waited as the last disappeared in the opening, fully expecting to hear shots fired.

But all was perfectly still, and Bigley was creeping slowly nearer and nearer to the opening when Bob Chowne made a rush.

"Here, you chaps get all the fun," he exclaimed. "I shall go in and see."

The two sentries laughed, for they were big brown good-tempered looking fellows, and in we all three went, to find ourselves in quite a long rugged passage, running upward and opening into a big hollow at the end, where the lantern was being used to peer in all directions, till it was evident that nothing was there.

"We're in the wrong hole," said the officer. "Now, my lads, forward!"

He went sharply out into the daylight again, to where the two sentries were on guard, and entered quickly, passing through the dripping water closely followed by his men.

But there was not room for all, and he backed out directly.

"There's nothing here," he cried angrily.

"Try the other hole," said Bob, running to where we had found the narrow opening behind an outlying buttress of rock.

Bob stepped in first this time, the lieutenant following, and then the man with the lantern.

"Bravo, boy!" cried the lieutenant; "this is the place. Rather awkward, but here we are. Come along, my lads."

The sailors scrambled in as quickly as they could, and we all followed rather slowly down what was a jagged crack in the rock about two feet wide and sloping, so that one had to walk with the body inclined to the right.

This at the end of about twenty feet opened out into quite a large rough place, which contained some old nets and tins, along with about a dozen half rotten lobster-pots, but nothing more.

"There must be another place somewhere," cried the lieutenant after convincing himself that there was no inner chamber. "Lead on, coxswain, with the light."

The man went on, and we were left to the last, hearing one of them whisper to his mate:

"This here's a rum game, Jemmy; don't look like much prize-money after all."

By the time we boys were out the lieutenant had disappeared with the coxswain in the first cavern, and his men followed, leaving my father outside.

"Sep," he said, as I joined him, "where do you think the men went in?"

"That first place," I said decisively.

"Yes," said Bob Chowne; "that's the hole."

"So I felt certain," said my father; and Bigley stood aside looking on, with his forehead full of wrinkles.

Another minute and the lieutenant was out with his men, the officer furious with rage.

"Captain Duncan, are you in league with these smuggling dogs, or are you not?"

"What do you mean, sir?" cried my father haughtily.

"Well, look here, sir," cried the officer moderating his tone. "You've brought us here on a fool's errand. Where's this cargo that you saw landed?"

"How can I tell, sir? You appealed to me as an officer to show you where it was landed. It was here. The men were going in and out of that cave for two or three hours."

"Then there must be an inner place," cried the lieutenant, stamping his foot with rage. "Come and search again, my lads."

They disappeared for another ten minutes or so, and then came back with the officer fuming with passion.

"Fooled!" he exclaimed aloud, "fooled! Here, back to the boat."

Everybody embarked again, and the boat was rowed back in silence to the Gap, where we landed, and the lieutenant stepped out afterwards leaving his men afloat.

"Now, then, Captain Duncan," he said, "before I go let me tell you that I shall report your conduct at headquarters. I consider that I have been fooled, sir, fooled."

"I had thought of doing the same by you, sir," retorted my father coldly; "but I do not think it worth while to quarrel with an angry disappointed man, nor yet to take further notice of your hasty words."

"What do you mean, sir? What do you mean?" blustered the lieutenant.

"Ha, ha, ha, ha, ha, ha! I see! Here's a game!" roared Bob Chowne, dancing about in the exuberance of his delight.

"What do you mean, sir? How dare you!" roared the officer turning upon Bob.

"Why, I know," cried Bob. "What a game! Don't you see how it was?"

"Will you say what you mean, you young idiot?" cried the lieutenant.

"Oh, I say, it wasn't me who was the idiot," cried Bob bluntly. "Why, you let smuggler Uggleston dodge back in the night. He was here about twelve or one, and he and his men must have been and fetched all the stuff away again, while you and your sailors were miles away in the dark."

"Sep," cried my father, as the lieutenant stood staring with wrath, "was Jonas Uggleston back here in the night?"

"Yes, father," I replied.

"And you did not tell me?"

"I have had no opportunity, father; and I did not think anything of it. He was here about one."

"That's it, then," cried my father. "Lieutenant, he has been too sharp for you. I noted that the sand was a good deal trampled. He has been back with his men and cleared out the place in your absence."

The lieutenant stood staring as if he could not comprehend it all for a minute or two, and then flushing with rage he stamped about.

"The scoundrel! The hound! The thief!" he roared. "I'll have him yet, though, and when I do catch him I'll hang him to the yard-arm, like the dog he is."

"Dog yourself," cried a fierce voice that we did not recognise, it was so changed; and Bigley struck the lieutenant full in the face with the back of his hand. "My father is a better man than you."

Chapter Thirty Six
The Lugger's Return

The lieutenant staggered back from the effects of the blow. But recovering, he whipped out his sword and made at Bigley, who hesitated for a moment and then dashed up the cliff-side, dodging in and out among the rocks, and he was twenty yards away before the lieutenant had gone ten, and gaining at every leap.

Seeing that he could not catch him, the lieutenant drew a pistol from his belt and would have fired, but my father caught his arm.

"Stop, sir," he cried; "he is but a boy."

By this time the coxswain and four men had leaped ashore and run to their leader's side.

"Up and bring him back," shouted the lieutenant fiercely, and wresting his arm free he fired at Bigley, but where the bullet went nobody could say, it certainly did not go very near Bigley, who knew every rock and crevice on the side of the headland, and wound his way in and out, and higher and higher, leaving his pursuers far behind.

"Forward! Quick!" roared the lieutenant; but it did not seem to me that the sailors got on very quickly, for they kept on losing ground, and it was so hopeless an affair at last that they were called off, and descended to follow their officer to the boat.

He did not come near us where we stood in a group, and we saw him spring into the gig; but all at once he leapt out again and walked swiftly to us.

"Here," he said authoritatively, as if he had forgotten something, and he pointed to the cottage. "Whose house is that?"

"Mine," said my father promptly.

The lieutenant looked disappointed, and turned sharply back again.

"It is my house," said my father as soon as the officer was out of hearing, and as if speaking to himself. "If he had said, 'who lives there?'

Devon Boys | 233

it would have been a different thing. He would have burnt and destroyed everything."

We stood watching the gig as the lieutenant returned and it was pushed off. It was not long reaching the cutter, whose sails were hoisted rapidly, and, filling as they were sheeted home, the graceful vessel began to glide away from the shore, and soon afterwards was careening over and heading for the west in pursuit of the lugger or luggers, whichever it might be.

"There, my lads," said my father, "you may go and look for your companion. He can come down safely now."

"Will the cutter come back, father?" I said.

"I daresay it will, to see if Uggleston's lugger returns; but I don't think the lugger will, and certainly Uggleston will not dare to return here to live for some time to come."

"Then what's to become of Bigley?" cried Bob Chowne.

"His father must settle that, my lad."

"But till he does, father?" I said. "Will he stay here?"

"Certainly, my boy. Why not? His father rents the cottage, and his son has a perfect right there."

"You will not turn him out, then, because his father is a smuggler?"

"I always try to be a just man, Sep," replied my father quietly.

"Ahoy!" came from high up over our heads, and, looking up there, we could see Bigley standing on the highest part of the headland waving his cap.

"Come down!" shouted Bob and I in a breath, and he heard us, gave his cap another wave, and disappeared.

He was not long in scrambling down to us, my father stopping till he came up looking very much abashed.

"Well, sir," said my father sternly. "What have you to say for yourself for striking one of his majesty's officers?"

Bigley's manner changed directly, his face flushed and he set his teeth as he raised his head boldly.

"He called my father a dog and a thief," cried Bigley fiercely, "and—and—I don't want to offend you, Captain Duncan, but I couldn't stand by and hear him without doing something."

"And you did do something, my lad," said my father, holding out his hand—"a very risky something. But there, I'm not going to say any more about it. Now, tell me; your father has given you some instructions, I suppose?"

Bigley hesitated a moment.

"Yes, sir; he said that he should not be able to come back here, but he would write to me."

"Yes; go on."

"And that I was to stay with Mother Bonnet as long as you would let me, and when you turned us out, we were to take lodgings in Ripplemouth."

"When I turned you out!" said my father angrily. "Pish! Ah, well, stop till I turn you out then. There, I must go now, Sep; this will be a broken day for you. Bring your two friends over to the Bay, and we'll have tea and dinner all together."

He turned off and left us, but I saw him give Bigley a very friendly nod and smile as he went away, and I felt sure that he rather admired what Bigley had done, though he kept up the idea of being very fierce and indignant with him for striking an officer of the royal navy.

As soon as we were well alone Bob Chowne threw himself on the ground and began to laugh and wipe his eyes.

"Oh, what a game!" he cried, as he rolled about. "Didn't old Big run?"

"Enough to make anybody run when a bullet was after him," I said.

"But how he did go up the rocks. Just like a big rabbit. I say, Big, you were frightened."

"Yes, that I was," said Bigley frankly; "I don't know when I felt so scared. Made sure he would hit me, and then that the sailors would cut me down with their swords."

This disappointed Bob, who had fully expected to hear a denial of the charge of fear, and he sat up and stared at the speaker, who turned to me then.

"Why, Sep," he said, "they must have worked hard in the night to get all those things away. Do you know, I'm sure that must have been the *Hirondelle*. I wonder how they managed to get off."

"I know," I said suddenly.

"Yah! Not you," cried Bob. "Hark at old cock Solomon, who knows everything."

"I don't care what you say," I replied. "I'm sure this is how they've got away."

"Well, let's hear," said Bob, and Bigley's eyes flashed with eagerness.

"Why, they haven't got away at all," I said. "They wouldn't dare to go down Channel after getting the cargo out of the cave, for fear of meeting the cutter just at daybreak."

"And you think they've gone up towards Bristol?" cried Bigley excitedly.

"Yes," I said; "and they are lying up somewhere over yonder on the Welsh coast till to-night, when they'll be off again."

"That's it," said Bigley. "I'm sure that's it."

"I don't believe it," said Bob sharply. "And if it is true, I'm ashamed of you both. Here's Sep Duncan taking part with the smugglers, and old Big hitting the officers in the eye, and bragging about his father. I shall look out for some fresh mates, that's what I shall do."

"Come and have some tea and dinner first, Bob," I said mockingly.

"Yes, I'll have some food first, for I'm getting hungry. My, what a game, though! How old Big did run when the lieutenant was going to give him a pill! Ha, ha, ha!"

We strolled about the shore, and then went into the cottage for a bit, and that afforded Bob another opportunity for a few sneers about this being Bigley's home now, addressing him as the master of the house, bantering him about being stingy with his cider, and finally jumping up as he saw my father coming down from the mine, and then we all went over to the Bay to our evening meal.

That night Bigley and I went part of the way home with Bob, and then I walked part of the way home with Bigley in the calm and solitude of the summer darkness.

We walked along the cliff path, and were about half-way to the Gap when Big caught me by the arm and pointed down below, about a quarter of a mile from the cliff, where, stealing along in the gloom, I caught sight of the sails of a small vessel, and directly after of those of another gliding on close at hand. They were so indistinct at first that I could see but little. Then I could make out that they were both luggers by their rig, and that one of them had three masts and the other only two.

Chapter Thirty Seven
Suspicions of Danger

Like all bits of excitement the coming of the cutter was followed by a time of calm. Bigley seemed to have settled down to a regular life at the cottage, spending part of his days looking out to sea, and the other part up at the mine, where my father seemed now to give him always a very warm welcome.

We saw the revenue cutter off the Gap now and then, and we had reason to believe that the crew had landed and thoroughly examined the caves again, but we saw nothing of them; it was only from knowing that one evening the little vessel lay off the shore about a mile to the west of the Gap, and Bigley went along the shore at next low tide, and said afterwards that he thought he could make out footprints, but the tide had washed over everything so much that he was not sure.

He heard no news of his father as week after week rolled by, till all at once came a letter from Dunquerque, inclosing some money, and telling him that he had got away safely, and was quite well.

"He said," Bigley told me in confidence, for he did not show me the letter; "he said that if your father behaved badly to me I was to go away at once with Mother Bonnet and take lodgings at Ripplemouth, just as he told me; but I don't think I shall have to do that."

I laughed as he told me this, and then asked him if he was going to write back to his father.

"No," said Bigley; "he says I am not to write, because it might give people a clue to where he is. I don't care, now I know that he is quite well."

Then the time glided on, with everybody at the mine leading the busiest of busy lives. I was there every day, and the men won the lead, others smelted it and cast it into pigs, then the pigs were remelted and the silver extracted and ingots cast, which were stored up, after being stamped and numbered, down in the strong cellar beneath the counting-house floor.

I did a great deal: sometimes I was down in the mine, whose passages began to grow longer; sometimes I was entering the number of pigs of lead that were taken over to Ripplemouth, and shipped at the little quay for Bristol; sometimes I was watching the careful process by which the silver was obtained from the lead, and learning a good deal about the art, while Bigley seemed to be growing more and more one of us, and worked with the greatest of earnestness over the various tasks I had to undertake.

"No news of old Jonas, father?" I said one day as we were walking along the cliff path to the mine, a lugger in the offing having brought him to my mind.

"No, Sep," said my father; "but I'm afraid that we shall have a visit from him some day, and a very unpleasant one."

"Why?" I asked.

"Because he will never forgive me about that cave business. I saw the look he gave me, my boy. He does not seem to have any very great ideas of the meaning of the word honour, and he evidently could not see then that I was bound to state what I had seen."

"But do you think he will owe you a grudge for that, father?"

"I am sure of it, my boy. He never forgave me for buying the Gap, and now I'm afraid this exposure of his smuggling tricks has made matters ten times worse."

"Oh, I hope not, father," I said eagerly.

"So do I, my boy; but I have very little faith in him, and I always dwell in expectation that some day or other, or some night or another, he will land with a strong party, and come up here to work all the mischief he can—perhaps carry off all our silver."

"But, father," I exclaimed, "that would be acting like a pirate."

"Well, Sep, there is not much difference between a pirate and a smuggler. They are both outlaws, and not very particular about what they do."

"Oh, but I hope we shall have no trouble of that sort, for Bigley's sake."

"So do I, Sep, but I feel this, that we are not safe, for we have made a dangerous enemy—one who can descend upon us at any time, and then get away by sea. What can we do if he makes such an attack?"

"Fight," I said bluntly. "We have plenty of arms, and the men will do just what they are bid."

"Yes," said my father; "but I should be deeply grieved for there to be any bloodshed. I've known what it is in my early days, Sep, and in spite of all that has been said about honour and glory there is always an unpleasant feeling afterwards, when in cool blood you think about having destroyed your fellow-creatures' lives."

"Yes, father," I said; "there must be, and we don't want to do it; but if anyone comes breaking into the mine premises to steal, they must take the consequences."

"Yes, Sep," said my father sternly, "they must, for I have enough of the old fighting-man left in me to make me say that I should not give up quietly if I was put to the proof."

I thought a good deal about my father's words, but though I regularly made Bigley my confidant, and told him pretty well everything, I did not tell him that, for I knew it would make him very uncomfortable, and besides it seemed such a horrible idea for us to have to be fighting against his father — our men against his.

The time went on, and we kept on hearing about the French war, but we seemed to be, away there in our quiet Devon combe, far from all the noise and turmoil, and very little of the news excited us.

We knew when there was a big fight, and when one side got the better of the other; but to read the papers we always appeared to get the victory. But, as I say, it did not seem to concern us much, only when the country traffic was a bit disturbed, and our lead began to accumulate for want of the means of sending it away.

"I don't so much mind the lead, Sep," my father used to say; "what I mind is the silver."

This was when the store beneath the counting-house became charged with too valuable a collection of ingots; and the second time this happened my father suddenly altered his arrangements.

"I can't rest satisfied that all is safe," he said, "when I am away at the Bay, and this place is only depending upon locks and keys."

"What shall you do then, father?" I asked. "Have a watchman!"

He nodded.

"Who? Old Sam?"

"No," he said; "ourselves, Sep, my lad. It will not be so comfortable, but while the country is so disturbed we will come and live over here."

No time was lost, and in two days the upper rooms of the counting-house and store had been filled with furniture, and Kicksey came over for the day, and went back at night, after cooking and cleaning for us.

As my father said, it was not so comfortable as being at home, but we were ready enough to adapt ourselves to circumstances; and any change was agreeable in those days.

Bigley was delighted, for it robbed his rather lonely life of its dulness, and he never for a moment realised why the change had been made.

But though we were always on the spot, my father relaxed none of his old preparations. Every other day there was an hour's drill or sword practice. Sometimes an evening was taken for the use of the pistols; and, by degrees, under my father's careful instructions, the little band of about twelve men had grown into a substantial trustworthy guard of sturdy fellows, any one of whom was ready to give a good account of himself should he be put to the test.

At first my father had been averse to Bigley drilling with us, but he raised no obstacle, for he said to me, "We can let him learn how to use the weapons, Sep, but it does not follow that he need fight for us."

"And I'm sure he would not fight against us, father," I said laughing.

So Bigley grew to be as handy with the cutlass as any of the men, and no mean shot with the pistol.

As for Bob Chowne, he came over and drilled sometimes, and he was considered to be our surgeon—that is, by Bigley and me—but he was not with us very often, for his father kept him at work studying medicine, meaning him to be a doctor later on; but, as Bob expressed it, he was always washing bottles or making pills, though as a fact neither of these tasks ever came to his share.

Four months—five months—six months had gone by since the adventure with the cutter, and Bigley had only had two or three letters sending him money, and saying that his father was quite well, but there was not a word of returning; and it struck me old Jonas must have had means of knowing that his son was still in the old cottage, or he would not have gone on sending money without having an answer back.

The rumours about the war seemed to affect us less than ever, and I was growing so accustomed to my busy life that I thought little of my old amusements, save when now and then I went out for an evening's fishing with Bigley, the old boat having been brought over from Ripplemouth, none the worse for its trip.

The mine went on growing more productive, and, in spite of the great expenses, it seemed as if my father would become a wealthy man. Lead was sent one way, silver another, and when the latter accumulated, as we were on the spot, my father dismissed his anxiety, and we were gradually becoming lulled into a feeling of repose, save when Bigley talked about his father, and then once more a little feeling of doubt and insecurity would slip in, as might have been the case in the olden times when the people near shore learned that some Saxon or Danish ship was hovering about the coast.

Chapter Thirty Eight
The Landing of the French

It was nine months now since the scene, at the little bay, when one soft spring evening Bigley and I were walking slowly back to the Gap, after seeing Bob Chowne part of the way home to Ripplemouth. The feeling of coming summer was in the air, the birds were singing in the oak woods their last farewell to the day, and from time to time we startled some thrush and spoiled his song.

Every now and then a rabbit gave us a glance at his furry coat as he sprang along, but soon it grew so dark that all we saw after each rustle was the speck of white which indicated his cottony tail, and soon even that was invisible.

The thin sharp line of the new moon hung low in the west, and the sea had quite a steely gleam in the dying day, while the stars were peeping out and beginning to look at themselves in the glassy surface of the sea.

Here and there we could see the coasting vessels going up and down the Channel, and just beneath the sinking moon there was a larger vessel coming up with the tide, but it was getting too dark to make out what it was. We kept along by the cliff path, and as we came to the descent that led to the cottage Bigley and I parted, little thinking what an eventful night it was to prove.

"You'll come up by and by," I shouted, when he was about half-way down; and he sent back a cheery reply that he would, as I went on along the Gap.

I found my father seated before his books entering some statement by the light of a candle, and as I came in he thrust the book from him wearily.

"Oh, there you are, then," he said good-humouredly. "Look here, young fellow, I don't see why I should go on worrying and toiling over this mine just to make you well off. I was happy and comfortable enough without it, and here am I wearing myself out, getting no pleasure and no change, and all for you."

"Sell it then, father," I said. "I don't want you to work so hard for me. I don't want to be rich. Give it up."

"No," he said smiling; "no, Sep. It gives me a great deal of care and anxiety, but I do not mind. The fact is, Sep, I was growing fat and rusty, and loosing my grip on the world. A do-nothing life is a mistake, and only fit for a pet dog, and him it kills. I wanted interesting work, and here it is, and I am making money for you at the same time."

"But I don't think I want much money, father," I said.

"Maybe you will when you grow older."

"I wish I could help you better," I said.

"Help me? Why, I am quite satisfied with you, my boy. You help me a great deal. There, put away those books, and let us have some supper. I find we have nearly eight thousand ounces of silver down below here, and it's far too much to have in our charge. We must get it away, Sep, as soon as we can."

"What would eight thousand ounces be worth?" I said.

"Somewhere about two thousand pounds, my lad. But there, let's have some supper, and then I should like to have a pipe for half an hour in the soft fresh air."

A tray was already waiting upon a side-table, and bringing it to occupy the place where the books had lain, we sat down and ate a hearty meal before we had done, after which I lifted the tray aside, and handed my father the tobacco jar.

In a few minutes he began to fill his pipe, and when he had lit it, I sat watching him and noticed how the soft thin smoke began to curl about his face, and float up between me and the row of cutlasses and pistols with the belts that were arranged along the wall.

"Now, let's have ten minutes' fresh air before we go to bed," he said rising. "You don't want to come, I suppose."

"Oh, yes, I'll come," I replied, and I stepped out with him into the soft transparent night.

"Ah, that's delicious!" he exclaimed as we walked a little way down the Gap, and then struck up the path leading to the high cliff track.

It was very dark, but at the same time clear; and as we paused after a time there were the lights below us in the new cottages, while above the stars shone out brilliantly and twinkled as if it was about to be a frost.

"What a calm peace there is over everything!" said my father thoughtfully. "Why, Sep, my very weariness seems to be a pleasure, it is so full of the promise of rest."

"I'm tired too," I said. "I've been walking a good way to-day. How plainly you can hear the sea!"

"Yes, the wind must be from the north. But how soft, and sweet, and gentle it is! What is that?"

"What?" I replied listening, for I had not detected a sound.

"That noise of trampling feet. Don't you hear?"

I listened.

"Yes, it is as if some people were coming along from the beach."

"What people should be coming along from the beach?" exclaimed my father in an excited manner.

"Or is it the murmur of the waves, father?" I said.

"No," he whispered after listening; "there are people coming, and that was a sharp quick order. Run down to the cottages and warn the foreman. Follow out the regular orders. You know. If it is a false alarm it will not matter, for it will be exercise for getting the men together against real trouble."

"Right, father," I said, and I was just about to run off to give the alarm to the foreman, who would alarm another man while I went to a fresh house. Then there would be four of us to alarm four more, who would run up to the rendezvous while we alarmed four more, and so the gathering would be complete, and the men at the counting-house and armed in a very few minutes.

I say I was just about to rush off, when a dark figure made a rush at us, and caught hold of my father's arm.

"Quick, captain!" he whispered. "The French. Landed from a big sloop. Coming up the Gap."

"Are you sure?" said my father in a low voice.

The answer came upon the soft breeze, and I stopped for no more, but ran down the slope as hard as I could go, dashed into the foreman's cottage, gave the alarm, and he leaped up, his wife catching up her child and following to go along the Gap, as already arranged, the woman knowing that the others would follow her so as to get to a place of safety in case of the enemy getting the upper hand.

It proved, as my father had trusted, but a matter of very few minutes before four men were running to the counting-house to receive the weapons ready for them, and for eight to follow, while the women and children were being hurried from the cottages and away inland.

The foreman and I were in front of the six men we were bringing, and as we ran and neared the dim grey-looking building that was to be our fort, we could hear the coming of what seemed to be quite a large body of men, who were talking together in a low voice, while from time to time a sharp command was uttered.

Then, all at once, and just as we reached the counting-house, there was a fresh order, and the sounds ceased, not a voice to be heard, and the tramp completely hushed.

"What did it mean?" I asked myself, as a curious sensation of excitement came over me, for it seemed that the strangers, whoever they were, perhaps the French, as Bigley had said, had halted to fire at us as we rushed to the counting-house door, and I fully expected to see the flashes of their muskets, and hear the reports and the whistling of the bullets.

But no, all remained still, and we paused at the door to let the others pass in first, and then, with a wonderful sense of relief, I leaped in, and heard the door closed behind quickly, but with hardly a sound.

It was a curious sensation. The moment before I felt in terrible danger. Now I felt quite safe, for I was behind strong walls, though in reality I was in greater danger than before.

There was no confusion, no hurry. The drilling had been so perfect, and my father had been for so long prepared for just such an emergency as this, that everything was done with a matter-of-fact ease.

Already as we reached the door the four first comers had been armed; now as the men entered they crossed over to the other side, and cutlass, pistols, and a well-filled cartouche-box were handed to each, and he took them, strapped on his belt, and then fell in, standing at ease.

"All armed?" said my father then, as we stood in the dark.

There was no answer—a good sign that everyone was supplied.

"The women and children gone?" said my father then.

No answer again.

"Load!" said my father.

Then there was a rustling noise, the clicking of ramrods, a dull thudding, more clicking, and silence.

"Now," said my father, "no man to fire until I give the word. Trust to your cutlasses, and I daresay we can beat them off. Ready?"

There was a dead silence.

"I would light the candles," said my father in a low firm voice, "but it would be helping the enemy, if enemy they are. Who's that?"

"It is I, sir, Bigley," said a familiar voice.

"I had forgotten you. What is it?"

"I have no weapons, sir."

"No, of course not. Boy, you cannot fight."

"Why not, sir?"

"Because—because—" I was close to them, and they were speaking in a low tone; "because—" said my father again.

"Because you think I should be fighting against my father," said Bigley sharply; "but I'm sure, sir, that it is not so."

"How do I know that?" said my father.

Rap, rap, rap, came now at the door, and a voice with a decided French accent, a voice that sounded familiar to me, said:

"Ees any boady here?"

"There, sir, it is the French."

"I don't know that," said my father. Then: "Stand fast, my lads."

"Ees any boady here?" said the same voice.

"Yes. Who's there?" said my father.

"Aha, it is good," came from outside. "My friends and bruders have make great meestakes and lose our vays. Can you show us to ze Ripplemouts towns?"

"Straight down to the sea and along by the cliff path east," said my father shortly.

"Open ze doors; I cannot make myselfs to hear."

My father repeated his instructions; there was a low murmur outside; and then there was a sharp beating on the door, as if from the hilt of a sword.

"What now?" cried my father.

"Le Capitaine Dooncane," cried a sharp fierce voice.

"Well?" said my father. "I am Captain Duncan."

"Open this door," said the same voice, speaking in French.

"What if I refuse?" said my father in the same tongue.

"If you refuse it will be broken down—directly."

"Is it the war?" said my father mockingly.

"It is the war," was the reply. "Open, and no harm will be done to you. Resist, and there will be no quarter. Is it surrender?"

"Monsieur forgets that he is talking to an English officer," said my father. "Stand back, sir; we are well-armed and prepared."

There was a low murmur of voices outside, and my father exclaimed:

"Sep, Bigley, upstairs with you and six men. Two of you to each window, and beat down with your cutlasses all who try to board. We'll keep the doors here. Now, my lads, tables and chairs against the doors. You'll find the wickets handy. I thought so; they're at the back door already."

He darted to the back room, helped place a table against the door, mounted upon it, and as the blows of a crowbar were heard, he placed a pistol to the little wicket in the panel high up, and fired a shot to alarm the attacking party.

The blows of the crowbar ceased, and a low suppressed yell from many voices broke out from all round the little stone-built place.

"That has quieted them for the moment," said my father; and, applying his eye to an aperture made for the purpose, he inspected the attacking force.

"French marines," he said quietly. "Well, my lads, they're outside and we are in. If they leave us alone we will not injure them, if they attack they must take the consequences. It is war time; they have landed, and we are fighting for our homes and all belonging to us. Will you fight?"

There was a low dull growl at this, uttered it seemed by every man present, and as my father's words had been distinctly heard upstairs, the men with Bigley and me joined in.

"That's good," said my father. "I thought so. Now once more trust to your strong aims and cutlasses. A couple of shots and then swords. They don't want loading again. If they break in we must retreat upstairs. If they prove too much for us and force their way up, we must hold out as long as we can, and then retreat by the north window and back up the west side of the valley among the big stones; but no retreat till I give the word. Now, my lads, do you want anything to make you fight?"

"Only the orders, captain," said the foreman, "or the French beggars to come on."

"All in good time. What are they doing?" said my father. "One shot can't have scared them off. Ah, the cowards! I expected as much."

For just then a dull light shone in through the window, and made every bar clear. The dull light became brighter, and the Frenchmen set up a cheer.

"They've fired the big shed roof, sir," said the foreman.

"Father," I cried down the stairs, "they have fired Sanders's cottage."

"Curse 'em," growled the foreman. "I'll make pork crackling of somebody's skin for that."

"Now they've gone on to the next cottage," cried Bigley.

"They're firing all the cottages," cried another of the men, and now the growl that rose from our little force was furious and fierce, and full of menace against the enemy, who had done this to give them ample light as I suppose.

"Never mind, my lads, they have forgotten that it will make it easier for us," said my father. "But hold your fire. It will be wanted here."

We could see each other plainly now, and it became necessary to look out cautiously, for fear of offering ourselves as targets for the Frenchmen's shots.

We could see that about a dozen well-armed men were in front, and another group of as many at the back of the house; but they were paying little heed to us for the moment, being engaged in watching their companions, who were running from cottage to cottage, firing them by thrusting torches under the thatch, and shouting and chattering to each other, as if these acts of wanton destruction were so much amusement in which they had delight.

Over and over again men made their pistols click, and were ready in their rage to send bullets flying amongst the wreckers of their homes; but my father uttered a low warning.

"Stand fast. Not till I say *fire*. Never mind your homes, my lads, we'll soon raise better ones, and your wives and children are all safe. Wait."

There was a low growl as if so many bull-dogs were being held back from their prey, and once more all was silent within.

Then there was a good deal of chattering and rushing, and the firing parties came back to where their companions were waiting, and we knew by the next order given that our time had come.

Chapter Thirty Nine
Desperate Times

In my heat and excitement I wondered that my father did not order his little company of men to begin firing at a time when every shot would tell, for there was a feeling of rage within me, roused by the wanton destruction of the cottages and every portion of the works that would burn; but I had not learned all my lessons then, and how a just and brave man, whether soldier or sailor, shrinks from destroying life until absolutely obliged.

My father came upstairs for a minute about the time when I was thinking this the most, and I could see a peculiarly hard stern look in his eyes as the fire flashed through the window upon his face.

"Mind: no firing," he said, "until they attack, and I give the word."

I felt afterwards how right he was, but then it seemed almost cowardly.

I soon altered my opinion, for all at once the French leader came up to the door and struck it with the hilt of his sword, as he exclaimed in French:

"Now, Captain Duncan, surrender!"

No reply was given.

"Open this door and pass out the whole of the silver bars you have there," was the next command, and this time my father answered:

"Come and take them if you can—*si vous osez*," he added in French.

There was no more delay. A couple of men were ordered to the front with iron bars, and they began to batter the door heavily, but without any further effect than to chip off splinters and make dints.

The men were called off, the rest standing ready to fire at anyone who should show a face at the windows, but we gave them no opportunity, for my father whispered:

"They are sixty. We are only just over a dozen. Wait, men, wait."

"What are they doing, Big?" I whispered to my companion, for he was in a better post for observations than myself.

"I can't quite see," he whispered back. "They've got a bag of something, and they're bringing it to the door."

I looked out quickly.

"Powder!" I exclaimed, and then I ran to the head of the stairs and called down to my father: "They are going to blow in the door with powder."

"Good!" said my father coolly, and issuing an order or two he drew all his men together into the back room. "Stay where you are, Sep," he whispered; "the explosion will not touch you, only, if we are hard pressed afterwards, come down with your men and take the enemy in the rear."

I felt my heart swell with pride at being treated like this, and the nervous sensation of dread grew less.

"Sooner the better, Master Sep," said one of the workmen. "Better keep away from the window, sir."

"No," I replied, "I must see what they are doing."

I felt that I must, and going to the window I stood upon a chair, and, keeping out of sight, looked down from the upper corner just in time to see a man run back from the door to join his companions, several of whom held rough torches of oakum steeped in tar.

"What are they doing, Big?" I whispered.

"That fellow has just laid a powder-bag by the door. But, Sep, you can't see any Englishmen there, can you?"

"No," I said hastily; "but I'm sure that's the French skipper Gualtière standing to the left of the French captain."

"So it is," whispered Bigley. "I thought I knew the face. Look out!"

"What are they going to do?"

"The men are being drawn back, all but the fellows with the lights, and one of them is coming forward to light the powder. Yes; now all the others are retiring."

"I can see," I whispered. "Now I can see the man with the torch. I say, will it blow the place up?"

"I don't know," said Bigley in a low whisper; "but I feel horribly frightened."

"So do I," I whispered back; "but don't let's show it, Big."

"I won't," he said sturdily.

Just then the man who had approached slowly made a dash in close to the house, and I was thinking that somebody ought to have shot him down when he dashed back again, and his friends received him with a loud shrill cheer.

As the cheer died away there was a low hissing noise from outside, and I knew it was the fuse burning, and then we all shrank together to the farthest corner of the room, waiting in the most painful suspense for the explosion, which we knew must follow, but which seemed as if it would never come.

It was only a matter of so many seconds, but they seemed to be minutes of terrible suspense, before there was a flash, the air seemed to have been sucked out of the room, and then, in the midst of a terrific roar, the floor was lifted up, and one end then fell, so that we all slid down into the room below in the midst of splinters, plaster, dust, and broken joists, just as the Frenchmen uttered a yell, and came dashing towards the open door.

What followed was one scene of wild confusion. It seemed that my father and his men came dashing out of the back room, and we were seized and dragged over the heap of broken wood-work and plaster, to be placed behind it, where we struggled to our feet, and then, in the midst of the clouds of blinding dust and choking gunpowder smoke, everybody made a breast-work of the damaged wood, and received the charge of the French sailors with pistol-shots and blows from the cutlasses.

This proved so effective that they fell back, running out as fast as they came in, and my father took advantage of the lull to have a few pieces of furniture dragged forward, and laid upon the heap of refuse so as to give us a better breast-work to fight behind.

"Hurt, Sep?" cried my father.

"No," I replied, "only shaken."

"That's well. Keep more back, my boy. Now, lads, cutlasses; here they come!"

There was a yell and a rush, the clashing of steel, with shouts and groans, and the Frenchmen were beaten back again.

"Time for breathing, my lads," cried my father, as we stood there in the darkness with the light full upon our enemies as they gathered at a short distance from the shattered doorway. "Who's hurt?"

"No one much, captain," growled the foreman. "A few chops and scratches. Here they are!"

For just then there was a yell, and the enemy rushed at us, coming in a little column, and this time led by an officer.

They could only come in two at a time; but, as they darkened the doorway and made their rush, they spread out as they entered like a fan right and left, and once more the groans, yells, and blows rang out.

It was clearer now, for the smoke and dust had floated out, and I could see something of the desperate fight that was going on, with men falling, and others of the Frenchmen from behind filling their places, for they kept on thronging in through the open doorway, till the counting-house was densely packed, and those behind literally drove their companions forward, till the rough breast-work was beaten and trampled down, and our little party forced back towards the wall that separated us from the inner room, in which there was a doorway leading into a back place, opening on to the cliff slope.

I can't pretend to describe what took place accurately. All I know is, that in the midst of a scene of shouting, yelling, and clashing cutlasses, I found myself crushed against the back wall with my sword above my head, and my ribs seeming to give way, as I was pinned there helplessly, till all at once there was a tremendous crash, and we were all driven backwards in a heap, friends and enemies together.

For the wood-work partition, already damaged by the force of the explosion, had given way, and we were precipitated into the back room.

What followed I hardly know, for as the men struggled up from the ruin the fight began again, and the result was that I found myself with my father and five men in the little back place of all, where the door opened out into the valley; but of course it was locked and barricaded inside, and the door into the back room was held by my father, the foreman, and two others, who were keeping about a dozen Frenchmen at bay, yelling and cutting and thrusting at them.

"Sep! Here! Quick!" my father shouted, without turning his head, for the enemy kept him occupied parrying their cuts and points.

"I am here, father," I said, getting close behind him.

"Right. Stand firm, my lads!" said my father. "We're beaten, but we must retreat in order. Ah, would you?"

This last was to a Frenchman who dashed in at him, but only to have his thrust parried, and to go down with an upward cut which disabled his sword arm.

"Sep," he whispered then, "open the back door. Be ready. We must now make a dash for the rocks. You lead; I'll keep the rear. Mind, my lads," he said to the stanch group about him, "keep together. If you separate you are lost. You'll be cut down or prisoners before you can raise a hand."

These words were all said in a jerky way in the midst of plenty of cutting and foining; for, though the Frenchmen did not attempt to pass the doorway, they kept on making fierce thrusts at us, though with little result.

I crept back and unfastened the door silently, so as not to draw the enemy's attention, and, holding my sword ready, I peered out, the noise going on drowning that I made with the lock and bolts.

To my dismay I saw that there were three of the enemy on guard, and, closing the door softly, I took a couple of steps back, and told my father.

"Only three!" he said coolly. "Oh, that's nothing. Now, then, to the door! Hold it ready. In a few moments you will see us make a dash and drive these fellows back. Then we shall turn and follow you. Dash out with a good shout, and strike right and left. The men there are sure to run. Then all for the rocks, and don't look back; we shall follow."

I obeyed him exactly. Just as I had the door ready to fling open, my father, the foreman, and the others suddenly sprang forward, as if about to drive the Frenchmen out of the counting-house, and they fell back.

Then open went the door. I saw our fellows turn round, and, sword in hand and feeling as if I was going to my death, I dashed right at the three men guarding the back, shouting "Hurrah!" at the top of my voice.

I felt sure that they would run me through, but my father was right. One ran to the left, another to the right, and the other straight on up the steep slope, and, as I cut at him desperately, down he went untouched, save by a stone over which he tripped, and we all went over him as we rushed up the valley side to the shelter of the rocks, and with the enemy swarming out and after us.

It was rough work, but we knew our way. The enemy were strange, and before we had toiled up a hundred yards they began to tail off. In another hundred we were some way up, and panting behind a clump of rocks that formed quite a little fort, while below us we could see the enemy gathered together in a group, and evidently about to return.

Chapter Forty
After the Fight

"Let's get breath first," said my father. "Sit down, my lads, anywhere. How many are we? Only six all told? Who's hurt?"

"Oh, I'm all right, captain," said the foreman; "only a bit of a cut."

"Only a bit of a cut!" said my father. "Here, hold your arm." My father drew out a bandage from his pocket, and tied up the foreman's arm, and he had no sooner done this than another man offered himself to be bandaged.

Just then a couple of shots were fired in our direction, and we heard the bullets strike the rocks not far away; but while our enemies were below, and in the full glare of the burning cottages, we were above them, and in the darkness of the shadows cast by the rocks.

So the shots were allowed to go unheeded, while the bandaging went on, every one having some injury which was borne without a murmur.

"Are you hurt, Sep?" said my father then, anxiously, after he had attended to his men.

"I don't think I'm cut anywhere," I said; "but my left arm hurts a good deal, and I can't breathe as I should like to."

"Breathe?" he said eagerly.

"Yes; it hurts my side here and catches."

"Humph!" he said. "Can you tie this round my shoulder?"

"Why, father," I said, "are you wounded too?"

"A scratch, my boy; but it bleeds a good deal."

He tore open his coat and tried to take it off, but could not, and we had to help him, and then roughly bandage his shoulder, where he had received a horrible cut.

"WHY, IT'S BIGLEY, FATHER," I CRIED EXCITEDLY.

"WHY, IT'S BIGLEY, FATHER," I CRIED EXCITEDLY.

I trembled as I helped, and forgot my own pains.

He noticed my trembling and laughed.

"Bah, Sep!" he said; "this is nothing. I'm afraid some of our poor fellows there are worse. Ah, who's that? Be ready, men; we must retreat, we are not in fighting trim."

For we could see a dark figure coming up after us, and it seemed to be an enemy; but directly after half a volley was fired at the figure, and we saw it drop and roll over.

"Down!" said my father with a groan. "Oh, if we were only fresh and strong! But they are six to one, my lads, and it would be madness."

"Look, father!" I cried pointing; "they are going back."

That was plain enough, and that they were going rapidly in answer to shouts of recall. So, encouraged by this, we were about to run down and help the man who had been shot, when by the glow of the fire we saw him rise up on his knees, and directly after there were a couple of flashes and reports, as he fired his pistols after the retreating foe, and then began to crawl up towards where we were.

"Why, it's Bigley, father," I said excitedly. "Ahoy!"

"Ahoy!" came back; and I saw my school-fellow get up and begin limping towards us as fast as he could come.

I ran to meet him, but stopped before I had gone many yards, for the painful sensation in my side checked me, and I was glad to hold my hand pressed upon the place, and wait till he came up.

"Oh, I am glad!" he cried, catching my hand. "I thought—no, I won't say what I thought."

"But you are hurt," I said. "Is it your leg?"

"Yes, I feel just as if I was a gull, Sep, and someone had shot me."

"And you are shot?"

"Yes, but only in the leg. Is the captain up there?"

"Yes," I said, "and three or four of the men. I say, Big, what a terrible night!"

"Yes," he replied, in a curious tone of voice; "but, I'm glad it's the French, and that no one else has done it."

My father had come down to where we were seated, and made us follow him to the shelter of the rocks.

"They may catch sight of you, my lads," he said, "and turn you into marks."

"Are you going to stop them now, captain?" said Bigley, following. "What are you going to do?"

"I'm ready to do anything, my lad," said my father sadly; "but what can half a dozen injured men, whose wounds are getting stiff, do against half a hundred sound?"

Bigley sighed.

"Couldn't we sit up here in the rocks and pick them all off with the carbines, sir?" he said suddenly.

"Yes, my lad, perhaps we could shoot down a few if we had the carbines, which we have not. No: we can do nothing but sit down and wait till we get well, comforting ourselves with the thought that we have done our best."

We were watching the French sailors now, not a man showing the slightest inclination to retreat farther, but standing like beaten dogs growling and ready to rush at their assailants if they could get the chance. Swords had been sheathed, but only while pistols were recharged; and then, as soon as these weapons were placed ready in belts, the cutlasses were drawn again; and just as they had obeyed the order to retreat, the men would have followed my father back, wounded as they were, to another attack.

Down below the Frenchmen were as busy as bees. We could hear the crackle and snap of wood as they seemed to be tearing it out of the counting-house; and then it was evident what they had been doing, for a torch danced here and there, and stopped in one place and seemed to double in size, to quadruple, and at last there was a leaping flame running up and a pile of wood began to blaze.

"There go years of labour!" said my father, speaking unconsciously so that the men could hear. "One night to ruin everything!"

"Nay, captain, such of us as is left 'll soon build un up again," said the foreman. "Women and children's safe, and there's stuff enough in the hillside to pay for all they've done."

"Ah! So there is, my brave fellow," said my father warmly. "You are teaching me philosophy."

"Am I, captain?" said the man innocently. "Think they'll find the silver?"

"I'm watching to see," said my father; "I don't know yet. Five minutes will show. I fear they know where to look."

Bigley was leaning on my shoulder at this time, and he gave me quite a pinch as his hand closed, but he did not speak; and there was no need, for I understood his thoughts, poor fellow! And what he must be feeling.

As the fires at the cottages were beginning to sink, the one the Frenchmen had lit by the counting-house blazed up more brightly. They kept feeding it with furniture, joists, and broken planks, about a dozen men running to and fro tearing out the broken wood-work and clearing the interior till we could see that everything had been swept away; and then there was a buzz of excitement by the ruined building while the hammer and clangour of crowbars could be heard, followed by the tearing up of more boards; and I knew as well as if I could see that the trap-door leading to the cellar was being demolished.

"They know where the silver be, captain," said our foreman; and once more Bigley started and I felt him spasmodically grip my shoulder.

"Yes," said my father between his teeth; "they know where the silver is. A planned thing, my man—a planned thing."

"None o' us had anything to do with it, captain, I swear," cried the foreman excitedly. "There wasn't a lad here as would have put 'em up to where it was hid."

"Hush, man! What are you saying?" cried my father. "As if it were likely that I should suspect any of the brave fellows who have been ready to give their lives in the defence of my works."

"But can't we get the rest together, captain, and stop 'em, or cut 'em off, or sink their boats, or something?"

"No, my lad, I'm afraid we can do nothing more than see them—Ah! They have found it!" said my father as a loud shout of triumph rang out from below. "Well, as you say, there's plenty more in the hillside, and we must set to work again, I suppose, and take warning by this and never keep a store here."

It was all plain enough. The silver was found, and the little boxes in which the ingots were packed in saw-dust were carried out and stood down by the blazing fire—twenty of them; and just as this was done there was the thud of a cannon away off the mouth of the Gap.

"Signal for recall," said my father.

It was quickly obeyed, for the French formed up round twenty of their party who shouldered the boxes. Four men with drawn swords went first, as if they were making a showy procession in the blaze of the burning fire; then came the twenty men carrying silver, then six more with drawn swords; then a group of about ten who seemed to be wounded, and four more who were being carried; and lastly some twenty or thirty, with swords flashing in the firelight, to form a rearguard.

"*En avant!*" rang out clearly in the night air, and away they went chattering and making plenty of noise, just as a second gun was fired and seemed to make the air throb as the report echoed up the valley.

"Why, there must be nigh a hundred on 'em. We may have a shot at 'em now, captain, mayn't us?" cried the foreman.

"What for, my man?" said my father kindly. "If we could save the silver I would say yes, but it would be only spilling blood unnecessarily. We made a brave defence and were beaten. We could not master them now, even if we could fire volleys every five minutes. It would only mean a fierce fight, and we should be hunted down one by one for nothing. No: they have won. Let them go now, but I should like to see them embark. A good-sized French man-of-war must be off the Gap."

"Come on, then, captain, and let's get over the mouth."

"No," said my father. "You go with my son and one of the men, but I forbid firing. See all you can. I must stay and look after our poor fellows here, unless they've taken them away as prisoners."

"Ah! I forgot them," said our man. "Come along, Master Sep. Let's go down here and cross, and get on the cliff path."

"Will you go, Big?" I said.

"No, I couldn't walk," he replied. "I can hardly get down here."

"I'll look after him," said my father. "Go on, but take care not to be caught."

"We'll mind that, captain," was the reply; and we descended as rapidly as pain would let us, reached the stream, crossed the path the Frenchmen had taken, and went on diagonally up the slope, getting higher above the enemy at every step, and talking together in a low tone about the fight, and how the poor fellows were whom we had missed.

"I hope and pray," said our foreman, "as no one ar'n't killed; and, my lor', how my arm do hurt!"

"So do I. Poor fellows!" I said, "how well they all fought!"

"Ay, they did. But the captain, Master Sep, he was like a lion all the time. Why, lad, what's the matter?"

"I—I don't want to make too much fuss," I panted; "but I'm broken somewhere, and it hurts horribly."

"Sit you down, lad, and wait till we come back," said the foreman kindly.

"No," I said, grinding my teeth, "I won't give up;" and I trudged on, knowing as well as could be that one or two of my ribs were broken when I was crushed against the wall, just before it gave way.

And all the time below us to the left wound the line of Frenchmen. It was so dark that we could not have told that they were there, but for the low babel of sounds that arose of voices and trampling feet, while now and then a sound more painful to us still came up in the form of a groan or a faint cry of pain, and after one of these outbursts the foreman said:

"I wonder whether that be one of our lads."

"Nay, not it," said our companion roughly; "it be a Frenchy. One of our lads wouldn't make a noise like that if you cut his head off."

I felt sure he was right, and I could not help smiling, but I was in too much pain to speak.

And so we trudged on, our paths diverging in a way that took us higher and higher towards where the track curved round the cliff at the east side of the Gap, while theirs, of course, kept down by the stream to the beach.

It was a weary painful walk, for the excitement was now gone, and my companions' wounds were stiffening, and giving them as much pain as my chest did me; but no one murmured, and we kept on till we were at the mouth of the Gap, high up above where four boats were lying, while half a mile away we could see the lights and dimly make out the hull of a large vessel.

In spite of our pain we had made most progress, and were waiting some minutes before the head of the column came up, and there, as we seated ourselves hundreds of feet above, we could watch the embarkation of the little force, and see in a dim way the boats run in, hear the plashing of feet in the shallow water, and then the sound of the boxes as they were laid in the bottom of one of the boats, this boat being then rowed out about a dozen yards to wait for the others.

"Only wish it was a storm instead of a calm smooth time," said our foreman. "Everything seems for 'em. I can't see why the Ripplemouth people haven't been over to help us. They must have seen the fires."

"No," I said, "I don't suppose they would. See how deep down in the valley the cottages are."

It was quite dark where we were sitting, but there appeared to be a pale light on the sea which enabled us to make out all that was going on below; and we watched the boats fill, and one by one push off, the wounded men being divided between the four. It was plain enough, and it made me shudder when some poor fellow was lifted moaning in by his comrades, who did not seem to be any too tender in their ways.

At last all were on board, and the word was given to start. There was a loud plashing as the oars dropped into the water, and we saw one boat lead off, and then a second follow, then the third and the fourth in single file, and making haste to join the big vessel, upon which signal lights were burning.

"Why, they don't know the way," I exclaimed, as I saw them bear off at once to the eastward instead of following right out the meandering channel of the little river.

"Don't know the way?" cried our foreman; "why, it's plain enough. They're at sea."

"They're over a lot of dangerous rocks," I said excitedly; "and if there don't happen to be water enough they'll come upon the Goat and Kids, and perhaps be upset."

"No fear," said the foreman; "they'll know better than that."

They were now about four hundred yards from the shore, and fading away into the darkness, heading for the lights of the French ship, and far to the east now of the course of the river, where it ran down through the sand and shingle—a course the lugger always followed when going out or coming in. But all seemed to be well with the boats, the regular beat of whose oars we could hear though they were quite out of sight, when all at once there came out of the darkness a tremendous yell, and we all started to our feet in alarm.

We could see nothing, but as we listened to the cries for help, and the shouting and splashing of the water, it was evident that an accident had occurred, and it needed very little imagination to picture the men of an overset boat struggling in the water, and being helped into the others.

"There's one of them capsized on the Goat Rock," I said excitedly.

"Think so, my lad?" said our foreman hoarsely.

"I'm sure of it," I cried. "Oh! If the day would break and we could only see."

As if in response to my wish there was a faint gleam out in the darkness just like a pale star, and then a blue glow which lit up the scene with a curiously sickly glare.

It made everything very plain, and by this light we could see that there were three crowded boats out in the blue circle of light, while we could just see the fourth beyond them upside down, the keel just above the water, and three men seated astride.

"Regular capsize," said our foreman. "Hope none of the wounded chaps aren't drowned. Don't mind about the rest."

The blue light burned out, but not before we had plainly seen that it was burning in the bows of the largest boat, and that the men on that capsized had been dragged into one of the others. Then, as we listened, the babble of voices ceased, the plash of oars recommenced, and gradually died away.

"Well," I said, "we may as well go back and report what we have seen. They've gone now."

"Yes," growled our foreman, holding his hand to his wound, "and they've left their marks behind."

Chapter Forty One
Amongst the Wounded

Weary as our walk down to the mouth of the Gap had been, that back seemed far worse, and we reached the fire by the counting-house, which still burned brightly, being fed with more wood, to find my father anxiously awaiting our news.

"Gone!" he said. "Yes, but they may return. Two—no we cannot spare two men, one must go and keep watch to warn us of their return."

"I'll go, Captain Duncan," said Bigley, limping up. "I can't walk about much, but I can sit down there on the top rocks and watch."

"Very good, my lad," said my father, "but take your pistols and fire twice rapidly if boats come in again."

As Bigley squeezed my hand and started off, my father exclaimed:

"Now I must have a messenger to go to Ripplemouth for Doctor Chowne. What man is not wounded?"

There was a murmur among the group assembled about the fire, a grim blood-smeared powder-blackened set of beings, several of whom had had their hair scorched away by the explosion. There was not a man who was not ready to go, but there was not one who was not wounded.

"I hardly know whom to send," said my father. "Sep, can you get over there?"

"I'll try, father," I replied from where I was sitting down on a piece of rock; but I spoke so faintly that my father came to my side, and caught my cold damp hand, and laid his upon my wet forehead.

"Madness!" he muttered. "Look here, my lads," he cried, "a couple of the women must be found at once."

"Ahoy! Duncan, ahoy!"

It was a distant hail from high up on the track.

"Heaven be praised!" cried my father, and then he shouted, "Chowne, ahoy!"

There was an answering hail, and in five minutes more Doctor Chowne came scrambling down the side of the ravine upon his pony, with Bob hanging on to its tail.

"My dear boy!" exclaimed the doctor, grasping my father's hand. "We heard the guns, and could make out the lights of a big vessel off here. I was afraid that something was wrong, and going up the hill yonder I could see the glow in the sky. That decided me, and we came over together. Anybody hurt?"

"Well, yes, a little," said my father grimly.

As he spoke the first grey dawn of morning was beginning to show in the valley and mingle strangely with the glow of the big fire and of the sickly flickering gleam above the burned-out cottages.

It was a doleful sight upon which the doctor gazed round as he stripped off his coat. My father, blackened, scorched, and blood-stained, was standing with the foreman, six men were sitting or half reclining on the ground, and four more lay on their backs as if insensible.

It was a ghastly answer to the question, "Is anybody hurt?" for there was no one without a serious wound.

"Ah! I see," said the doctor grimly. "Well, is anybody killed?"

"Heaven forbid!" cried my father.

"Amen," said the doctor. "Here, Bob, bandages, scissors. Fine lesson in surgery for you. Now, captain, you first."

"No, no—the men," said my father.

"Here, I've no time to waste," cried the doctor. "Now, then, who's worst?"

"Mas'r Sep," cried the foreman loudly; and there was a sort of chorus of "Ay, ay!"

I tried to protest, but I felt sick, and as if I should faint, and the doctor cried:

"Hold your tongue, sir. Now then, what is it—bullet or sword cut?"

"Oh!" I shrieked, for he had seized me rather roughly.

"There, eh?" said the doctor, "that's it, is it? Here, knife, Bob."

"What is it?" said my father excitedly; "an operation?"

"Yes," said Doctor Chowne, "on his coat. Only going to rip it off, man. What a fuss you do make about your boy!"

"But tell me, Chowne," cried my father, "is he badly hurt?"

"Badly hurt? No. A few ribs broken seemingly. I'll soon bandage him up."

He did, and very painful it was; but at the same time it seemed to give me strength and confidence, as he wound the stout bandage round and round and left Bob grinning at me as he fastened the ends, while he went to another patient.

"Been a regular fight, then?" said Bob, who kept on questioning me, and making me tell him everything, though I felt as if I could hardly speak.

"Yes," I said, "terrible."

"But old Big; where's he?"

"Wounded, and keeping watch where the Frenchmen went."

"Old Big wounded, eh? And a regular fight—French and English too. Well, of all the shabby mean beggars that ever lived, you and old Bigley are about the two worst."

"What do mean?" I cried angrily.

"There, don't wriggle that way or I shall stick the needle in you. To go and have a big genuine fight like that and never let me know."

"Here, Bob, quick!" cried the doctor, and my old school-fellow had to go and help bandage another's wound.

"He will have his grumble," I said to myself, smiling as well as I could for one in pain.

The daylight grew broader, and the blackened counting-house and cottages more desolate-looking, the whole place seeming to be suffering from the effects of some terrible storm, and as I lay there I saw the doctor go on busily bandaging the poor fellows' wounds, every one suffering the pain he was caused without a murmur. The worst cases he temporarily bandaged, leaving the rest till the men were better able to bear it, and at last he came round to my father, who was wounded in two places.

"Die? No: there are some ugly chops and holes, but I'm not going to let any of the brave fellows die," cried the doctor cheerily. "Now the first thing is to get the women back and a roof over that long shed in case it should rain. I'll have a lot of ling cut for beds, but I must have some help. Perhaps I had better ride over to the village—no, I'll send my boy. But I say, Duncan, I think you ought to have given better account of the Frenchmen."

"Why, they had to get fifteen or sixteen wounded men away," I cried, and then winced.

"And serve 'em right," said the doctor. "Here, Bob!"

Bang, bang!

"What's that?"

"Bigley's signal; and by the way, doctor, the poor lad is wounded too. Come along and see."

"No, I'll go," said the doctor. "You are not fit."

"But I'm going all the same," cried my father; and I saw them go off along the cliff path.

"Here, Mars Sep," said our foreman, "I'm going to climb up yonder to see what's going on; will you come?"

"I don't think I can do it," I said, "but I'll try;" and with the help of his hand now and then I managed to climb up the west slope of the Gap right to the very top, where, in the bright sunny morning, we saw a sight that filled us with horror, for a couple of well-filled boats were rowing towards us from the side of a large sloop of war, from whose port-holes projected a row of guns that seemed to threaten fresh destruction to our coast.

But all at once we saw a flag run fluttering up to the peak and then blow out clear, with the result that the boats began to alter their course, turning completely round and rowing back to the man-of-war.

As they were going back we could see sail after sail drop down from the yards of the sloop; and as the boats reached her and were hoisted up to the davits, she began to move swiftly towards the west, her canvas growing broader minute by minute till she passed out of our sight.

"Why, she's gone," said our foreman. "Is she coming back?"

"I hope not," I cried. "Look!" I pointed towards the east over a depression in the Gap side through which we could catch a glimpse of the sea, and there in the bright sunlight we could make out a couple of vessels crowding on under all sail; and, little as I knew of such matters, I was able to say that one was a small frigate and the other a man-of-war cutter that looked very much like our old friend.

"After the Frenchman—eh?" said our foreman, gazing hard, wide-eyed and open-mouthed, as his cheeks flushed and he seemed to forget his wounds. "Well, then, all I can say is, that I hope they'll be caught."

"Let's get down," I said. "See, there's the doctor bringing Bigley Uggleston back on his pony. I wonder how he is."

Chapter Forty Two
A Fight at Sea

We descended slowly and painfully, to get down in time to receive a severe scolding from the doctor, while my father confirmed the news, as Bigley was half-lifted off for Bob to mount the pony and go off for help.

The British ships had had news brought them of the attack, and had started at daybreak in full chase, and an hour afterwards all who could climbed to where we could catch sight of the sea, to find out the meaning of the firing that was going on.

It was plain enough. A large three-masted lugger was in full flight with the frigate after her, and sending shot after shot without effect, till one of them went home, cutting the lugger's principal mast in two, and her largest sail fell down like a broken wing, leaving the lugger helpless on the surface. Then a boat was lowered, and we saw her going at full speed, pulled as she was by a dashing man-o'-war crew, and we watched anxiously to see if there was going to be a fresh fight. But no; the man-o'-war long-boat pulled alongside and the men leaped aboard to send up the English colours directly, while the frigate went on in full chase of the French sloop, and we soon after saw that the lugger was being steered towards the mouth of the Gap.

But meantime the doctor had been busy with poor Bigley, who had been laid upon a soft bed of heather to form his couch while his wound was examined.

"Why, you cowardly young scoundrel!" he cried cheerfully, "the bullet is embedded in the muscles of the calf of your leg, and it came in behind. You dog: you were running away."

"So would you have run away, doctor," I said warmly, "if half a dozen Frenchmen were after you and firing."

"Never, sir!" cried the doctor fiercely, as he probed the wound; "an Englishman never runs. There, I can feel it—that's the fellow."

"Oh, doctor!" groaned poor Bigley.

"Hurt?" said Doctor Chowne. "Ah, well! I suppose it does. And so you, an Englishman, ran away—eh?"

"English boy," said Bigley grinding his teeth with pain, while I felt the big drops gathering on my forehead, and was wroth with the doctor for being so cool and brutal.

"English boy!—eh?" he said. "Well, but boys are the stuff of which you make young men. Ha, ha, ha! What do you think of that?"

"You're half-killing me, doctor!" groaned poor Bigley.

"Not I, my lad. I've got the rascal; come out, sir! There you are—see there! What do you think of that for a nasty piece of French lead to be sticking in your leg? If I hadn't fished it out it would have been there making your leg swell and fester, and we should have had no end of a game."

As he spoke he held out the bullet he had extracted at the end of a long narrow pair of forceps; and, as Bigley looked at it with failing eyes, he turned away with a shudder and whispered to me, as I supported his head upon my arm:

"I'm glad Bob Chowne isn't here to see what a miserable coward I am, Sep. Don't tell him—there's a good chap!"

I was about to answer, but his eyes closed and he fainted dead away.

"Poor lad!" said the doctor kindly. "Why, he was as brave as a lion. I talked nonsense to keep up his spirits and make him indignant while I hurt him in that cruel way. Poor lad! Poor lad!"

"Doctor Chowne," I cried with the tears in my eyes, "I felt just now as if I hated you!"

"Just you say that again!" he cried, laughing grimly. "You forget, you young dog, that I have you by the hip. You are my patient, and I have as tight a hold of you as an old baron in the good old times had of his prisoners. There! He is coming to, and I sha'n't have to hurt him any more to-day."

"Will he have to lose his leg, doctor?" I whispered.

"What! Because of that hole? Pshaw, boy! The bullet is out, and nature has begun already to pour out her healing stuff to make it grow together. I'll make him as sound as a roach before I have done. Now we must see to getting our wounded under cover. I didn't think the Gap would ever be turned into such a hospital as this. Why, Sep, it's quite a treat to get such a morning's practice in surgery. There! I'll go and wash my hands, and I must have some breakfast or I shall starve."

Breakfast! Starve! At such a time as this! I looked at him in horror, and he read my thoughts and laughed.

"Why, you young goose!" he exclaimed, "do you think I can afford to be miserable and have the horrors because other people suffer? Not a bit of it. I'm obliged to be well and hearty and—unfeeling—eh? Ah, well, Sep! I'm not such an unfeeling brute as I seem; and I'd give fifty pounds now to be able to find those poor fellows breakfast and shelter at once."

The doctor was able to supply his patients with refreshments without the expenditure of fifty pounds, for Mother Bonnet had just come up to announce that she had been back to the cottage to find it untouched, after going away in alarm when the Frenchmen landed, and she said that she had the fire lit and coffee and tea on the way for every one who wanted it.

"Mother Bonnet, you're a queen!" cried the doctor; and then turning to me: "Rather strange that they should have spared the cottage and old Jonas's goods, eh, Sep? There's something behind all this."

We were not long in finding out what was behind all this. I had my own suspicions without the doctor's, and they were soon confirmed by the coming of the big three-masted lugger, which was brought close in by the man-o'-war's men, who landed with a lieutenant at their head, and came up the Gap to see our condition.

He was a bright, manly fellow, and my father and he became friends at once, while he was quite humorous in his indignation.

"The cowardly scoundrels!" he cried. "Oh, if we had only been here! How delighted my Jacks would have been to have a go at them!"

"Do you think so?" said my father smiling.

"Think so, sir? Why, my boys have been half mad with disappointment. Poor fellows! Just about a dozen of you. Well, there's no mistake about your having made a brave defence, Captain Duncan. Not a man unhurt. Sir, I'm proud to know you."

"My men behaved better than I did, sir," said my father modestly.

"Oh, of course, sir," cried the lieutenant laughing; "but avast talking. What can we do for you? I'm here ashore with the lugger and prisoners till my ship comes back, so what shall we do? You don't want doctoring, I see?"

"We want covering in first of all, sir," said the doctor, pointing to the unroofed shed.

"Of course you do," cried the lieutenant; "and all your men wounded. Here, heave ahead, my lads, and half of you run back to the lugger and bring up all the spare sails and spars you can get hold of. If there are no spars bring the sweeps."

"Ay, ay, sir," cried the sailors; and half of them went off at the double back along the valley, while the others, under the command of their officer, set to work and shovelled and brushed out all the burnt charcoal and smouldering wood from the long shed, and then from the counting-house, and after that they were busy at work cutting ling and heath with their cutlasses, when the men despatched to the lugger came back loaded with sails and spars.

At it they went, and in a very short time had rigged up a roof over the shed for our poor fellows, carried in a quantity of ling, and spread over that more sail-cloth, making quite a comfortable bed with room for a dozen men, and ample space for the doctor to go between.

Then, with the tenderness of women, the great bronzed fellows lifted the wounded men who could not walk, slipped under them a hammock, and one at each corner carried them in and laid them down.

"There you are, messmates," said the biggest of the men; "now, then, a quid apiece for you to keep down the pain. Make ready: pockets, 'bacco boxes," he shouted, and his comrades laughingly obeyed.

"Thank you, my lads, thank you," cried the doctor, going round and shaking hands with all in turn; "why, it would be a pleasure to have to do with such men as you. But there, you're safe and sound."

"At present, sir," said the big sailor; "but hark! They're at it yonder."

We listened and sure enough there was the distant sound of heavy firing coming from the west.

"And we not in it, mates," said the big sailor dolefully.

The wounded being cared for and the miners' wives beginning to come back, we left them in the doctor's charge, and, in response to the lieutenant's invitation, went back with him to the lugger.

"I'll send your fellows up all I can," he said, "but you two come to the lugger cabin, and I think I can scrape you up a bit of a meal."

We were ready enough to go for many reasons, one of them being curiosity; and having shaken hands with Bigley, and asked my father to do the same, for the poor fellow was very miserable and despondent, away we went.

"The rascals!" said the lieutenant, "they've got all your silver then? How much was it worth?"

"Nearly two thousand five hundred pounds' worth," said my father.

"What a haul!" exclaimed the lieutenant, "and so compact and handy. Never mind, captain, hark at our guns talking to them. They'll have to disgorge. But, I say, some one must have told them where to come."

"I'm afraid so," said my father.

"Who was likely to know?—this smuggling rascal that we have got in the French lugger?"

"Who is he? An Englishman?"

"No, sir, a Frenchman who speaks English pretty well. The officer on the revenue cutter knows him. A Captain Gualtière, I believe."

"Oh!" I exclaimed.

"You know him then?" said the officer sharply.

"Yes," said my father; "he picked up my son and two companions one day after their boat had been blown out to sea."

"He seems to have picked up something else beside, sir," cried the officer—"knowledge of where you kept your silver. And you may depend upon it his lugger has been playing leader to the French sloop, and showed the captain where to land. Two thousand five hundred pounds in bars of silver! We must have that back."

"I'm afraid you are not quite right, sir," said my father sadly. "I think we shall find that the betrayal of my place was due to a smuggler who used to live in yonder cottage, information respecting whose cargo landing I was compelled, as a king's officer, to give to the commander of the cutter. It has been an old sore, and it has doubtless rankled."

"Oh, father!" I said sadly, "do you think this really is so?"

"Yes, Sep," he replied, "and so do you; but don't be alarmed, I shall not visit it upon his son. The poor lad thinks the same, I am sure, and he is half broken-hearted about it." We reached the beach soon after, where a couple of Jacks were in charge of the boat, and soon after we were pulled alongside of the lugger, to find that the men left on board, in charge of a midshipman of about my own age, had been busy repairing damages, *fishing*, as they called it, the broken spar, while the lugger's crew sat forward smoking and looking on, in company with their skipper, who rose smiling, and saluted.

"Aha! Le Capitaine Dooncaine," he cried; "and m'sieu hees sone. I salute you both."

"Salute me?" cried my father angrily. "After this night's work?"

"This night's work, mon capitaine?" he said lightly. "Vy node. I am prisonaire; so is my sheep, and my brave boys. But it ees ze fortune of var."

"Yes; the fortune of war," said my father bitterly.

"I do node gomplaine myself. You Angleesh are a grand nation; ve are a grand nation. Ve are fighting now. If ze sloop sail vin she vill come for me. If she lose ze capitaine vill be prisonaire, and behold encore ze fortune of war."

"Sir," said my father, "it is the act of pirates to descend upon a set of peaceful people as your countrymen did last night, thanks to your playing spy."

"Spy? Espion? Monsieur insults a French gentleman. I am no spy."

"Was it not the work of a spy to bring that French sloop here to ravage my place and steal the ore that had been smelted down?"

"True, saire, it vas bad; but ze espion was your own countrymen, saire. Ze Capitaine Gualtière does no do such not you calls dirty vorks as zat."

"Jonas Uggleston! It was he, then?" cried my father. "I felt sure of it; but I believed you to have had a hand in it, Captain Gualtière."

"A hand in him, sair. Ze Capitaine Ugglee-stone ask me to join him, it there is months ago, sair; but I am a smugglaire, and a shentilhomme, node a pirate."

"Captain Gualtière," said my father, "you once saved my boy's life, and I have insulted you—a prisoner. Sir, I beg your pardon."

My father took off his hat, and before he realised what was about to take place, the Frenchman had thrown his lithe arms about him and kissed his cheek.

"Sair," he exclaimed with emotion, "I am a prisonaire, but I look upon ze Capitaine Dooncaine as a friend."

They then shook hands, and my father coloured up as he saw the officer of the frigate look on as if amused.

"Monsieur," said Captain Gualtière; "I am no longer the maitre here; but you vill entaire my cabine, and I pray you to take dejeuner—ze breakezefast vis me."

The result was that we had a surprisingly good meal, and very refreshing it proved, though I was in terrible pain all the time, and kept on wondering whether I ought to eat and drink.

The lieutenant from the frigate kept getting up and going on deck to listen to the firing, which was very heavy in the distance, though nothing could be seen, and he exclaimed once against the great headland, the Ram's Nose, which shut off the view.

"It's so hard," he said; "here have I been longing for an engagement, and the first one that turns up I am away from my ship, and cannot even see the fun."

I saw my father, who was wincing with pain, smile at the lieutenant's idea of fun.

"Why, you are safer here," he said.

"Safer!" exclaimed the lieutenant contemptuously. "Now, Captain Duncan, would you have liked it when you were on active service?"

"That I certainly should not, sir."

"Ah, well," said the lieutenant, "I suppose I must be contented with our little prize here. This Gualtière has long been wanted. A most successful smuggler, sir."

The conversation was ceasing to interest me, so I went on deck, when the middy came up to me directly from where he was standing listening to the firing.

I looked at him with the eyes of admiration, for his uniform, dirk, and pistols gave him a warlike aspect, and besides he was in temporary command of the sturdy Jacks who were overawing the smuggler's men.

"Won't you sit down?" he said, turning up a little keg.

I sank upon the seat with a sigh, for I felt weak.

"Ah! You are a lucky fellow," he said.

"Why?" I asked.

"Why? To be in a fight last night and get wounded."

"Oh!" I exclaimed laughing.

"Ah, you may laugh!" he said. "I call it first rate. You're only a landsman, and get all that luck. It's of no use to you. Why, if it had been me, of course

I am too young for promotion, but it would have been remembered by and by. I say, tell us all about it."

I told him, and to my surprise I found before long that all the sailors were listening intently.

"Ah!" exclaimed the middy as I finished; "don't I wish we had all been there."

"And don't I wish you had all been there!" I said dolefully; "our place is regularly wrecked."

"Never mind," cried the middy, shaking my hand. "They ar'n't getting much by it. Hark! How our old girl is pounding away at 'em. I'll be bound to say that the spars and planks are flying, and—oh, don't I wish I were there!"

Chapter Forty Three
Bigley Feels his Position

During the day, after leaving an adequate guard over the prisoners in the lugger, the lieutenant came up the Gap twice, and worked hard with his men to get our poor work-people in a more comfortable state, though now plenty of the Ripplemouth folk had been over, and help and necessaries were freely lent, so that the night was made fairly comfortable for the wounded and their families. We slept in the ruins of the counting-house, whose roof was open to the sky, for my father had not the heart to go home and rest there; and when he sent Bigley over, and I felt that I should like to go and keep the poor fellow company, I, too, had not the heart to go and leave my father alone.

The next morning the lieutenant came to fetch us to breakfast on board the lugger; but we made a very poor meal, our injuries being more painful, and I felt weak and ill; but there was so much to see and hear that I kept forgetting my sufferings in the interest of the time.

There were our men to go and see, and sit and talk to where they were too poorly to get up. There was Mother Bonnet to speak to when she started for the Bay to attend on Bigley; and I had her to see again when she came back, all ruffled and indignant, after a verbal engagement with our Kicksey, who would not let the old woman interfere, because she wanted to nurse Bigley herself.

Then towards afternoon, when the lieutenant had nearly gone mad with suspense about the frigate and at being bound to stop there with the lugger, according to his orders, news came by a fishing boat, that there had been a desperate engagement, and the frigate had been sunk.

But on the top of that came news by a man who was riding over from Stinchcombe, that it was the French vessel that had been sunk.

This stopped the lieutenant just as he was putting off in the lugger, and soon after a fresh news-bearer came in the shape of another fisherman, who announced that the Frenchman was taken.

There was a regular cheer at this, and I saw Captain Gaultière's brow knit; but he passed it off, and sat with the officer straining his eyes to the west in search of the prize to our flag.

It was no wonder that he looked as triumphant as our people seemed chap-fallen when towards evening the frigate appeared alone, with every stitch of canvas that she could show spread to the western breeze, but the spy-glasses showed that she was in anything but good trim, for her main-mast was gone by the board, only a short stump rising above the deck, and as she came nearer, her shattered bulwarks told of a desperate fight.

There was a signal of recall flying; and at this the lieutenant shook hands warmly, and with the middy bade us good-bye, setting sail directly after with the prisoners in their own vessel, and towing the frigate's boat behind.

We learned afterwards that there had been a most desperate engagement, far away to the west, and that the Frenchman was becoming hopelessly beaten with half her guns silenced, and that she was on the point of striking her colours, when a lucky shot from one of her big guns cut through the frigate's main-mast, and it toppled over into the sea, whereupon the French sloop made her escape, sinking the cutter which bravely tried to check her, and carrying off her crew as prisoners.

We only obtained this information in driblets; but one thing was certain, the French sloop had got right away, and my father frowned as he thought of his lost silver.

He bore up famously for a few days, working hard, in spite of Doctor Chowne's orders, in trying to make his wounded work-people comfortable, and then when by the doctor's orders I was lying at home on a sofa in the same room as Bigley, my poor father broke down and took to his bed.

"I'm not surprised," Doctor Chowne said to me shaking his head. "You're all a set of the most obstinate mules that ever kicked. I should have had you all well by now, only young Bigley there would walk on his crippled leg and irritate it; you would keep rolling and dancing about and keeping your ribs from mending; and your father has gone on walking about just as if nothing was the matter, when all the time he ought to have been in bed."

"But a little rest will soon set him right, will it not, doctor?" I said anxiously.

"A little rest? He'll be obliged to take a great deal now, and I'm glad of it. Hang him: I'll bring him in a bill by and by!"

The doctor was quite right; we had all been very disobedient, and suffered for it; but in spite of the pain, and fever, and weakness, that was a very pleasant time. How we used to lie there listening to the birds! Sometimes it was the blackbirds piping softly in the garden. Then from high up over the hill we could faintly hear the skylark singing away, and then perhaps mingling with it would come the wild querulous *pee-ew! pee-ew!* Of the grey and white gulls, as in imagination we saw them gliding here and there about the cliffs.

But there was war in our cottage at the Bay—desperate war. Mother Bonnet coming every morning with fish and cream and chickens and fruit for her boy, as she called Bigley; and our Kicksey snorting and indignant at the intrusion, and telling old Sam that it was just as if master was too poor to pay for things.

Then by degrees my father grew well enough to sit out in the little battery by his guns, and breathe the soft sea-breezes that came in from the west; and here he used to receive our foreman, who came over every morning to report how much lead had been smelted and cast, and how the mine was growing more productive.

For as fast as the men grew well enough, they returned to their duties. The cottages were restored as quickly as was possible, and every day the traces of the French attack grew less visible; but still my father did not get quite well.

Bob Chowne was over with us a great deal, and I believe he did both Bigley and me a vast deal of good from being so cantankerous. He would do anything for us; fetch, carry, or turn himself into a crutch for Bigley to lean upon, as he hopped down the garden to a chair; but he must be allowed to snarl and find fault, and snarl he did horribly.

One day when I was beginning to feel quite strong again, and I was able to take a long breath once more without feeling sharp pricking sensations, and afterwards a long dull aching pain, I went down the garden to find Bigley standing before my father with his head bent and listening patiently to what seemed to be a scolding.

"I've told you before, my lad. Ah, Sep, you there?"

"Yes, father," I said. "I beg your pardon. I did not know."

"There, stop," cried my father. "It is nothing that you may not hear. Bigley Uggleston is talking again about going, and I am bullying him for it."

"I can't help it, Captain Duncan," cried poor Bigley passionately. "I want to be frank and honest; and it always seems dreadful to me that, after what has taken place and your terrible losses, I should be staying here and receiving favours at your hands."

"Now, my good lad, listen to me," said my father. "Do you think that I am so wanting in gentlemanly feeling that I should wish to visit the sin of another upon your head?"

"No, sir; but I am in such a strange position."

"You are, my lad; but you see your father has always had the worthy ambition to give his son a good education, and make him something better than he has been himself."

"Yes, sir, but—"

"Hear me out, Bigley. It has been my misfortune twice over to give him deadly offence, and the last time he visited it upon me by giving information to the French, which led to, as you call it, my serious losses."

"Yes, sir," cried Bigley, "and I am miserable. I feel as if I could not look you in the face."

"Why not?" said my father kindly. "Yours is a good, frank, honest face, my lad, and you have always been my boy's companion and friend. Come, come, no more of this nonsense. I have right on my side, and some day your father will awaken to the fact that the information I gave was given in the way of duty, and have a better opinion of me. As to you—"

"I must go, sir—I must go," cried Bigley, "I cannot stay here any longer."

"No, you must not go," said my father firmly. "It is evidently your father's wish that you should stay, or he would say so when he sends you money so regularly. There, come, we'll say that he has done me a great deal of injury, and caused me a very heavy loss."

"Yes, sir, that is always on my mind."

"And that kept you from getting better, my lad. So now I'm going to make a bargain with you. Get quite strong again, as I hope to be myself before long, and come and help us at the mine to recover the lost ground again."

"May I?" cried Bigley eagerly.

"Of course," said my father; and as I saw quite a cloud disappear from poor Bigley's countenance, I tossed up my cap and cried, "Hurrah!"

Chapter Forty Four
Bigley Makes a Discovery

The time glided on and the war did not trouble us, for we were too busy in the Gap, where everything had been restored and even improved, and my father was fighting bravely to recover from the terrible loss the French descent had caused to the property, for the rebuilding of cottages and repairs of machinery, after the store of silver had been taken, left him very much impoverished; but, as he used to say, it was only a question of time to get right.

Bigley worked regularly with me, living at the smuggler's cottage with Mother Bonnet for his housekeeper; and he used to hear regularly from his father, who expressed no intention of ever returning, merely saying that he was glad that his son was doing so well, and quite accepting the position. He used to send money, but now Bigley had ceased to use it, for he received a regular payment from my father, and this other money used to be sent to a bank.

The mine was fairly productive, but I knew that my father had been compelled to borrow a good deal, and this preyed upon his mind so much that one day he said to me:

"Sep, I think I shall be obliged to sell the Gap, with the mine and all it holds. I don't like this life of debt, and the prospect of years of toil before I can clear it off."

"But it would be such a pity, father," I exclaimed.

"It would, my boy, but I am not so sanguine as I was. That terrible night shook me a great deal, and if it were not for the thought of you I should give up at once."

He repeated this to me two or three times, and it made a very unpleasant impression that troubled me a very great deal.

Bob Chowne, who was shortly going up to London to study at one of the hospitals, came over one evening, and we all three, as in the old days, had tea at the smuggler's cottage, Mother Bonnet beaming upon us, and never looking so pleased as when we wanted more of one of her home-made loaves.

Then after tea we decided, as the sea was so calm, to have a few hours' fishing, and taking the boat we rowed out as far as the Goat and Kids, the grapnel was thrown out, and we began to fish.

It was a glorious evening, and we took rock-whiting, pout, and small conger at such a rate that I cried, "Hold, enough!"

"No, no, keep on," said Bob Chowne. "Let's see how many we can catch."

"It will be a good feast for the work-people," said Bigley, as I hesitated; and knowing how glad they all were of a bit of fish I turned to again, throwing in my baited hooks, and hauling in the fine fellows every minute or two.

But at last the darkness forbade further work, so the lines were reeled-up, the fish counted over into the two baskets, and Bigley proceeded to haul up the grapnel.

The intention was good, but the grapnel refused to be hauled up. The boat's bows were dragged right over it, and Bigley stood up and tugged till the boat was perceptibly pulled down, but not an inch would the grapnel budge.

"It has got between a couple of rocks, I suppose," said Bigley.

"Here, stand aside!" cried Bob Chowne, "let the doctor come."

He caught hold of the stout line, stood in Bigley's place, and hauled till his wrists ached.

"Here, come and pull, Sep," he cried; and I joined him and hauled, but in vain.

Then we changed the position of the boat, and dragged and jerked in one direction and then in another. Every way we could think of did we try, but could not stir the anchor, and as we were giving up in despair Bob said:

"I know; some big sea-monster has swallowed the hook and he won't move. Here, let's get ashore."

"But we must not lose a new grapnel," cried Bigley. "Here, I know what we'll do."

He hastily unfastened the rope from the ring-bolt in the bows, and secured it to the boat-hook by a hitch or two, and then cast it overboard.

"There!" he said; "that will buoy it, and I'll come out to-morrow and get it up somehow."

Then taking the oars he rowed us ashore, where a couple of the mine men were smoking their pipes and shining like glowworms as they waited to see what sport we had had.

The news spread respecting our exceptionally good fortune; and as soon as the two men had helped to haul the boat right up beyond the reach of the tide, as the grapnel was gone, they ran up to the miners' village and came trooping back with the rest, armed with baskets, dishes, and in some cases only bare-handed, to receive their portions of our big haul.

They gave us a cheer, and soon afterwards we parted, Bob Chowne to sleep at the smuggler's cottage, while I went back to the Bay.

I woke at daylight next morning, and not feeling disposed to sleep, I dressed and started off for the Gap to rouse up Bigley and Bob and propose a bathe; but as I came in sight of the Gap mouth I found Bigley already astir and just going down to the boat.

I shouted and ran down to him waving my towel, to which he answered by waving another, showing that he had risen with a similar idea to my own.

"I thought I would have a bathe, and do some business too," he said; and then, in answer to my inquiring look, "Try and get up the grapnel," he added.

"Oh!" I exclaimed; "but why didn't you rouse up Bob?"

"Rouse up Bob!" he said gruffly. "Go and try and rouse up that block of stone!"

"What! Have you tried?" I said.

"Tried! I've shaken him, and punched him, and done everything I could but drenched him, and that would be a pity. He don't want to get up; so let him lie. Here, help me run the boat down."

I laid hold of one side, we balanced her on an even keel, and as it was down a steep slope we soon ran her into the water, jumped aboard, and began paddling out down the narrow part that formed the bed of the river on the seaward side of the pebble ridge.

The tide was very low, the sun up bright and high, and the water so clear that there was every rock below us so close that it seemed as if we could not go over some of them without touching.

"We'll row out to the buoyed grapnel," said Bigley; "make fast, and while you have your bathe I shall dive down, follow the rope, and see if I can find out how the grapnel has got fast."

"If you can," I said.

"Well, I'm going to try," replied Bigley. "I don't suppose it's above three fathoms deep."

"You can't dive down three fathoms?" I said.

"Can't I?" replied Bigley laughing. "I'm going to show you. Look here!"

He pointed to a big long stone in the bows of the boat weighing some twenty-pounds. To this a thin line was attached, and I saw his meaning at once.

"Yes," I said, "that will do it, only don't forget to let go."

"No fear," he replied; and we paddled on, with the beautiful view of the cliffs opening out as we rowed farther from the shore.

We had nearly a quarter of a mile to go before we struck against the floating boat-hook close to the now exposed rocks, when Bigley threw in his oar, hoisted the rough buoy aboard, unhitched the rope, ran it through the ring-bolt, and hauled on till he had the boat's stem right over the grapnel, which still refused to come; so we made fast.

Bigley then began to undress rapidly, while I proceeded to work more slowly, being curious to watch what he was doing.

I had not long to wait, for after making fast one end of the thin line to the thwart of the boat he poised the stone on the gunwale, leaped in, and then putting his left arm round the grapnel rope he got well hold of the stone, and drew it over to descend with it rapidly to the bottom.

I crept to the bows and looked over to see his white body far below in the clear water, and then he came up again to rub his eyes, pant, and hold on by the side of the boat.

"Why, what's the matter?" I said; "seen a shark?"

"No," he cried, "but I've seen something else. Here, haul up the stone."

"Bother the stone!" I exclaimed, "I came to bathe."

"Haul it up quickly," he said; and I obeyed, and afterwards lifted it on to the gunwale.

He seemed very excited, but he would not speak about what he had seen, only beg me to do what he told me, which was to untie the line from the stone and then make a running noose and put it loosely round.

I did all this, wondering at his mysterious way, but only expecting that it was to fasten round the grapnel so as to pull in a fresh direction.

BIGLEY UGGLESTON AND SEP DUNCAN MAKE A DISCOVERY.

As soon as I had done he took hold of the loop that was round the stone, drew a long breath, and asked me to lift it over into the water.

This I did, and he went down head-first, while I again watched him below among the waving weeds all indistinct in the troubled sea.

He was down for a full minute as I crouched there with my head over the side. He seemed to be so long that I began to grow alarmed lest he had become entangled, and I was about to haul up the line attached to the stone. I looked down anxiously with my face closer to the surface, but only to make him out in a bleared indistinct manner, and then he shot up like a line of light and swam to the side and held on.

"Thought I shouldn't be able to do it," he said; "but I've got the line round."

"Well, what next?" I said. "But I say, is a grapnel worth all this trouble?"

"A grapnel?" he said with a peculiar smile.

"Yes."

"Wait a minute till I am in the boat."

He climbed in, and came to my side.

"Now," he said; "haul up steadily. I think she'll come."

I tightened the line, and for a moment or two there was a dead resistance. Then something heavy began to stir, and I hauled away steadily, hand over hand.

"I've got it," I said as I gazed down. "It was right in amongst some strong weed. Here it comes."

I pulled away till I had nearly got it to the top, and then Bigley came to my help, reached over, and the object I was dragging up bumped against the boat, slipped out of the noose, and went down rapidly just like a mass of stone.

"What did you fasten the line to that for?" I said.

"What did I do it for, Sep?" he panted. "Didn't you see what it was?"

"No," I said bluntly.

"What did it look like?"

"Box covered with sea-weed," I replied.

"Well, don't you see now?"

"No," I replied.

"Why, Sep, how dull you are this morning!" he cried. "Didn't you see that you had hold of one of your father's silver chests?"

"*One of my father's what?*" I roared.

"One of the silver chests. Sep, it was over these rocks, against that one, I suppose," he cried, pointing to a huge block just below the surface, and a favourite haunt of conger, "that the Frenchman's boat capsized."

"What, the one with the silver?" I cried.

"Yes, and I believe all the chests are at the bottom there."

"And they were coming back to try for them when the frigate came in sight!" I shouted.

"Yes, yes, yes."

"Hurrah! Hurrah! Hurrah!" I cried, leaping up in the boat, and waving my arms about like an idiot. "Why, Bigley, it will set father free of all his troubles. Here, I'm half mad. What shall we do? Hold hard a moment: I'm going down to see."

I had only my breeches on, and tearing these off, I stepped on to the gunwale, leaped up, turned over, and dived down into the clear cold water, trying with all my might to reach the bottom, but only describing a curve, and coming up again about twenty feet from the boat.

I swam back to have another try, but Bigley stopped me as I was about to dive off.

"No, no," he said; "it's of no use. You can't get down there without a killick or some other weight."

"But I'm not sure it is the silver," I cried in a despairing tone.

"But I am," he said. "The boxes are lying all about. They look like stones if you stare down, because they are all amongst the weed; but when I got down to feel for the grapnel I was right upon them. It's in amongst them somehow. That was why I came up again and tried to fasten the line round one."

"But are you quite sure, Big?" I said, trembling with eagerness.

"Quite sure," he said. "There can't be any mistake about it. The Frenchman's boat ran on the rock and capsized, and all the chests must have gone to the bottom like a shot."

"And my poor father suffering all that worry, when here lay all his silver at the bottom, close to the shore. Here, what shall we do, Bigley? We must stop and watch it, for fear anybody else should come and find it."

"No fear of that," he said, drawing the rope once more through the ring-bolt, and then securing the boat-hook to the end, and throwing it overboard to act as a buoy. "Here, let's dress and go and tell him."

"Yes, yes," I cried, trembling with eagerness, and hurrying on my clothes, as he did his, we rowed ashore, and after hauling the boat back to its safe place, climbed up the slope, and prepared to walk to the Bay.

"Big," I said; "I'm afraid to leave it. Suppose while we are gone someone goes and takes it all away."

"Ah! Suppose they do," he said. "But it isn't such an easy task. Nobody knows of it but us, Sep, and we can keep the secret."

"You are right," I said. "Come along, and let's make haste and tell him."

We strode along the cliff path that morning faster, I think, than we had ever gone before, and when we came in sight of our place I was going to rush in and tell my father, but something struck me that it would be only fair to let Bigley go, as he had made the discovery, so I told him to go first.

He would not, though, and we went up to the cottage together, to find Kicksey kicking up a dust in the parlour with a broom.

"Is father up yet?" I cried.

"Yes, my dear, hours ago, and half-way to Barnstaple before now."

"What!" I cried.

"He's going to London, my dear, and here's a letter that Sam was to bring over to you if you didn't come back to breakfast."

I tore open the letter and read it in a few moments.

It was very brief, and merely told me that he had had a letter the past night making so stern a demand upon him for money that he had decided to go up to London at once and sell the mine.

"Big," I said dolefully; "we've come too late. What shall we do?"

I gave him the letter to read, and he wrinkled up his brow.

"Go after him and catch him," he cried.

"Yes; but how?"

"I don't know," he panted; "let's try."

"But the silver?"

"Is locked up safely where we found it, lad," he cried. "It is a secret. Come on."

"But how, Big? He is riding."

"Then we must walk. A man can walk down a horse. Now, let's see if it can't be done by boys."

Chapter Forty Five
Trying an Impossibility

We two set out to perform an impossibility: for though, starting together on a long journey, a good steady walker might tire out a horse carrying a man, and in a fortnight's work, before we had got half-way to Barnstaple, I knew that my father would have arranged to catch the coach, and I remembered that the coach would change horses every ten or twelve miles; and as all this forced itself into my mind, I sat down on a stone by the road-side.

"Tired?" said Bigley, wiping the perspiration from his face.

"No, not yet; but I've been thinking, and my thoughts get heavier every moment," I replied.

"What do you mean?" cried Bigley.

"That we cannot do this," I said; "and we should be doing something far more sensible if we go back home, and write a letter to my father. Why, it would get to him days before we could."

Bigley took off his cap and rubbed his ear.

"I'm afraid you are right," he said; "but I don't like to go back."

"Then let's go on to Barnstaple, and write to him from there."

"To be sure!" cried Bigley, jumping at the compromise. "Come along."

"No, I said; it will not do. I've left his letter behind, and I don't know where to write."

"Oh, Sep!" cried Bigley reproachfully. "Then, we must go back."

We stood looking at each other just as we had made a fresh start, and the weariness we were beginning to feel brought with it a strange low-spirited sensation that was depressing in the extreme.

"Come along," I said. "Let's get back, or we shall lose another day before we can get off a letter."

"Wait a minute," said Bigley; "there's the half-way house not a quarter of a mile away. We'll go on there and have some bread and cheese and cider, then we shall be able to walk back more quickly."

It did not take us long to reach the pretty little road-side ale-house, where the first thing I saw was the doctor's pony tied up to the gate by the rough stable or shed.

"Some one ill?" I said. "Shall we tell Doctor Chowne what we were going to do?"

I had hardly spoken these words when my father appeared at the door.

"Why, Sep, Uggleston!" he exclaimed; "you here?"

"Why, father!" I cried, catching him by the arm. "I thought you had gone."

"The pony broke down, my boy," said my father, "and I have had to bring him back here—walking all the way; and I was undecided as to whether I should pay someone to take him home, or lead him myself, and make a fresh start to-morrow."

"Come back," I said with a look full of delight. "He ought to come back, eh, Big?"

Bigley nodded and smiled, and then I eagerly told him all.

"It was Bigley's doing, father," I exclaimed. "He found it out."

"My lad," said my father huskily, "you have saved me, for I could only have sold my property at a terrible loss."

"And you will come back with us, father," I said.

"Come back, my boy? Of course. Why, Bigley, my lad, you have always looked at me as if I felt a grudge against you for being your father's son; now, my boy, I shall always have to look at you as a benefactor, who has saved me from ruin."

Bigley tried to say something about that dreadful night, and the attack on the mine premises, but my father stopped him.

"Never mind about all that," he said; "let's get back and see if you are right, and that it is not a solitary chest which the Frenchmen have left us."

"No fear of that, sir," cried Bigley. "I was down long enough to see that there was quite a lot of them."

"Or of pieces of rock," said my father smiling. "I'm older than you are, my lad, and not so sanguine."

"But I feel so sure, sir," cried Bigley.

"That's right, my lad. I'm glad you do; but you have seen them, I have not."

"But Sep saw them too."

"I saw the box we hauled up," I said; "but I could not be sure about what was at the bottom amongst the rocks and weeds."

Bigley looked so disappointed that my father smiled.

"Come," he cried; "you think I am ungrateful, and throwing cold water upon your discovery, when there is plenty over it as it is. So come, let us assume that the treasure is there, and begin to make our plans about how to recover it."

At the last moment we had been obliged to leave the pony at the little inn, and we were walking steadily back as this conversation went on.

"Well, sir, it will be very easy," said Bigley eagerly.

"Not so easy," said my father. "We shall want a couple of men who can dive."

"Oh no, you will not, sir," replied Bigley. "I have thought it all out. All we shall want will be a clear day with the sea smooth."

"Yes, highly necessary, Bigley," said my father.

"Then we should want a very long smooth pole, and if we could not get one long enough two poles would have to be fished together."

"And then you'd fish for the boxes?" I said.

"No," said Bigley seriously; "you would have to sink the pole just down to where the chests lie, and rig up a block at the top, run a rope through it, hold one end of the rope in the boat to which the pole is made fast, and at the other end have a thick strong bag made of net."

"Well, what then?" said my father.

"Why, then you would put a big pig of lead in the bag, let me take hold of the bag, let the rope run slack, and I should go down to the bottom in an instant. Then I should lift a box into the net-bag and come up, leaving it there for you in the boat to haul it up."

"Yes, that sounds very simple," said my father; "but could you do it?"

"Could I do it!" cried Bigley. "Why, sir, we did get one up to the top without any proper things. I can dive."

"Yes, he can dive, father," I said eagerly. "You need not be afraid about that."

My father looked at us both, and grew very silent, as we trudged on, to reach the cottage at last utterly tired; and though Bigley proposed that we should go on and see whether the buoy we had left was all right, my father said that it might very well wait till morning, and Bigley stayed for the night.

"I thought your father would have been ever so much more eager and excited about it," said Bigley, speaking to me from the inner room where he slept, the door having been left open.

"He is excited," I said in a low voice, for across the passage I could hear him walking up and down in his own room; and that kept on till I dropped off asleep, and dreamed that the French had landed with four large boats and a great pole which they lowered down into the sea. Then they seemed to have got me fastened to the rope that ran through the wheel-block at the head, and they had fastened a pig of lead on to my chest, which pressed upon me as they hauled me up out of the boat, and then let go.

It was all wonderfully real. I felt myself suspended over the water, which looked black as ink instead of lit up by the sun as it was when Bigley went down. And as I hung there, the oppression from the pig of lead was terrible, and it seemed to please Captain Gualtière, who was there in a boat opposite, giving orders and laughing at my struggles to escape. "Now," I heard him say in his Frenchy English, "cease to hold ze ropes, and laissez let him go."

Then there was a dull splash, and with the weight always upon me I seemed to part the waters and go down, down, down, into the deep black depths, which appeared to have no bottom. There was a growing sensation of suffocation; my boots hurt my feet, and the blister I had made upon my heel smarted, and all at once the pony, as it stood at the half-way house door, kicked out at me, just as I was beginning to suffocate; and this broke the rope, and I shot up to the surface.

In other words, I started up awake, to find that I had been lying on my back, that I was bathed in perspiration, and that my father was still walking up and down his bed-room.

"What stuff to go and dream!" I said to myself, as I felt very much relieved. "That comes of eating cold beef and pickled cucumber for supper."

I turned upon my side to settle myself off to sleep again; but I could not doze off; and do what I would, the thought of being sent down into the black water with a pig of our lead upon my chest, and the pony down below ready to kick out at me kept haunting my mind, while across the passage there was my father still keeping up the regular tramp.

Just then the clock at the bottom of the stairs began to strike, and I thought that it must be a dark morning and about four, but to my astonishment it struck eleven, and I felt sure that it must be wrong.

And all this while there was the restless pace up and down my father's room, making the jug in the basin rattle faintly, and after turning over three or four times I made up my mind that it was impossible to sleep, so I would dress, and then go and wake Bigley and sit and talk.

I had just made up my mind to this, as it seemed to me, when Bigley stood in the doorway and said:

"Now, Sep, old fellow, wake up."

I started up in bed and stared, for the room was flooded with sunshine, and I knew that I must have been sound asleep, while from across the passage came the regular pace of my father walking up and down, and the jug clattered in the basin.

"Has he been walking up and down all night?" I said sleepily.

"Oh, no!" said Bigley. "I have only just called him, and heard him get up. But make haste. It's a splendid morning, and the sea's like glass."

"And the skin's all off my heel," I said; "and it's as sore as sore, and so is one of my toes."

"Sep!" shouted my father just then; "make haste down, and tell Ellen that we want the breakfast as early as possible."

"Yes, father," I said; but at the same moment Kicksey's voice came up the stairs as she heard what he said, and it was to announce that breakfast would be ready in ten minutes' time.

Chapter Forty Six
Treasures from the Deep

It was a glorious morning. There had been no wind for nearly three weeks beyond pleasant summer breezes, and the water was as clear as crystal, which is not so very often the case on our shore.

My father had soon completed his preparations, there being a fine larch in the woody part of the Gap; and this was soon felled, stripped, and cleared of branch and bark. Bigley soon found a suitable rope and block in his father's store, and a couple of boats were got ready, with a suitable bag of rough canvas, in which several holes were cut out so as to allow the water to pass readily through.

All this was got ready in a couple of hours, three pigs of lead were placed in the boat, in case one would be lost, and with the foreman to help, and a couple of men to pull, we set off from the beach with no lookers-on, and in a short time we were fast to the line that marked the spot where the boxes were supposed to lie.

Bigley gave vent to a sigh of satisfaction, for he had been in a terrible fidget, telling me over and over again that he was sure the boat-hook which served as a buoy had been washed away, and totally forgetting that the cluster of rocks known as the Goat and Kids were so familiar to the fishermen about that the spot could easily have been found again.

However there we were. The line was hauled tightly in over the bows of our boat, the pole thrust down straight to the bottom, but only to keep rising up until one of the pigs of lead was lashed on to the thick end, when it consented to stay. The block with its wheel had already been secured in its place, and the rest of the gear being ready nothing remained but to make the first descent, and for which Bigley was eager.

"I scarcely like to send you down, Bigley," said my father just at the last. "I hardly feel justified in doing so."

"Why not, sir?" cried Bigley. "It's only like diving for fun."

"But if anything happened?"

"Why, nothing can happen, sir. It's as easy as can be."

"One moment," said my father; "let's see how the tackle works."

He gave the word, the men slackened the rope, and the bag with the pig of lead in it went down with a splash and sank rapidly to the bottom, where it was allowed to stay for a few minutes and then hauled up.

"There, sir, that goes right enough, only when it went down it would have taken me with it, and when it came up it would have brought the first chest of silver."

"If you have not been mistaken," said my father drily. "Well, sir, we shall see," said Bigley colouring; and standing up in the boat he made a spring and dived off, curving down and rising again like a seal before swimming back to the side with a mastery over the water that I never could approach, though there was a time when I could swim and dive pretty well.

"Now, then," cried Bigley, taking hold of the bag without waiting for farther orders, "let the rope run quite clear, and don't haul till I come up and tell you."

"Do you feel sure that you can do it, my lad?" cried my father eagerly. "Oh yes, sir!"

"Then, mind, if there is any difficulty you will give up at once."

"I will not do it, Captain Duncan, if I cannot," said Bigley laughing. "Now, then, off!"

The bag, which with the lead inside had been resting on the gunwale, was lowered into the water; Bigley seized it, and in an instant over he turned to go down head-first, with the line running rapidly through the block, and then all at once growing slack.

My father and the foreman held the end, but like the rest they leaned over the side of the boat to watch the movements of the white figure they could indistinctly see far below, for the water was of course disturbed, and our movements in the boats kept up a series of ripples which blurred the surface.

My heart beat fast, for Bigley seemed to be down a long time, though it was only a few seconds before he rose rapidly to the surface and swam to the boat.

"Well, my lad," cried my father excitedly, "there is nothing, then?"

"I couldn't manage it the first time," panted Bigley. "I got hold of a box, but it was awkward work getting it into the bag. I could not hold it and get the chest in too. Haul up, please."

"But are you sure you can do it?" said my father.

"I am certain, sir," replied Bigley; and the men began to haul up the bag.

As Bigley was about to give the word to let go once more there came a loud "Ahoy!" from the shore; and turning my head I saw that Bob Chowne had come over and was asking to be fetched.

"It is impossible," said my father—"he must wait;" and I knew as well as if I were listening to him that Bob was saying something about our always having all the fun.

"Let go," cried Bigley; and away he went again, the weight drawing him down so rapidly that I felt a little envious, and as if I should like to make one of the trips.

He was up again more quickly this time.

"Haul up," he cried; "it's of no use. I can't get the box into the bag. Here, I see!" he cried, "make fast that maund to the rope and put the lead in there."

He pointed, as he held on by the boat's edge, to a fish-basket in the stern of the boat; and as soon as the bag had been hauled aboard the rope was set free and fastened, scale-fashion, to the basket.

Bigley's countenance brightened at this, and seizing it directly he gave the word, declaring that he was all right; and away he went once more, and came up again so quickly that we felt there was something wrong.

"What's the matter?" I cried.

"Haul up and see," was his reply; and as the men hauled, everyone held his breath till the basket came up slowly and heavily to the surface.

"It's a box or a stone," I cried; and then I gave a shout, in which all the men joined, for there was a square box in the basket and my father lifted it out.

"He's right! He's right!" cried my father excitedly. "Bigley, my dear lad, I could not believe that it was true!"

"Over with the basket, sir," cried Bigley; "quick!" and he went down again and once more rose.

"All ready!" he cried; and so it was, for another box was hauled in—another unmistakable case of our silver, for there were the marks upon it; and my heart beat with pride and pleasure at our success.

"How do you feel?" cried my father. "Don't go down more than you can bear."

"I feel like this, sir," cried Bigley seizing hold of the two handles of the basket and going down once more, to come up again almost as quickly, and another box was hauled up.

Just then there was a cheer from the shore, and on looking in that direction there was the doctor now beside Bob Chowne, and they evidently realised what was taking place, for both shouted and waved their hats.

They would have come off to us, but there was no boat to be had nearer than Ripplemouth; so they watched us while Bigley went down again and again till ten boxes had been recovered, when my father refused to let him go down any more, in spite of his prayers and declarations that he was all right and could go down as often as we liked.

My father was determined, though, and made him dress himself and help row ashore with us so as to carry the chests up to the cottage; but as soon as they were landed my father sent up to the mine and all the men were fetched to bear the silver up, and it was placed in safety in the restored cellar.

The spot had of course been left buoyed, and a couple of men were awarded the task of watching the place till after dinner, when towards four o'clock we all went down again, Bigley declaring himself ready to dive.

By this time I had come to the conclusion that I was behaving in a very cowardly way in letting him do all the work, and without saying a word I determined to quietly undress ready, and take the next turn.

The doctor and Bob Chowne, who had said just what I anticipated, joined us this time, while everyone occupied in the Gap came down to see the astounding fact that the Frenchmen had not got the silver after all.

We rowed out and made fast as before, and Bigley went down; but instead of paying any attention to his dive I let the others watch him, got ready, and then, as a fresh box was recovered, I leaped overboard, crying, "My turn now!" and swam to the basket.

"You, Sep?" said my father in a hesitating tone.

"Yes, father," I shouted. "Let go."

The men obeyed, and almost before I could realise it, I felt a snatch at my arms, and was dragged rapidly down.

In spite of my preparation I was so surprised that I almost lost my presence of mind; but, as luck had it, the basket settled down close to a box, and somehow or another I got one hand under it and tilted it over into the basket, to which I was holding on tightly the while.

Then in a blind confused way, with the water seeming to thunder in my ears, I loosened my hold, and almost directly my head popped out into the fresh air, and I swam to the boat amidst a furious burst of cheering.

I felt quite ashamed, and hardly knew what was said to me, for the idea was strong upon me that I had failed. But I had not, for the next minute one of the little chests was hauled up and into the boat, my father leaning over and patting my bare wet shoulder.

"Bravo, Sep!" he exclaimed; and those two words sent a glow through me, cleared away the confusion, and made me think Bigley a long while down when he took his turn, I was so impatient to begin again.

He was soon up, another hauled in, and this time I did not let the weight drag at my shoulders, but plunged with it, went down, shuffled a chest into the basket more easily, and came up.

Then Bigley obtained another, and suggested that the next dive should be from the stern of the boat.

He was quite right, and in the course of about an hour we had gone on turn for turn and obtained nineteen of the chests, so that there was only one more to recover.

The doctor had twice over suggested that we had been too long in the water, but everyone was in such a state of excitement, and there was so much cheering as box after box of silver was recovered, that his advice was unheeded, and in the midst of quite a burst of cheers I seized the basket by the handles and took my fifth plunge into what seemed to be a sea of glowing fire, so glorious was the sunshine as the sun sank lower in the west.

I knew where the last one lay, just where it had been shot when the boat overturned, and it was on its side in the midst of a number of blocks of stone tangled with weed. The boat had been shifted a little, and I came down right by it, turned it over and over into the basket; but as I did so

I slipped, and something dark came over me. My legs passed between a couple of stones, and then as I tried to recover myself and rise the darkness increased, a strange confusion came over me, and then all was blank till I heard someone say:

"Yes; he'll do now."

My head was aching frightfully, and there was a strange confused sensation in my head that puzzled me, and made me wonder why my feet were so hot, and why my father was leaning over me holding my hand.

Then he appeared to sink down out of sight as a door was shut, and I heard him muttering as I thought to himself, and he seemed to say something about being better that everything should have been lost than that have happened.

I couldn't make it out, only that he was in terrible trouble, and his face looked haggard and thin as he rose up again and bent over me to take me in his arms as he looked closely in my face.

Then, as he held me to his breast, I could feel that he was sobbing, and I heard him say distinctly in a low reverent tone:

"Thank God—thank God!"

Chapter Forty Seven
Last Memories

I heard all about it afterwards; how they had hauled up quickly as I did not rise to the surface, in the belief that I might be clinging still to the basket; but though the last chest was there, that was all.

Bigley seized the handles and went down, staying so long that everybody grew cold with horror, and when they hauled up he was helpless, and with one hand holding fast to the side of the basket.

It was our foreman who went down next, and managed to get his arm round me, where I was entangled in a tremendous growth of sea-weed, and with one of my legs hooked, as it were, between and round a piece of rock. By great good fortune he was able to drag me out, and rise with me to the surface, but so overcome that he could hardly take a stroke; and as for me, Doctor Chowne had a long battle before he could bring me back as it were to life.

I have little more to tell of my early life there on the North Devon coast, for after that time rolled on very peacefully. We had no more visits from the French, not even from Captain Gualtière, and we saw no more of old Jonas Uggleston. He had settled in Dunquerque, he told his son in his letters, and these always contained the advice that he was on no account to leave the service of Captain Duncan, but to do his duty by him as an honest man.

And truly Bigley Uggleston did do his duty by my father and by me, for year by year we grew closer friends, the more so that Bob Chowne drifted away after his course of training in London, and finally became a ship's surgeon.

As for us, we led a very uneventful life, going steadily on with the management of the mine, which never was productive enough to make a huge fortune, but quite sufficient to keep my father fairly wealthy, and give employment and bread to quite a little village which grew up in the Gap.

For the recovery of the silver was the turning-point in my father's mining career. After that all went well.

As I said, Jonas Uggleston never came back, but one day a bronzed white-headed old sailor was seated at the door of the smuggler's cottage when I went to call on Bigley, and this old fellow rose with quite a broad grin on his face.

I stared for a moment, he was so foreign-looking with his clipped beard and quaintly cut garb. Then I realised who it was: Binnacle Bill come back to his old wife, Mother Bonnet.

"Couldn't leave the master before," he said. "But now I've come, and you'll give me a job now and then, and Master Bigley, I should like never to go away no more."

Binnacle Bill did not go away any more, for he was at once installed boatman, and bound to have boat, tackle, and baits ready every time Bigley and I felt disposed to have an hour or two's fishing in the evening.

If Bob Chowne came down his work grew harder, for Bob was as fond of fishing as ever. He used to come to see his father sometimes, for he was devotedly attached to him, and the old doctor's place was full of the presents his son sent him from abroad.

But Bob always came over to the Bay, grumbling and saying that he was sick of Ripplemouth; and then he grumbled at old Sam and Kicksey about the dinner, or the fruit, or the weather, and then he used to grumble at his two old school-fellows as we walked along the cliff path, or went out with him in the boat.

"Ah, you two always were lucky fellows," he said to us one day, when I told him that I was going to spend my winter evenings setting down my old recollections with Bigley Uggleston's help. "Nothing to do but enjoy yourselves, and idle, and write. But what's the good of doing that? Nobody will ever care to read about what such chaps as we've been, did in such an out-of-the-way place as this."

"Never mind," I said, "I mean to set it all down just as I can recollect; and as to anybody reading it—well, we shall see."

"Ah, well," said Bob, "just as you like; but if I was a grumbling sort of fellow, and given to finding fault, I should say it's just waste of time."

This was too much for Bigley, who burst into a hearty fit of laughter, in which I joined.

Bob stared at us both rather sulkily for a moment, and then uttered his favourite ejaculation, which was "Yah!"